iniquity

Trobador Publishing
Wakefield, MA 01880
www.normanggautreau.com
Copyright © 2012 by Norman G. Gautreau
ALL RIGHTS RESERVED

ISBN 978-0-9856885-1-6

Past Praise for the Author's Work

" ... absorbing, moving and thoughtful ...rich in the qualities of character and setting that allow the reader to enter into the lives and moral dilemmas he portrays." — *The Historical Novels Review*

"... [Gautreau has] a strong eye for detailed atmosphere ... the characters are wonderfully rendered." — *Publisher's Weekly*

"...stands out for [his] ability to bring both place and character to life for the reader." — *Massachusetts Center for the Book*

"...transports the reader back in time when integrity and a higher purpose in life was not merely an aspiration but an honorable resolve ... exquisitely written." — *David Baldacci, New York Times bestselling author of Last Man Standing and Absolute Power*

"[He] perfectly captures [the] struggle with the elements as a way of life, the fury and the bounty of the ocean and the tough, basically good-hearted folk who understand life at its most basic ... core."
— *Curledup.com*

"... well and truly told, vivid, engrossing and edgy as life can get. The reader cares about the people, about their place ... a tale worth the telling, people worth the meeting. One of the few books I've read recently that I read twice—once because I cared so much how it came out and the second time for sheer pleasure."
— *The Courier-Gazette, Bangor, ME*

"Characters, both major and minor, are vividly drawn ..."
— *Library Journal*

"... very highly recommended ..."
— *Library Bookwatch*

"Setting and characters intertwine nicely ... a fast moving novel ..."
— *Portland (ME) Press Herald*

By the same author

Sea Room
Island of First Light
The Sea Around Them
Francesca Allegri

iniquity

A novel

Norman G. Gautreau

Trobador
Publishing

Contents

Self, so self-loving were iniquity.
—Shakespeare, Sonnet 62

Part 1

March–April, 2nd Year of the Baxter Administration

He that is proud eats up himself. Pride is his own glass,
His own trumpet, his own chronicle, and whatever praises
Itself but in the deed, devours the deed in the praise.
—William Shakespeare, Troilus and Cressida, ii, III

Chapter 1—The Voice of the Moon

Only later would Secret Service agents realize they'd missed the signs that spring day, else they would surely have noticed the man in blue OR garb—gown, booties, cap, surgical gloves—roaming the grounds of George Washington University Hospital on four consecutive days with a shock of red hair spilling from under his scrub cap and carrying a cigarette between latex-covered fingers as he drifted among pedestrians like second-hand smoke. And if the man escaped the attention of the people whose very job was surveillance, it's not surprising the general public took little notice of the man. Maybe they were distracted by the warming weather: trees coming into leaf on 23rd Street; cherry blossoms blooming around the Tidal Basin; warm breezes wafting the flags on government buildings. Or else they were wary, as they scurried across the street, of the streams of traffic spinning off Washington Circle.

Perhaps, also, their thoughts lingered with a patient several stories above them in the hospital.

Even those who had seen him many times because they had encamped for several days outside the hospital, keeping vigil for the dying, wildly popular First Lady—the religious among them murmuring prayers— even these people appeared to pay him no heed, apparently assuming he was as devoted to Grace Baxter as were they.

But what about the people whose job it is to protect the president of the United States and his family? With their suspicious and keen eyes peering through ubiquitous sunglasses surely they, of all people, should have noticed that on each of the last four days—days when the president visited his dying wife in the hospital—this same cigarette-smoking, latex-gloved surgeon was lurking in the area when the president's motorcade arrived, despite the fact that they varied the time of the president's arrival as well as the entrance he would use.

Had they examined the surveillance photos from each of those days more carefully, they would have seen this same man in many of the digital images and they might have known that the assassin was announcing himself.

Later, with the benefit of hindsight, and on closer scrutiny, they would see the obvious.

But it would be too late.

What if a man gained the White House after forty years of struggle—first in the House, then in the Senate—and it all turned out to be nothing but a big mistake? Then, another thought came to him: *President Angus Baxter*. As if to validate who he was … what he was.

He hunched the collar of his jacket against the sea breeze off Maine's Penobscot Bay and nodded grimly, mumbling to himself, "This is why they call it the *trappings* of the presidency." A wry chuckle at his own pun. *The ball and chains of the White House.* Several years before, it had been a buoyant dream, a proud dream to be counted among the greats—Lincoln, Jefferson, Roosevelt—but now the leaden weight of the office threatened to take him under.

That, and the worsening condition of his wife.

He glanced at the gibbous moon riding low over the serrated tips of the spruce. Every few seconds it flared the feathers of a seagull white. It glinted off the white hull of the Coast Guard cutter and the gray hulls of the warships stationed a mile off Baxter Island to guard his person. The moon glared back at him—a half-hooded, unblinking eyeball; it was like the constant gaze of his protective detail, or the deck officers who, at that very moment, were probably watching him through binoculars pressed so hard to their eye sockets that they left rings. He remembered the famous photograph of the earth taken by the Apollo 13 crew as they orbited the moon—*Earth Rise*. How small the earth appeared and how miniscule he must now look in the single eye of the moon, this man standing on the edge of an ocean. On the edge of a continent.

On the edge of a life.

A sea of troubles. He gave a wry laugh at the cliché, the self-editor of his mind always alert. But at the moment he wasn't feeling the famous eloquence of speech that had won him so many admirers. Erato, normally his reliable consort, was absent on this night.

A sea of troubles. His wife failing; his domestic agenda filibustered into fragments; military actions in Africa and Central America threatening to evolve into quagmires (already, pundits were drawing comparisons to Vietnam, Iraq and Afghanistan); the Mideast peace talks more difficult than he imagined even in his most pessimistic moments…. He was like a swimmer desperately clinging to a navigation buoy in a rip current.

A half mile offshore a red bell buoy rolled in the swell with muffled, arrhythmic clangs. Seagulls, illumined by the moon, flitted around it.

How had they done it, those few—those very few—great men who had come before him? Was it just the times that make the man, or was there something lacking in himself? Was he destined, like most of his predecessors, to be merely mediocre—a caretaker of the office until the next great president came along? If that was the case, the job wasn't worth the agony, the terrible price he and Grace had paid.

Shifting his gaze to look out beyond the warships, he hoped to see the telltale phosphorescent streak of a passing whale. *Solitary. Free to roam.* Perhaps he would join himself to the whale like Ahab. Sound deep into the dark, soothing waters. *Escape.*

The beam from the Baxter Island lighthouse swept across his face every two seconds—the slow, weak rhythm of a failing heart.

Grace lay in a hospital bed back in Washington. What would he do without her? If any president ever needed a First Lady, he was that man. She had always been his mooring against the cyclones of depression that occasionally raged in his mind. She was the one who ensured he wasn't swept out to sea by a rip current of problems or pulled under by the crashing surf of opposition.

Waves rolled in from the bay, respirating against the shore with pebbly rattles in their throats. As he strode barefoot through the wet sand his footfalls made soft sucking sounds. He studied the exquisite regularity of the tiny rounded crests sculpted by the oscillating waves. An odor of decay rose from the rimpled mud that gleamed wetly in the moonlight; it was the same smell that had penetrated his senses years before at Cape Split in Nova Scotia.

Two days earlier, when he'd visited Grace at the hospital, she'd reminded him of Cape Split. After the doctors left her room, he had said, in a voice low enough so not to be heard by the agents outside her door, "I don't know how I would go on without you."

"*Will* go on, not *would* go on," she'd replied. "It's not conditional." When he didn't answer, she continued, "You *will* go on, Angus, because you *have* to. Do you remember Cape Split?" She gazed into his eyes. "Of course, you do. You willed yourself to go on then, you'll do it again."

"*You* willed me to go on."

"No. I only begged you. You made the choice." She grimaced.

"But I had you to support me then," he said. "Are you in pain?"

She shook her head. "They've loaded me up with morphine. It's just that it's difficult to stay awake."

"Sleep. We'll talk again later."

"Back then, you were a new congressman with limited responsibilities, and we didn't have children. Now, you're the president and we've been blessed with children and grandchildren. You have many more people depending on you, plus a whole country, the whole world. You *have* to go on." She said it with a weakening voice.

"You should sleep," he whispered.

She nodded.

He studied her face as images of Cape Split passed through his mind, as fresh as if it had happened the previous day.

He had been a newly elected congressman when he and Grace, on vacation, stayed at a seaside cabin on a bluff overlooking the Bay of Fundy and the Minas Channel. On the morning of the second day he woke confused and disoriented, caught in the undertow of another depression. Perhaps because he was exhausted from the recent, hard campaign—that he'd nearly lost because of scurrilous ads produced by a Super PAC—the sense of hopelessness was stronger than it had ever been. Careful not to wake Grace, he stole out of bed, dressed, and slipped out the door into a fog-bound world. As he felt for the path leading down the gentle side of the bluff to the bay, he heard what the locals called "the voice of the moon"—the roar of the turbulent tidal currents coursing through the Minas Channel. He stumbled down the path toward the sound.

Ten minutes later, he was more than a hundred yards out on the exposed mud flats, his mind as befogged as the bay. Soon, he knew, he would be inundated by the incoming tidal current which, at times, can travel at an astonishing eight knots.

A quick, merciful end; that was all he wanted—a quick, merciful end.

That's when he heard Grace call to him. Her voice, thin and weak in the moist scrim of fog, seemed to come from another universe.

"Go back," he yelled, peering toward where her voice had sounded.

But she kept coming. Another call of "Angus!" Nearer.

"Go back," he pleaded weakly.

But she appeared wraithlike out of the fog, running and slipping on the slick tidal flats. When she reached him, she asked, breathless, "What are you doing?"

"Please go back."

"The tide … you'll drown." Her eyes were moist with fear.

"Grace, please—"

"—No. I'm not going back without you." She looked over her shoulder as the roar of the current grew.

"I can't …." he said.

"You *can*. You're just overtired from the campaign. Don't do this, Angus. It won't solve anything." She grabbed his arm and tugged.

"Grace, I—"

"—Come. Let's go back to the shore." Her voice was quavering, pleading. When he resisted, she pulled harder. "I'm not leaving you. If you drown, I drown."

It had taken almost fifteen minutes to coax him to dry land.

That very morning they checked out of the cabin and she drove him back to Maine where, with a combination of psychiatric counseling and medications, he gradually recovered his enthusiasm for life.

For forty years Angus and Grace managed to keep the secret of his depressions lest it destroy his political career, and the psychiatrist was bound by medical ethics never to speak of it. Not even their closest friend, Matt, knew.

Not long before his inauguration, he drew encouragement from a book titled *Lincoln's Melancholy: How Depression Challenged a President and Fueled His Greatness* in which the author argued that Lincoln's depression gave him the fortitude and hard-headedness to avoid unwarranted optimism. The author also argued that a lifetime of living with the depression strengthened Lincoln's moral will and in that way contributed to his transcendence.

Now, as President Baxter walked near the dark waters of Penobscot Bay, a shredding cloud, weightless as a desperate thought, passed before the moon.

"You can cancel the meeting."

Baxter whirled to see Matt Cannon standing behind him. "Jesus, Matt, you startled me. What are you doing up at this hour? It can't be much later than four o'clock."

"Couldn't sleep. Saw you walking down here," Matt said. "Angus, I think I know what you're going through … Grace and all. As I said, you can cancel the meeting."

Baxter shook his head. "It's too important, Matt. When peace is mercifully established, how do we explain to those who buried loved ones on the last day of hostilities that we could have acted a day sooner? How do we explain it to the people who buried loved ones the day before that, or on the day before that?"

It was something he'd been saying a lot lately—in private conversations, in speeches, in briefings—a simple turn of phrase that summed up for him (and, he hoped, for others) the urgency of the newly emerging problem in the Middle East—only the last in a long series of setbacks. It always amused and annoyed him that the enormous political and diplomatic complexities of the world had to be reduced to simple rhetorical turns of phrase if any progress was to be made, if people were to be won over. Thank heaven for speech writers! *Sound bites and platitudes.* He shook his head forcefully. "No, Matt, Grace is fully informed about the meeting and she'd be bullshit if I squandered this opportunity."

"Postpone, then. You need to go see her."

"Eyuh, but I can't," Baxter replied with a touch of his famous Maine accent. He placed a large, bony hand on Matt Cannon's shoulder. "It would send the wrong signal." It had taken too much to get the Palestinian, Ahmad Bakhit, and the Israeli, Jehu Golani, to meet. Baxter instinctively felt he had only this one chance to broker a new peace agreement—the kind of strong one that had eluded every president since Carter; the peace agreement that would burnish his legacy; that would answer Grace's prayers. He could not allow his personal agony to stand in the way of what he thought might be his best, and perhaps, his last chance, and he was strengthened by the sure knowledge that Grace would agree with him.

"What wrong signal?" Matt asked. "That you're a human being who loves his wife? Christ, even the president has a right be with his wife at a time like this."

"You're wrong, Matt, Grace and I gave up certain rights long ago when we chose this life."

"But, for Christ's sake she's—"

"—She's dying!" Baxter squeezed his eyes shut. A heaviness came to his chest. "Looks that way. But not yet; the doctors say there's time."

"All the same, Angus, it's—"

"—No, it's not all the same, damn it! You *know* Grace. Just ask yourself: what she would say if you proposed to her that I cancel this meeting in order to be with her?"

Matt gave a wry smile. "She'd tell me to shove it up my ass."

Baxter nodded. "She sure would. She knows how important this is. Hell, she's worked for it every bit as hard as I; the most effective First Lady this country's ever had." The president gazed out to sea. Arms of fog, moist and heavy, rolled in from the outer islands, curling around the lighthouse like a gossamer octopus. A few droplets of fog gathered on his face. He turned and started back toward his Baxter Island home, now the Downeast White House code-named Omaha by the Secret Service at the president's request. "Some time ago we agreed you wouldn't be part of my administration—"

"—so I'd be free to do things your aides couldn't do, operate behind the scenes, back channels, all that," said Matt. "What of it?"

"That was meant to apply only to politics, but this—this is one of those times, too. Except for me and the children, no one is closer to Grace than you are. I want you to go to her, tell her how the meetings are going, every detail—she'll want to know—and tell her I'll call every chance I get."

"Of course."

"Get her thinking about the Bakhit-Golani problem."

"Of course, Angus, but—"

"Maybe if she has something to look forward to ...."

Matt gazed softly and sympathetically at Baxter. Surely, he can't believe ...?

"And there's another reason you're not in the administration," Baxter said with a chuckle after a long pause.

"What's that?"

"I like people around me who can call me 'Angus.' You and Grace are the only ones. 'Mister President' can get tiresome."

"Bullshit! You love it."

Baxter smiled. "Tell her the minute the meetings are over, I'll be there."

The man in blue surgical garb wasn't fooled in the least. He knew who the Secret Service agents were; they were all dressed alike and wearing similar pilot's sunglasses, almost as if they were a required item in the uniform. It couldn't have been more obvious if they were in police uniforms or in army camouflage. And, he thought, they all wore that expression of intense nonchalance, that who-gives-a-flying-fuck stare that may have fooled other people, but not him. It was probably an expression they learned in Secret Service school and practiced in front of a mirror.

And because he knew who they were, and they had no idea about him, he was free to wander around and figure out, by the pattern of the entrances they used for the president in the last four days, which one they would use next.

It would be the emergency room entrance.

His attitude toward them wasn't all disdain, however. He fully admired the way they concealed the weapons he knew they carried, the compact Sig Sauer P229s. His brother Billy had one in his collection.

And that was another way you could tell who the secret agents were: on warm days they were the only ones wearing jackets.

It would be the emergency room entrance and he would be ready.

Angus Baxter sat alone in the living room of his island house. Soon, he would have to prepare himself for the conference with the Palestinians and Israelis, but for now his thoughts were with his wife.

They'd done it together, he and Grace, through a lifetime of dreams and plans and plots; through thousands of choices about the seesaw balance between their public and private lives, always counting what they were gaining, never measuring what they were losing.

Now, with Grace about to die, he felt lost in his present world and unable to remember his world before politics. There was a time, in the anonymity of his youth, when he knew the names of constellations, the set of the tides, the plants and trees on his family's island, the sea birds and the song birds. But these were all lost to a lifetime of political intrigue, to the callusing effects of iniquities committed and iniquities suffered. The most connected man in the world, he felt utterly and painfully disconnected.

And he felt that old acquaintance, the one from the Bay of Fundy, speaking with the voice of the moon, begin to hook into him with its pincers.

The double sweep of the Baxter Island lighthouse strobed the ceiling of the semi-darkened room with a fog-filtered light—like a searchlight at a concentration camp. He imagined men in a watchtower guarding against his escape. Raising his left wrist before his eyes, he pressed a button on his watch. The digital face emitted a ghostly green light—4:37. He followed the strobe of light with is gaze. He counted the seconds before the next double flash, if only to assure himself of his place in the order of things. Anywhere along the coast you can count the seconds between lighthouse flashes, see the pattern of the flashes, and know the precise latitude and longitude of your existence on Earth—if, that is, you hadn't forgotten all those things you once knew.

Most everyone in the sprawling compound would be asleep except for the night guards, the military aide in the next cabin, and the men holding watch on the small flotilla of warships a mile off the coast. And, of course, Leonard, Baxter's favorite cook, who would be making preparations for breakfast—and, perhaps, his visitors from the Middle East who might be suffering jet lag. He glanced at his watch, did a quick mental calculation, and concluded it was just coming up on noon in Jerusalem.

He went again to the open window where a chintz curtain, fanned by a sea breeze, brushed his arm. Even in the semi-darkness he saw again how the fair weather of the previous day had turned foul with patchy fog and filthy air. Trees twitched and squirmed in the cold wind. In the distance, revealed only by the diffused beam of the lighthouse, long white combers curled in from the gray sea. It all belonged to another world, one from which he was shut out by the monuments and marble and heavy drapes of his usual Washington existence—shut out by the airframes of *Air Force One* and *Marine One*, and by the bulkheads of bulletproof limousines.

The faint lights of the ships bobbed on the slowly heaving sea.

He had an urge to step outside again, walk down the path to the shore as he had so many times in his childhood when he felt in tune with the rhythms of the sea. Despite the fog, there was still enough scattered light for a walk; the moonlight wasn't as miserly as it sometimes could be. But they would follow him again. Discreetly, yes. At a distance, yes. But follow him they would, just as they had a half-hour before. No, once was enough; if he went a second time, it would raise their concerns and they would guard him even more closely. Anything unusual, anything at all out of the ordinary, alarmed the Secret Service people.

If Grace had been with him, they would have gone together to the shore, perhaps hand in hand as in the old days, and the others would smile indulgently and not follow. The chief of the protection detail would raise his wrist near his lips and announce into the microphone, "Osprey and Owl moving, keep a distance," using the code names for the president and first lady. But people seldom trust a man wandering alone—president of the United States or no—not if (as some of his closest aides knew) he was a man subject to fits of strange behavior. The Secret Service had probably been discreetly instructed by Baxter's chief of staff to keep a close eye on him. Maybe they had even been instructed secretly by Grace.

It was Baxter himself who suggested the code name 'Osprey' to the Secret Service. He told them that every year an osprey made a nest atop the pilings of a day mark warning mariners about the rocks at the entrance to the cove at Baxter Island.

They quickly accommodated the new president and, as was their long-held practice, assigned names beginning with 'O' to members of his family and to protected locations, such as 'Omaha' for the Downeast White House, which he had requested anyway. What he didn't tell them was that there had been a belief in the Middle Ages that fish were so mesmerized by the osprey that they turned belly-up in surrender. It was probably this myth Shakespeare had in mind when he had Aufidius say of Coriolanus:

> *I think he'll be to Rome*
> *As is the osprey to the fish, who takes it*
> *By sovereignty of nature.*

The house used to make sounds, murmur to itself in the wind; windows used to rattle in their frames—all sounds that had brought comfort to him from his earliest days on the family island. But after he'd made the mistake of designating the house his official retreat, the Secret Service had surrounded it with cabins for staff and guests and had taken it upon themselves to seal the house up tightly.

Now it was as silent and dead as a marble crypt; now there was no sound but the muttering of the sea when he forced a window open.

Somewhere within the compound the cook's dog barked. Doubtless Leonard would leave his stove to tend to the animal. Or someone else on the staff would find it and feed it so it wouldn't disturb the foreign guests. Everything was controlled in his sealed-off world. Everything.

With a break in the fog, moonlight shone through the rectangle of skylight above his bed, lending a pearling light to the white sheets. It was the kind of light that always made Grace smile. He wondered if the same moon shone into her room at the hospital. *Uhrlicht.* He wondered if she was smiling.

Staring up through the skylight, he thought it would be so easy to give up his responsibilities and live out his days here—he and Grace, just the two of them except for occasional visits from the children and grandchildren. They had given up so much to win the White House, now he wondered if it had been worth it. How nice it would be to escape, to live in peace and comfort with Grace.

If only she would survive.

But the doctors at GWH offered no hope.

Jim Stockton, the White House physician, offered no hope.

What's more, Baxter's own hard-headed mind—forged by a lifetime, like Lincoln, of coping with depression—offered no hope.

Muttering a curse, he rose from the bed again and stepped outside into the night air. The fog enfolded him like a sweat-bodied, weightless Sumo wrestler. He imagined lowered voices saying into microphones, "Osprey is moving again."

The doctors called it Glioblastoma Multiforme, a ten centimeter brain tumor that was large enough, like a swollen thumb held at arm's length, to totally eclipse the moon, the sun ... their entire universe.

After taking a few deep breaths, he returned inside and lay back down.

"Osprey back inside."

He must have drifted off for a long while because when his eyes fluttered open again, he saw through the skylight a whitening of the mist—the first hint of dawn. At the same time, he heard a shuffling in the adjoining room. Undoubtedly, Edward was laying out his clothes and placing fresh towels by the shower stall ... and mixing him his morning Bloody Mary about which only Edward, sworn to secrecy, knew. He eased into the morning routine, preparing to put his public face on as he had done nearly every morning for as long as he could remember. On this day he would try to inch the Israelis and the Palestinians closer to that elusive permanent peace that for decades had only been a dream. It was something he owed the world; something he owed his children; something he owed himself. And he felt he was the only man who could achieve it.

It was something he owed Grace.

When he last visited her, two days before, he had ushered people out of her room so they could be alone—so that if he should climb into bed with her and hold her in his arms, nobody would be there to witness and inevitably leak to the press. And when he did climb into her bed to enfold her in his arms they had talked mainly about the Middle East. She had said, "Angus, go to the island. Meet with Bakhit and Golani. Don't leave it to staff and State. I'll still be here when you return. I promise. In the meantime, the children will be here for me; Matt will be here ...."

"Bakhit and Golani aren't the only problem," he'd replied. "With all the blood that's been shed since Carter's Camp David, I think I can get them to go along with a different approach. After all, nothing else has worked. One of the biggest problems is right here."

She nodded. "It means you're going to have to commit the United States like it's never been committed before."

He nodded. "And that's where the real problem comes in: Congress. It's going to be like pulling teeth to get the Hill to agree to the costs, never mind the tremendous ramp-up of aid to both Israel and the Palestinian people. Especially once Haskins revs up his opposition."

"Haskins is a problem, I agree, and he has more than half the senate with him. But you have to push ahead," Grace squeezed his hand. "We've worked so hard for this, you and I, and there's not much else I can contribute to your legacy—*our* legacy."

Her words still echoed in his mind as he left the main house.
"Osprey moving."

The fog was lifting, a streak of sunlight slashed the cloudbank on the eastern horizon. As he moved through the compound toward the main building, a converted barn, where the breakfast meeting was to be held, aides appeared from all sides briefing him on the latest developments and on the agenda for the meeting.

He took a deep breath and donned his public mask and stepped back into the mud flats of politics. Back to his familiar existence, an existence so full of compromises that the breath of iniquity always followed close behind, as close as the aides breathing hotly on his neck.

The sting of the Bloody Mary lingered on his tongue. He guessed Edward must have slipped with the Tabasco sauce.

THE PRESS SECRETARY: "I'll have a few words on today's agenda then I'll open it up for questions. The president woke at five-thirty and had only a tomato juice instead of his usual breakfast because, as you know, he will meet with President Bakhit and Prime Minister Golani this morning over breakfast, after which the three gentlemen will hold a press conference. Following that, President Baxter will return to Washington. I have no news about the First Lady beyond what I reported last night. The doctors at George Washington will hold their own press conference this morning at ten-thirty. And that's about it. Any questions? Yes, John."

"You said tomato juice?"

"Yes, tomato juice."

Chapter 2—Billy Scroggs; Matt Cannon

Billy Scroggs stared at the ringing phone, his pulse quickening. He knew it might be the bank; they'd been calling several times a day for a week. After the fourth ring, the answering machine kicked in. He heard his wife's recorded voice, "We can't come to the phone. Please leave a message and we'll call back."

A man's voice said, "This is the Bass Run Savings Bank. It's important that we talk to you about a serious matter. Please return our call as soon as possible at—"

Scroggs quickly lifted the receiver. "Hello?" It was as good a time as any. At least Mary-Ann and Annie were out; they wouldn't have to hear him plead.

"Is this Mr. Scroggs?"

"Yes."

"Good afternoon, Mr. Scroggs. I'm calling about your mortgage payments. You're three months behind. When can you bring your account up to date?"

"I need a little time. I got laid off, but I'm lookin' for work. Maybe a month or two." He had been employed as a software engineer for a small firm, Creative Software Associates, west of Bangor, but like so many jobs in technology it had been out-sourced, as he would say, to some fucking, brown-skinned, slant-eyed Malaysian. He didn't know what the man on the other end of the line looked like, but he pictured Angus Baxter. When

American jobs go to foreigners, it's the fault of the politicians with their open trade policies and that asshole Baxter was always jabbering on about a so-called global economy. The man was destroying America.

"I'm afraid we need at least two payments this week or we're going to have to initiate foreclosure proceedings."

"But that's impossible; I ain't got the money right now."

"I'm sorry."

"Listen, goddamn it. I'm an American. I fought for my country." His hand tightened around the receiver. Images of Iraq flashed in his mind.

"Sir, I don't have to listen to your cursing."

"Cursin'? Jesus Christ, all I said was goddamn it."

"If you can't control your language, I'm going to have to hang up."

"Well, go ahead. Hang up the goddamned phone." He paused, struggled to control himself. "Wait. Wait. Let's talk about it. Look, you gotta give me a break. I'm lookin' for a job."

"I'm afraid we've been as patient as we can, Mr. Scroggs. You have one week to send us two payments or we'll begin foreclosure proceedings. Have a good day."

Scroggs slammed the receiver into its cradle. "Fuckin' asshole!" His hand shook. *What about providing a home for Mary-Ann and Annie? What about that? What would they do without the house? There was no place they could go.* It was all falling apart again and it was happening just after he'd begun to feel, in the last several years, that he'd finally gotten his life together. After Iraq, he'd spent years rehabilitating in one military hospital after another followed by more years blurred by drugs and booze. But then, at age thirty, he'd met Mary-Ann and things started to get better.

He took a course in computer programming, proved brilliant at it, and quickly landed a job. They had Annie a few years later and life finally seemed worth living; the job was going well and he was able to put some money in the bank for Annie's education with enough left over to buy Mary-Ann some things. He was even able to add a few pieces to his gun collection.

But no sooner had he started to feel comfortable than the company began shifting jobs out of the country. He hung on for more than a year in constant fear that he would lose his job. And then it happened—late on a Friday, just before everybody left for the weekend, giving him no opportunity to vent his anger and hurt. He'd had to wait through the interminable weekend to go in and talk to them about the possibility of another job.

And when he went in on Monday to explore the possibility of another job, he was met at the door by security people who insisted on escorting him while he was in the building.

Then, his former boss left him with no hope.

The HR director left him with no hope.

What's more, his own embittered mind, formed by a lifetime of disappointment, left him with no hope.

That had been more than a year before, a year in which his bitterness had grown like a tumor. And now the money was gone. Annie would never get the breaks she deserved.

To add to his worries, his brother Donnie, who had also lost his job, had disappeared, leaving Billy mystified. As he often did, Billy pulled from his wallet a photograph of Donnie with that shock of red hair and stared affectionately at it. In the picture his older brother was talking with a well-dressed man in front of a table containing what looked like militia literature. Wondering if the man was somehow connected with Donnie's disappearance, Scroggs had asked all the people he could think of if they knew the man whose clothes labeled him an outsider, but the man remained a mystery.

Since Mary-Ann and Annie weren't due for another hour, he decided to go down to Bob's Bar for a beer to calm his nerves before they returned. He left the house, letting the screen door slam behind him, hopped into his old, battered Dodge Ram pickup, and tore out of the front yard onto the dirt road leading into town. Gravel spat from under the rear tires. When he rolled the window down, the wind blew through his wispy blond hair. The air carried the brutish smell of the deep forest—pines and animal piss and centuries of decay, a hint of skunk. Again, he pictured Angus Baxter.

At Bob's Bar, Zeke was tending the bar as usual. Vernon Ludlow and Huey Figg sat hunched over beers. A television, suspended high in the corner at the end of the bar, was tuned to Fox News but there was no volume. Filling the screen was an image of President Baxter speaking at a podium that bore the seal of the President of the United States.

Reflections from the shifting light of the television screen played in the puddles of spilled beer on the varnished counter. "What's that lowlife talkin' about now?" Scroggs asked.

"Afternoon, Billy," said Zeke, looking over his shoulder at the TV. "Who the hell knows?"

"Probably tellin' us he's screwin' us again," said Vernon Ludlow as he raised his beer toward Scroggs.

"Him and his goddamned so-called global economy," said Huey Figg. "All it means is the Indians and Chinks got our jobs."

"Naw, I think he's talkin' 'bout the Middle East," Zeke said.

"Same difference. Then it's the Jews and Arabs get the jobs. Anyway you cut it, we get screwed."

"Eyuh, ain't that the truth?"

"But the guys who own the companies don't get screwed. They get big, fat bonuses," said Scroggs.

"They're like all the others. They don't give a shit about people like us."

"They all have ins at the White House."

Huey Figg and Vernon Ludlow were also without jobs. They had both worked in a small plant that manufactured after market car parts and, though the plant was still there, most of the shop floor jobs had been sent to Indonesia where labor could be hired at $2.50 an hour instead of the $12.00 an hour they'd been making.

"Billy, you heard from Donnie?" asked Zeke.

"Not a word."

"Where the hell could that idiot be?" Huey Figg asked.

Anger suffusing his cheeks, Scroggs glared at Figg. "Hey Huey, I don't want to hear no more shit like that, you got me? My brother ain't no idiot; he's smarter than anyone in this fuckin' room."

"Yuh, Billy," said Zeke, with a kindly smile. "He's sharp, all right. But you gotta admit, he's a bit of a fruitcake."

"He's different, that's all," said Scroggs. "Ain't nothin' wrong with that." *Donnie has every right to be a little loony after the beatings he took from our asshole of a father. And many times he was only protecting me.*

Scroggs stayed long enough to have two beers and talk half-heartedly with the others about hunting and guns. Then, seeing the fading light outside and judging that Mary-Ann and Annie would be home soon, he left. He wanted to beat them home so he could rinse his mouth with Listerine. Mary-Ann didn't like it when he drank before nightfall; they couldn't afford it.

All the way home he replayed the conversation with the man at the bank, his anger building. He gripped the steering wheel, imagining himself walking into the bank and blowing the guy away. He had the guns for it, and he'd shot people before. Although it had been during the war, it hadn't been difficult, not at all, not like he'd expected. But this bank man—he had no idea what he looked like. He was faceless, just a disembodied voice at the other end of the line. All the same, he burned with an ache for revenge.

He pulled into the dirt driveway, relieved to see that Mary-Ann and Annie hadn't returned yet, and mounted the rickety stairs to the porch. He let himself in and went upstairs to take a shower and brush his teeth. When he emerged, the smell of beer gone from his breath, Mary-Ann and Annie were unpacking grocery bags in the kitchen. Annie ran to greet him and he lifted her into his arms. "How's my little girl?" he asked with a laugh.

"Mommy let me buy some peanut butter cups, Daddy. Want one?"

Scroggs frowned at his wife who merely shrugged her shoulders. "They were on sale," she said. "It was only a little more than a dollar. I had enough food stamps for the rest."

Scroggs squeezed Annie. "Sure, I'll have one." He lowered her to the floor and she ran to search through the bags.

Scroggs looked at his wife. It angered him to see the lines of worry around her eyes. Once more, a wave of humiliation came over him. He was a man who had always cared well for his family but now Mary-Ann was growing old before his eyes and Annie was walking around in clothes that barely fit. In another few months he would have to find a way to buy her at least one or two decent outfits for the coming school year. He closed his eyes, remembering the voice of the man from the bank who might as well have said, "I'm gonna see to it your daughter never goes to college."

Later, Scroggs and Mary-Ann ate mostly in silence while Annie described to her father the trip to the food market. But as much as he tried, Scroggs couldn't drive the phone call from the bank out of his mind. When they finished eating, he rose and said, "I'll be in the basement."

"Don't you ever get enough of your guns?" Mary-Ann asked.

He shrugged, said nothing.

"Can I come, Daddy?" asked Annie.

"No," Mary-Ann said. "You stay here and help me clean up."

"Aw, Mom!"

Scroggs descended the basement stairs. The basement room, where he kept his gun collection, was windowless. He pulled a string to light a single naked bulb. The bulb swayed in a slow arc, sweeping a weak light over the guns arranged on a long table. In a corner was an old metal cabinet housing boxes of ammunition. As always, the sight of the guns and ammunition brought a sense of comfort to him. He may not have the money to ward off the vultures, but at least he could defend himself and his family if someone came to take the house away.

He vowed that wouldn't happen.

What he needed was a plan of action.

Years before, when he was in Iraq, he'd always had a plan to get back at the motherfuckers who made his life miserable, who seemed determined to get him and his buddies killed. Now it was time to plan again. It wasn't his fault that his job had been given to some brown-skinned, slant-eyed Malaysian. He wasn't to blame if the owners of the company cared only about the bottom line and not in the least about the lives they destroyed while they raked in obscene profits. The news he'd seen about executive salaries and bloated bonuses and about corporate abuses only served to heighten his sense of righteousness. And now, with Baxter's globalism, things seemed even worse for little guys like him.

He needed a plan and he put his brilliant programmer's mind to it. It was something he owed Mary-Ann; something he owed himself.

Most of all, it is something he owed Annie.

Walking briskly, Matt Cannon approached the main entrance of the George Washington University Hospital. He inhaled deeply the spring air, filled with the scent of burgeoning life, as if to inoculate himself against the suffocating, conditioned air, tinged with disease, he knew he would find inside the hospital. When he reached the revolving doors, he hesitated; he wasn't quite ready to see Grace Baxter. Mingled with the aromas of spring was a drift of acrid cigarette smoke and it awakened a latent urge in him. Though a dedicated runner, he occasionally allowed himself a cigarette to calm his nerves; the inconsistency often baffled people to whom he would simply say, "I'm just a complicated guy."

He turned and saw, to his surprise, that the smoker was a doctor judging by the scrubs and surgical cap he wore. Matt approached the man. "Any chance I can bum a cigarette from you?"

With an unfriendly look, the man proffered a cigarette from a red Marlboro box held in a latex-gloved hand.

Matt slipped it between his lips, took the book of matches the doctor held out, cupped his hands around the cigarette and lit it. "Thanks," he said, returning the matches. "Nice day."

The man said nothing as he tucked a strand of wild red hair under his surgical cap.

"Yuh…well, thanks again," Matt said. He moved some distance down the sidewalk, taking quick, shallow drags on the cigarette. When he had smoked only half of it, he stubbed it out, squared his shoulders, and made for the hospital entrance.

Matt smiled at the red-haired doctor as he passed, but the smile wasn't returned.

Filled with trepidation, he emerged from the elevator at the VIP floor, turned right, and walked along the familiar corridor. Not that Grace Baxter wouldn't want to see him; she was always cheered by his visits. But each time he'd seen her, she'd changed—her eyes more deeply sunk into their sockets; the red rim around them redder still; her skin more parchment-like; her lips drawn more thinly. It was as if a sudden gust from the opening door could reduce her to dust. Each time he'd seen her, he was convinced she couldn't live much longer, that it would be the last time he'd see her alive and it saddened him beyond telling for he had known her since the beginning of Baxter's political career when he worked on that first campaign for the state senate and she was his dearest friend. This was even more true since Baxter became president, creating a certain formal distance between him and Matt.

While Baxter had acquired some of the remoteness of the presidency, Grace had remained as she always was—warm, open. It was she who had insisted Matt not be a formal part of the administration because it would have opened an even greater gulf between the two men. She had sensed that her husband would need someone, in addition to her, to turn to when everybody else was pressing a personal agenda. Matt was forever grateful for her wisdom.

He passed the nurse's station. A board listing patients, their attending physicians, and their nurses, showed no evidence that the First Lady was on the floor. It was a requirement of the Secret Service and it brought a wry smile to Matt's face because he couldn't imagine anyone being fooled by the absence of her name, not with several armed agents posted outside her door at the far end of the corridor. The agents, two men and a woman, nodded solemnly as he approached. Because he wasn't familiar with the First Lady's protective detail, the only one he recognized was Walter, a tall, athletic man who had the bearing of a Hollywood leading man. Matt was aware of what the wags said about the president's protective detail: that they wore two holsters under their jackets, one for their guns and one for their hair dryers.

"Is Owl alone?" Matt asked, barely suppressing a smile.

"Yes sir, Mister Cannon," replied the female agent.

"Do you know if she's awake?"

"I believe so; the doctor left just a minute or so ago."

"Thanks." He approached the door and tapped lightly.

A frail voice, thin as a cobweb, came from the other side. "Come in, Matt."

He opened the door and slipped into the room. The air was fusty with sickness. Two metallic, silver balloons swayed slowly like mourning dancers as the breeze from the closing door caught them. They bore inscriptions: *Get well, Grandma. We love you, Grandma.* Several pictures, crudely drawn with crayons, decorated the far wall. The broad windowsill was crowded with get-well cards. One of them shivered slightly in the updraft from the built-in heating duct.

"How did you know it was me?" Matt asked.

Grace Baxter gave a weak smile. "After so long in this room I've come to recognize how people knock." She was propped up with three pillows supporting her head.

"How are you feeling today?"

"Prodded and poked. The doctor just left and, before him, a young man came by to take some blood. If those vampires take any more blood I'll dry up and blow away." She reached for his hand. Her's trembled slightly. "How's my husband?"

"I talked with him this morning. He'll be in to see you as soon as the meeting's over and he can fly back to Washington."

She stared at him a minute then rolled her head to the side and gazed out the window. "Good. He's needed here."

Something about the way she said it alarmed him. He gripped her hand tighter. "Is there something I should know?"

"No, no, it's not about me," she said with a weak smile. "If he's going to make any progress with negotiations he's got to win over Senator Haskins. That's where the sticking point to the Middle East is going to be. He needs to be back here." She spoke with a breathless intensity, as if she were trying to force her words through a small tube.

"Well, I'm sure that's on his mind. But you can bet the first thing he does is drop in to see you. Haskins can wait," Matt said. "Have Max and Kyla been by today?"

"They're coming tonight. And they're bringing the grandchildren. But you'll never guess who did come by today."

"Who?"

"Julia Haskins."

"You're kidding!"

"Her husband and Angus may hate each other, but she, herself, is a very nice, warm person."

"Besides, it—"

"—It what?"

"Nothing."

"You were going to say something."

Matt merely shook his head.

"You were going to say it will play well with the press. 'Senator Haskins' wife puts aside politics to visit First Lady on her deathbed'."

"No, Grace. I—"

"—I trust her sincerity. I don't think it had any hidden purpose. When you're standing on the bank of that mythical river as I am, you want to believe in people."

"The River Styx?"

She nodded, turned her head to the side, murmured, "You want quite desperately to believe in people."

"Isn't Styx the entrance to the underworld?"

She gave an arch smile. "My dear man, I've spent a lifetime in politics; where the hell else would I go."

He squeezed her hand. "Do you think the president can win over Haskins?"

She shook her head slowly. "The man will probably run against Angus again in the next election. He'll oppose him at every turn. It's not so much that he wants to win; it's that he wants Angus to lose."

Matt knew how important the peace process was to her and how bitterly disappointed she must be to be dying before any lasting progress could be made.

They talked for a while longer. Several times, Grace drifted off to sleep only to awaken moments later with an apology. "It's the medication," she said. Her eyes brightened momentarily. "Have you and lovely Marcie set a date yet?"

He smiled. "You ask me that every time I see you."

"You two should get married. Have children."

He didn't tell her how, for a long time, he had been aching to father children. He flashed a smile and said, "There you go being a busybody again." But what he didn't say was how he and Marcie had talked about it endlessly in the past year, worrying about how it would affect each of their careers. Nor did he tell her how just two nights before, after making love, Marcie had said, "I think it's time, Matt, we've been putting it off too long."

"Are you saying you'll finally agree to marry me?"

"I want to have your children."

Just the memory of it, so fresh, thrilled him. He decided perhaps he should share his joy with Grace Baxter, but her eyelids were drooping again and when he said he would leave because she must get some sleep before her children visited, she closed her eyes without protest.

Matt returned to his car filled with a sense of foreboding. He prayed Baxter would return soon.

Three days after the phone call from the bank, Billy Scroggs drove his truck into the parking lot of a small shopping center at 11:30 in the morning. In addition to a Hannaford's Supermarket, a Rite Aid pharmacy, a Dunkin' Donuts shop and a pizza place, the complex also housed the Bass Run Savings Bank plus, in a separate building to the side, the offices of Creative Software Associates.

Scroggs drove slowly around the perimeter of the lot until he found what he was looking for: a black BMW 5 Series sedan angled so that it took up two parking spots. "Asshole!" muttered Scroggs. There were many times when he wanted to key the car just to show the jerk, Lloyd Feinstein, that he couldn't prevent scratches by taking up two slots. But now he had a better idea. He knew that many men in his situation, guys who had been screwed, went into an office with guns blazing. But that was plain stupid—the sign of a man who let his emotions run away with him—and he was far too smart for that.

He stopped the truck behind the BMW. Fortunately, again to preserve his pristine paint job, Feinstein always parked in the remote part of the lot where security cameras didn't reach. Now, Scroggs' truck hid him from any human eyes that might be looking his way. Quickly, he slid the package of explosives under the BMW, then went around his truck making like he was inspecting the tires in case anyone was watching. Finally, he climbed into the truck and drove out of the parking lot.

A half mile down the road, he turned onto a smaller road that doubled back, meandering uphill to a pizza shop that overlooked the shopping center, which was only a hundred yards away.

Inside, He took a seat by a window and ordered two slices with pepperoni and a coke.

When he finished the second slice, it was already past noon. He had counted on Feinstein's habit of always driving off to lunch at exactly noon. Where was the man? Not wanting to look suspicious by lingering, Scroggs ordered a third slice of pizza and a second coke.

But before they could be delivered, Feinstein appeared. He walked to his car and circled it, apparently inspecting for scratches. Then he reached for the door handle.

That's when Scroggs squeezed the button of the remote detonator in his jacket pocket.

The following day the newspaper reported that a bomb had gone off under a BMW and that a vice president of Creative Software Associates, who'd had the misfortune of approaching his car at the wrong time, had been killed. Several people inside the glass-enclosed lobby had been seriously injured. It even made the national news.

In the week that followed, as expected, the police questioned everybody who had been laid off from Creative Software. But they came up with nothing. Scroggs was in the clear.

Meanwhile, a notice of foreclosure appeared in his mailbox.

The man in blue surgical garb dropped a spent cigarette to the pavement and ground it under his heel. He had been walking up and down 23rd Street in front of the George Washington University Hospital—his footfalls soft in the surgical booties—evaluating all the possibilities, calculating angles, and trying to confirm the pattern he thought he had detected in the way the Secret Service chose entrances to the hospital for the president. It had amused him greatly that as he walked along the sidewalk, several people had said, "Good afternoon, Doctor."

In keeping with his doctor's pose, he had privately dubbed himself *The Scalpel* because he was God's instrument for cutting out the tumor in the society that was the president of the United States.

It would be elective surgery—*his* elective—and he had scheduled it for that night. The prospect of dying in the process didn't bother him in the least because Baxter and people like him had already made his life not worth living. His only regret was that people might compare him to those Muslim extremists who also sacrifice themselves for a cause, like those motherfuckers who flew planes into the Twin Towers and the Pentagon. But there was a big difference—he was laying down his life for God, not Allah.

The Scalpel took a deep breath, adjusted his surgical cap, lit yet another cigarette, and pondered his choices. By the time he'd smoked the cigarette down to the filter, he had made his decision: as he'd thought before, it would be the emergency room entrance that night. He was sure of it.

Having made his decision, his next task was to prepare the scene—something like prepping the patient before surgery.

After buying a newspaper from a street vending machine, he strolled into the Emergency Department reception area and took a seat as though he were waiting for a patient to be delivered to him. One of the people behind the counter—perhaps she was a triage nurse—gave him a quizzical look. But he ignored her. *What was wrong with a doctor having a seat in the ED waiting area and reading a newspaper?* He flashed the woman a smile, opened the paper, and pretended to read. With each turn of the page, he lowered the paper momentarily and scanned the area. Finally, he made his choice: the soda machine.

Satisfied, he left the hospital and descended into the Foggy Bottom Metro station to take the train under the Potomac to his hotel across the river in Arlington. On the subway platform, and again on the train, people smiled at him. There were more smiles as he passed the reception desk in the hotel—the cheapest he could find—to take the elevator up to his room where he retrieved his Walther P-99 semi automatic pistol and tucked it into the briefcase he had brought for the purpose. He left the hotel and re-entered the Metro.

By the time he walked back into the ED reception area, no more than an hour had elapsed. Now it was time for stage two of his plan. He went into the men's room, waited for another man to leave, then emptied the paper towel dispenser. Carrying an armful of paper towels, his briefcase cradled against his chest, he shut himself into a stall. He took the newspaper that he'd stuffed into his briefcase, spread it across the floor, scattered the paper towels over it, and held a match to the pile until it erupted into flames. Hurriedly, he left the men's room and took a seat near the soda machine.

Minutes later, the fire alarm went off. As patients, visitors, and hospital personnel ran around trying to figure out what to do, *The Scalpel* calmly tucked the Walther P-99, with its snub nose, behind the soda machine.

He would retrieve it later when, as he expected, everyone became distracted by the sirens announcing the arrival of the president of the United States.

President Angus Baxter, sitting alone in the Oval Office, the phone clutched to his ear, said, "Thank you, Doctor, we'll be there shortly." After lowering the phone to its cradle, his hand lingered on the receiver as if to let go would be to yield to something he didn't want to acknowledge.

Not now. Please God, not now.

Yet after a lifetime in politics, a life that demanded he always face situations clear-eyed and dispassionately, he could no longer deny his wife of forty years was about to die. When he had visited Grace the previous day, after returning from Maine, he'd been shocked at how much she'd declined in just a few days. Now, this latest call confirmed his worst fears. The realization swamped his mind the way a sea fog swallows the land—moist, viscous.

He was glad he asked Matt Cannon to wait in the outer office while he took the call; he needed this time alone to compose himself, to clear his mind. He touched the polished wood box containing his father's Congressional Medal of Honor.

Courage.

Just a few days before—when the truce he'd thought he had brokered in the Middle East had collapsed almost as soon as it had been concluded and he tossed in bed for hours, his wife, from her own hospital bed, had phoned and said, consolingly, "Great men suffer greatly because their dreams are great." And now, indeed, he suffered. But not as a great man. At this moment he was an ordinary man who was about to lose the person he most loved in the world. With a deep, shuddering sigh, he pressed the button on the intercom.

"Yes, Mister President?"

"Is everything ready?"

"Yes, Mr. President. Matt's waiting for you."

"Yuh." The word choked from his lips. One word only because he knew his voice would falter on more words. Wearily, he levered his lanky frame from the chair and leaned for a moment on his desk. It was a custom-made desk Grace had persuaded him to commission rather than use one of the four desks—the Resolute, the Wilson, the Theodore Roosevelt, and the C&O—that had been used by nearly every president in the past hundred years. Only LBJ before him had commissioned his own desk. Baxter wondered if Grace had been sending him a message about the dangers of overweening pride by linking him in that way with Johnson.

The revolving globes of the anniversary clock that she'd given him as an inauguration gift swept reflections across his sharp cheekbones and flared in the reading glasses resting at the tip of his nose. He walked to the sideboard, crossing the carpet bearing the seal of the president, opened the door, removed a bottle, and poured himself a finger of scotch. He closed his eyes and drank it in one swallow, focusing on the burning in his throat. Taking a deep breath, he went into the Oval Office bathroom where he swirled a mouthful of Listerine. Spitting it into the sink, he squared his shoulders and walked to the outer door. When he opened it and entered the anteroom, Matt Cannon bolted from a chair and came to him. "The motorcade's ready, Mister President."

Baxter nodded. The anteroom and the corridors were strangely deserted. Baxter felt a surge of gratitude for the understanding and discretion of the White House staff that usually crowded the place. Doris, his secretary, held out a card. "It's for the First Lady," she said. "It's from all of us."

Baxter swallowed. The taste of Listerine was sharp, unpleasant, on his tongue. He took the card, nodded, forced a tight smile, then hurried from the room before tears overwhelmed him. He was not a man easily given to tears, but from the moment he first heard Grace's diagnosis, they'd come freely, usually in the solitude of the family quarters.

When he emerged onto the portico, an aide popped an umbrella open and held it over Baxter's head. Matt took the umbrella from the man and walked with the president to the limousine where Baxter folded his frame into the back seat. Matt rushed round to the other side of the car and slipped in beside him. The windshield wipers made a rhythmic, clicking sound above the purr of the idling engine.

When Baxter had visited Grace the day before, her cheeks had been hollow but her eyes had been bright. She hadn't been heavily medicated. Either the pain had subsided or she had refused to yield to it. She said she was comfortable, but he knew she'd say that anyway. He just couldn't tell. After forty years of marriage there were still times when they held secrets from each other; it was a kind of love—each not wanting to worry the other.

The motorcade snaked out the long driveway onto Pennsylvania Avenue. People stood silently along the sidewalks, holding umbrellas, watching him pass.

The day before, alone in her hospital room, holding hands, they'd talked about the grandchildren. "Angus, promise me," she'd said with a smile, "promise me when your second term is over you'll spend time with them. They love you. They need you."

He squeezed her hand. "I will, Grace."

Wind-driven rain had spattered against the window. He'd watched thin rivulets of rainwater—illumined blue, red and white by the flashing lights of his waiting motorcade—slither down the pane of glass.

"No big projects like Carter or Clinton. At least not for a while."

"No big projects."

"You'll have plenty of time later to be an active ex-president. But for now, Peter, especially, needs you. Natalie and Jeremy, too. You can relax and write your memoirs."

He nodded.

"I'm afraid Maxwell and Kyla are much like we were. Too busy with life to spend the time they should with their children. We were that way, you know."

"Yes, I know."

"It's a steep price we paid for what we wanted to do. Maxwell and Kyla suffered for it."

"Were we too ambitious?"

Grace smiled, a smile filled with regret and longing. "It's too late for us to question it now, Angus." She reached across her body and placed her cold hand over his. She closed her eyes, breathing deeply, evenly. Baxter knew it was his wife's way of mastering the pain. As he gazed at her frail hands—veins and bones defining deep valleys, macula spots—they morphed into the hands that, soft and smooth, had once warmly cradled his body after lovemaking; that, sprinkled with baby powder, had expertly changed Max's, then Kyla's, diapers; that had held a pen confidently over a notebook. She stirred. Her eyes opened. "We ... we did a lot of good, too, Angus. Remember that. We paid the price for a public life but we got the rewards also."

"I promise you, Grace, I'll get your education bill passed."

"Bakhit and Golani ...?"

"I'll bring them together again if it's the last thing I do. The Middle East has seen enough bloodshed to last many lifetimes."

"If you can achieve that, you'll be recognized as one of the truly great peacemakers."

"I intend to win Haskins over."

"Do that, and I'll be content. I want so much for you to bring peace where all the others have failed. It belongs to you, it defines you, the way slavery did Lincoln and World War Two did FDR. And when all that's done ... Peter, Jeremy, and Natalie."

He gave her a sad smile. "You have my promise."

She squeezed his hand weakly. "I worry about you, Angus. I worry what you'll do without me. The Bay of Fundy; it seems so long ago now. But still ...."

He leaned over and kissed her on the forehead. "Don't worry about that," he murmured. His heart felt as though it was fluttering around his vocal cords, tapping against the walls of his throat.

They talked for a while longer, then she said, "Now you must go. You're still the president and there are things to do."

He rose, leaned down and brushed his lips against her cheeks. "I love you, Grace. I'll be back tomorrow evening." He walked to the door.

"Angus?"

He turned.

"I love you, too, Angus. I always have. Remember that."

He smiled, nodded, and started toward the door again.

"Angus?"

He turned.

"Angus, you'll be okay without me." It was said on a rising inflection, halfway between an assertion and a question. "I've never forgotten the Bay of Fundy. Cape Split."

For a long moment, Baxter said nothing.

"Angus?"

"You need to get your rest now."

"There's so much good you can still do. I wouldn't want—"

"—I'll be fine, Grace. Sleep now; I'll be back tomorrow night."

Now, through the rain-pelted windshield and the sweep of the wipers, he saw they were approaching Washington Circle. He couldn't wait to see her, to hold her hand once again. To say to her what he wanted to say. To tell her what she'd meant to him all these years. Just to see her face.

As they came off Washington Circle, Baxter saw the sign for the GWH's emergency entrance up ahead.

Chapter 3—Multiple GSW

By Matt Cannon's watch it was precisely 8:26 in the evening when the presidential limousine turned off Washington Circle and onto 23rd Street. He'd had no real reason to look at his watch; it was merely habit. The president was there beside him, and for once there was no strict schedule to maintain, no demands from the White House staff. Because on this night, the president had cancelled all his appointments.

Yet, Matt would have cause to remember that time of 8:26 forever.

A passing thunderstorm, just a few minutes before, had left the road wet and glistening, the air cleansed. The solid authority of the red and blue lights on the Secret Service car ahead of them reflected wetly in the washed road.

Pedestrians with umbrellas paused to watch the speeding motorcade. They appeared distorted through streaks of rain slanting back on the limousine's windows. The varicolored umbrellas were luminescent in the rinsed air—intense reds, greens—soft, rounded blooms of light. Even the black umbrellas seemed to glow.

Matt turned from the window and looked at his friend. The president stared straight ahead. His drawn, gaunt face looked older than his seventy years. He rested his gnarled hands on his knees which, because of his famous long legs, rode high as though the seat in which he sat was designed for a much smaller man.

Overriding the luxuriant smell of the limousine's leather seats was another fragrance, heady, pungent. Matt looked at Baxter. "Is that cologne I smell?" He couldn't recall ever smelling cologne, or even after-shave lotion, on Baxter.

Baxter gave a faint smile. "Old Spice. Back when we first started seeing each other, Grace loved it. Said it made her think I was some romantic sailor. I'd put it on only when …." He turned to look out the window.

Matt stared at the back of Baxter's head for a moment then gazed out the windshield past the driver's shoulder. Ahead of them were two lead cars occupied by Secret Service men. They followed a cordon of motorcycles turning toward a side entrance of the hospital. Matt felt the president's sadness as a tangible presence.

He had been with his friend through many bad times and knew him to be a man of profound sensibilities, one who cared deeply for people. He had seen his anguish when people died—whether soldiers killed in some mission he'd authorized, or an old friend and mentor like the former U.N. ambassador, or even a murderer whose death sentence he felt obliged not to commute. Baxter would brood for days under a heavy mantle of sadness. But never had he seen the man so weighed down as now. On this night, Matt heard none of the usual banter about baseball between the president, a Red Sox fan, and the secret service agent driving the limousine, a Yankees fan.

In the past month, there had been many visits to the hospital; enough to have the agents nervous about establishing a pattern. But Baxter would only agree to vary the times of his visits, necessitating a disruption of the customary schedules of the administration.

The regular meetings with the National Security Council and with the Cabinet, the president's daily briefing, phone calls to senators and house members—all formerly precisely scheduled—now occurred at odd hours, and the reshuffling had had a ripple effect throughout the administration. Staff meetings of the department secretaries were re-scheduled on short notice; trips overseas were changed, even Baxter's daily exercise routine now occurred at strange hours, sometimes in the middle of the night. Only state visits were held sacrosanct. But even then, the president often had others stand in for him at the preliminary meetings leading to the final conference between heads-of-state.

This created some friction between the president and Katherine Moore-Paterson who resented playing the role of a ceremonial vice president.

Matt glanced at his watch again. 8:28. At that moment, Marcie would probably be slipping his missed dinner into the oven at low heat to keep it warm. She had told him not to worry about being late; being with the president at this time was more important.

When this was over they would sit down and plan a wedding date. It would be in the near future because they were in a hurry to have children; Marcie was in her late thirties and Matt was approaching fifty. It was now or never. He wondered if their relationship could ever evolve into one as tight, as all-embracing, as that between Angus and Grace Baxter.

As they pulled up to the hospital's emergency entrance, marked by a red sign, the president took a deep breath. He appeared to be steeling himself.

Whenever the presidential limousine arrived somewhere, the agents in the car with the president stayed put until agents from the control van, an unmarked, armored Suburban with smoke-glass windows, secured the area and surrounded the limousine, forming the inner perimeter of protection in the three-perimeter philosophy of the Secret Service.

As Matt and the president waited for this to happen, Baxter said, "You do surely bar the door upon your own liberty if you deny your friends your grief … Hamlet … Rosencrantz."

Matt knew his friend well enough to understand this was the man's way of thanking him for being there. He gave Baxter an encouraging pat on the knee. "Be strong."

Matt was relieved to see they didn't use the entrance to the morgue this time. He understood the need for a varied routine but when they used the morgue it always gave Matt the chills. He glanced at his watch. 8:29. He lowered his head to look out at the roofs of the buildings around the hospital and saw several of the sharpshooters, dressed in black, that constituted the outer perimeter of the protection package.

At last, an agent skillfully opened the door on Matt's side of the limousine. Skillfully, because there was a trick to opening the doors that only Secret Service agents knew—another level of security. Matt stepped out. He was startled by the freshness of the air, the clean smell of rain, a faint odor of lingering ozone. Several agents huddled around the open door to the limousine, glancing warily about. Matt turned to wait for Baxter to emerge with the help of the lead agent. The doors to the limousine closed with solid thumps, a heavy, familiar, satisfying, bullet-proof sound.

"Good evening, Mister President," said Mike Padilla, the president's lead Secret Service agent and a man Matt enjoyed for his unusual sense of humor. "I'm so sorry about Mrs. Baxter."

Baxter nodded.

"Follow me, please, sir."

They started to walk toward the entrance.

Behind a barricade on the sidewalk, opposite the entrance, a small clutch of people stood solemnly watching, umbrellas folded. Every several yards an agent stood facing them, watching for anything that looked suspicious. No matter how much the Secret Service tried to vary the president's arrival patterns—both time and entrance—there were always people around. The people seemed to sense the gravity of the moment; there were none of the cheers and calls of "Mister President" that Baxter's arrival usually elicited, only a distant murmuring. It was as if the entire nation was participating in a death vigil.

Several of the agents rushed to place themselves between the small crowd and the president, their rubber-soled shoes squeaking on the wet pavement. For the umpteenth time since Baxter became president, Matt was impressed by how the cocoon around the man always seemed to be one of sound, and a sense of electric excitement.

Before them, the flashing lights of the idling motorcade were reflected in the doors of the emergency entrance. Ahead and to Matt's right, a man in blue surgical scrubs emerged from a small clutch of hospital staff standing to the right of the entrance under the EMERGENCY sign. Matt would always remember the shock of red hair spilling from under the man's cap as he rushed toward the railing overlooking the presidential party coming up the ramp—took a single step then pulled a gun from under his doctor's coat. A blue police light flashed along its barrel. In that split second, Matt recognized the man he'd cadged a cigarette from.

A frenzy of movement.

Shouts.

Mike Padilla yelled "Down!" and jumped to his right to place himself between the president and the man.

Matt turned to his left to push the president out of the line of fire.

A gunshot reverberated from the entryway.

Then another.

And another.

Mike crumbled to the ramp.

"He's shooting!" someone shouted.

"Get him!"

"Oh, shit!"

Several more shots.

Matt felt as though somebody hit him in the side with a baseball bat. Then he felt a biting pain in his groin. He was stunned to see the ramp rushing up toward him. He felt helpless, as though being slammed to the ground by some invisible force. He hit the ramp hard, his head coming to rest against one of the railing's metal stanchions. He was vaguely aware of a flurry of gunshots; men shouting and cursing; feet scuffling and scraping around his head. Everything happening in some space far above him. He tried to grab the railing and lever himself upright but the pain was searing.

Several more shots.

Oh God, Angus! He tried to roll over. His cheek brushed the wet metal of the stanchion. It felt cold. Moments later, several people were bending over him, their voices sounding as though coming from a distant place. Someone touched his side and he winced. A voice shouted, "Multiple GSW … right side … groin. Let's get him inside. Now!"

"The president?" Matt gasped. But no one answered.

He started to ask again, but a wave of pain sliced through him like a heavy, sharp sheet of ice. His body heaved involuntarily. Tears formed in the corners of his eyes. Again, the scraping of feet rushing all around him. He heard another voice to his right. "GSW to the head. Unresponsive. Trauma Bay One, now!"

The president? Angus?

Another scramble of feet. He feared they would kick him in the head. But he was unable to raise his arm to shield his face. And from further away: "Multiple GSW to the chest. No pulse. We're gonna need a thoracotomy tray."

A shock of fear ran through Matt. "The president!" he cried through grimaced teeth. And under his breath he murmured "Angus!" He knew that GSW meant gunshot wound. "Jesus, Angus. NO!"

A woman's face was close to his. She loosened his tie, opened the top buttons of his shirt. Her gloved hands were covered in blood. He felt other hands working at his waist. Undoing his belt. "You'll be alright," the woman said. "Try to relax. We'll take care of you."

"But the president?" he moaned. *Why won't anybody answer?* He thought of Marcie. His dinner in the oven. An overwhelming need to be there, to be with her, swept over him. He hoped they would hurry and do what they had to do so he could go to her. All he wanted to do was go to her. Go to Marcie. Talk. Let her help him understand. "The president?" he asked again, more weakly this time.

But the woman attending him was already barking orders to somebody and Matt felt himself being lifted into the air. All at once he was inside the building and he saw ceiling tiles speeding by overhead, heard the shouts of doctors and nurses, the thump as the gurney crashed through swinging doors. He felt cool air on his chest and was surprised to realize his upper body was bare; he couldn't remember them taking his jacket and shirt off. He started to reach out with his arm but cried out with the pain.

"Try not to move, sir."

"Please, will somebody please tell me about the president?" he moaned.

The nurse, stuffing something against his side said, "We just don't know. Everything happened so fast."

He felt a sharp prick in his arm. "Oh God! I need to—" His words were cut off by something appearing over his nose and mouth. It bit into his skin. He felt like he was choking. He was conscious of swallowing spittle and he felt the wetness of it on his cheeks. His eyes opened wide, fearful. He was staring into a bright light. He was blinded by the brightness of the light.

And now he felt himself sinking into the gurney as though it was made of quicksand. The voices around him receded ... far away ... hollow ... leaden .... pain dissolving away ... warmth.

Now, a velvet blackness.

Billy Scroggs just had to get out of the house. The news he'd seen on TV gave him a bad feeling and he didn't want Mary-Ann to hear it in case his worst fears were confirmed. She never took news, especially bad news, well. He also didn't think it would be good for Annie to see the news.

Just in case.

He decided to go to Bob's Bar, his habitual refuge, and watch the news there. He switched the TV off, went upstairs and called through the bathroom door where Mary-Ann had just finished taking a shower. "I'm goin' down to Bob's for a beer."

"Ain't there beers in the fridge?" she called out.

He pretended not to hear and hurried down the steps before she came out of the bathroom, his combat boots making loud thuds on the treads. He paused in the living room to turn the TV on again, switch it to a game channel, then turn it off once more. He knew she'd turn the TV on when she came downstairs and, once into a game show, she wouldn't change stations. It was an addiction of hers.

He had his consolations, she had hers.

Outside, the last vestige of sunlight was slipping from the high, serrated pine ridge. Only a thin, lurid bruise of red illumined the rim of sky. A hunter's moon in the east already gave the deep valley a spectral appearance. Scroggs' nose twitched at the faint odor of skunk lingering in the air. It was a smell that always made him think of the unrelenting fight for survival taking place in the murkiness of the forest—predators and preys. In the distance he heard a dog bark.

Twenty yards up the road a woman sat in a late model, shining white Mercedes parked by the side of the road. She was looking at the house and writing in a spiral note book. A vulture preparing her bid for the foreclosure.

Scroggs climbed into his truck and drove past the woman. They exchanged glances—her's haughty, his hate-filled. He wanted to kill her on the spot, but he accelerated past.

In the gloaming, the truck's headlights cut a swath of light along the rutted dirt road. Some creature of the woods dashed across the road, caught momentarily in the sweeping bloom of light, then disappeared on the other side. Around a bend, the headlights picked out two beads of light low in the middle of the road. *Eyeballs.* Scroggs slammed his foot on the accelerator. The truck lurched forward. He aimed for the eyeballs, but the animal disappeared.

Like Iraq.

Like militants in the night.

Fuckin' insurgents!

Five minutes later he swung the truck into the parking lot at Bob's Bar. As he walked toward the door, the glare from a pair of headlights swept across his face. He turned to watch. The woman in the Mercedes sped past. He followed her with his gaze, then entered the bar.

About a dozen men sat on stools and at tables. The TV blared. Most of the men had their heads turned in its direction, beer bottles clutched in their hands. He looked at the digital time on the lower part of the TV screen and saw it change to 9:37. He climbed onto a bar stool and almost instantly a bottle of Budweiser appeared before him. He acknowledged Zeke, the bartender with a slight nod. "Can you turn the volume up?" Scroggs asked.

"Sure, Billy. Some kinda shit, huh?"

Scroggs didn't answer. He took a long swig from the bottle and lowered it to the counter. Absently, he slid the bottle back and forth through a ring of suds on the gleaming surface of the bar. It made small skating sounds and a click, click, each time it passed over the catchphrase, roughly carved in Greek, into the wood: μολων λαβέ. His head was cocked toward the large-screen television which showed people milling about near the entrance to a hospital which was girded by police tape.

An off-camera voice said, " … numerous shots. Several people were hit, including, it's feared, President Baxter." He paused, then said, "Now this just in: exclusive footage of the shooting."

The screen now showed the emergency entrance to the hospital, a crowd of people, flashing motorcade lights, then a sudden outburst of chaos as a gunman in doctor's clothes, highlighted in a circle of digital brightness, opened fire. Then the images jumped all over, showing the sky, the top of a building, someone's shoes, as the cameraman apparently started running.

But the few seconds the shooter was on screen had been enough to send a jolt of recognition through Scroggs.

"That looks like your brother, Billy," said a man several stools to Scroggs' right. "Ain't that your brother?"

"Fuck! That is your brother, Billy!" said Huey Figg. "He ain't no doctor!"

Scroggs didn't answer; his entire focus was on the television screen as he gripped the bottle hard by the neck, sliding it back and forth along the counter, clicking over the carved phrase.

They replayed the assassination scene numerous times and even if the image of his brother hadn't been clear, he would have had no difficulty recognizing the peculiar way Donnie held his body, the way he held his gun. It was exactly the same as when they played Cowboys and Indians years before … or the way Donnie would hold himself when facing off to their father, halfway between prepared to charge and prepared to run.

Everyone in the bar turned toward Billy. Zeke lifted Billy's bottle, wiped the spill of beer, and placed the bottle back down. "You know Donnie was gonna do that?" he asked in a soft voice.

Billy shook his head slowly. "He never said nothin', Zeke."

Of course, he and Donnie had talked about it—talked about the need to get rid of Baxter before he destroyed the Constitution; before he sacrificed American sovereignty to the United Nations; before he let immigrants take over the whole fuckin' country; before he let foreigners take all the jobs— but Billy had no idea Donnie would follow through with it.

"Jesus, Billy," said an older man. "This means the goddamned feds'll be here in Bass Run, you realize that? They'll have all kinds o' questions. Maybe you oughta get the fuck outa here for a while."

"Why?"

" 'Cause you're his fuckin' brother! Shit, man!"

"And 'cause you got a big, fuckin' stash of weapons," added Zeke. "They'll want to know about that."

"Eyuh, Billy. They'll fuckin' try to frame you."

Let them, thought Scroggs. After Reno and Clinton took out all those people at Waco; after what the FBI did at Ruby Ridge; after Bush killed Tim McVeigh; this would be just be another thing building toward the ultimate revolution. All the same, he thought of that hunting shack deep in the woods. Maybe he should move the weapons there for the time being.

"What gun was he usin', Billy?" asked Huey Figg. "Was that his Glock? Could you tell?"

"Fuck you, Huey!" Scroggs shot back.

"Oh, shit, listen!" said Zeke.

But Billy was already listening to the latest news bulletin. ".... just been confirmed: the gunman, Donald A. Scroggs has died on the operating table. He had been shot a minimum of five times by Secret Service agents trying to protect the president."

"Jesus, Billy!"

"God," said Zeke. "That poor, fuckin' sweet, loony fool."

Vernon Ludlow came over and put a hand on Scroggs' shoulder. "Jeez, Billy, I'm real sorry. I know we all thought he was a bit wacko, but he was a good man, sharp as anybody."

Billy Scroggs' eyes watered. He looked down at the new puddle of beer under his bottle, trying to hide his face. It felt as though someone had reached down his throat and twisted his guts, like the time when he was a small boy and his father, in a fit of rage, punched his mother and the blood came gushing from her nose. Donnie had pummeled his father's back with his fists as Billy watched in horror. *Donnie.* He had always been there for Billy. He had always been the one to look up to and to depend on, the one who had comforted him later when their father was killed in an auto accident, and again when their mother took off with some joker from Canada.

Now Donnie is gone.

And it's Baxter's fault.

He'd always known something terrible was bound to happen when Haskins lost the election to Baxter. But this?

"Christ, Billy, what're you gonna do?"

Again, Scroggs didn't answer. He couldn't imagine life without Donnie, but somehow he would have to make it right. If he were still in Iraq he'd know precisely what to do: find some fucking officer, frag him. Make the motherfuckers pay for their betrayal. He would have to be careful, keep a low profile for a while. But he knew that somehow, someday, the feds would pay for this. He would see to it. A rage started to build in him. It was like an animal gnawing at his insides, climbing up his gut, burrowing under the skin of his face, heating it, blushing it.

Chapter 4—Karl Zacher; Wayne Haskins

On Capitol Hill it was nearing midnight when an elevator jolted to a stop and the doors slid open with a metallic hiss. Karl Zacher, stout and balding, emerged onto the third floor of the Richard B. Russell Senate Office building. He walked down the long, deserted, dimly lit corridor toward the familiar door to Senator Haskins' office, his footfalls echoing from the walls. He had walked this corridor many times before, though never at such an ungodly hour.

He pulled the door open, entered the senator's suite where three people lingered at the secretary's desk atop which sat an open pizza box, one slice uneaten. A half dozen empty soda cans littered the desk.

"Mister Zacher," said the senator's secretary, a young, attractive brunette. "I'm afraid there's only one slice left, but it's all yours."

"No, thanks, Kathy," he said with a smile. "You folks are working late." Though a wealthy financier and a major contributor to Haskins' campaigns, he had nothing to do with the day-to-day operation of the senator's office. All the same, he couldn't imagine they often worked this late; something unusual kept them here and he had a damned good idea what it was.

"He's called the entire staff in," replied Kathy. She reached for a can of soda. "Want a coke or something?"

"No, thanks. Just ate. Stuffed," he replied. "It's about Baxter, right? What happened at the hospital?"

Kathy nodded grimly. "It's been quite a shock even if we have no use for the man." She rose from her chair. "The senator was just talking with BATF about the whole mess; that's Alcohol, Tobacco, and Firearms. They are—."

"—I know who they are."

"Yes, well I'll see if he's finished and tell him you're here." She disappeared into Senator Haskins' inner office.

Moments later, several staff members filed out of the senator's office. The last one, Haskins' press secretary, a tall, bespectacled man who didn't like Zacher and made it obvious every time they met, said, "He wants to see you. Alone."

Zacher smiled. "Good evening, Tom. Nice to see you're in such good spirits."

Tom said nothing.

Senator Haskins, usually an affable backslapper who would rise and meet visitors in the middle of the large room, remained seated behind his massive mahogany desk, a grim expression on his jowl-cheeked face. Another open pizza box sat on his desk, this one only half-eaten.

Zacher approached the desk. "May I?" He reached for a slice.

"Do you know anything about this, Karl?" Haskins asked.

Zacher shook his head. "I'm as shocked as you are." He folded the pizza slice in half and took a large bite. A string of cheese stretched between his mouth and the pizza. He pinched it from the slice and fed it into his mouth, then reached into his back pocket for a handkerchief.

Haskins said, "I just got confirmation from the ATF folks about what was reported a little while ago on FOX—that this Scroggs guy was active in the M-4 militia group."

"I know; I heard that, too," said Zacher, wiping his mouth with the handkerchief.

"I figured you would. Christ, you give enough money to those goddamned people."

"Not for this, I don't. Not assassination. Besides, I've never given any money to this group, M-4. I hardly even know who the hell they are."

Haskins rose from his chair and walked around his desk to stand before Zacher. "Karl, I hope you're telling me the truth here, and the whole goddamned truth, because if you aren't, we're going to have a boatload of trouble on our hands."

Zacher felt heat rising to his cheeks. "I'm telling you the truth, Wayne. I've never sent any money to this M-4 group."

Senator Haskins gazed at his friend for a long moment. "Well, that's good. Because if you did, that would link you to this thing and if you're linked, then I'm linked."

"Well I'm not linked," Zacher snapped. "So you're not linked."

"Okay, okay. All I'm saying is if there happened to be a check or a bank transfer or something, even if it wasn't to support this assassination thing, we would be linked in the public's perception."

"Well, you don't have to worry, Wayne. There's no fucking linkage, no checks, no transfers. Not a fucking thing."

"Except that you've been known to support militia groups in the past," said Haskins. "And don't use that kind of language in my office. I've asked you before."

Zacher shrugged.

"We're going to need some spin on this," Haskins said. He returned to his desk. "I suggest you stop support for any group until this thing blows over."

"Sure, no problem," said Zacher. "Makes sense."

"And I want you to meet with Tom. You need to develop a story just in case the media hounds come after you."

"Tonight?"

"Yes, tonight. The fan's spinning; the poop's in the air. You've got to be ready by morning."

"And what are you going to say?"

"I'm going to say you're a key supporter but I had no knowledge of your relationship to certain militia groups and that I will demand you terminate all such relationships or I'll refuse all future support."

Zacher nodded. "Okay, plain enough. I'll get to work on my story." He started to leave the office, stopped, turned, and said, "But you know, between you and me, none of this means I don't think Baxter deserves what he gets."

Haskins frowned, glared at his friend. "Karl, I'll say this once and in a way I hope you'll understand. There's no room in politics for this crap, no matter what you think about the other man. You got that? This isn't the godforsaken Roman Republic."

Zacher nodded. "Right, got it, Wayne." An insipient smile formed at the corners of his mouth.

The senator looked into the eyes of his friend, apparently trying to decide if he was being honest. Finally, he asked, "By the way, have you any idea what this ..." He raised a pair of reading glasses to his eyes and peered at a sheet of paper. " ... this M-4 name stands for?"

Zacher nodded, smiled. "The McVeigh Memorial Militia of Maine. Four 'm's. M-4. The M-4 is also an assault weapon."

"McVeigh, the Oklahoma bomber?"

"That's the sweetheart."

"Frig it, that's all we need."

The dead-stone sensation of anesthetic was dissipating. Matt Cannon's eyelids fluttered when the first trickle of pain seeped into his consciousness. As he stared at the ceiling in the dimly lit room, the pain started to flow more heavily, like a stream freeing itself from ice. He groaned. At first, his thoughts were confused. He knew he was in a hospital bed, that something had happened to him, but he couldn't grasp what it was; it lay just beyond the outer rim of his consciousness.

He called for a nurse. When no response came, he called again, "Nurse." He was confused when the sound came out garbled.

A young woman entered the room. She pointed to a white rectangle of plastic on his tray. "Press that button when you need a nurse. Are you having pain?"

He nodded.

She handed him a cord at the end of which was a button. "It's a PCA pump. When you're feeling pain, press the button. You're hooked up to a morphine drip."

"What's a PCA pump?" he managed to ask.

"PCA stands for patient controlled analgesia. It means you're the one who controls how much morphine you get."

He frowned at her, pressed the button once, then a second and third time. The nurse smiled. "It's okay. There's a governor on the pump so you don't OD."

He dropped the device beside him on the bed and waited for the medicine to take effect. As his bewilderment left him, he became conscious of another discomfort. With a confused expression, he felt the tip of his nose. "Don't touch," the nurse said. "You need to leave that in." When he furrowed his brow inquisitively, she said, "It's a nasal-gastric tube. It's draining stuff from your stomach."

"Why?" he whispered hoarsely.

"One of the bullets pierced your bowel. It's called an ileus. The doctor will explain it to you." She turned to leave.

Bullets?

Suddenly, it all came back to him.

The president!

Angus!

He tried to call the nurse back but she was already gone, closing the door behind her. He fumbled for the call button, but it had slipped off the bed. Although the morphine was already kicking in, he became aware of a throbbing pain in the area of his groin. He tried lift the blankets and raise his head, but he was unable.

What's happened to me?

What's happened to Angus?

A heavy drowsiness descended on him as the morphine took control of his being. He closed his eyes.

It was three in the morning when an aide dropped Wayne Haskins off at his home in McLean, Virginia, on the outskirts of Washington. So not to wake his wife and the three grandchildren who were visiting with them, Haskins had the aide drop him off at the foot of the long driveway. He thanked his driver and started up the gravel surface. His footfalls emitted a soft crunch with every step. He tried to walk lightly, but it was difficult to control his two-hundred-and-fifty pound frame. As he came round the turn in the driveway, he saw that Julia had left the front lights on. Their bloom softened the severity of the flattened and fluted columns on each side of the front door of the huge Georgian Colonial. Drawing nearer, he saw insects flitting around the lights.

He was about to unlock the door when it opened and Julia appeared before him in her nightgown. Her white hair was tousled and she had a look of concern that deepened the wrinkles around her eyes. "Oh, God, Wayne," she whispered. "I'm so glad you're home." She threw her arms around him and pulled him close. "It's so awful!"

"Do the children know?" he asked.

She shook her head. "They were in bed by the time the news came on."

"Good. I'll talk with them in the morning. I don't want them to be too frightened."

"Do you have any news?"

"It looks like it was just one idiot from a militia group in Maine."

"Scroggs, they said his name was."

"Yes."

"Does this mean your security detail will be strengthened?"

"For the campaign? I wouldn't be surprised."

Julia Haskins shook her head sadly. "And the poor man's wife in the hospital, dying."

"They say she was about to pass. Obviously, he was on his way to say goodbye when it happened." Haskins felt his throat tighten, his words were strained.

"Dear God," Julia whispered, holding her husband closer. "Oh, how I hate the way things have become."

"Me, too … when it's like this. I guess that's the difference between men like Baxter and me, and men like Karl."

"Karl Zacher?"

"I just don't trust the man. I saw him at the office a few hours ago. He assured me nobody he knew was involved in this. But, still, he has the reputation for supporting militia groups."

"Wayne, you should get rid of him. He's no good for you."

"Ah, my dear, but that's politics. He not only contributes a great deal of his own money, but he's the best fund raiser I've ever known."

"But what if they find he is involved in this?"

"Well, that's exactly why I insisted he assure me he wasn't. I'd have to cut him loose just like that." Haskins snapped his fingers. "Otherwise, the public would get the impression I condoned this sort of thing."

"That would be so unfair. You are not that kind of man!" Julia stepped back, looked into her husband's eyes. "Do you believe him? Zacher?"

Haskins nodded. "I'm pretty good at reading people. That's why I had him come to my office rather than talk with him over the phone."

Julia sighed. She gazed at her husband for a few moments then asked, "Can I fix you something to eat?"

"We had pizza delivered to the office."

"Well, how about a glass of milk to help you sleep?"

"In an hour. I've got to gather my thoughts. The media will be all over me for comments in the morning."

"I'll stay up with you. You can bounce ideas off me. Maybe we can even fix martinis."

Haskins kissed Julia on the forehead. "I just don't know what I'd do without you. As much as Baxter and I have been political enemies, I've felt so badly for him with the First Lady in the hospital. Now, this has to happen." He sighed deeply. "Julia, is it alright if I look in on the children first?"

"Of course. Just be very quiet."

Together, they mounted the stairs to the second floor room they had renovated for the grandchildren. Carefully, Haskins eased open the door to the children's bunk room. The three boys were snuggled under their blankets. Haskins gazed at them for a while, his eyes moistening. He took a deep breath and gently closed the door with only the slightest click. "I just wanted to breathe some innocence for a change," he whispered to his wife. "I hope they never lose it."

She gave a wry, sad smile.

They descended the stairs into the living room. Julia fluffed up a cushion and persuaded her husband to settle himself onto the sofa.

"You know," said Haskins, "I've often said I don't want to leave my grandchildren the kind of country that Baxter envisioned. But it's a damn sight better than one in which assassins run around on the loose."

Footsteps ....

Voices ....

In a daze of semi-consciousness, Matt tried to place the sounds. His thoughts wouldn't focus. There was a buzzing in his ears like the drone of bees. Human sounds.

People outside the room?

But what room? His office in Georgetown? He tried to open his eyes, but his lids wouldn't move.

A clearer sound: *ba-diiiinng, whirrr.*

An elevator. Where am I?

A hospital? Yes, of course.

Even as his mind surfaced into a semblance of clarity, he heard more footsteps. A sudden rush of feet echoing in the corridor. Then it all came flooding back to him.

The shooting.

The shouts.

A scuffle of shoes around his head.

A squeal of tires.

"Multiple GSW to the chest...." Oh, God! *Angus....*

He loved the man more than could be said. Since childhood Baxter had been like an older brother, or even a father. There was nothing Matt Cannon wouldn't do for his friend. Nothing.

He would die for him.

Matt sensed a presence hovering over him. He tried to open his eyelids but they were still heavy. He had a vague, uneasy feeling, but he couldn't quite place it. His eyelids flickered open. He tried to focus on the face looking down on him. Slowly, it resolved into a familiar, smiling countenance, a deeply sad smile.

"Angus?"

"Hello, my friend," said President Baxter.

"I thought you ...." He attempted to speak despite the NG tube in his throat.

"Thanks to you and Mike Padilla, I wasn't touched. You, Mike, and the shooter were the only ones hit. You're a brave man, Matt."

Matt struggled to raise his head. It was like pushing through something viscous. He dropped his head back on the pillow. "Thank God, you're safe."

The president nodded, said nothing. Past Baxter's shoulder, Matt saw Marcie. Weakly, he extended his hand toward her. She took it. Matt fixed his eyes on the president "How's Mike?"

Baxter shook his head slowly. His eyes turned even more sorrowful. They were moist. "He didn't make it. Neither did the shooter."

Matt closed his eyes. Clarity was returning rapidly to his mind. "Jesus, Mike's wife is eight months pregnant. God!" Marcie squeezed his hand. Matt asked, "How many were there?"

"Just the one guy," said Marcie. "He was posing as a doctor." She leaned over and kissed him on the forehead.

Matt nodded. "I recognized him. He was hanging around outside when I visited the First lady."

A nurse came into the room. "Excuse me, Mister President, Ms. Gaudet, but I have to draw some blood. Then he'll need to sleep."

Baxter reached down and patted Matt's hand. "Listen, you sleep. I'll come by after the National Security meeting tomorrow. I'll slide the ambassador from Italy an hour or so. Given the circumstances, he'll understand." He turned to leave, looked back, and said, "And Matt, thanks. You saved my life."

"Angus ... the First Lady?"

Baxter's eyes welled.

Marcie shook her head sadly.

"Oh God, I'm sorry, Angus," Matt said. "I'm so, so sorry."

Baxter nodded, turned slowly, and left.

Marcie watched him go then turned to Matt. "She died before he got to see her."

"And he's having National Security meetings? Going on with his schedule?"

"He released a statement saying the First Lady would have wanted it that way because she believed so passionately in what they were doing."

Matt frowned. Fleetingly, he wondered if his friend was so obsessed with the idea of greatness that he would play on the nation's sympathies even at a time like this—a sad, Lincolnesque figure sacrificing himself for the country. He asked, "When is the funeral?"

"The day after tomorrow," Marcie replied, starting to withdraw her hand.

But Matt gripped it more tightly. "How long did they say I'll be here?"

"About a week," she replied. "They had to repair your bowel."

"Damn!"

"That tube is so you don't pass anything through it until it heals. I'm afraid that means no food." She pinched another tube lightly between finger and thumb. "This is all you get until then."

He followed the tube to where a needle entered a vein on the top of his hand. He sighed. A nurse entered the room, checked the intravenous bags, then applied a cuff to take Matt's blood pressure.

Marcie said, "I'll be right back. I've got to step outside and call the office to tell them I'll be late. They don't allow cell phones here."

Five minutes later, when she returned, the nurse was still in the room. Matt said, "You know what I've been thinking? When I get out of here, we'll go home, get a pizza and a bottle of wine, then we'll slip into bed and see if we can make a baby. Grace Baxter wanted that for us. If it's a girl, we'll name her Grace."

Marcie frowned and shot a glance at the nurse who had inserted a needle into the median cubital vein on the inside of Matt's right arm and was now drawing blood into a vial.

"Don't worry about her," Matt said. "I'm sure she's heard things like that before. Haven't you?"

"I'm Emily," the nurse replied with a look of commiseration. She withdrew the needle, folded Matt's arm back, and pressed a cotton gauze against the puncture. She looked up at Marcie. "We should let him sleep. Later, the doctor will come in and explain things to him."

"Explain?" Matt asked. "What things?"

"Your wounds," the nurse replied. "What they did in surgery. What the recovery will be like."

"Wounds? Plural?"

"The doctor will explain," replied the nurse as she attached a label to the vial then left the room.

"What's she talking about?" Matt asked.

Marcie stared at him as if debating whether to speak. Finally, she said, "Matt, there were two bullets. One entered your side and injured your bowel. That's why you have that tube down your throat."

Matt had a sense of unease. "The other bullet?"

"Physically, it's not a serious wound. They said it only hit soft tissue."

"What soft tissue?"

Marcie hesitated. "Matt, the other bullet destroyed your testicles." She spoke rapidly. "It grazed the front of your right thigh, passed through your testicles …."

"What are you saying?"

"… then lodged in the inside of your left thigh. They say—"

"—Marcie, what are you saying?"

She put a comforting hand on his forehead. "Matt, they couldn't save them."

Matt stared at her while he tried to take in what he just heard. His face flushed with anger.

Marcie bent over and hugged him around the neck. "We'll get past this," she whispered in his ear. "We can always adopt. And the good news is you'll still be able to … to function."

Matt remained silent for a long while. Finally, he reached for the pain control button and pressed it urgently four times in quick succession. He closed his eyes tightly, turned away from Marcie, and slammed the pump cord onto the bed.

Mary-Ann Scroggs heard the four quick shots and clutched her daughter close. She flinched every time a rifle shot ruptured the air and echoed off the hills surrounding their house. Even before the reverberations of one shot died away, Scroggs fired off another round and Mary-Ann held little Annie closer still. "I'm scared, Mommy," Annie said. "What's Daddy doing?"

"He's just angry, Sweetheart. He's sad and angry that Uncle Donnie got killed."

"I wish he would stop."

"I know, Sweetheart," Mary-Ann said, stroking Annie's hair, "but he's gotta get it outa his system."

"Can you make some banana bread? He always stops everything if there's banana bread."

"He'd be finished by the time the banana bread was done, Sweetheart."

"I don't care," said Annie, sliding from her mother's lap. "I'm gonna get the bananas and flour ready." She ran to the cupboard and began shifting items around in search for the all purpose flour.

"Okay, Annie, I'll make banana bread. But first, I'm gonna go out and tell Daddy to come in and help us make it the way he likes to do."

"Oh, that would be good," said Annie. "Can I come with you?"

"No, Honey. You just get everything' ready."

Filled with trepidation, Mary-Ann went out onto the porch and called out, "Billy ...."

He ripped off another round. A sliver of bark exploded from the white pine he was using as a target.

"Billy, I'm comin' to talk. Please put the rifle down. Please."

Scroggs looked over his shoulder from the rocking chair he'd dragged into the yard, hesitated, then rested the rifle across his lap. As she approached, Mary-Ann saw at least two dozen spent cartridges scattered at his feet. And she saw tears coursing down his cheeks. It was something she'd never seen before and it sent a frisson of fear through her. She stood behind the rocking chair, leaned over the back, and pressed her cheek to his. "My poor man," she said as she stroked the side of his neck.

"I loved him," Scroggs muttered.

"I know you did. You gotta right to feel this way." She placed a hand on his shoulder.

He reached back and placed his hand over hers. "All this shootin'—am I scarin' Annie?"

"Uhm hmm. She wants us to bake banana bread together. It's to make you stop."

He gave a sad grunt. "Okay, Honey, let's go in. But I promise you this: somebody will pay for what happened to Donnie. You can be sure of that."

The following morning Matt was feeling much more alert and sitting up in bed when President Baxter and Marcie appeared. The president gave the same sad smile as the previous day. "You're looking a lot better, Matt."

There was a doctor in the room so Matt said, "Thank you, Mister President." Only in private did he call the president Angus.

Marcie came forward and touched Matt's forehead. She leaned over and kissed him softly on the lips. "I was here again last night, but you were gone to the world. They must have used up their whole supply of morphine on you."

He smiled weakly, placed his hand on her wrist.

The president asked the doctor, "How's he doing?"

"He'll be fine, Mister President. There's no sign of infection and the repair work on the bowel went perfectly."

"Good," the president replied. He turned to Matt. "You'll be back on your feet in no time."

Matt said, "Mister President ... Grace ... I'm so sorry." He saw Marcie turn an empathetic gaze on the president.

Baxter gave a weak smile. He turned to the doctor. "May we have a few moments alone, Doctor?"

"Certainly, Mister President." The doctor left, ushering a nurse out the door before him.

"Would you like me to leave, Mister President?" asked Marcie.

"No, of course not," Baxter replied. He turned to Matt. "After the shooting, they hustled me back to the White House. By the time they'd secured the area and I was able to return ... well, Grace was gone."

"God ...."

Baxter's face contorted into an expression of hatred. "That son-of-a-bitch robbed us of a last goodbye. I'll never forgive him for that."

Matt glanced at Marcie, thought of the children they'd wanted, and flashed on his own reason for not forgiving the shooter. Turning back to the president he asked, "Was Grace alone?"

Baxter shook his head. "Maxwell and Kyla were with her all day. They're taking it very badly. But at least they were with her when she died. They said her last words were for me." He paused. "She said, 'Tell Dad I love him and … tell him never to give up on the things we talked about.' "

"That sounds so much like her."

Marcie placed a hand on the president's shoulder.

"I'm going to rename the education bill the Grace Baxter Bill," Baxter said with a forced smile.

Matt gave a wry smile in return. "Haskins will have a tough time scuttling it with that name. Public sentiment will be all on your side."

"I hate to play politics with her death, but it's what she wanted more than anything. It'll be a tribute to her." Baxter walked to the window, drew the curtain back. "Speaking of Haskins, the ATF folks tell me this shooter belonged to a militia group in Maine."

"What does that have to do with Haskins?"

"Not with him, but he has supporters known to have ties with certain militia groups."

"Karl Zacher?"

The president nodded. "I have people looking into it. If there's any connection there, any connection at all …."

"Haskins would have a tough time explaining his relationship to Zacher. The First Lady would have loved it."

"I told the ATF folks I want them to move fast on this. If we find out anything, anything, I'm going to take that son-of-a-bitch Zacher down … and Haskins with him."

"I hope you do, Mister President," said Marcie.

Matt said. "I can't think of anything I'd like better."

"Yes, well …." Baxter placed a hand on Matt's arm. "I'm going to leave you two alone now. Get all the rest you can. Listen to the doctors." The president turned to Marcie. "You should see if you can arrange a vacation. Spend some time together." He paused, looked at them both, and added "Time is precious."

Part 2

Be it by gins, by snares, by subtlety,
Sleeping, or waking, 'tis no matter how,
So he be dead; for that is good deceit
Which mates him first that first intends deceit.
—William Shakespeare, Henry VI, iii, I

Chapter 5—Alexandra Lake

Traveling alone, Alexandra Lake drove to the abandoned sawmill on the Dead River near the outskirts of Bass Run, Maine. For this ATF agent and militia infiltrator, it was the first visit to the mill where former M-4 members frequently met. Former members, because shortly after the attempt to assassinate President Baxter by one of its own, the M-4 militia group had quietly suspended activities.

It was part of a larger pattern throughout the country starting with the Oklahoma City bombing and the execution of Timothy McVeigh. In the face of widespread public outrage, the steam had gone out of the militia movement. Almost universally, they decided to lay low for a while.

However, ATF and the Justice Department had been seeing alarming signs of its re-emergence recently. So they assigned Alexandra the task of infiltrating, if possible, the area in Maine where the former M-4 group had been centered. The government needed early warning of any revival of this group, which had already spawned a potential assassin, and which seemed to sense a greater freedom now that the government's radar was focused mainly on foreign terrorist groups.

Alexandra enjoyed a strong reputation among her colleagues at ATF. After graduating with a Master's degree in Political Science from Georgetown University, she joined the ATF and entered the physically and mentally challenging Special Agent Basic Training at the Federal

Law Enforcement Center in Glynco, Georgia, where she quickly earned a reputation of excellence. Among her first assignments was to infiltrate and report on a little-known militia group in California.

She was so successful, that she continued to be assigned similar tasks. Now, to infiltrate the Maine militia she had persuaded the people at ATF that as a woman it would be easier for her to infiltrate because she would attract less suspicion, pose less of a threat to the men of the group. If they were on the lookout for government agents, they wouldn't be expecting a woman. It also helped that there were already a lot of woman among the militia groups, so she wouldn't stand out.

The part that everybody left unspoken was the fact that, with her trim, athletic body, brown hair cut in a short, pixie style (what her hairdresser referred to as "gamine") and her blue eyes, she was a very attractive woman—so much so that, as she'd long ago discovered, men didn't *want* to find her suspicious. Her hairstyle in particular, reminiscent of a World War II resistance fighter, suggested a woman who meant business, who might be willing to take up arms when the time came. Also, it had been her experience that the women of militia groups were more willing to talk to another woman and thus likely to divulge more information about the group's activities.

At first, her superiors had wanted to pair her with a man but she persuaded them she'd have a better chance if she was alone and told people she'd just left her man on the west coast and wanted to strike out on her own on the other side of the country. She didn't say it, but she knew this cover story would not be what the militia people would be expecting and in that way it would be more believable. Sometimes the best lie is an improbable lie, for why would somebody take the trouble to lie only then to make it uninventive. Besides, this story would scream "availability" to the single militia men. Married ones, too, for that matter.

The government knew the assassin's brother, Billy Scroggs lived in the area and was still angry about his brother's death. The Deputy Assistant Director, Field Operations—East, of the Bureau of Alcohol, Tobacco, and Firearms (BATF) had told Alexandra the man bore watching and the event she was about to attend, an anniversary memorial service for Donald Scroggs, promised to be a good source of information about the current strength and sentiments of the militia movement in that part of Maine.

During the long drive, the windshield had become juiced with squashed bugs. Some were so big, she could hear the soft pops as they kamikazied themselves into the windshield. She pressed the windshield washer button, and a spray fanned out over the curved glass followed by rapid sweeps of the wipers. But the only effect was to smear the bug juice into two symmetric arcs because the wiper blades had long needed replacement. What had been a perfect, crystalline day had now taken on a smudged appearance.

As she neared the mill, she saw, through the blotched windshield, several dozen cars and pickup trucks parked along the rutted dirt road leading to the main meeting area. Many of them were bedecked with bumper stickers:

GET US OUT OF THE UNITED NATIONS
SUPPORT YOUR LOCAL POLICE,
AND KEEP THEM INDEPENDENT
WAKE UP AMERICA! READ YOUR CONSTITUTION
THE UN IS NOT YOUR FRIEND

In the center of this last one was a grinning skull wearing the blue U.N. combat helmet displaying a globe flanked by olive branches.

Alexandra knew she was in militia country.

As had become his habit in the year since Grace died, Baxter wandered the halls of the White House late into the night; it had become too painful to stay alone in the living quarters. His children and grandchildren visited often, but there were still many lonely times when the natural solitude of the presidency was magnified to nearly unbearable levels.

On this night, dressed in pajamas, robe and slippers, he searched a shelf in the dimly lit library on the ground floor of the residence. The bookcase contained the complete collection of Shakespeare he had shipped from the Baxter Island residence. As he searched, the golden lab puppy his grandchildren had given him for company nuzzled at his leg. At last, Baxter pulled out the Oxford Complete Sonnets and

Poems. He carried the book to an easy chair and sat. He patted the seat of the chair, "Come, Beatrice," he said.

The dog scampered into the chair and licked Baxter's cheek. Baxter turned away from the wet assault and lifted a tall glass of scotch and water from the lamp table. He took a long draught and started to search through the heavy volume, finally inserting a bookmark when he found the sonnet he wanted. He rose from the chair and said, "Let's go, Beatrice. Time to entertain the guards."

The dog stared at him.

Baxter gave a flick of the wrist. "Go, Beatrice; lead the way."

The dog turned and scurried from the room. She confidently led Baxter down the central hall, past the map room, the palm room and through the press corps offices of the west wing. Finally, they descended to the subterranean passages where it was said Lyndon Johnson had held wild parties.

Baxter was aware of the Secret Service officers discreetly following him, but he was used to them. They were infinitely better than that other thing that pursued him, that sense of death pestering at his heels like a cat wanting to be fed. Or like a sea fog rolling in.

To him, the White House felt like a tomb. In the months after Grace died he'd thought several times of resigning the office, but he couldn't bring himself to do it. He and Grace had worked so hard, waged so many campaigns for the House then the Senate, ultimately to gain the presidency, that to leave now would be a betrayal of Grace's memory. And it would have been a betrayal of the American people. Would Washington have quit? Jefferson? Lincoln? Roosevelt?

Nevertheless, the temptation was great. What did he have to live for, anyway? In the last year there had been no progress on his most cherished ambition: a permanent Mideast accord. In fact, matters had deteriorated significantly. Even the Grace Baxter Education Bill had unexpectedly run into heavy opposition. Surprisingly, little of the sympathetic reaction to her death translated into votes for the bill. That was a consequence of the increasing polarization of American society which meant that most seats in the House and the Senate were safe because they naturally fell to one party or the other or they were gerrymandered that way. The result? Few politicians needed to worry that their opposition to the Grace Baxter bill would cost them in the long run.

And, of course, the military actions in Africa and Central America dragged on and on with no exit in sight. He was spending increasingly more time signing sympathy letters to parents and spouses of dead soldiers, or else visiting the severely wounded at Walter Reed.

Not for the first time he found himself wishing that the assassin had succeeded. Katherine Moore-Paterson would have moved into the Oval Office and at least his legacy, though brief and incomplete like Kennedy's, would not have suffered any more blows. Indeed, it might have improved because Moore-Paterson might have been able to get some legislation through Congress when the nation rallied around her the way it did with Johnson after Kennedy was killed.

But now he was in danger of losing any shred of a decent legacy because he'd lost the will to fight and all the great things he'd hoped to accomplish were imperiled or already moribund. It was something he only admitted to himself under the covers in the darkness of his bedroom, but he was beginning to see doubt creeping into the faces of the White House staff. More than once, his personal physician had warned of the dangers of depression and had prescribed Paxil, but Baxter seldom took it. Everyone had noticed how his famed upright posture had slouched, how he was more bent, how his back was more rounded, how his shoulders sagged.

He turned a corner of the corridor and faced a wall of darkness. No lights lit the connecting corridor. He remembered the cave he and Grace had visited in southwest France decades before. They'd marveled at the prehistoric paintings of bison and horses, how they seemed to suggest an intimate connection between the soul of the painter and the soul of nature. It came to him that all the impedimenta of the presidency, all the trappings of office, were just so many layers of separation between him and the people. Between him and the truth. Between him and himself. He was many times more removed from the essence of life than were those painters of bison and horses. How he longed to pass his remaining days fishing or sailing, the way it used to be in Maine.

No intermediaries between him and the clean embrace of nature, no layer upon layer of insulation, of isolation.

He was aware of what they were saying. Already his opponents were raising whispered questions about his competency to continue in office. He also knew the Secret Service wondered about his night wanderings and he could never fully trust them to be silent—not after the Clinton-Lewinski scandal when Secret Service agents were grilled.

He heard an echoing click and the corridor was flooded with light. He smiled ruefully, gave a perfunctory wave to the men somewhere behind him, and continued to slouch along the corridor.

Senator Haskins lowered the phone and frowned at Karl Zacher. "He's wandering the White House again."

"They say Johnson did that when his presidency was falling apart."

"You think Baxter is losing it?"

"You mean mentally? Does a bear shit in the woods?"

Haskins rose from his chair, strolled to the window, and looked out on the Washington night. "You know, in the past year I've come to respect the man. When Julia and I attended Grace Baxter's funeral, I put all our differences on the back burner and just tuned into the man's anguish. You can't do that with someone and not come away seeing him simply for what he is—a good and decent human being who is suffering. I can only imagine how I would feel if, God forbid, anything happened to Julia." At the sideboard he poured whiskies for himself and Zacher. "But to answer your question: yes, a bear does poop in the woods; he's really losing it."

"The media has commented on how the hostility between you and the president seems to have cooled."

Haskins shrugged.

"But he is a political opponent."

"Yes … I haven't lost sight of that," Haskins said matter-of-factly, "and frankly given his mental state, I worry for the country."

"Then you should do something about it."

"Yuh, but what?"

"Persuade him to resign?"

Haskins gave a short laugh. "Me? Oh sure, he'll listen to me." He took a long sip of whisky. "They say he recites Shakespeare to the White House guards but substitutes some of his own words."

"So impeach him for messing with the bard. Look, he's bound to screw up. There's an opportunity in it for you."

Haskins nodded. "Don't you think I know that? The man should resign; the people would understand."

"What if his medical records somehow became public?"

Haskins snapped a glance at Zacher. "What do you mean?"

"Chances are pretty high he's being treated."

"But those records are confidential."

Zacher shrugged.

Haskins stared at him. "Are you suggesting you could get a hold of them?"

"Anything can be done. Most of the records, of course, will be at the White House in his personal physician's office and we couldn't get our hands on them. However, they're not equipped the way a hospital is and they would have to send a lot of tests out."

"And will his medical records give us the ammunition we need to force him to resign? If we get them into the right hands, I mean."

Zacher shrugged. "Can't say without seeing them. Depends on what the tests are, what the results are. But my guess is we can make inferences."

"How soon?"

"Soon."

"And you can make sure it can't be—"

"—it can't be traced to you. Of course."

"As long as you understand that," said Haskins. "The records need to end up in the hands of someone in his own party so it doesn't look like a political maneuver. I'll figure out who if and when you get the records."

President Baxter followed Beatrice down the newly lit corridor. Halfway down, he stopped under a light fixture near a glass-paneled door, opened the book of sonnets to where he had placed the bookmark, and started to declaim in a strong voice that echoed from the walls:

Sin of self-love possesseth all mine eye
And all my soul, and all my every part;
And for this sin there is no remedy,
It is so grounded inward in my heart.
Methinks no face so gracious is as mine,
No shape so true, no truth of such account;
And for myself mine own worth do define,
As I all other in all worths surmount.

He stopped and stared at his reflection in the door's window:

But when my glass shows me myself indeed
Beated and chopp'd with tanned antiquity,
Mine own self-love quite contrary I read;
Self so self-loving were iniquity.

He closed the book and in a low voice, the words slurred with whisky, he said, "Grace ... Oh, Grace. Grace, methinks no face so gracious as thine ... Grace, methinks so face no gracious as thine ... Grace ... me ... unnhh ...?" He looked up startled. Before him, further up the corridor, was the indistinct figure of his wife, wraithlike, wearing all white, radiant, drifting away from him down the corridor.

He stumbled after her, Beatrice scampering before him. He reached out a hand and called in a loud voice, "The glorious lady of my mind! *La gloriosa donna della mia mente! La gloriosa ...Oh, Grace methinks no face so, so, so gracious as thine ....*"

His voice trailed off to a breathless gasp.

The following night, Haskins poured himself and Zacher drinks. "I think he's seeing ghosts."

"What makes you say that?"

"I got a report that he shouted something real strange to an empty corridor. 'The glorious lady of my mind.'"

"What the hell does *that* mean?"

"I put my staff on it. That's what Dante called his dead love, Beatrice: 'the glorious lady of my mind.'"

"The name he gave to his dog?"

"And in *The Inferno*, Dante's guide to paradise."

"Fucking east coast intellectual!" said Zacher. He took a long sip of his whiskey. "I've been thinking. There may be a way to get the leadership of his own party to twist his arm."

"You mean get him to resign?"

"Yuh."

"If we could get proof he's being treated for some mental disorder. Maybe even alcoholism ...." Said Haskins.

"It can be done," replied Zacher.

Haskins stared at him a long moment. "Is this one of those things I'm better off not knowing about?"

"Just leave it to me."

Alexandra Lake parked the car and stepped into the close, oppressive heat. Squinting, trying not to breathe too deeply, she walked through a swarm of gnats to where a platform had been erected in front of several rows of folding chairs. She guessed there would be speeches and it would be easy to pick up the mood of the crowd by hearing what the speakers had to say and taking note of which phrases listeners responded to. Off to the side, near a pile of rotting sawdust, planks had been placed atop a disused and rusted saw bench—the long kind used to quarter whole logs—where various items were on display for sale. There were stacks of Stormfront T-shirts, black and white, with a Celtic cross and the slogan *White Pride World Wide.* Alongside them was a box of embroidered patches bearing the same design. Huey Figg, wearing one of the T-shirts, wet with sweat, said, "What do you say, pretty lady? Only fifteen bucks and part of the proceeds goes to Donnie Scroggs' brother."

"What for? Missing the asshole?"

Huey frowned. "Now, Lady, that ain't fair! Did you even know Donnie?"

"I meant Donnie missing Baxter, not his brother missing Donnie."

"Oh."

Alexandra nodded toward the T-shirts and said, "Okay, I'll take one. Medium." She reached into her pocket, pulled out a twenty dollar bill and handed it to the man. "Where can I change?" she asked.

Huey laughed. "What's wrong with right here? This ain't New York or San Francisco. Ain't nobody gonna get worked up seein' a lady in a bra." He gestured toward several women who were walking by wearing halters.

Alexandra smiled. "Sure, why not." She whipped off her short sleeve camouflage shirt, causing her unfettered breasts to jiggle, donned the black T-shirt, and smiled at the gawking man. She made a point of glancing at his crotch. "You're right, nobody seems worked up ... yet."

Huey blew out a long breath. "You're new around here," he said.

"Me and my man were with a group in California. I split up with the asshole and figured I'd get as far away as possible, find a new group."

"Can't get much farther away than Maine, I guess."

"That's what I figure."

"Well, look around, see if you want to hook on with us."

"Yuh."

Alexandra strolled past the table, examining other items, and came to a section reserved for literature of various kinds: several books—*Global Tyranny: The United Nations and the Emerging New World Order; The Insiders: Architects of the New World Order*; and *The Blue Book* of the John Birch Society. There were also pamphlets whose covers were adorned with photographs of aborted fetuses. Next came a small selection of jewelry, mostly Celtic crosses of various kinds in silver and pewter. She thought of buying one, but figured the T-shirt would be enough cover and she didn't need to spend any more money that she might not be able to include on her expense report. She imagined the entry: one Celtic cross, pewter, for espionage purposes.

She came to a table cluttered with firearms. She stopped and perused them. The elderly man behind the table said, "I'm Harold Larson. This here's my personal collection."

Alexandra made a show of admiring the guns, then moved on.

Mary-Ann Scroggs, with unkempt blond hair and a haggard look around her eyes, stood behind a plank set on sawhorses for the selling of coffee, donuts, and several kinds of juice. Alexandra purchased a cup of coffee and chatted with the woman. "Looks like there'll be speakers," she said.

Mary-Ann nodded. "You bet, honey. Billy Scroggs is gonna speak and a few others, includin' Gary Molesworth."

Alexandra recognized the name—a notorious militia type. "Gary Molesworth?"

"Yep. From Michigan. Somewhere near Traverse City, I guess."

"I never met him," said Alexandra. "What's he look like?"

"That's him there, in the camouflage fatigues, talkin' to Billy."

Alexandra looked to where the woman was pointing and saw two men. It wasn't hard to recognize Billy Scroggs; he bore a strong resemblance to his brother. She studied the other man, registering his features, so she'd remember them when she had a chance to jot the description down in her notebook.

"Sugar and cream are at that end of the table."

"Oh, thanks. Billy Scroggs? Isn't that the brother of Donnie?" She had meant to say "ain't" but forgot. She resolved to do better.

"Sure is," Mary-Ann replied, adding, "And also my husband." She brushed at a stray strand of hair plastered to her sweating forehead and locked eyes with Alexandra.

"Oh … Well, pleased to meet you, Mrs. Scroggs."

"Where you from?"

"California."

"What brings you here?"

"Needed new scenery."

Mary-Ann eyed her for a moment, shrugged, then turned to a man who had come for coffee.

Alexandra noted an open jar containing coins and dollar bills. A sign behind the jar said it was a collection to build a proper memorial for the fallen hero, Donald A. Scroggs. As she dropped a five-dollar bill inside, she wondered how she would record it on her expense report. *Donation to honor failed assassin, $5.00.* She guessed it would show up as a couple of hamburgers instead.

"Thank you," said Mary-Ann.

"Ain't no problem. I think it's only right to honor your brother-in-law."

"Well, at least he tried," Mary-Ann replied in a resigned voice. "Just some other turkeys got in the way. Wasn't his fault."

"Yuh, right."

While she waited for the speeches to start, Alexandra roamed through the crowd, listening to conversations, trying to sense the mood of the people. Every now and then, she looked in the direction of the makeshift stage and noted that Billy Scroggs and Gary Molesworth were still huddled in conversation.

The day was growing unbearably hot and she went several times to the juice table. She stood sipping her juice, slapping at a bothersome bee that hovered around the sweet rim of the bottle, and listened to conversations. To her surprise, there was very little talk about the kinds of issues represented on the literature table. Instead, people talked of ordinary things like their children or their cars or their gardens. She heard nothing about abortions, new world orders, the overbearing federal government ... or the president. Except for some scattered discussions about automatic weapons, the gathering could be mistaken for a small town fair anywhere in the country.

That is, until Billy Scroggs spoke.

The man mounted the speaker's platform to great cheers. As he spoke, frequently dabbing at his sweating face with a bandana that he also used to wave at the ever-present mosquitoes, people responded enthusiastically. He railed against the government, saying, "Baxter and his rainbow pals are plannin' to trash the sacred Constitution and sell America's freedom to the United Nations."

The sneer with which he pronounced "rainbow" captured Alexandra's attention. She knew it was a code word that encompassed Jews, homosexuals, lesbians and African Americans and perhaps a wide variety of other groups that stoked the hatred and fear of these people.

"My brother," Scroggs continued, "tried to do his part to preserve our freedoms, to steer us away from this insane, sick, politically correct path the nation is on. And what did they do? They killed him. And with his death, a little bit of the Constitution died. But don't think for a minute that's gonna stop us. No."

The audience burst into enthusiastic applause.

"Not on your life. Not on my brother's life. Instead, when they killed him, it gave us strength. When they martyred him, it guaranteed that everything he lived for will go on. He may be dead, but his spirit is alive in each of us. And I tell you this, I ain't afraid of takin' up where he left off."

Again, he was greeted by wild applause and cheers. There were shouts of "Down with Baxter!" and "To hell with the U.N!"

"I'm not about to stand by and see our country raped by a bunch of flag-burning perverts who murder babies in the womb and who hug not only trees, but homosexuals and lesbians and Jews and niggers. It's time we take this country back for the people who belong here, for the people who made it what it is."

More cheers. Some people waved American flags. A few waved Confederate flags.

Scroggs lowered his voice. "And on a personal level, I want to tell you that I believe in honor and honor tells me a brother's death must be avenged. As it says in Jeremiah, '... we shall prevail against him, and we shall take our revenge on him.' They killed more than eighty folks in Waco; they killed Vicki and little Sammy Weaver at Ruby Ridge; they executed Timmy McVeigh. They killed Donnie. I say it's time we take our revenge on them." Scroggs pumped his fist in the air and was accompanied by more enthusiastic applause and flag waving.

Although Scroggs was, by far, the most effective speaker, everyone who followed sounded the same themes, punctuating them with their own messages about abortion, the second amendment, world trade, immigrants. The most compelling were Gary Molesworth, who spoke passionately of the urgent need for a new American Revolution, even if violence was required, and Jim Claxton from Gary, Indiana, who spoke of purifying the American government of people like President Baxter.

After the speeches, Alexandra stayed for another hour, repeating the names—Gary Molesworth, Jim Claxton—often to herself for when she could be alone to enter their names in her notebook. All the time she was there, she saw that Scroggs, Molesworth, and Claxton, remained huddled together off in a corner. She would have given anything to be able to hear what they were saying.

By the time the meeting started to break up, Alexandra had decided she needed to get her information to the right people in Washington, ASAP.

She was walking toward her car when she was intercepted by Huey Figg. A few steps behind him were Billy Scroggs, Gary Molesworth holding a

German Shepherd on a leash, and a man she knew as Andy McBride. McBride, like her, was a BATF plant. She exchanged a microsecond glance with him, all that was needed to assure each other their covers were safe.

"I want you to meet some guys," said Huey Figg. He repeated each of their names to her.

"My wife says you're from California," said Scroggs.

"Word gets 'round." She bent down to pat the German Shepherd. "What's her name?" she asked Molesworth.

"Blondi."

Alexandra smiled at him. "Same as Hitler's dog. Nice."

Scroggs spoke. "My wife says you were admirin' Harold Larson's guns. Want to see my collection?"

"Is that something like 'Do you wanna see my etchings?'"

"I'm married," said Scroggs. "Got a daughter."

"I ain't married," said Huey Figg.

"How lucky can womankind get?" said Alexandra.

While Figg gave her a confused look, she said to Scroggs, "My ex was a collector. I seen all I need to see. Nice to meet you boys." She turned and walked toward her car.

Ten minutes later and several miles down the road, Alexandra pulled over. She took a small digital recorder from her pocket and pressed a few buttons. She heard Scroggs' voice: "Baxter and his rainbow pals are plannin' to trash the Constitution and sell America to the United Nations ...."

She pressed 'Stop' and smiled.

Chapter 6—Roger Anderson; Air Force One

Shortly after two in the morning, in a pathology lab at the Bethesda Naval Hospital, a nervous man in his late twenties sat at a computer terminal. A familiar, faint, electronic smell—fried ozone—came from the monitor as it displayed a page of cryptic numbers and letters. Large, moist saddlebags stained the underarms of the man's shirt. His palms were sweaty and his normally sure fingers fumbled at the softly clicking keyboard. He made several typing errors before he took a deep breath and rolled his armless chair away from the computer. Interlacing the fingers of his hands, he cracked his knuckles, trying to loosen himself up. As he did so, he noticed that his hands were shaking. He told himself to concentrate, to think of his wife who at that moment would be snuggled in their bed surrounded by their two dogs. He thought of the baby she was carrying. It was for her—for them—for their marriage, that he was doing what he was doing.

For them he kept reminding himself.

He had so much hope, so many dreams, for their future; he wasn't about to let it be ruined. He had to do this.

Every sound—normally so familiar he'd hardly notice them—made him edgy. There was the deep-throated whisper emanating from the air-conditioning duct; the ping of an elevator registering floors; and, from the next room, the hum of a centrifuge spinning blood samples.

There was the sound of his breathing.

He was about to lean over the keyboard again when he heard an even more alarming sound: approaching footsteps in the corridor. He held his breath. At this time in the morning, the lab was running on a light staff—only enough people to service STAT orders. His three colleagues had left just a few minutes before for a bite in the cafeteria, and for the first time that night he was alone. It was the only chance he'd have of accomplishing his task, and he wondered now if he'd missed his opportunity as the light footsteps came closer. The door opened. He froze. *Damn!*

"Forgot my money," said Sharon Miller, the senior pathologist on duty. "You sure you don't want anything, Roger? A cup of coffee? A soda?" She started toward him.

Quickly, he clicked on the close box and the screen went into desk-top mode. Familiar icons. Nothing suspicious. "No, thanks," he replied.

Sharon placed her hands on his shoulders, giving him a light massage. "You're all tense. Working too hard. Why don't you take a break?"

"I will. I just want to get a few things done."

"Okay, then. See you in fifteen." She gave his shoulders a final squeeze and headed for the door.

He spun around in his chair. "On second thought, Sharon, will you get me a coffee—milk, no sugar … and, say, a bagel—toasted?" He figured that might give him an extra minute or two.

She smiled. "That's more like it. I worry about you sometimes."

When the door closed with a reassuring click, Roger Anderson turned back to the computer keyboard. Working as fast as he could, with frequent glances toward the door, he typed into the name field:

jastockton

He pressed "enter" and the cursor flipped to the password field. He typed 983652, pressed "enter" again.

He held his breath as the computer displayed a new screen. On the top, in bold, black letters, was the name James A. Stockton, MD. Moving the mouse quickly, he gave two rapid clicks on "patient list" and then again on "print."

The printer came to life with a whirr and after a moment, two laser-printed pages floated into the output tray. Anderson rushed over, whipped the pages from the printer, folded them into fours, and stuck them into his hip pocket.

He scurried back to the terminal and typed his own name and password into the computer, bringing up a new screen, one that nobody would question.

In a few hours he would deliver the pages to Karl Zacher and maybe then he could wash his hands of this whole business once and for all.

Angus Baxter walked across the south lawn and smartly returned the salute of the two marines at the base of *Marine One's* boarding door. With him were Matt Cannon, several of his White House staff, and his military aide, a Navy commander who carried the "football," the emergency satchel which contained retaliatory options, launch codes for nuclear weapons, and several other items the president might need in case of enemy attack. The football could never be far from the president, which is why the military aide always accompanied him everywhere.

Once seated, Baxter gave a nod to the pilots and within moments *Marine One* lifted off from the lawn. Once airborne, it was joined by three identical "white tops" that had lifted off from the Marine Corps Base at Quantico, thirty miles to the southwest. Once *Marine One* rendezvoused with the other three helicopters, the four took turns at the vanguard to disguise which one carried the president.

Less than half an hour later, *Marine One* settled onto the tarmac at Andrews Air Force Base with a whirl of blades and an upwelling of dust, President Angus Baxter gazed out the window. Before him, squatting outside Hanger 19, was one of the two specially configured and stately Boeing 747s that, as soon as he stepped aboard, would become known as *Air Force One*. It was silhouetted majestically against the brightening red of a morning sky. The rim of the sun had just appeared above the horizon and the glittering blue and white flanks of the giant aircraft took on a rosy hue.

Of all the perks of the presidency, this was surely one of the grandest. For him, the plane had become a kind of private sanctuary, a place where he could relax outside the constant gaze of the public and the press—even if there were almost always press aboard. It had been one of Grace's favorite places, too. In the first year of his presidency, *Air Force One*, Camp David, and, especially the Downeast White House, were the only places where they could recapture, if only briefly, the warm intimacy they had enjoyed in a more private life.

It was odd that this should be so, for *Air Force One* was certainly not lacking in the grandeur and pomp of the presidency. Indeed, it was one of its most powerful symbols. Its gravity was reflected in the number and quality of the crack Air Force mechanics and flight crews whose mission it was to ensure that the plane on which the president flew was the safest in the world. Its seriousness of purpose was made palpable by the total lock-down imposed on Andrews by the Secret Service as soon as the president's helicopter lifted off from the south lawn of the White House for the air base. And, considering the several C-141s that had taken off from Andrews in the previous forty-eight hours, carrying the president's armored motorcade as well as Secret Service advance teams, a flight of *Air Force One* became the modern day equivalent of a mediaeval king's progress. It was not just the president who was traveling, but the entire power and authority of the White House.

The luxurious plane was also an effective political instrument. On this trip, he was using it for campaign appearances disguised as presidential visits to areas recently devastated by a major earthquake. The plan was for him to announce, with *Air Force One* sitting in the background confirming his power as president, his declaration of parts of California as major disaster areas and his directive that FEMA make substantial funds available—more than a billion dollars—for relief. That single, high-profile event should be enough to virtually guarantee California's electoral votes on election day.

In addition to such obvious uses of the plane, came another, more subtle advantage. Virtually no politician was immune to the seductive power of an invitation to fly with the president. And, once aboard *Air Force One*, these politicians were unusually vulnerable to presidential persuasion.

If Baxter had some program to push, or a senator or a congressman to woo, an invitation to fly with him could often prove irresistible. Such was the case on this trip to California. Baxter had invited Senators Philipps and Westmacott to join him. Both men were opponents of the Grace Baxter Education Bill and both were friends of Senator Haskins, his assumed rival in the next election. He, of course, didn't expect to change their friendship with Haskins, but he did hope, if not to win their support, at minimum blunt the vehemence of their opposition to the education bill which was in deep trouble. Perhaps he could at least persuade them not to attach poison pill ammendments to the bill.

He owed it to Grace's memory.

As Baxter stepped through the yawning door of the plane, the chief steward greeted him. "Good morning, Mister President, everyone is on board."

"Good. Thank you, Anthony."

"As soon as we reach altitude, I'll be serving breakfast."

Baxter placed his hand on Anthony's shoulder and gave him a sly wink. "In the meantime, Anthony, how about bringing me a Bloody Mary? Make it look like a plain tomato juice, okay?"

"Yes, sir. Of course, sir."

Baxter poked his head into the cockpit. "Good morning, Larry ... Jack ... Sandra. Looks like good flying weather today."

"Clear all the way to California, Mister President," replied Sandra, the flight engineer.

"Excellent. You may take off as soon as you're ready." As was his habit, he strapped himself into the jump seat for takeoff. He enjoyed watching the practiced skill of the crew as they brought the lumbering giant into the air; it was another of the perks of the presidency. He'd been told the elder George Bush, an old fighter pilot, had often flown in the cockpit.

When they reached cruising altitude, Baxter made his way aft, passing his executive suite—which contained his stateroom, shower, and office—and entered the combination conference / dining room where his staff and guests were already assembled for breakfast. As he entered, they all rose. "Good morning, Mister President."

Anthony appeared with a tray on which were arrayed glasses of tomato juice. With a wink, he placed one before Baxter, then distributed the others around the table. Baxter gave him a smile of gratitude. Anthony had quickly learned to disguise the Bloody Marys by giving tomato juice, in identical glasses, to everyone else.

The president looked around the table. As he had instructed, Senators Philipps and Westmacott had the seats closest to him. The others around the table were Matt Cannon, a half dozen members of the White House staff, and four hand-selected members of the media—two print, one radio and one television. At the far end of the table was his personal physician, Commander Jim

Stockton, who always traveled with him and who presided over the specially designed medical compartment that included everything needed for minor emergencies, including an operating table and lamp which folded up into the bulkhead like a Murphy bed.

Baxter spent most of the breakfast chatting with his two visiting senators about their families and their home states. He knew better than to push them on the education bill immediately. He'd wait until later, perhaps after they'd had a few drinks with him at lunch or at dinner when they would be flying from San Francisco to Los Angeles. He, in the meanwhile, had consumed an additional two Bloody Marys and by the end of breakfast was finding it challenging to form words, so he excused himself and went into his suite for a mid-morning nap. A few morning drinks then a nap was a luxury he also permitted himself in the White House, but there it was more difficult to hide.

Alcohol was a problem he'd wrestled with nearly all his life. However, in the first few years of his administration, feeling the immense responsibility of his office, he had been completely abstemious. But now, ever since the night of Grace's death and the attempted assassination, he was drinking as heavily as ever. He'd learned to pace his drinking throughout the day so that at no time did he feel incapacitated or unable to make crucial decisions. Or, so he persuaded himself. He never became roaring drunk as, it was said, Lyndon Johnson did.

A knock sounded on the door of his suite. "Come in," Baxter said.

The door opened and Jim Stockton appeared. "Can I have a word, Mister President?

"Sure, Jim. What's on your mind?"

"Mister President, I'm not going to beat around the bush. You were slurring a few words in there."

"Do you think others noticed?"

"No, I don't think so. I'm just attuned to it."

"Good, then there's no problem, is there?"

"I'm afraid I disagree, Mister President," Stockton said, his voice betraying his nervousness. "The drinking is one thing, but I think it only masks a deeper issue, one far more serious."

"A deeper issue?" asked Baxter testily.

"I'm sorry if it upsets you, but I think you're showing signs of severe depression and—"

"—Oh, Christ, not that again."

"As your personal physician, it's my duty to tell you what I think."

"Okay, you told me."

"Won't you consider seeing a psychiatrist? It—"

"—No."

"It can be arranged discreetly. No one need know about it."

"I said no, Jim."

"But—"

"—Jim, I have a world of respect for you, but on this one I'm simply not going to budge. Understood?"

Stockton sighed deeply. "Yes, Mister President."

"I understand your concern, but it's misplaced. I'm unhappy, Jim, not depressed. There's a difference. I miss her more than I thought possible, so I drink, but I'm fully capable of doing my job. Nobody ever said you had to be happy to be effective."

"Of course, Mister President."

Baxter stared at Stockton for a long while. Finally he said, "Jim, It's okay for me to be unhappy. I loved her."

"Yes, sir."

"I appreciate your concern," said Baxter. "And, Jim … don't ever stop."

"I won't, sir."

"But now let me get a little nap."

Stockton slipped out the door, closing it quietly.

When Baxter woke from his nap, it was time for lunch. Over salmon and several bottles of white wine, the president managed to persuade Senators Philipps and Westmacott not to attach their proposed amendments to the education bill, which would have assured its failure, but rather to let it come to a full floor vote as drafted, so he was feeling good about himself when they landed in San Francisco.

As the plane taxied, Baxter was sitting in his office going over his remarks when he heard a characteristic knock on the door. "Come on in, Matt," he called. When Matt entered, Baxter asked, "How are you feeling?" It had become his customary greeting. Though Matt had healed long before, it was Baxter's way of reminding his friend of his appreciation and respect.

"I'm fine. Are you ready with the speech?" asked Matt.

Baxter nodded. "No problem."

"How about reading it quickly to me," said Matt. "You know ... just a warm up. Loosen the lips."

Baxter smiled. "You know, Matt, for a lawyer you are so goddamned transparent that I wonder how you get away with putting things over on judges sometimes."

"What do you mean?"

"You want me to read the speech to see if I'm slurring the words."

"No, no. I just thought—"

"—Well, stop your worrying. I'm perfectly fine."

"I saw Philipps and Westmacott exchanging glances. I think they're wondering if you've had too much to drink at lunch."

"Why? Just because I can handle twice as much as they can? That's *their* problem. Tell them to listen to my speech and then ask them what they think. And while you're at it, tell them to count the electoral votes flying away from their friend Haskins as I speak. That ought to give them something else to think about." He paused, noticing Matt's raised eyebrows. He didn't have to ask what the matter was, for he'd heard it himself: the 's' in 'something' had come out like a 'z.' Baxter stuffed his notes into the inner pocket of his jacket and crossed to the door. As he passed, he patted Matt on the shoulder and said, "And you listen closely, too. I'll give you a hundred dollars for every word even slightly slurred." He concentrated on 'slightly slurred' and got it out right.

Matt smiled. "I guess if you can say 'slightly slurred' without slurring, you'll be okay."

The speech went perfectly and an hour later they were airborne for Los Angeles. More wine over dinner persuaded the two senators to excuse themselves with self-conscious grins and retire for the night. However, Baxter kept going with several appearances in Los Angeles that lasted until the small hours of the morning, exhausting everyone who'd accompanied him.

He owed it to Grace. He owed it to his legacy.

Roger Anderson parked on Jefferson Drive and was soon walking slowly along the gravel path of the Mall past the Air and Space Museum and the National Museum of the American Indian.

Ahead of him, the Capitol Building shone white under the lights that still flooded it in the hour before dawn. The Mall was mostly deserted except for a few joggers and the human silence was as complete as he'd ever experienced in the center of Washington D.C. In its place, he heard a cacophony of bird calls in the trees and was filled with a strange envy.

How good it would be to live from day to day with no worries other than whatever it was birds worried about. No powerful man holding a gun to your head. No blackmail. No threat to your marriage. He sighed deeply.

He saw a car slow to a stop where 3rd Street SW crossed the Mall opposite the Capitol Reflecting Pool. A man emerged from the driver's side, leaving the lights and motor on. The man circled around the front of the car where the headlights illumined his dark suit for a moment before he continued around to the side where he leaned back against the car and folded his arms. Anderson recognized Karl Zacher merely by the man's posture, the haughty angle of his head.

The same attack of nerves Anderson had experienced in the pathology lab returned to him. He felt his heart begin to race. It seemed to flutter in his throat. Powerful men always frightened him, made him feel weak and defenseless. All he wanted was to be out of this place and to go home to his wife. Looking to his left and right, he advanced toward Zacher.

"Do you have the list?" Zacher asked.

"Yes, Mister Zacher," replied Anderson, reaching into his pocket.

"Good boy. Let's have it."

Anderson handed the man the list, wishing his hands were not shaking so much that they caused the sheet of paper to flutter.

Zacher walked round to the front of the car and lowered the list so the headlights shone on it. He studied it for a moment, then looked up at Anderson. "So that's his entire patient list?"

"Yes, Sir."

"There are only a couple dozen names on the list."

"Like I told you, Mister Zacher, Doctor Stockton hasn't taken any patients since he became the head of the White House Medical Office. The other names are mostly White House staff."

"Excellent." Zacher said, scrutinizing the list again.

"Can I go now?" Anderson asked, cursing himself for the whining tone in his voice.

"Of course you can. And, good work."

Anderson turned to go. He'd taken only a few steps when Zacher said, "I'll call you when I need you again."

Anderson turned back to the man. "Please, Mister Zacher, don't. I don't want to do this anymore. I could lose my job." Though he tried to deepen his voice, it still came out as a whimper.

"I'm sorry, Roger, but your work is not nearly finished. This is only the first step. I need to know when a new name appears on this list."

"But I told you, Doctor Stockton doesn't take new patients."

"I have reason to believe a new name will soon appear on this list and I want to know about it when it does."

"But I can't be doing this. My job ...."

Zacher placed a hand on Anderson's shoulder. He squeezed it with a surprisingly strong grip that caused Anderson to flinch. "If you're careful, you won't get caught. Don't worry."

"But—"

"—Roger, listen to me carefully. There's only a tiny chance you'll lose your job over this. On the other hand, if you don't do it, there's a one hundred percent chance you'll lose your wife. One hundred percent! Do I make myself clear?"

A cold current ran through Anderson. "Yes, sir."

"Unless, of course, she's the most understanding woman in the world ... or unless you two have agreed on an open marriage. Do you have an open marriage?" Zacher removed his hand from Anderson's shoulder and held his two hands out, palms up, as though balancing something. "Look, a small risk here versus a certain, big risk here," he said raising each hand in succession. "Doesn't that make sense? Don't be a fool."

"Yes, sir."

"Now you have my number. Check the file daily. I want to know the instant a new name appears on the man's patient list. Got it?"

Anderson nodded.

"The very instant. It's crucial, understand?"

"Yes, sir. I'll have a program running in background that'll alert me when that happens."

"Good thinking. And when it happens, I'll have one more thing for you to do immediately," said Zacher, patting Anderson on the shoulder.

"Perhaps a little modification to your program, and then you'll be free of me forever. Okay?"

"Okay."

"Good, now go home to your wife."

The vice president, Katherine Moore-Paterson, sat opposite President Baxter in the Oval Office. She was a slender woman with close-cropped, kinky, salt-and-pepper hair. Because she had said she wanted a few private minutes with the president, they'd asked the staff who would normally sit in on such discussions, to wait down the hall in the cabinet room for the meeting that was scheduled to begin in fifteen minutes. "Well, what's on your mind, Katherine?" asked Baxter.

She leaned forward. Reflections from the revolving armature of the president's anniversary clock swept across her ebony skin. "Two things, Mister President ...."

"Angus, when we're alone. Okay?"

She smiled. "Okay, Angus. As I was saying, there are two things I wanted to discuss. First is the ceremony at the Lincoln Memorial."

"I understand we're moving it from the King Memorial site."

Moore-Paterson nodded. "More space for people."

"That's August twenty-eighth?"

The vice president nodded. "The anniversary of the King speech. It's the program for that day that I wanted to talk about."

"You want the major speech," Baxter said with a smile.

She laughed. "Angus, why do I always get the feeling you're two steps ahead of me? Yes, I do. As the first African-American woman—"

"—You got it."

She gave a bemused smile. "Just like that?"

"Hell, Katherine, it only makes sense. Will you have me make some introductory remarks?"

"Of course."

Baxter smiled. "You know, Katherine, these are going to have to be among the best speeches we've ever made. We'll be standing in front of a statue of one of the greatest orators the world has ever known and just to our right will be a statue of another great orator."

"I know. I've already started to work on mine."

"You're going to write it yourself? No speech writer?"

"For this one, Angus, no speech writer."

Baxter pursed his lips, nodded. "Perhaps I'll do the same thing." He glanced at his watch. "Now, what was the second item?"

Moore-Patterson hesitated. She took a deep breath. "Angus, I hope you don't get angry, but there's something I need to tell you. Some of my people have heard rumblings—most notably, recently, from aides to Senators Philipps and Westmacott—that your attention seems to wander in meetings and that you're drinking quite heavily."

He tilted his head to look into her moist, nut-brown eyes for a moment before asking, "What do you think, Katherine?"

"About the drinking I don't know. As to your seeming distracted at times, I've noticed it too, but I put it down to everything that's happened in the last few years—the assassination attempt, Grace, the collapse of the Middle East thing, the trouble with the education bill, the messes in Africa. But I certainly don't think it affects your ability to do the job."

"But is that what others think?"

"Only the ones who want you out of office. They're grasping for anything to nail you with."

"And?"

"Well, Angus, I think you should be careful about giving them any ammunition. Appearances count a whole lot more than the truth in this city. Hell, you know that better than anybody."

Baxter smiled, said, "Thanks for the warning. Believe me, I appreciate it." He glanced at his watch again. "Now we're five minutes late for the cabinet meeting. Shall we go?"

Alexandra Lake felt the easy part of her job was done; she'd uncovered a threat on the life of the president. Of course, she couldn't be sure if it was a specific threat or a general threat, real or vague. Scroggs never actually came out and said, "I'm going to kill the president," but in her opinion he'd come close enough. Fortunately, it wasn't a decision she had to make.

In the towering bureaucracy that was the government, she knew the question would be decided somewhere up the chain of command. Her responsibility was to nudge and poke the information upward until it reached the right ears. How fast it got there, of course, she couldn't control. It was entirely dependent on the people who occupied the various rungs of the ladder. If they were good, diligent people, her information would reach top levels speedily.

But if, along the way, the information was horded by just one person who was jealous of his or her prerogatives, or by a subordinate who insisted on waiting for a superior to return from a vacation, or an illness, or a trip, then who knew how long it would take? Yes, she thought ruefully, this was by far the more difficult part of his job. She had never been comfortable with the workings of bureaucracies, especially when something crossed departmental lines as this one would between Justice and Homeland Security. She had only a vague idea how it all worked—*if* it worked. All she could do was start the ball rolling and wait for a response.

Her first step was to inform the head of the Portland Office, Special Agent Bruce Campbell. But this, fortunately was only a formality because she and Campbell were friends and all it took was a quick phone call to get the okay to bring her information to the Deputy Assistant Director, Field Operations—East, of the Bureau of Tobacco, Alcohol, and Firearms (BATF).

His name was Arthur Byrd and Alexandra now sat outside the man's office on Causeway Street in Boston in a vinyl-covered chair next to a plastic plant. ATF pamphlets were spread out on the marred coffee table in front of her. There was no one else except Byrd's secretary in the small anteroom. On the opposite wall, framed photographs of President Baxter and the Secretary of Homeland Security hung on both sides of an American flag hanging limply from a pole planted in a metal base.

While she waited, she tried to remember the Organization Manual and what it told her about the route her information would have to take before it got to someone who could take action. Within BATF, it would have to go to the Assistant Director, Field Operations in Washington. The information would go up the line to the Deputy Attorney General and probably the Attorney General himself, perhaps after making a stop at FBI. It would then cross over to Homeland Security where the Secret Service was housed and maybe even to the CIA, yet another agency.

Jesus!

Billy Scroggs, who probably didn't need to consult a soul, would be given a generous head start in planning if, as she believed, the man was serious about avenging his brother's death. She took a deep breath and gave an exasperated sigh.

"It shouldn't be much longer," the secretary said in a weary voice.

"No, no," she replied. "I was thinking of something else."

"There's coffee and powdered creamer over there if you want," the woman said, nodding toward a small room that looked more like a supply closet. Through the opening Alexandra saw a copy machine.

"No thanks, I'll just wait." Perhaps she was just being pessimistic. Maybe she could persuade the Deputy Assistant Director so passionately that he would rush the information to Washington with equal conviction and, for once, things would happen without an ungodly delay. After all, if she was passionate in her conviction that the president's life could be at stake, maybe she could convince them as well. She would soon find out.

Ten minutes later, she was called into Byrd's office. The man stood to welcome her. He was a tall man with an out-of-date crewcut. "Good to see you, Alex. You're looking well. How are things up in Maine? Bruce said you have something important to report."

"I believe it's of vital importance," she replied. She told Byrd of the event for Donald Scroggs and the speech made by his brother.

"Were those his exact words: 'I'm not afraid of taking up where my brother left off'?"

Alexandra nodded. "Exact words. He also gave a quote from the Bible talking about revenge and then said, 'a brother's death must be avenged.' "

Byrd strolled to the window, gazed out at the traffic. "I agree," he said, finally. "I think we need to move this up the line immediately. Only problem is Tolliver is on vacation and the last time I went past him, I got hell from his boss, Louis Harper."

"He's the Director of Field Ops? I can't keep them all straight."

"Yes, and a stubborn son-of-a-bitch. Plays it by the book all the time." He turned and smiled at Alexandra. "I tell you, if what we have in this organization is an information artery, then he's an embolism in that artery."

Alexandra frowned.

"Don't worry just yet, though. I'm not afraid of taking heat from him. I'll try. All I'm saying is he'll just tell me to go through channels."

"What about going past him?"

Byrd laughed. "Sure. I could do it. Once. Then as soon as Tolliver found out I'd be shuffling papers somewhere in South Dakota." He paused, smiled, said, "I'm afraid I can't do that."

"For Christ's sake, Arthur, we're talking assassination!"

"Alex, I—"

"Screw you!" Alexandra said. "I'll go to Washington myself!" She took several steps toward the door.

"Hold on, Alex. Don't you think you're overreacting just a little bit?"

"But this is really important and you're—"

"—I know it's important, but you don't have to chew the scenery to make your point." He paused, then said, "You're right. I'm being chickenshit. Fuck it, I'll do it."

Roger Anderson's knees trembled as he approached Karl Zacher at the usual meeting place on the Mall. A slow drizzle had darkened the early morning hour and Zacher's car, still running, clicked out time with its windshield wipers. It seemed unnaturally loud to Anderson, as though mocking the throbbing of his heart. Zacher greeted him cheerfully. "Another early morning rendezvous. We've got to stop meeting like this."

Anderson didn't smile. "I hope so."

"Oh, now, you should feel good about this. I can't tell you exactly how, but you're doing a great thing for your country." Zacher patted him on the shoulder. "Believe me."

Anderson waited for a car to go by, then said, "I have the list."

"Good man." Zacher held out his hand. "Give it here."

Anderson gave the list to him and stood back while Zacher held an umbrella over it and examined it in the bloom of the headlights. He asked Anderson to hold the umbrella while he ran his finger down the list of names. After a moment, he said, "Excellent."

"The new name is John Smith," Anderson said.

"I can see that. How very imaginative!" Zacher ran his finger down the list again, apparently counting names. "Uhm hmm, just one new name. This has got to be it." He reached into his Burberry and pulled out an envelope. He handed it to Anderson. "Now here's the last thing you need to do, then you're free to get on with your life. Whenever you get test requests from Doctor Stockton for this John Smith, just do what it says in this envelope. It's a simple matter, really. The results of a CBC, a complete blood count—"

"—I know what a CBC is."

"And also blood chemistry results, a peripheral blood smear—"

"—Mister Zacher, I can't—"

"—And, because if I guess correctly there will also be results for a cytogenetic analysis and immunophenotyping."

Anderson's jaw went slack. "Let me get this straight," He said with a strangled voice pitched artificially high. "You want me to report to you all the results of every test?"

"It's a simple matter. Read what's in the envelope and you'll know what we need."

"Oh, Jesus Christ! I can't do that."

Zacher frowned. "That's too bad. And you've come so far. I'd really hate to have to go through with what we discussed."

"What ... what are you going to do?"

Zacher shook his head, sighed. "Roger, I told you at considerable length what I would do."

"But my wife would leave me."

"Perhaps. We all have to pay for our mistakes. You only get Mulligans in golf. Unfortunate, but true." Zacher paused, then said, "It's really too bad that one tiny mistake and .... But you know, this is one time when you can get a Mulligan after all. All you have to do is what I ask, then your mistake is wiped clean. Your lovely wife will never know about it and you can start all over."

Anderson shifted his feet, stared at the ground. "Damn," he muttered. He looked up, glared at Zacher, and said, "All right, goddamn it, I'll do it. But it's got to end right here." His voice didn't come across as strong as he'd hoped.

"If you do it right, it will end here."

"If I ever get caught ...."

"I know, I know," said Zacher with mock sympathy. "But you won't. And when you've done this small thing, you'll never, ever, see me again.

That's a promise. All this thing's going to do is create confusion with the media, that's all. Keep them guessing, make the administration have to answer a lot of questions."

Anderson gazed at the man for a long while. The urge to run was almost irresistible. But in the end he tucked the envelope into his pocket, turned, and started to walk away.

Zacher called after him. "One more thing, Roger ...."

Anderson turned, frowned.

"Keep your background program running."

"Why?"

"Because when Stockton sees those results, my bet is he'll want to repeat the tests."

Mary-Ann Scroggs hated to hear what she was hearing again. Her husband frequently took target practice out back, but lately it seemed an obsession. He was spending nearly every spare moment shooting. That, coupled with what he'd said at Donnie's memorial service, left her uneasy. She wondered if he was planning something drastic and, if so, how she could talk him out of it. She flinched as another shot ruptured the air and echoed off the hills. She exchanged glances with Annie who, like before, was worried. Mary-Ann lifted the checkered cloth covering the banana bread she'd removed from the oven and tested its heat. It was still hot, but it would do. Nervously, she undid the knot in her apron and went to the door. Then she changed her mind and said, "Annie, go tell Daddy the banana bread is ready."

Annie said, "Okay, Mommy." She pushed her chair back with a scrape across the worn linoleum floor. The screen door squeaked when she opened it. Mary-Ann heard her daughter call out between rifle shots, "Daddy, Mommy has banana bread ready. She wants you to come in and have a piece."

Moments later, he appeared. As always, he let the screen door slam behind him. It was like a final, late echo from the last round he'd fired off. He leaned his M-4 carbine against the wall in the tiny mud room, lifted Annie to hug her, and took a chair at the table with his daughter in his lap.

Mary-Ann placed two small dishes with slices of banana bread in front of them, opened a jar of grape jelly, and handed him a knife.

"You want Daddy to spread some jelly on your banana bread?" Scroggs asked his daughter.

"No, I want to do it," she replied. "I'll do yours, too." She slipped from his lap and took a chair of her own. With her tongue protruding in concentration, she lathered grape jelly on the two slices and handed one to her father.

Scroggs laughed. "Have some banana bread with your grape jelly."

"Is it too much?"

"No, Sweetheart, it's just perfect."

Mary Ann watched them eat. When they finished, she told Annie to go out and play. After the screen door swung shut, she turned to her husband. "Billy, all this shooting," she said, trying to make her voice sound casual, "what's it for?"

"Just shootin'," he muttered before gulping a large glass of milk.

"It's makin' me and Annie nervous."

"Ain't nothin' to be nervous about."

"You also made me nervous at Donnie's memorial service what with all that talk about finishing what he started."

Billy laughed. "You think I'm practicin' so I can assassinate Baxter?"

"Ain't you?"

"Listen here, Mary-Ann, someday I'm gonna get that son-of-a-bitch. It's the patriotic thing to do. I sure as hell don't want Annie growin' up in the kinda world Baxter wants to create. Besides, it's what God wants me to do."

"Has He been speaking to you again?"

"All the time."

"And you're sure this is what He wants you to do?"

"Yuh, I'm sure."

Mary-Ann studied her husband's face. When that bomb went off at the Creative Software building, Billy had started acting strangely. She never asked him about it—she was afraid to—but she had her suspicions. Then Donnie got himself killed and Billy's anger grew even greater. It scared her. The only times she'd seen him smile was when he was able to use some of the money people donated to Donnie's memorial fund to keep up with the mortgage.

Scroggs reached for another slice of banana bread, slathered grape jelly on it, and placed the knife across the edge of his plate. "I'm waitin' for the

Good Lord to give me the sign which I know will come." He looked at her. "You know that, don't you?"

She frowned, nodded, and looked through the screen door to where Annie was playing on the tire swing Billy had hung from the big oak.

Billy continued. "But I see it like this here: I might as well kill two birds with one stone, as they say."

"What do you mean?"

"Meaning I'll do it when somebody pays me to do it. I'm tired of us livin' this hand-to-mouth existence. I want to give Annie the kinds of things other kids get."

"But who would pay you?"

Billy laughed. "Oh, come on, Mary-Ann. There's thousands of well-off people who'd love to see that man dead, the way everything he does destroys just a little bit more of our freedoms. All I gotta do is find the right person."

"How're you gonna do that?"

"Well, for one, you heard my speech. That there was a marketin' message. Sure as hell it'll get around that Billy Scroggs is willin'. Plus, I've already got word out through the various militia groups we're in contact with."

Mary-Ann laughed wryly. "What'd you say? Gun for hire?"

He gazed at her, his expression solemn. "Exactly," he said. "Don't worry, God will send somebody my way."

"But what about Annie? She loves you. She needs you."

"I ain't gonna get myself killed like Donnie. He was off his rocker. I'll plan better than that. Don't worry about Annie. In a way, this thing's for her. I ain't about to ruin it by gettin' myself killed."

Karl Zacher entered Senator Haskins' office waving a sheet of paper. "Got it right here," he said triumphantly.

"Got what?" asked Haskins.

"The list of Stockton's patients. There's a new name. Get this. It's John Smith."

"How original."

Zacher gave a sardonic laugh. "That's what I thought. He couldn't be more obvious if he included a photograph."

Senator Haskins came out from behind his desk to take the paper from Zacher. He examined it and asked, "So you think that's him?"

"Who the hell else would it be? Stockton's not taking any new patients and after the media circus when Grace Baxter's test results got out, Stockton was bound to use an assumed name just like we thought. Baxter's name is also there but what do you want to bet no tests ever show up with his real name again?"

"So if Baxter's being treated for depression or alcoholism, we'll know?"

Zacher gave an enigmatic smile.

"I said, we'll know?"

"Even if he's treated by a psychiatrist in total secrecy," Zacher said, "it'll hit his personal physician's files. That's the way it works."

"And your man will get the info to you immediately?"

"He's designing a computer program that—"

Haskins held up a hand. "I don't need to know. As long as it does the job. I want them scrambling to answer questions. Divert their attention."

"Oh, it'll do that all right." Zacher chuckled to himself. If Haskins didn't want to know about a simple computer program, what would he think if he knew what was in the package he'd given Anderson? No, that's another thing Senator Wayne Haskins didn't need to know.

"But I don't want it getting out. If the man's suffering from depression that's affecting his performance, I'll confront him with it personally. Man to man. No media. You hear me?"

"Don't worry. I'll handle it."

"Good. I'll try to persuade him to resign for the good of the country. He might go along with it because I'd be hurting myself. I happen to think Moore-Paterson would be a more formidable opponent, and I think Baxter knows that."

"You'd be willing to hurt your own chances?"

"Karl, you may find this hard to believe, but sometimes the good of the country does trump personal ambition—either mine or his. And right now the good of the country requires a president who's on top of his game."

"Like you?"

"I'm not even sure I'd get the nomination. After the last campaign I have as many enemies on the Republican side as Baxter has among the

Democrats; I had to campaign away from my base to have any chance. If Baxter resigns and plays it right, it would give Moore-Paterson a huge sympathy boost. The party might think someone younger than me is needed to run against someone so dynamic especially if she's running as an incumbent."

"But you wouldn't turn down the nomination."

"Of course not."

Zacher gave a cynical smile. "I disagree with you. It's Baxter who has the sympathy boost. Hell, when Grace Baxter died it was like the nation lost a favorite grandmother. To use Clinton's phrase, everybody feels Baxter's pain. You'd lose to him if he didn't resign. You want to run against Moore-Paterson. What's more, there's no way in fucking hell you'll ever persuade Baxter to resign by having a heart-to-heart with him."

"Karl, I've warned you repeatedly about using foul language in my office."

"Sorry. But all the same, you're not going to get him to resign unless his medical records somehow go public. You'll talk with him alright, but only to let him know what you've got and that you'll release it."

Haskins gave a sardonic laugh. "Okay, so you see through my argument."

"It isn't that difficult."

"Which means we're back to square one," said Haskins. "We need something strong enough to persuade Baxter to resign and that will be difficult."

Zacher slipped into his coat and went to the door. "Oh, I don't know. It might be easier than you think."

"What do you mean by that?"

Zacher opened the door, paused, raised a hand, and said, "Like you said before, you don't need to know."

"Zacher, you worry me sometimes."

"Don't worry, Baxter will resign and you'll get elected. What more could you want?"

Senator Haskins returned to his desk, sat down in the high-backed leather chair, and gazed at a photograph of his three grandchildren. "You know," he said, "sometimes I hate politics. It's just a damned dirty business. It's not like what it used to be."

"And it's people like me who make it dirty?" asked Zacher.

"I didn't say that."

"No, but it's what you think. You figure if you didn't need so damn much money every time you run for office then you wouldn't have to put up with men like me and all the interest groups and lobbyists that plague your day. Then you could all have a nice, gentleman's debating society where no one gets hurt except, perhaps for a small thing like pride." Zacher walked up to the desk. He placed both hands on it, leaned forward, and said, "But it's not ... it's not fu ..., freaking, like that, so you'll just have to put up with me."

"I don't need you to tell me what politics is like."

"Good. Then how about trusting me to get the job done and stop worrying about how I might do it?"

Haskins glared at Zacher. He knew the man was right; he would just have to hope that Zacher didn't get carried away by his hatred of Baxter. The last thing he needed was to get entangled in something nasty. It wasn't the kind of legacy he wanted to leave his grandchildren.

Chapter 7—AG Ken Nesbitt; Dr. Jim Stockton

Matt Cannon sat in the Oval Office with Baxter as they waited for the attorney general to show up. To kill time, Baxter recounted a story about his father. He held out the case containing his father's Congressional Medal of Honor. "I never knew him, you know."

"I know. You were only four when he was killed on Omaha Beach and he had already been gone for a couple of years." Matt hoped that by filling in details himself he could shorten the story he'd heard so many times.

"After I became president, I had some people research the names of the men in his unit. I had the ones who were still living visit the White House to tell me about Dad."

"I know. I was there."

"They said they'd never seen courage like he showed. They talked about the night before the invasion when they had already boarded the ship that would take them across the channel. They were forbidden communications with the shore, but a British nurse standing on the docks used semaphore flags to send them one word."

Matt saw a tear course down Baxter's cheek.

"That one word was 'C-O-U-R-A-G-E.' They said Dad used that incident to rally his men for the next morning."

"They say he gave a beautiful speech," added Matt. "It must be in your genes."

"They landed on Omaha: Able company, 116th Infantry, 29th Division, a little after six the next morning. A thousand yards from the beach they started to take hits from artillery shells. Boats exploded, men drowned. The ramps of the Higgins boats dropped and guys were ripped apart by machine gun fire before they even got a few yards.

When some of them finally made shore, Dad told them to make for the bluff at the top of the beach. But he didn't go with them. Instead, he went back and pulled a wounded man ashore. Then he went back for another. He helped them to the bluff and, miraculously, they made it."

Baxter paused and stroked the sides of the medal box. He strolled to the windows and gazed out across the south lawn to the Washington Monument for a long time before saying, "After they were reinforced by Baker and Charlie companies and the waves of troops that followed them, Dad rallied his men and led them up a trail that, according to the invasion maps, would take them to the village of Les Moulins and a dirt road marked on the maps as Exit No. 3. A couple of men were hit and Dad went back to drag them to cover one after the other. Then a third man was hit and, again, Dad went back."

Matt waited, silent, for several long minutes.

Finally, the president said, "That's when he got it." Baxter returned to the desk and placed the medal-of-honor box down. His hand was shaking. "How is it possible to emulate courage like that? How is it possible?"

The phone on the desk buzzed. Baxter pressed a button. "Yes?"

Doris' voice came through the intercom. "The attorney general is here."

"Okay. Give me a moment."

Matt said, "Will you forgive me if I say something?"

"Say it."

"You'll never win a Congressional Medal of Honor. You can't repeat that. But there is one recognition that would be almost as important and it's my guess that it is what drives you."

Baxter gave a reluctant smile. "So now you're my analyst? Okay, what is it?"

"The Nobel Peace Prize."

"Never even thought about it."

"Bullshit! You pull off what nobody else has ever been able to do, win an enduring peace in the Middle East, and it's yours. I'm thinking that it's always lurking in your mind. How else could you equal—?"

"—All right, Matt, that's enough." He pressed the intercom. "Doris, the attorney general can come in now." He turned back to Matt. "Please get the door for Nesbitt; he doesn't know how to open it." As with the presidential limousine, there was a trick to opening the doors to the Oval Office; it was another level of security.

Cannon stared at him for a few moments, then went to the door, opened it, and waved the Attorney General in. Kenneth Nesbitt was a fat, balding man whose clothes were rumpled and who wore long-out-of-style neckties in thin, drab colors. He'd been a second choice, a compromise appointment in the spirit of bipartisanship after the senate had turned down Baxter's first choice, mainly at the urging of Senator Haskins. Baxter soon found that he didn't like Nesbitt and their relations were, at best, cordial, though cool. His sentiments were shared by Matt who'd had several distasteful dealings with the man in the private sector.

"Good morning, Mister President. You're looking well."

"You said it was urgent," said Baxter. "Have a seat and tell me about it." He directed Nesbitt to a sofa and propped himself on the edge of the desk fingering the case that held his father's medal.

When Nesbitt was seated, he leaned forward, elbows on his knees, and said, "Mister President, I just came from a meeting between my organization and Homeland Security. As you know, the folks in ATF have been keeping an eye on the militia groups around the country. One of their agents reported up the channels that the M-4 group. That's the one that—"

"—that this guy, Scroggs, belonged to," said the president. "Yes, I know. Go on."

"Yes, well it seems they're starting up again. At least that's what the folks from ATF think."

"What makes them think that?"

"This agent attended a memorial event for Donald Scroggs. Jesus Christ, can you imagine that? They give the asshole a memorial event because he tried to assassinate you and died in the process."

"Was it crowded?" Baxter asked with a chuckle. "Hell, I could think of at least a hundred people who'd be only too happy to honor the guy, most of them in this city."

Nesbitt seemed unsure what to say. He glanced at the rotating crystal globes and appeared temporarily mesmerized by them. He stammered for a moment before saying, "There were speeches. Apparently, they were filled with hatred for you, sir."

"Are you sure this wasn't the Senate?"

Nesbitt laughed uncomfortably. "No, sir. Scroggs' brother, especially, gave a vitriolic speech in which the ATF agent thinks he made a direct threat on your life." Again, he watched the crystal globes flashing a regular pulse.

Baxter walked to the other end of the desk and sat against it, directly in front of the clock. "What did he say?"

Nesbitt pulled a paper from his briefcase. He scanned it for a moment, then said, "He said about his brother, quote, 'He may be dead, but his spirit is alive in each of us. And I tell you this, I ain't afraid of taking up where he left off.' That sounds like a direct threat to me, Mister President."

"I don't know. To me, it sounds like empty bombast."

"Well, he didn't specifically say he was going to assassinate you, sir, but his meaning was pretty clear. And any threat of assassination is a crime." Nesbitt paused a moment then said, "I recommend we go after him. Put him out of commission."

"You mean call the FBI on him for exercising his free speech?"

"There are limits to free speech, Mister President. You can't yell 'fire'—"

"—Yes, yes, I know: you can't yell fire in a crowded theater," Baxter said impatiently.

"Right. And you sure as hell can't threaten to assassinate the President of the United States."

"But that's not how these folks see it. You'd only be making a martyr of him and that would give a spark of life to the whole militia movement when, at last, it seemed to be dying down."

"But Mister President, we could arrest him on other grounds. I'm sure he's got a stash of weapons that is illegal as hell; they all do. We could get the ATF guys on it."

"Same thing. You make him a martyr. Don't you remember the flak Janet Reno took with Waco and Ruby Ridge? Do you truly want the federal government to go through all of that again?"

Nesbitt looked to Matt for help, but Matt was staring at the president, a bemused look on his face. In his right hand he held a glass of soda. Flashes from the rotating crystal globes brushed across its surface.

Baxter continued. "Listen, I don't want you to touch this guy. At least for the time being. Get ATF to send their man back in there and monitor the situation."

"The agent is a woman, not a man. Her name's Alexandra Lake. One of the best."

"Whatever. The last thing we need to do is fire up the militia movement. Then you'll have at least a dozen potential assassins on your hands."

Nesbitt protested feebly for a few moments, but when Baxter made it clear he was immovable, the man gave up. He rose and the president came forward to shake his hand then guided him to the door. "Keep me informed though, Ken."

"Of course, Mister President," Nesbitt said.

After the Attorney General left, Matt asked, "Don't you think you should take him more seriously?"

"Him or this threat?"

Matt laughed. "Okay. The threat."

"Look, it comes with the territory," replied Baxter. "Besides, I meant what I said. Moving on this guy would only galvanize the militia types."

"Don't you think you should at least consult the Secret Service on something like this?"

"If it went through channels as Nesbitt said, they already know about it and, if they thought it was clear and present, they would have come to me themselves."

"All the same. I think you should—"

"—Matt, enough! We have more important things to talk about right now. For example, what the hell am I going to do about this?" He waved a National Security report about a fresh wave of violence in the Middle East.

Matt wanted to pursue the issue, but he knew when his friend's mind was made up, there was nothing that would budge him.

A week later, the attorney general saw Senator Haskins at a party at the French Embassy. Many of the Washington in-crowd were there, including a number of senators and members of Congress, as well as some key people from the Baxter administration. Because of the later, Nesbitt had to wait nearly two hours before he could find an opportunity to talk privately with Haskins; he didn't want members of the administration to hear what he had to say or, for that matter, to see him huddling with the opposition senator, because his loyalty to the administration was already suspect.

The reception room was bedecked with French and American flags and an odor of lemon-scented furniture polish mixed with the tannic aroma of wine, a medley of seductive perfumes, and the salty smell of caviar. Nesbitt spent his time chatting with a variety of people and, in particular, practicing his French with the wife of the ambassador who had applied copious amounts of a beguiling perfume to her shoulders and neck.

Finally, he was standing near Haskins when he overheard the senator ask a drinks waiter, *"Pardonnez-moi, ou est la toilette?"*

The waiter directed him to an unmarked room next to the library. Nesbitt followed a few moments later and stood at the entrance. At last, he heard the flush and a moment later Haskins emerged from the bathroom. Nesbitt went up to the senator. "Can I have a minute with you, Senator Haskins?"

"Sure Ken. What's up?"

He motioned the senator into the small, book-lined study that also smelled of furniture polish. He closed the door and said, "Senator, I wanted to tell you about a meeting I had with the president last week. I informed him we have evidence that the M-4 militia group was re-forming."

"The assassin's group?"

"Yes. And the assassin's brother, a guy named Billy Scroggs, is one of their leaders. It seems this man gave a speech in which he promised to finish the work his brother started."

Senator Haskins raised his eyebrows. "That's a direct threat on the president's life!"

"That's what I said, but the president doesn't see it that way."

"What do you mean?"

"I told him I planned to raid the group, but he said he wanted me to hold off. Said it would just stir them up."

"That's ridiculous! You can't let somebody get away with threatening the president."

"My feelings exactly. But Baxter was adamant. Even Matt Cannon seemed confused."

Haskins frowned. "Does Baxter think he's immortal? Does he think he's Charles de Gaulle riding through Paris in an open car?"

"You got me," replied the Attorney General. "But I thought it was such strange behavior, I wanted to tell you about it. I can't get it out of my mind that he's playing some kind of game."

Haskins nodded. "If he is, it's a dangerous game. I mean, I certainly have no love for the president and I wouldn't shed any tears if he was out of the way, but certainly not that way. An assassination? That would be an unmitigated disaster. It wouldn't be good for the country and it sure as hell would be a major headache for me."

"How so?"

"Come on, think about it. He gets himself killed and Moore-Paterson becomes president. Then in the election she gets a huge sympathy vote. It would be Lyndon Johnson all over again. And that's not to speak of the president's programs that would get a tremendous boost—all because of national sympathy. If we were lucky enough and those militia jerks missed like the last time … well just look at the big bounce in popularity he got when that Scroggs guy tried to assassinate him."

"I understand all that, but Baxter refuses to take this seriously. Either he's blind or he's up to something."

"He's sure as hell not blind."

"So what do you think he's up to?"

Haskins gave a sardonic laugh. "Well, I'd like to think he's so afraid of me that he'd risk his life to bring me down. But that's totally absurd." He paused, then said, "No, I can't believe he's playing a game here. He's just not seeing it clearly. Maybe he is blind. Maybe his wife's death … his drinking …."

"What should I do?"

"Ignore him for his own good, for the good of all of us. Persuade the folks at Homeland Security and Justice to either arrest this Scroggs guy or keep a close eye on him. And I mean a real close eye."

Nesbitt laughed. "I never thought I'd hear you show such concern for the president's safety."

"Look, he's a good man. I don't happen to agree with a damn thing he does, but that doesn't mean I want to see him killed."

As they drove home from the French Embassy in a steady rain, Haskins and his wife were silent. She knew how difficult it was for him to drive in such conditions. The senator leaned forward over the steering wheel, peering through the rain-splattered windshield as the wipers kept a steady, fast, slap-slap rhythm. Though he wore eyeglasses, he suffered from poor vision at night. Lights appeared as blurred splotches that he was unable to resolve into sharp images. Both his shoulders ached, and occasionally he had to blink hard to dispel the phantom images he kept imagining floating in the road ahead of him.

"I had a strange meeting with Ken Nesbitt at the party," he said, rotating his shoulders to ease the ache.

Julia Haskins leaned across and placed her hands at the base of her husband's neck. She massaged vigorously. "Tell me about it," she said.

"Ahh, that feels good," Haskins said. "Thanks." He told his wife about Nesbitt's meeting with the president and how Baxter had seemed to take the news of a possible assassination threat lightly. "Even Matt Cannon appeared baffled by the president's response, according to Nesbitt. He said it was very clear in Cannon's eyes."

"You would think that after the last assassination attempt he'd take such a thing more seriously."

"Exactly," replied Haskins. "Especially when this threat involved the brother of Donald Scroggs."

"His brother?"

Haskins nodded. "Now you see why the president's reaction is so strange?"

"I should say so!"

"Nesbitt thinks he's up to some sort of game."

"What possible game could he be playing that he'd allow his own life to be threatened?"

"That's the obvious question. And no matter how hard I try, I can come up with only one possible answer."

"What's that?"

"It doesn't matter to him because he knows he's not running for a second term. As soon as he makes an announcement to that affect, any threat of assassination goes up in smoke. If I'm a potential assassin, I'd say, 'What's the point?'."

"Not running for a second term? Baxter? Why would he make such a decision?"

"Well, I have it from very reliable sources inside the administration that ever since Grace Baxter died, his attention and focus isn't what it used to be. He tends to wander in meetings, especially lately."

"So you think he may realize this and is prepared to resign because he can't do the job the way he wants?"

Haskins flipped the right directional for the exit off the Dolly Madison Boulevard and said, "He's an honorable man with a strong sense of reality. If he felt he wasn't up to it, he'd do the same thing I would do in his position: resign."

"You'd really resign?"

"Yes, *really*. Some things are more important than the office. If I thought the country would be better for it …."

"But if Baxter resigns that means the vice president would take over. What would that do to your chances?"

"She's pretty popular and could be real tough as an incumbent. All the same, given the political landscape of the last election, it might help."

"How so?"

"Well, they'd feel obligated to give Moore-Patterson the nomination, she being the incumbent VP. But I'd stand a good chance of beating her in the electoral vote. Baxter beat me by less than a percentage point in several states that might not go for a black woman. They represent a couple dozen electoral votes and I lost the election by seven votes."

"And you can beat her in those states?"

"I think so. I might even pick up a few other states I lost by narrow margins last time around."

"That makes a lot of sense, yet it all depends on Baxter resigning."

"True," said Haskins. "But I have reason to believe he'll be persuaded."

"What makes you say that?"

Haskins glanced sideways at his wife. "Sweetheart, that's one of those things you said long ago you'd rather not know about."

"Some kind of political trick?"

He put a hand on her knee, smiled, and said, "Let's just put it this way: There's a good chance the man you'll soon find beside you in bed will be the next president of the United States." He leaned over and kissed her on the cheek. "I've always wanted to sleep with the First Lady."

When Marcie Gaudet woke, she decided to go in late to her job as vice president of operations at the First Bank of Arlington. Matt Cannon stirred beside her, rolling over and, in the process, pulling the sheets across her body. The silken friction sent a frisson of delight through her. She rolled over and placed her lips on the round pucker of skin where the bullet had entered his side a year earlier. She traced her tongue around the periphery of the wound, feeling its rough edges. It was her signal that she wanted to make love. The wound to his groin may have made him sterile, but it didn't deprive him of erections. She reached under the sheets to stroke him while nuzzling his neck. A stale, musky odor rose from his body, exciting her.

Matt opened his eyes, stretched. "Uhmm, what a nice way to wake up." He gazed at his runner's watch. "Four-thirty already?"

"Uhm hmm. Time to get our running shoes on." Most mornings they ran together between five and seven miles along the B&O canal. "Unless, of course, I can interest you in something else …."

He smiled. "Let's see … running … or Marcie … running … or Marcie. What will it be?"

She kissed him on the lips and said, "I'll be in the shower when you decide." She slid out of bed and strolled naked toward the bathroom.

Matt propped himself on one elbow and watched her, admiring the tautness of her runner's body, especially her firm buttocks and her well-defined thigh and calf muscles. At every Washington party, she drew the attention of men. And that was without them seeing her as he now saw her. She went into the bathroom, leaving the door open, and soon he heard the shower running.

He hauled himself out of bed, went into the bathroom, and pulled the curtain back to join her. They soaped each others' bodies, lingering in the sensitive places, stopping to kiss several times. Matt licked at a drop of water suspended from Marcie's eyebrow and reached behind her to grasp her soap-slippery buttocks. She closed her eyes and gave him a dreamy smile. Her medium length, blond hair was plastered to her skull, exposing her ears. He nibbled one of them.

A phone rang.

"Oh no," groaned Marcie.

Matt closed his eyes and frowned. "Shit," he muttered. "That's the drop phone." He was referring to a special phone directly linking him to the White House. It had a distinctive grating sound.

"There's only one person in the White House who would dare call at this hour," said Marcie. "You better get it. Something must be up."

"You mean besides me?" he asked ruefully. He climbed out of the shower, threw a towel around himself, and went into the bedroom, trailing small puddles of water. He picked up the phone. "Hello?"

"Matt? It's Angus. Sorry if I disturbed you. I was afraid you'd be out running already."

"No problem, Mister President. What's up?"

"How about a round of golf?"

"What?" asked Matt, his voice falsetto. "When?"

"Now. I need to have a talk with you."

"On the golf course?"

"Can you think of anyplace more private, given my position?"

"Uh, no, I guess not."

"Matt, I need you. Now."

"Of course. I'll be there as soon as I can get dressed." He hung up and returned to the bathroom.

"What's happening?" asked Marcie. She leaned against the bathroom door frame, a towel cinched around her body.

"He wants me to play golf."

"Are you kidding? Why on such short notice?"

"He wouldn't say over the phone. It's obvious he wants to talk about something, but not in the White House."

"Well, I hope it's not another crisis that'll keep you away for days. Doesn't he realize you're not even in the administration?"

"Sometimes that's what makes me so useful to him. I can come and go without drawing much attention. And I'm not recognized outside the Inner Belt."

As Matt dressed, Marcie asked, "By the way, how is the president doing? Emotionally, I mean."

Matt shook his head. "It's been a year since Grace died, but he's not over it yet. Not even close. I don't think he'll ever recover. They tell me he sometimes drifts off in meetings. He's never done that before."

"It's too bad Haskins killed the education bill. It would have been a great tribute to the First Lady. God, how I hate that man."

"You and I both. But the president? He's almost obsessed with bringing Haskins down, especially since that business with that education bill. It gets to the point where I worry about him."

"What do you mean?"

"It's that drifting off thing. Lately, when I meet with him, even if we're alone, I get the feeling he's not really present. It must have been like that in the last years of the Reagan administration."

Marcie knitted her brow. "You can't mean you think he's in the first stages of Alzheimer's?"

"No. At least, I don't think so," said Matt, fumbling with the knot of a necktie. "But he did have a doctor's appointment that he deliberately kept from me. He's never done that before, too."

"How do you know he had an appointment and that he kept it from you? And, why would he tell you in the first place?"

"He wouldn't," Matt replied. "Except that I went into the Oval Office a few weeks ago just as Jim Stockton was leaving. Jim gave me a quick hello then rushed off which was very unlike him; he's usually very cordial. Then, when I went into the Oval Office, the president seemed upset. So I asked him directly if he'd just had a medical discussion with Jim and he said no. I pressed him on it because he and Jim aren't close; there's nothing else they would meet about except a medical issue. But he still denied it."

Marcie helped him with the knot. "Why do you suppose he did that?"

"It's obvious. Because he's got some kind of health problem he doesn't want me, or anybody else, to know about."

"So it *could* be Alzheimer's?"

"Could be, I suppose; he's seventy. But I think it could be some kind of clinical depression. That would make more sense, and it would be something he'd want to hide." He kissed Marcie on the forehead and made for the door.

"Well I hope everything turns out all right," Marcie said, blowing him a kiss. "Give him my best. Tell him I'm thinking of him."

Angus Baxter peered out of the oval office windows at the Washington Monument just now beginning to emerge from the gloom. The first roseate light of dawn brushed the monument's severe surfaces making it appear soft and welcoming, nothing like what it truly was—a cold, stately, monument to a dead president. The brass ornaments at the tops of the flagpoles ringing the obelisk reflected gold in the low sunlight. Below them, the flags stirred with an awakening breeze. In another couple of hours the monument would be swarming with tourists. A mile away, the dome of the Thomas Jefferson Memorial glowed with a flush of pink. A solitary jogger, her face and ponytail alight with the new sun, crossed the Ellipse. The dog running before her on a leash was still in shadow.

Baxter wondered idly if there would ever be a monument for him. *Unlikely.*

Twenty minutes after receiving the call from the president, Matt, dressed and clean shaven, drove down Pennsylvania Avenue toward the White House. Because he had his golf clubs with him, Matt decided to drive rather than walk as was his custom. Despite the early hour, the city was enfolded in an oppressive embrace of early summer heat. As he passed a trash truck, he saw that the shirts of the men heaving plastic bags into the maw of the truck were wetly plastered to their backs.

Soon, he pulled up to the East Gate. After a friendly greeting to the guards, he entered the White House and made his way to the West Wing.

Baxter thought all those who win the presidency must harbor fantasies of greatness. Yet most presidents have turned out to have a higher opinion of themselves than history eventually accorded them. The irony was those who earned themselves monuments—Washington, Lincoln, Jefferson, FDR—probably were far more modest about their achievements than others who were seduced by their own grandiose visions. Baxter wondered where he fit among his predecessors.

It required the shock of the doctor's report a few weeks earlier to force him to confront his own limited achievements and question whether he ever would attain what he'd set out to do.

He saw a flight of birds flit past the monument, their wing tips stirring the new light. The hairs on his back prickled. When was the last time he'd even noticed such beauty, such simple life, let alone be thrilled by it? He'd begun seeing things in a new way shortly after Grace died. Frequently he found himself remembering how she would often comment about the scent of the morning air or the way the stars looked through the skylight at the Maine residence. And she would reminisce about their time in Congress when they had taken long sailing vacations. She would recall in amazing detail the feel of the wind in the sails, the motion of the boat, the sound of the salt water hissing along the hull. One night shortly before her death, she'd reminded him in rapturous detail of the time they sailed alone down Vineyard Sound between Edgartown and Tarpaulin Cove, an easy distance of about fifteen nautical miles. As they rounded West Chop on Martha's Vineyard and set a course due west, the setting sun was low on the horizon ahead of them at the same time that a full moon rose above the eastern horizon. "It felt like we were on a wire stretched taut and humming between the sun and moon," she'd said. That had led her to recall a similar time in Maui when the sun and moon had been low at opposite ends of the sky and she'd stayed up all night writing a poem about it. The week before her death, alone in the hospital room with the Secret Service agents discreetly outside in the corridor, he'd curled up with her in the bed while she recited the poem from memory:

> *Now the moonrise came lilting*
> *to the lead of sunset and the earth*
> *was made to quaver on a slender*
> *thread spun from the moon*
> *by the sun and all things*
> *living quaked with lingering joy*
> *as the day's life-making fire*
> *was quenched by a rinse of moonlight.*

He wondered: did it take the knowledge of one's impending death to fire the senses, to awaken the spirit? What was it that Samuel Johnson had said: "Nothing so focuses the mind as the prospect of being hanged in the morning"? Is that what it took to live fully? What a pity if it were true. But then again, Grace's senses had been open and receptive that night in Maui when they were much younger. They'd made love on the beach in a wash of moonlight. Was it something you lose with age? Was it something that several senate campaigns, a presidential campaign, and the presidency itself had sapped from them? Or had she, even then, back in Maui, felt somehow close to death?

As he passed the Roosevelt Room, Matt saw Jim Stockton walking just ahead of him toward the Oval Office. "Jim, wait up," he called out. "What are you doing here this early?" This was the second time in recent weeks he'd seen Stockton in the area of the Oval Office at an odd time.

Stockton stopped and waited for him. "Hello, Matt." His voice was subdued, his manner grim.

Matt furrowed his brow. "Something's going on. What is it?"

Stockton nodded toward the Oval Office. "I'll let him tell you." He continued down the corridor.

Walking beside Stockton, Matt said, "You won't give me a heads up so I can be prepared?"

"Sorry, Matt. I'd like to, but I just can't. You'll learn in the limo on the way to the golf course."

"The limo? We're not taking *Marine One*?"

"We're not going to Holly Hills," replied Stockton, referring to Baxter's favorite course which was not far from Camp David. "Instead, we're going to Andrews."

"Still, he usually takes *Marine One*."

Stockton shook his head. "Motorcade this time."

"What's he doing, economizing?"

Stockton didn't answer. They had arrived in the President's Outer Office to find a woman sitting nervously in an arm chair. Matt walked up to the woman, who rose to meet him, and offered his hand. "Hello, I'm Matt Cannon and this is Commander Stockton."

"I'm Alexandra Lake," she replied.

"Are you here for the golf?" Matt asked.

Lake gave him a surprised look. "Uh, no."

"So, what are you doing here?"

"I … I really don't know," Alexandra replied.

Matt gave her a quizzical look. Outside the window, beyond the Rose Garden, he saw the motorcade already lined up and Secret Service agents milling about. He shook his head. Nothing Baxter ever did was without purpose.

Was it possible he chose the courses at Andrews Air Force Base—which he did not prefer to Holly Hills—because it was much closer and he could travel by motorcade rather than *Marine One*? That was the only difference Matt could imagine, and it wasn't much of a difference because Holly Hills by *Marine One* and Andrews by motorcade required about the same amount of time.

Then it came to him: On *Marine One*, everyone in the president's secure package—secret agents, military aide, physician—traveled inside the same airframe. Consequently, there was little opportunity for secret discussion. In the motorcade, however, the secure package traveled in support vehicles, leaving the occupants of the president's limo free to discuss anything they wanted in total secrecy. That's it, Matt thought, the president wants to have some kind of important conversation, one he doesn't want to have inside the White House with staff crawling all over the place, nor any other place where there was a remote possibility of being overheard. As far as Matt knew, there were only four places in Baxter's confined world where this could happen: the White House residence, Camp David, the Down East White House, and the motorcade.

Matt turned to Stockton. "The president wants to have an ultra secure conversation."

"Yes."

"And you're going to be in the limo with him and me."

"Yes."

Matt turned to Alexandra Lake. "And you?"

Alexandra spread her hands. "I have no idea."

Matt turned back to Stockton. "Camp David provides plenty of privacy. Why not there instead of the gold course?"

Stockton shook his head. "I have no idea."

Angus Baxter chuckled. The utter absurdity of his idea, its theatricality, was trumped only by its irrefutable, cold logic. He'd been wrestling with it for the previous two weeks and it reminded him of the urge for a cigarette when he quit smoking some forty years earlier—the little beast of an idea kept rearing itself every half-hour or so. Like a persistent fly.

And every time this new idea surfaced, he tried to find a hole in it, some logical inconsistency, but he couldn't. It just made too damn much sense. The idea was like a tensile web that wrapped his mind, trapping itself in its own tangle. Eventually, he'd yielded himself to it.

Matt, of course would laugh at first. He'd wonder why the president had called him just after dawn for a sudden golf date only to make such an absurd, sick joke. Then he would grow more and more incredulous; his jaw would drop; creases would form on his forehead; he would finger the ragged edges of the side wound through his shirt; and he would stop in the middle of the fairway or on a green as if somebody had struck him.

Baxter knew his friend intimately after so many years and he could almost predict, to the smallest gesture, the man's every reaction. And it was Matt's expected reactions to what he would say that ruled out the White House, Camp David or even the Downeast White House as places for this meeting. In all those other places there would be staff all over the place and, though he and Matt could undoubtedly speak in private, people would notice Matt's disposition, even long after the conversation, and would know something serious was going down and would wonder why they weren't involved. There were just too many complications, so it had to be the golf course.

Since Andrews was a military base, the Secret Service could impose a lock down and they could position the Counter Assault Team, dressed in black with binoculars pressed to their eye sockets, all along the golf course. What this, in turn, meant was that the Secret Service would accommodate the request (order?) he planned to make: that they give him a hundred yards of space all around.

Baxter went to the desk and lifted the pewter-framed picture of Grace. As always, small tears formed in the corner of his eyes as he gazed at her smiling image. The rotating crystal globes of the anniversary clock reflected in the glass protecting the photograph.

He replaced the picture of his wife and took up the polished wooden box containing his father's Medal of Honor. He ran his finger across the gold bar and arrow shafts that contained the word VALOR, felt the blue ribbon with its embroidered stars, fingered the green-enameled ring. The citation and a picture of his father stood next to the box at the right front of the desk where they were sure to be seen by any visitor to the Oval Office.

He knew the words of the citation by heart:

Awarded posthumously to Lt. Colonel Maxwell Baxter for extraordinary valor on June 6th, 1944 when he repeatedly led men off Omaha Beach in Normandy ....

How he wished he had known his father!

He always made sure the open box with its medal was on display, especially when the Joint Chiefs were in the office.

Valor.

"It looks like it's my turn to see if I've got it in me, Dad," he said aloud. "I only wish it could be the pure, simple kind like yours. But it isn't going to work that way, is it?"

He looked at his watch. *5:30.* Matt should be outside the office.

Alexandra Lake was utterly unfamiliar with the White House, and had had difficulty finding the correct entrance. She had to get directions from a policeman who, unsure of the woman, escorted her to the East Gate. There, Alexandra showed her badge to the agents and they consulted a clipboard while the policeman waited. Finally, one of the agents nodded and let her pass. She had been nervous. At other times, entering even the Department of Justice building had impressed her with a sense of the power inherent in a place of authority, but this far exceeded that.

It had taken more than three weeks for her report on the M-4 militia group to reach the top levels in Washington. When it finally did, she'd expected some sort of task force would be organized to conduct a raid—perhaps ATF, or maybe FBI, or, more likely still, some combination of the two. But a personal interview with the president, himself? That was the last thing she'd expected. She couldn't imagine what this was about. Without doubt, the Director of the Secret Service, and probably the Homeland Defense Secretary, and the Attorney General, had already informed the president of her discoveries. What did the president need with her?

Once inside the White House, she'd been directed by a couple of uniformed Secret Service agents to a room and told to wait there. She didn't know much about the layout of the White House, but she guessed she was somewhere in the West Wing, perhaps outside the Oval Office itself. The thought sent a shiver through her. She studied the furnishings and the paintings on the wall. She noticed from the parallel lines left by a vacuum that the carpets had recently been cleaned. She was amazed at how spotless the place was, wholly unlike any other government building she'd been in.

Wouldn't her mother get a thrill out of this, she thought. Unless, of course, she was in some kind of trouble. That thought further unsettled her. She sat back in the chair, crossed and re-crossed her legs, and waited with the two men she had just met.

The door to the Oval Office opened and Baxter stuck his head out. He looked at Alexandra., She jumped to her feet.

"You must be Ms. Lake," he said.

"Yes, Mister President," she replied quickly.

"Good. Welcome to the White House." Baxter turned to Jim Stockton. "Jim, we'll be leaving in ten or fifteen minutes. You're welcome to sit in the limousine or hang around the Rose Garden."

"Yes, Mister President," Stockton said. He walked out to the Rose Garden through one of the doors in the president's secretary's office.

"Ms. Lake, join me and Matt Cannon, here, in the Oval Office." He held the door for her as she passed into the room. "Please, have a seat," said Baxter, gesturing toward a sofa.

Alexandra felt her knees trembling a little as she sat in one of two sofas that faced each other. Between them was a coffee table with a large floral arrangement. In the carpet at the end of the coffee table was the seal of the president which only made her more nervous.

Matt Cannon took a seat on the opposite sofa and President Baxter sat in a chair with its back to the fireplace which was opposite the presidential desk.

Baxter said to Alexandra, "Now I want you to tell us everything you know about this Billy Scroggs guy."

Alexandra drew in a breath. Haltingly, she told her story. She described the memorial event in detail and especially Billy Scroggs and his speech. She also described the little town of Bass Run and what she could of Scroggs' house. "I only saw it at a distance, but it looked pretty rundown to me."

"In need of repairs?"

"Oh, yes, sir. Substantial," replied Alexandra.

Baxter paused a moment then said, "Now what Scroggs said at this event, Do you think this man was serious?"

"I have no doubt about it, Mister President. That's why I reported it up the line."

"Of course. What do you think he's waiting for? If I'm as dangerous as he says, he hasn't got a moment to lose."

Alexandra pursed her lips, she wasn't sure how to answer. Was he making a joke she was supposed to laugh at? She chose not to laugh. "Well, that's hard to say, Mister President. If I had to guess, I'd say it's money. As I've described, the man is dirt poor, doesn't have a job. And, excuse me, sir, but to assassinate the president you just can't come into town on a bus one day and do your business like you were going to the fair or a museum or something. Not after nine-eleven. He would need money to disappear for a while, to change his identity, to stay in hotels, you name it. If he wanted to survive, that is. And since he has a family, I assume he'd want to survive."

"I see," said Baxter. "So, in short, he needs a sponsor?"

"Something like that, Mister President."

Baxter glanced at Matt, raised his eyebrows. Then he turned back to Alexandra. "Well, thank you for coming in, Ms. Lake. I wanted to hear it all from the horse's mouth, so to speak, and you've done admirably." He laughed. "Not that you're a horse, of course. Only an expression."

"Yes, sir," she replied. "Do you want me to follow up, Mister President?"

"No, we'll take it from here," Baxter said, as he started to usher her out of the Oval Office. At the door, he stopped and asked one more question. "Tell me, if he's going to come after me, what weapon do you think he'd use?"

Alexandra creased her forehead. "Weapon, Mister President?"

"Yes. What would he use?"

"I suppose he'd use a gun. He's known to have a large collection."

"One of those assault rifles?"

"Probably, sir."

"How many bullets does one of those things hold?"

"It varies. The AK47 has at least a thirty round magazine, but you can fit it with larger magazines. Roughly the same deal with the M4."

"Does that mean if he came after me other people standing close to me would be in danger?"

Alexandra hesitated a moment before saying, "No, I don't think so. First, he's known to be a good shot and, second, he has a wife and kid, so he's not going to want to stick around and shoot things up. He'll probably plant himself some distance away, take his one or two shots, then beat it the hell out of there."

"I see," replied Baxter. "Well, thank you for coming in and remember: this was a secret meeting. You're not to tell anyone, even your superiors about it. Understand?"

"Yes, Mister President."

She left the Oval Office more confused than ever.

After Alexandra Lake left the Oval Office, Matt asked, "What was that all about?"

"You'll know soon enough," Baxter replied. "Let's get going to Andrews." He left Matt standing, momentarily stunned, as he went through the door and out onto the west colonnade.

Matt hurried after Baxter and soon they were climbing into in the back of the limousine where Jim Stockton was already seated.

Baxter usually like to chat with the agents who occupied the front seat, but this time he hit the switch to close the sound proof window between them and the front seat.

An uneasy feeling came over Matt.

At that moment, Jim Stockton would have given anything to be somewhere other than in the president's limousine waiting to do the president's bidding. The last few weeks had been the most painful time in his medical career, surpassing even the grim frustration of being an emergency physician in New York in the hours after the 9/11 attacks and having mostly nothing to do. Nothing. Too few survivors.

Just as there was nothing he could do about Baxter's diagnosis. It had all been there in the pathology slides and confirmed by two specialists who, of course, had no idea whose slides they were viewing. The slides and the test results had been so shocking that Stockton had insisted on repeating the tests, but the results came out the same. He had gone to great lengths to preserve the president's privacy and he prided himself in having succeeded.

He chuckled to himself at his deliberately unimaginative choice of a pseudonym—John Smith. If you want to hide something, put it in plain view. But he took no pleasure in the cold, hard, irrefutable science of the slides and the test results. And he was heartbroken.

Back in the White House medical office, after reviewing the results, he had pulled his wallet out of his hip pocket. Studying the photograph of his wife and two children, he found it hard to imagine the depths of the president's pain, his only reference being how he imagined he, himself, would feel if Olivia died or if one of the kids died. But then he would have to add on top of that the diagnosis he'd been compelled to give President Baxter and what it meant. Never had talking to a patient been so gut-wrenching. He had to be careful to hide his distress from the other physicians and from the nurses in the medical office.

Now, in the limousine, he was about to include Matt Cannon in on the secret only he and the president shared and he would rather have been almost any other place.

They were scarcely off the White House grounds when Baxter said, "Jim has something to tell you, Matt." He gave a nod to Stockton.

Stockton hesitated a moment, glanced at the president, then turned to Matt. "I'm sorry to inform you that we've diagnosed the president with leukemia—specifically acute myeloid leukemia," he said.

Matt looked from Stockton to Baxter, then back to Stockton again. "How serious?"

"In the president's case, I'm afraid it's incurable and untreatable."

"God!" Matt whispered. He turned his gaze on the president who wore a passive expression.

"Tell him the rest, Jim," said Baxter.

Stockton took a deep breath and said, "I'm afraid the president has no more than six to nine months."

"Jesus!" muttered Matt, "Jesus Christ! Are you sure?"

Stockton nodded sadly. "Medicine's not a precise science. I ..." He paused, then said, "Oh, hell. I'm as certain as can be, damn it! I ran the tests three times, hoping there was some mistake." Stockton's eyes turned moist.

Matt stared at him for a long moment then turned to Baxter. "Angus ... Mister President ... I don't know what to say."

"What's there to say? It was a shock at first; I refused to believe it for a long time, but I'm resigned to it now," said Baxter. "At least, for the most part. I have to admit, however, there are times when I feel like destroying something—not a good state-of-mind for a somebody who has an army, navy and air force, not to mention those nuclear codes Commander Headley is carrying in the car behind us." He gave a bitter laugh. "We've had a number of setbacks since I took office. We've always dealt with them head on."

"Yes, but this?"

"True, this trumps all the others by a country mile. But we'll deal with it like any other crisis."

Matt was silent for a moment, looking for words. Finally, he asked, "How long have you known?"

"About two weeks."

"Who else knows?"

"Just the three of us," said Baxter. "You, me, and Jim. And that's the way it's going to stay."

"The vice president?"

"Of course Katherine will have to be informed eventually, but only when it's absolutely necessary."

Matt turned to Stockton. "But you said you did the tests three times. What about pathologists, lab technicians, other doctors?"

"All tests were done under a false name and through an intermediary. The president and I agreed to that after his bout with pneumonia two years ago raised such a fuss in the press. Also, who can forget the media circus when the First Lady's medical records got out."

Matt looked at Baxter. "Maxwell? Kyla?"

"My family knows nothing and I intend to keep it that way."

"You said you need to tell the vice president eventually. What about others in the administration?"

"No. Beyond Katherine, absolutely nobody must know of this. Not the Cabinet, not the Chief of Staff, not a soul in the administration."

"But surely you can trust the Cabinet? Delores Northcote?"

"I trust you. Beyond that, I just don't know."

Confused, Matt studied the president's face. Never before had he heard such evidence of paranoia. His own chief of staff? "When do you plan to tell Katherine?"

"Only when we have no choice. We have to protect ourselves from leaks. If Haskins and his cronies sensed a transition coming, who knows what they'd do? It would leave Katherine weak, vulnerable. Not to mention the destabilizing effect it would have on foreign relations."

"So why tell me?"

"Matt, we've known each other most of our lives and, as I've said, I trust you completely. Your grandfather fought with my father at Omaha Beach. I thought you should know." He didn't add what Matt already knew—that Lt. Colonel Baxter had been in the act of saving Sergeant Cannon's life when he was killed, part of the action that had won him the Congressional Medal of Honor. "And there are certain things you can help me with," Baxter added. He turned to Stockton. "Jim, thanks for accommodating my strange request to meet in the limo, but I could think of no other place private enough."

Stockton furrowed his brow. He could think of a dozen places where the three of them could have had this conversation without any of it getting out. But who was he to question Baxter? "You're welcome, Mister President. Please call me if there's any change in your condition—any at all."

"I will, Jim. Now I'm afraid you're going to have to wait with the Secret Service folks while Matt and I shoot a round of golf."

Chapter 8—The Courses at Andrews AFB

When the motorcade turned onto West Perimeter Road and pulled into the clubhouse parking lot of The Courses at Andrews, Matt saw that agents of the Counter Assault Team, all dressed in black and heavily armed, were already at their posts. He knew he would see more of them all along the golf course.

Of the three courses—South, West, East—the Secret Service asked Baxter and Matt to play the South course because it was furthest from the Route 5 freeway and thus easier to protect. They had already stationed Counter Assault Team agents all along the perimeter and consequently felt comfortable honoring Baxter's request to give him and Matt at least a hundred yard buffer zone.

The first hole, about four hundred yards, was a slight dogleg left and both Baxter and Matt placed their drives on the left edge of the fairway almost two hundred yards, or so, out.

As Matt drove the golf cart down the fairway, he said, "I'm still reeling from what Jim said back there in the limo. I don't know what to say."

"Do you remember when I was pitching for the Sox, that one year I was in the show?"

"I've heard all your baseball stories many times over, Angus," Matt said with a frown. He knew about Baxter's quick rise through the minor leagues after high school, his one year in the major leagues, and the career-ending injury that freed him to go to college and begin a new career. "Do you really want to talk about that now?"

"Top of the ninth and we're leading by one run in a game we had to win to stay in the pennant race. Bases loaded, no outs."

"Tough situation," said Matt. He couldn't fathom where Baxter was going with this and the last thing he wanted now was another repeat of Baxter's baseball story.

"Roger Maris is up. The end of his career, but still dangerous. He works me to three and two. The catcher calls for a changeup. What I end up throwing is a changeup that does nothing, just hangs fat and pretty over the plate, a meatball. Well, Maris is so hungry for it, he over-swings, hits a soft liner to third and the third baseman snags it, tags third, catching the runner off base, fires to second and we get that runner, too, because he had a huge lead. Triple play. Game over. Everyone thought I was brilliant but it was about the worst pitch I'd ever thrown—the biggest, fattest, juiciest meatball ever."

"So you've said before." Matt stopped the cart alongside Baxter's ball.

Baxter climbed out of the cart and stood over his ball, gazing at the green. "What do you think?" he asked. "Fairway wood from here or an iron?"

"Wood," replied Matt, knowing that Baxter was unusually adept with his 3-wood. He watched as Baxter addressed the ball, took a few warm-up swings, then hit the ball with a satisfying thwack. The ball landed on the front edge of the green exactly equidistant between the traps that bordered the green on each side. "Great shot!" said Matt.

Baxter climbed back into the cart and Matt drove toward his ball which was twenty yards further up the fairway. "So what's the point of the Maris story?" he asked Baxter.

"Let's finish this hole, then I'll tell you."

Matt hit an equally good second shot and both were soon on the green with opportunities for a par 4. However, neither one putted well and Baxter ended up with a bogey while Matt double bogeyed.

As they drove from the tee after their drives on the long, par 5 second hole, Matt again asked, "So what about the Maris story?"

"Eyuh, well as I said, I sure as hell didn't mean to serve up a meatball to Maris, I can tell you that." Baxter paused, looked across to Matt, grinned, and said, "But I do intend to serve a real fat one up to Haskins' friend, and see if he swings at it."

"I guess I don't understand."

"I'll get to my plan in a minute," said Baxter. "First, I want to do some scenario thinking with you. Stop the cart."

Matt stopped the cart. He looked back to see the president's protection detail standing on the tee they'd just left. With them was Jim Stockton and Commander Headley. He turned to look at Baxter who was staring into the distance. He waited a moment, then said, "Angus?"

Baxter turned. "Sorry, just distracted for a moment." He paused, then said, "So tell me, what happens six or nine months from now when this damned leukemia thing gets me?"

"God, Angus, I don't even want to think about it."

"What happens, damn it?"

Matt was startled by Baxter's sudden, uncharacteristic anger. "What do you mean, what happens?"

"How will the nation respond?"

"Well, I expect there'd be an outpouring of grief. Shit, Angus, this is too much to take in."

"Stay with me, Matt. How about Haskins and his crowd? How will they respond?"

Matt gave a bitter laugh. "At first, they'll put on a show of deep, heartfelt sympathy. They'll try to look noble by suspending opposition during difficult times for the nation. They'll back off for a while so as not to look too eager to take advantage of . . . of a national tragedy." Matt's eyes became moist. "Damn it, Angus!"

Baxter put a hand on Matt's shoulder and gave him a nod. After a momentary pause, he asked. "And that'll last for how long—Haskins backing off and all?"

"A few months."

"Then?"

"Then he'll be all over the vice president . . . the new president . . . with fangs bared. It'll be worse than the last campaign."

"Which I won over him by one percentage point," said Baxter. "One percentage point! We can assume he's running next time around. What chance does Katherine, as good as she is, have against him?"

Matt made a plosive sound with his lips. "It's hard to say. Given history, none, zilch, nada. As good as she is."

"Because we're still a nation that has problems with women leaders, especially African-American women leaders. Oh, Haskins wouldn't come out and run against her gender or race explicitly, but it would be there in insinuations, off-handed remarks, all the things his people are good at. And right wing talk radio and cable TV would be all over it with their high-pitched coded messages, but their meaning would be abundantly clear. Katherine would get much of the woman vote of course. The key would be Haskins' core constituents. If they came out in droves to prevent a woman from becoming president, then I'm afraid some states we won last time—North Carolina, Florida, maybe even Indiana—would swing the other way."

Matt nodded. "He'd win. It's as simple as that."

"And everything we've worked for goes down the drain. And that's just the domestic side of things. With his xenophobic thinking I can't even imagine what would happen to foreign affairs."

"Damn!"

"Right. All of that happens when I die from this goddamned leukemia."

"But what the hell can we do about it?" asked Matt.

"I can die from something else."

"Come again?" Matt tilted his head, stared at Baxter with an incredulous expression.

Baxter gave a slight nod toward the Secret Service agents. "Let's drive up to our balls before they think something's wrong and come to rescue us.

Matt drove up to the balls which were close to each other. They each took their second shots and both found the trees—Baxter to the left and Matt to the right of a small gap almost two hundred yards short of the green.

They drove first for Matt's ball which they quickly found. But as Matt pulled an iron from his bag and prepared to take a layup shot because he had no clear line to the fairway before the green, Baxter put a hand on his shoulder. "Hold off a minute. Pretend we're still looking for the ball."

Matt looked back up the fairway and saw Jim Stockton, Commander Headley and the agents standing around their idle golf carts well more than a hundred yards away. He turned to Baxter and shook his head. "You can die from something else? What does that mean?"

"Let me paint you another scenario," said Baxter. "Let's say, for the sake of argument, that I was assassinated and Haskins' friend, Zacher, was indirectly implicated."

"You're hallucinating."

"Bear with me. Just say it happens. Theoretically, of course."

"You can't be serious. He's not that stupid."

"No, but is there any doubt in your mind he'd love to see it happen?"

"Haskins?"

"No, of course not. We have our political differences, but in the end he's a decent man. I mean Zacher."

"Zacher? No, no doubt whatsoever."

"In fact, there's no way we can prove it, but I know you share my strong suspicion that Zacher was involved indirectly in that last attempt, right?"

"I'd give anything if we could take down that lowlife. But he's not stupid enough to be directly involved. He'd just give money to militia groups, water the garden, and hope that something comes up."

Baxter nodded. "That's his method."

"But he's not your main enemy. Haskins is."

"Right, Haskins. Most Americans think of him as a ruthless man who would stop at nothing for the presidency."

"You painted him with that brush beautifully during the campaign."

Baxter smiled. "Rule number one: always define the other man before he defines himself. And the voters bought it."

"Because there's an element of truth to it. Just look at the attacks he ran against the First Lady's education plan."

"Actually, Matt, to be fair, they weren't bad at all. They focused on policy, not personality. I appreciated Haskins for that."

Matt shrugged. "But you were implying he has a perception problem ...."

"Right. We know Haskins wouldn't get himself involved in an assassination plot, but it would be credible to a large segment of the population because they know he has a connection with Zacher."

"Damn it all, Angus, where's this getting us? Why are you bringing me through all this so soon after dropping a fucking bomb on me?"

"I'll get to that. First, let me ask you again, for the sake of argument of course, what would happen if I were assassinated and the American people even suspected Zacher might be involved?"

"He'd be destroyed."

"Exactly. And?"

"Serious questions would be raised about Haskins."

The president smiled, nodded.

Matt shook his head. "I still don't see where you're going with this."

"If Zacher's not stupid enough to directly arrange an assassination, let's arrange it for him. Let's serve him up a meatball. Triple play. Game over."

Matt stared at him, but said nothing.

"That's the way I thought you'd respond," Baxter said with a chuckle. "That's why we're meeting out here. I'm saying, let's make it happen for him."

"Angus," said Matt, with a nervous laugh. "you can't be serious."

"Matt, I'm dead serious."

Matt stared at his friend for a long time, a look of incredulity on his face. He shook his head emphatically. "No," he said raising his arms as though in surrender. "This is too much. I can't believe you're serious. I know you're not serious."

"Don't make gestures like that," Baxter said, looking back up the fairway. "I'm serious."

"You're playing games with me."

"Matt, I'm dying of cancer. I have only a few months to live," said Baxter. "Do you think for one moment I'd joke around about something like this at this time? … With my best friend?"

"No, of course not. It's just—"

"—I know. It took me two long weeks to get used to the idea once it first came to me. Believe me, I've thought about this from every conceivable angle, every angle imaginable."

Matt stared at Baxter for a few moments then said, "Okay. Let's say I buy what you're saying. "Have you considered what would happen to the country? It would be plunged into crisis."

"What crisis? That's journalists' hyperbole. We've survived assassinations, assassination attempts, resignations, impeachments. All that happened was the country went on in an orderly way."

"But still—"

"—Matt, I will die in office. If you want to call that a crisis, go ahead. But, however I die, the country will survive … grow stronger, even. And Katherine will take over in a so-called crisis and the country will settle down and her standing with the public will be raised immeasurably."

"But Angus, this is too much to take in. I—"

"—Listen, I'm going to die. Get that through your beautiful, sweet head, my dear friend, my dearest of friends. I'm going to die! I know there's supposed to be this denial-anger-grief-acceptance progression, something like that, but I'm asking you to short-circuit it."

"That's asking a lot."

"I know, but I need you to accept the situation real fast. I'm going to die. The only thing is, unlike most people, I have a chance to choose the method. If there's any advantage to being told you have a terminal illness, that's got to be it. Now I could choose to die of the leukemia, and suffer through the end stages, and everything we dreamed of goes up in smoke. I don't think Katherine would survive a strong challenge from Haskins. On the other hand, if I die by an assassination in which Haskins' friend is implicated, the country rallies around Katherine. Our legacy survives. It's as simple as that."

"Simple? Fucking simple? Shit!"

Baxter put a hand on Matt's shoulder and motioned for him to lower his voice. They fell silent. Matt walked out from the trees and onto the fairway, then back again. Finally, he said, "Everything you say makes some kind of weird sense. But all the same—"

"—All the same, it just seems crazy?"

"Exactly. And even if I said 'sounds great, let's do it', how the hell would we actually do it?"

"Well, it's about time you asked. I've been thinking a lot about that, too."

"I was afraid you were going to say that."

"Let's keep moving and finish this hole so we don't overly worry our keepers. That will also give you a chance to digest what I've said so far."

They each finished the par 5 hole with double bogey sevens. As they came to the short par 3 third, Baxter remained silent and Matt decided not to press him. He hoped Baxter would realize how insane his idea was and would drop it, leaving them free to play out the rest of the round as if it were a normal golf outing.

Matt sliced his 7-iron and the ball landed in the water short of the green. His second tee shot bent left of the fairway. Baxter lofted a sweet 6-iron onto the apron of the green, then said nothing further about his idea as they finished the hole and played through the fourth in silence. Baxter remained silent until they had driven up to their balls that, after their second shots, sat squarely in the middle of a fat part of the fifth fairway where it made a severe dogleg left. Finally, as they sat in the cart, he said, "Well?"

"Well, what?" asked Matt.

"Have you figured out how to shoot down my idea? You've had almost a half-hour to think it through."

"And I have been thinking about it," Matt replied. "What I don't get is how you make it happen."

"Well, as I said, I've given that a lot of thought. Of course we know about Karl Zacher's connections to militia groups."

"It's a real problem for Haskins."

"That's the point. Now Zacher may not be stupid enough to go for the meatball, but these militia guys are Olympic champions of stupidity. And probably every last one of them would love to see me dead because of our involvement with the United Nations and my position on the second amendment."

"Okay, I'll grant you that. They'd love you to disappear. But so what?"

"We arrange for one of these guys to accept a contract on me and we rig it so he gets paid by Zacher and it's traceable. Bank transfer authorization, something like that."

"A sting?"

Baxter nodded. "A sting. We get rid of Zacher who, we have reason to believe, was involved in the last assassination attempt and, given Haskins' association with Zacher, doubts about him will be sky high. He'll be forced to do something dramatic to quell those doubts. He can always say he knew nothing about it, which would be true, but I guarantee that well more than fifty percent of the voters wouldn't believe him. So what would you do if you were Haskins?"

Matt thought a moment. "I'd condemn the assassination, I'd make a loud call for unity behind the new president, I'd wait a few weeks before continuing the campaign, then I'd go real light on attacks on Katherine knowing that, under the circumstances, they would likely backfire."

"You've got it. In other words, he's de-fanged."

Matt shook his head incredulously. "I hate to say it, but it makes some kind of sick, fucking sense. But the assassin would have to believe he's being hired by Zacher without Zacher knowing anything about it. How the hell do you pull that off?" He paused, shook his head, and said, "Jesus Christ! I can't believe I'm actually talking about this like it's some kind of real plan."

"But you are."

"Okay, okay. So how do you pull it off? Theoretically, I mean, of course."

"*I* can't."

Matt gazed at Baxter with an incredulous expression. "Oh no! No, no, no, NO!"

"Keep your voice down," Baxter said. "It has to be you, Matt."

"Do you realize what you're asking?" Matt asked with a forced whisper. "You're asking me to arrange to have my best friend killed." He gazed at Baxter, anger sharpening his features. His eyes welled.

Baxter's eyes also became moist. "I'm asking you to help your friend die the way he wants to. A split second of pain rather than months of pain. A death that leaves a legacy rather than one that destroys a legacy."

"God, Angus ...."

"I know. It's almost unbearable to contemplate. What's more, it's illegal... assisted suicide ... inciting a presidential assassination. If it were discovered, it would mean big trouble for you. And, of course, I wouldn't be around to shoulder the blame."

Again, they fell silent. The implications of what Baxter had said hit Matt like a punch to the solar plexus. At first, he was consumed by the horror of the proposition, but now the danger of it fell full force on him.

Baxter said, "I know I shouldn't ask you to do this, but I can see no other way. There's not one single other person in this world I could trust to be silent, not one. Maybe I'm blinded by my concern for my legacy; maybe I have an overblown sense of how important my programs are for the country and how dangerous Haskins' ideas are. Presidents have been known to be blinded by the office. If you think I'm wearing blinders, Matt, help me see the truth."

Matt remained silent.

Baxter said, "Matt, for once in my life I'm confused. It's all just too much. Tell me how this idea is off the tracks. I want to know, damn it!"

"I—" Matt started to say, but he stopped, merely shaking his head.

"It's plaguing me," Baxter said, his voice quavering.

Matt merely shook his head as if trying to dispel a nightmare.

Baxter gazed at him for a moment, then said, "Listen, Matt, I'm asking you as a friend, not as Special Counsel to the President or whatever title it was we gave you. This is in no way an order. I wouldn't do that."

"I appreciate that. Truly, I do."

"And I'll understand if you refuse. Hell, I don't know what I'd do if the situation were reversed."

"Angus … I simply can't do it."

Baxter stared at him for a long moment, then said, "Take your shot."

They finished the hole, teed off on the sixth, and were standing in the fairway over their balls when Baxter said, "Matt, strip away the presidency, assume for a moment I'm just an ordinary man who's dying of a painful disease—just your best friend, a retired man who's your golfing buddy. And assume I said, 'I want to choose my own way of going. I don't want to linger … be a burden. And I don't want to suffer. I *don't* want to suffer!' And assume I asked you to help me die. Would you do it as a friend?"

"If that's what you wanted … I guess I'd—"

"—Let's say I was on life support and you visited me at the hospital and I asked you to pull the plug. Would you?"

"Again, if that's what you wanted …."

"Or I asked you to persuade a doctor to help me die."

Matt remained silent.

"Or I just said, 'Please close the garage door for me. I'll start up the fucking car myself.' "

Again, Matt said nothing.

"How many ordinary people in my position just take a gun and … one split second? How many? I'll tell you—lots. If I asked, would you get me a gun?"

"Angus, stop grilling me; I need time to think about all this!" cried Matt. He looked at his watch and laughed sardonically. "A few hours ago, I was looking forward to talking with you about your new education bill strategy. Now …." He shook his head, the incredulous look still on his face.

"I know just what you mean. When Jim gave me the diagnosis, I had a profound sense of how one minute, one measly second, can completely turn a life upside down. You're pitching a no-hitter in the ninth in a scoreless game and one bad pitch, one meatball, one split-second swing of the bat ... homerun, and it's all over."

Matt nodded and looked away.

"After we finish this round, take the day off," Baxter said. "You need time to get over the shock. Otherwise the people in your office will know something bad is going down. I don't want you to be answering questions."

"Is that the reason for the limousine and for the round of golf? You were worried about my reaction and what others might think?"

Baxter gave a sardonic smile. "You should see your face right now. If we were at the White House or Camp David or anywhere else, people would certainly know something important was going on and they'd be pissed at me for leaving them out of the loop."

"I need time to think about this," Matt replied with a nod. "Alone."

"Yes, and 'alone' is the operative word. This is something you have to decide on your own. On this one, you get no advice. Not even from Marcie. I'm sorry to put you in that situation, but there it is."

"I understand."

Shielded by the cart from the eyes of the Secret Service agents, Baxter offered an embrace. They hugged. Matt gave a bitter laugh. "The only time we ever hugged like that was at my father's funeral."

"Yes. It's something we men seem unable to do except when death is staring us in the face." Baxter paused. He stared into the distance thinking of his father's Medal of Honor.

"And Alexandra Lake? What was that all about?"

"I wanted you to hear what she had to say. If you decide to go ahead with this, you have your candidate."

"First you give me the motive, then you give me the means."

"If you decide to go ahead."

"*If* I decide to go ahead, Angus—*If.*"

"I'll be waiting for your decision."

By the time they finished the eighteenth hole, Matt had to give Baxter credit for anticipating his reaction and making sure he was in a setting where he had time to regain his composure. Any remaining strain on his face could be explained by the fact that he had shot one of the worst rounds of his life.

When Matt arrived back at his Georgetown house, he parked the car and, rather than go inside, he decided to take a walk.

The trees along Wisconsin Avenue were in full leaf and birds flitted among the branches. As he walked, he was passed by several joggers who were chatting good-naturedly about something. At one corner, an old couple sitting on a bench laughed with delight as they threw bread crumbs to a flock of pigeons. It struck Matt as a great irony that all around him were signs of life even as he was faced with the imminent death of his best friend. And his president.

He wondered how Baxter felt, how it must be to know the approximate date you are going to die. At least with a terminal illness, there's always the hope of one more day, and maybe another day after that, but if he went through with the president's mind-boggling plan, they would be forced to wake up each day on which a public event was scheduled figuring it could be the last day of the president's life. He wondered how either of them would bear that kind of pressure, that kind of certainty tinged with uncertainty. The idea was almost too much to comprehend.

He remembered a case he had tried years before when he defended two police officers who had shot and killed a man. A terrified woman had called the police on her cell phone because her estranged husband, against whom she had taken out a restraining order, was carrying a rifle and prowling the mall parking lot where she'd left her car. At the same time, they received several more calls from shoppers and mall security. When the police arrived, they found the man standing beside a car, rifle pointed at the ground. He made no effort to escape. Instead, he stared at them with a haunted look in his eyes. As they approached, he raised the rifle slowly, pointing it at them. They shot him in self defense. He'd had every opportunity to fire his rifle, but he didn't.

In researching his defense of the police officers, Matt found that such events as victim-precipitated suicide, otherwise known as suicide-by-cop, were not nearly as unusual as he might have thought.

One study, by the University of Southern California, of fatal shootings by police officers of the Los Angeles County Sheriff's Department, showed that in an eleven-year period as many as ten percent of police shootings were precipitated by a suicidal person, roughly fifty in five hundred. It was a well-known phenomenon in police circles.

What was President Baxter's plan if not simply suicide-by-cop on a much grander scale—and with motives that, on the surface at least, seemed entirely logical? And then there was the leukemia. As the president had said, assisted suicide among terminally ill patients—ones facing a painful end—was also not at all uncommon. By the time he arrived home, Matt had partially convinced himself that the president's plan made some sense.

He was surprised to find Marcie home. The door was unlocked and when he entered he saw her in the kitchen reading the newspaper over a sandwich. "How was the golf?" she asked.

"Okay. What are you doing home?"

"Forgot some papers. Decided to have lunch at home. What about you? Are you going in late?"

"I'm taking the day off."

Marcie put the newspaper down. Creases appeared on her forehead. "What's wrong, Matt? You look like your best friend just died."

He gave a sardonic laugh, but said nothing.

Marcie rose from the table, went to him, felt his forehead. "Are you feeling ill?"

"No, I'm fine. I just have a problem to figure out."

"What is it?"

"I'm afraid I can't tell you. The president asked me to keep it to myself."

"So there really is some sort of crisis?"

"Of sorts, yes."

"So if that's the case, shouldn't you be with him at the White House? I'm afraid I don't understand."

He shook his head. "It's not that kind of crisis. It's something I have to work out for myself."

"Did you and the president have some sort of disagreement?"

"No, nothing like that." He gazed at her for a long moment. "All I can say is he's asked me to do something that I find extremely difficult and he's given me the option of refusing him. In other words, it's entirely up to me."

"Is that why you're home?"

"Uhm hmm. We both thought I should take the day off to think about it."

Marcie placed her arms around him. "Why do I get the feeling it's one of those political games you hate so much? It sounds painful. I wish I could help."

Matt held her close then leaned back to look into her eyes. "Can I ask you a few questions?"

"Of course."

"These are only hypothetical, okay?"

She tilted her head, narrowed her eyes at him. "Hypothetical? Already I'm getting an uncomfortable feeling."

"Hypothetical, okay?"

She nodded.

Matt asked, "Given your position at the bank, I figured you're the right person to ask. Is it possible to transfer funds from someone's account to another account without that person's knowledge?"

"Sure, piece of cake," Marcie replied with a frown. "But you do know it would be illegal as hell?"

"Of course, but could it be done?"

"Well, eventually the person would find out if he or she reviews the monthly statement. If it were a large amount, I don't see how anyone could miss it. Then, at that point, the person who did the transfer would be in deep trouble."

"That could be traced?"

"In most cases. It's done through the computer and each terminal is identified with a particular clerk."

"But computers can be hacked."

"It's done all the time. And at that point, it would be far more difficult to trace." She put her hands on his cheeks, gazed into his eyes. "This is all hypothetical, isn't it? You're not contemplating something like this are you? Surely, this isn't what the president asked you to do?"

"No, no, it's all hypothetical …."

"Why am I getting the uneasy feeling that the words 'for now' were left unspoken just then?"

"I'm sorry, Marcie. I just can't say any more at the moment."

"At the moment …." She echoed with a frown.

"Maybe when you get back from work, I'll have sorted this thing out and we can talk some more."

She nodded. "Okay. But I hate to see you so obviously suffering like this. I hope I can be of more help later on. What do you say tonight we call out for pizza and get a bottle of wine and just talk?"

"Sounds good."

"Why don't you go for a nice long run along the canal? You always say you think better when you're running."

In fact, Matt had been thinking the same thing. While he had been walking back to Georgetown, he thought that a good ten- or fifteen-mile run would be needed to even begin to think this proposition through. He hoped the extra blood flowing through his brain, awash with endorphins, would flush out an answer because he sure as hell didn't have one at the moment.

Chapter 9—Matt Cannon's Dilemma

Presenting his best friend with such an agonizing choice left Angus Baxter with a profound sense of guilt. Several times, he thought of calling Matt Cannon at home and telling him to forget the whole thing. But after forty years of political life, his mind had locked into a logical way of thinking and he couldn't escape the cold logic of his plan. Once he had accepted the judgment of his disease, every political instinct in him had said to make the best of it, to protect his programs, to ensure his legacy. *"If life gives you lemons ...."*

As a public person, he could see no other way of consolidating his place in history than by going through with his plan, bizarre as it was. And there was something else that moved him as a private person: he didn't want to spend the last months of his life in pain, wasting away, and becoming a burden on everybody. It would put himself, his family, his administration, and the country through a long period of uncertainty during the death vigil. Little would get done because nobody in Washington would be sure who was in charge at the White House. Better to have it done quickly and relatively painlessly. A single instant of pain.

Of course, he could simply resign, but that wouldn't produce the same kind of immunization for the vice president; she would still be left vulnerable. Plus, that wouldn't solve the problem of a lingering death. He recalled how, twenty years before, a friend, dying of pancreatic cancer, had one day simply closed the garage door, started his car, and died peacefully and with dignity. He'd always admired that simple act of courage and always thought he would make the same choice given similar circumstances.

He was reminded of the Terri Schiavo case and how dignity was sacrificed to the baser instincts of politicians and the media. Now, he'd been presented with a strange variation of the situation. But as President of the United States, certain options, such as carbon monoxide, were not open to him. What might be dignified and right for a private person didn't work for a public person on whom the entire world would make a judgment. Suicide in his case would be seen as cowardice, a way out, rather than courage. As a public person, his legacy was at stake and that meant more than just how history would view him; it meant the very survival of the programs and policies he had worked his entire adult life to put in place. It would mean betraying the progress that he and Grace had made.

Yet, as a public person, he had an option far better than carbon monoxide, one that, crazy as the idea might be, had the same result while also helping to preserve all he'd achieved.

In fact, it would be a form of immortality because his work would go on after him. And what was he sacrificing for it? A few weeks or months of life that would probably be filled with pain and suffering—not only for him, but for the people he loved most. As he saw it, it was a far more sensible exchange than that made by suicide bombers, or by zealous assassins with fantasies of virgins in heaven, who otherwise might have lifetimes ahead of them.

But there was something else that differentiated this thing he was contemplating from an act of suicide by an ordinary person—others were involved. In that way, he was like a suicide bomber. In destroying himself, he would also most likely destroy the assassin. (It didn't help when he'd learned that Scroggs had a wife and a daughter.) Certainly, he would destroy Zacher—that was the whole point—and, probably, Haskins as well.

Of course it occurred to him that if there was any morality at all attached to such an act, it was only the morality of the greatest possible good, only the morality that the ends justify the means. It was his only measuring stick. Religion—real religion, not the appearance of it for political purposes— had long ceased to be relevant to him.

And as to social prohibitions against what he was contemplating? Well, they worked only when there was a penalty to pay. But here, there was no penalty. There would be no public shame, no approbation, because that would all fall on Zacher and the others. There was no possibility of being punished for a crime because the leukemia diagnosis had removed the opportunity for imprisonment. He simply wouldn't be around to suffer the consequences of his actions.

So if there were no religious constraints (because he didn't believe in an afterlife or hell), no social constraints (because shame and punishment were not possible if he were dead), and no instinct of self-preservation (because what was the point if he was going to die anyway?), then what was there that could stop him? The inescapable answer was: nothing. It was a frighteningly liberating thought. He wondered if others felt as free of constraint when they knew there was nothing—nothing at all—to lose.

Of course, in the last few weeks, facing death, he had reexamined the question of a god, but came to the conclusion there was none. In a strange way, it was meeting Grace that persuaded him against the idea of a god—the notion that there was intelligent design in the universe. Even as a young boy he had spent hours sitting on the rocks of Baxter Island contemplating the capriciousness of things—calculating the chances of separate events occurring at precisely the same time in the long stretch of eternity. Such as the time he saw a whale breach about a half mile off the coast. He wondered about the impulse that led the whale to rise from the depths exactly when he, himself, followed a vague urge to wander down to the shore and sit on a rock looking out to sea.

Projecting back a hundred, a thousand years, long before either he or the whale existed except for potentialities in their respective gene pools, he guessed the chances of all their ancestors being born and surviving and eventually producing them—coupled with the chances of they themselves—he and the whale—coming together after years of random wanderings; he calculated these chances at being something like one in a number approaching infinity.

He played mental games like that all the time. Then, when he met Grace, he marveled at how, given an infinity of possibilities, their beings could have emerged from eons of mingling and conceptions and ancestral wanderings to come together in the same time and in the same place just when they were each ready for a union. He concluded it was pure chance, albeit a happy one for which he was grateful. But one thing this awareness of the chaotic randomness in the world did was blunt the edge of any possible belief in a greater, intelligent being.

Given the infinite possibilities to explain everything that occurs in the universe, from the appearance of stars to human evolution, there was no reason to postulate the existence of a god. Evolution, random change and chance could explain everything.

Once he decided that logic was an invention of the human mind that evolved in order to impose order on such chaos, dispassionate, rational thinking became the touchstone of his life. It was with this logic that he postured at having a belief in god, because to do so would help him get elected. No overt atheist has the possibility of being elected president of the United States. At least, not yet.

That said, he was free to choose a religion based not on its affinity with his own beliefs, but based on the electoral map of the country. It was with such logic that he developed the policies and programs that would guide his administration. And it was with such logic that he was able to justify sending young men and women into military action. Of course, he felt the emotions of things—he did, after all, count himself as human. He felt deep sadness and a tinge of guilt when soldiers died carrying out his orders. And, certainly, he felt the terrible pain of Grace's death. But in the end, he distrusted emotion, believing that when it overrode clear, rational, human-invented thinking, events would start to spiral out of control.

So, no, he had nothing to lose. He would simply cease to exist and nothing would have happened except that one of those infinite threads of possibility would have ended. No surviving the leukemia. No rewards after life. No virgins in heaven. No walking on clouds.

The only rational thing left was to take the action that would assure the better part of his possible greatness in the only life he had. His assassination—an ugly word to which he was becoming accustomed—coupled with its potential to promote his plans and policies (especially peace in the Middle East and Grace's education bill) would persuade history of the greatness he always knew was in him. It would be a great act of selfless courage worthy of the son of a man who sacrificed his life on Omaha Beach to save others. And it would leave a better world for his grandchildren.

But what would Matt lose? Could he do that to his friend? In the end, he persuaded himself (because he wanted to?) that Matt wouldn't agree to do it unless he truly believed in the virtue of it. If Matt agreed to do it, it would be because he understood the cold logic of the greatest good … and because he understood it would cause Maxwell and Kyla and the grandchildren much less pain; they wouldn't have to witness his gradual, painful decline. After being forced to watch their mother and grandmother waste away over months, the last thing they needed was to go through the same thing all over again with him.

Baxter's wavering resolve once more hardened, he went up to the family quarters to have breakfast with his son and his daughter and their families, a breakfast that now was part of a countdown. How many more times would he be able to enjoy the company of his children and grandchildren? Seeing Martha, the breakfast cook, in the west sitting hall walking toward the kitchen he called out, "Good Morning, Martha."

"Oh, good morning Mister President," she replied. "Your favorite omelet today, tomatoes and mushrooms."

"Sounds wonderful. Are the others up?"

"They're already in the dining room, Mister President."

He entered the dining room. Cups of coffee and glasses of orange juice were already sitting on the table. His son Maxwell and his son-in-law Richard Tausen rose to shake hands while Kyla and his daughter-in-law, Sarah rushed forward to embrace him. "We're so glad you could make it, Dad," said Kyla. "When we learned you were in the Oval Office, we were afraid there was some kind of crisis."

"I wouldn't miss it for the world," Baxter replied. He went to each of his grandchildren in turn—Maxwell's two, Natalie and Jeremy, and Kyla's son, Peter. "Well now, Petey, are you going to have omelets with us or is it to be, ahh …." He looked to Kyla for help.

"Cocoa Puffs, Dad," said Kyla.

"Oh, right. Cocoa Puffs," he said, shaking his head in mock disgust.

From the kitchen, Martha called out, "Cocoa Puffs are not something a president's grandson should be eating."

"I keep telling you, Martha," said Baxter, "presidents and their families are normal people, too."

"Normal people don't live in the White House, Mister President. Normal people don't have cooks like me."

Her remark roused a flush of sadness in him, but he let it pass. He had an image of himself at the stove making pancakes, like numberless men on a Saturday morning, then taking his grandchildren to soccer practice. He tried to remember if he'd ever done that with Maxwell and Kyla.

How he hated the walls of the White House!

"I'm going to have an omelet like you, Papa," said Peter.

"Great. No Cocoa Puffs, then. Satisfied, Martha?"

"Yes sir, Mister President."

An overwhelming sadness swept over Baxter. He was struck by the realization that he would never see his grandchildren grow up. He struggled to shake off the thought. He smiled and said, "The topic for this morning's breakfast meeting is … vacation."

"For me?" called out Martha with a laugh.

"If we go on vacation, it'll amount to a vacation for you, Martha. With full pay."

"I do like your policies, Mister President."

"Are you planning a vacation, Dad?" asked Maxwell.

Baxter settled into his seat at the head of the table. "We get to spend so little time together as a family, I thought a vacation where we could be truly alone together would be wonderful."

"You mean without the Secret Service."

"Well, we can never escape them entirely. But I have an idea how to keep them pretty much at arm's length."

"What do you have in mind?"

"How would you all like a sailing vacation? We can get a big boat that will sleep all of us—maybe somewhere around Nantucket or Martha's Vineyard—and the Secret Service guys can stick themselves in some kind of powerboat. At least the water would be separating us."

"That sounds great."

"It's been years since I've sailed," said Baxter.

"It would be like Mom was still with us," said Kyla. "She used to love sailing so much."

Baxter felt his throat tighten. "That's one reason I thought of it."

Martha came in from the kitchen rolling a serving cart before her. She looked at the president, her brows knitted. It was a look of deep sympathy. "Not a day goes by when I don't pray for Mrs. Baxter," she said. "Such a fine lady." She distributed the plates of omelets around the table.

"Thank you, Martha," said Baxter. "We all pray for her."

"As it should be, Mister President."

Maxwell asked, "When do you want to do this sailing vacation?"

"How about in a few weeks?"

They looked around the table at each other. Maxwell said, "Wow, that's pretty short notice. Would, say, August, be better?"

Baxter shook his head. "The sooner the better. As the summer wears on, I've got some really important things coming up. A few heads-of-state, your mother's education bill that I've got to try to push through Congress again, that sort of thing."

"In that case," said Maxwell. "I'll make the time." He looked at Kyla and the others. "What do you say?"

"I'm game," she replied and was quickly followed by the others.

"Great," said Baxter. "I'll get some of my people on it right away. We'll find a nice boat—have a wonderful time together." He looked at his grandchildren. "We're going to make sailors out of each of you. Then you can be on the sailing team in college like I was." Except, he thought, I won't be around to see it.

Through the remainder of breakfast, Baxter focused his attention on his family. He observed details of gesture he'd never fully noticed before, habits of speech, ways of lifting food from the plates. He was trying to burn them into his mind. Of course, somewhere in the back of his mind he had been familiar with all these things, but for the first time he was making an effort to bring them to the forefront of awareness. He noticed how Kyla curved her wrist around the glass of orange juice; probably a habit from when Peter used to habitually knock glasses over. And he noticed how Peter's light hair matched the tones of his Danish father rather than the deeper brown of the Baxter hair; and how Natalie and Jeremy kept eyeing each other, to be sure the one didn't get more omelet than the other.

He saw how everybody in the generation after him seemed to defer to Maxwell. He was sure his son was a natural leader and he wondered if he might consider giving up his architecture practice to run for office some day. He would be proud to have his son follow in his footsteps, like the Adams or the Bushes. Perhaps he would have a long talk with Maxwell when they were on the sailboat. Not once during the entire breakfast did he divide his mind by thinking of the National Security meeting scheduled to start in an hour or the Cabinet meeting shortly after that. He gave no thought at all to his war with Senator Haskins. And, for once, the words of an unwritten speech were not swimming around in his head while he was talking with his family. In fact, the only words going through his head during the lulls in conversation were from one of his wife's poems: *Now the moonrise came lilting to the lead of sunset* ....

Before picking the sailing dates, he had consulted the almanac to ensure the moon would be full for some of their time on the boat. But toward the end of breakfast, one troubling thought intruded. It was about Matt and the dreadful position he had been forced to put his friend in. Again, he felt a pang of remorse.

Except for his long run along the C&O Canal, well past Fletcher's Boathouse and the Chain Bridge, Matt spent the rest of the day in his home without turning the TV on to check the news. For this one day, he would divorce himself from all current events; let the world and the White House go on without him. Instead, he spent the day staring at the walls and contemplating the mind-numbing proposition Baxter had put before him. And when things seemed too confusing to figure out, he resorted to an old trick—he sketched the problem out on paper, filling in boxes and triangles with the pros and cons of the problem, looking for a way out. But he found none.

As Baxter had said, the logic of the idea was irrefutable even if the sentiment was abhorrent. He remembered what Baxter had said about being blinded and he wondered if, after several years in the White House, his friend was no longer able to see things clearly.

It seemed to Matt the concerns of the presidency with its national and global issues—where events affected whole populations and geographies—were so far distant from ordinary life that those involved temporarily lose the ability to stay in touch with things whose natural dwelling place was the individual human soul.

That, it seemed to him, was the key to the situation.

He couldn't think of it solely in terms of the political impact; he had to consider what it meant to him and to Baxter. And, finally, he persuaded himself that, despite all the logic, it came down to the personal wishes of a friend. He shifted the problem, imagining Baxter was not the president but just a dear friend who was dying and lacked the resources to choose his own way out, to grace his death with the dignity of choice.

Under those circumstances, would he help his friend by obtaining the necessary pills? Would he even go so far as to help his friend take those pills? And the answer was a painful yes. To do anything else would be to disregard the wishes of a man who was perfectly capable of thinking this kind of thing through. In fact, it would be denying his friend the opportunity to exercise an extraordinary courage, the opportunity to do what, in his heart, he felt was right for himself, his family, and his country. If Baxter was blinded, it was by a sense of what he perceived his duty to be.

But what about the cost? What about the things it would do to others? He didn't spend too much time thinking about Scroggs or Senator Haskins. And as for Zacher, Matt thought about the last year with Marcie—his dry, ineffectual orgasms, their shattered dreams of parenthood—and his suspicion that Zacher was somehow connected. His hatred for the man, always smoldering, flared up every time he thought about the assassination attempt and he would have no regrets at having a hand in destroying the man.

But what about Baxter's children and grandchildren? What about the country?

What about himself?

There was the crux of the matter. He'd already decided Baxter was right about the positive things that would happen concerning the country. He even persuaded himself that it would be better, less painful, for Maxwell, Kyla, and the grandchildren. But what about himself? What would it do to him? He could think of nothing good coming of it, except, perhaps, the comforting knowledge that he was honoring the wishes of his friend. And when it was over, he would have to live with it. It would be difficult—it might even be impossible—but that's where his own courage came in.

Matt decided he had to do it.

Late that afternoon, the telephone rang. Seeing that the caller ID was the White House, Matt answered it right away. "Hello?"

"Matt? It's Jim Stockton."

"Oh … Hi, Jim."

"Matt I need to talk with you. Can we meet somewhere?"

"I assume it's about this morning's discussion?"

"Yes."

Matt paused. Did he really want to go through all that again now that his mind was made up? "Can you get to the Four Seasons in Georgetown?"

"Sure. Say half an hour?" Matt agreed to the time and hung up.

Alexandra Lake had been awed at being in the Oval Office in the presence of the president and Matt Cannon who everybody acknowledged was the president's closest friend. She recalled an article in Time Magazine that talked about the president's inner circle and Cannon, though not a formal part of the administration, was prominently featured.

But beyond awe, she was also befuddled, even a little suspicious. The president had called her in to fill a role that should have been filled by the Director of the Secret Service, the Homeland Defense Secretary, or the Attorney General—perhaps all three—plus his national security advisor and his chief of staff. Was he trying to keep them out of the loop? Why in God's name would he do that? It was his life that was being threatened, yet he chose to exclude the very people whose responsibility it was to protect him.

Also, he had seemed weirdly calm about the whole thing, as if he didn't regard Billy Scroggs as a serious threat, yet by his questions to her it was clear that he did take the thing seriously. He had been much more relaxed, even nonchalant, than certainly Matt Cannon who, despite trying to appear unfazed, looked as if he had just been told that World War III had started.

Then there was the president's odd question about the kind of weapon that Scroggs would use and his concern for the safety of the people around him. It was almost as if he was resigned to being killed as long as no one else was hurt.

She was worried. As she climbed into her car and prepared to head back to Maine, she decided she had better make damned sure she knew where Billy Scroggs was at all times and, if possible, what he was thinking. And there was only one way to do that: she had to complete her infiltration and wangle her way into his confidence.

When Matt arrived in the lobby of the Georgetown Four Seasons, Jim Stockton was already sitting on a cream-colored sofa. The wood-paneled lobby was bustling with businessmen and women, so Matt suggested they take a walk along the C&O Canal. They emerged behind the hotel and onto the old tow path bordering the canal. However, they were still not alone; there were too many joggers. It was only after the path turned from brick to crushed stone and dirt that there was enough gap between the joggers for them to talk in private.

"Matt," began Stockton, "My first responsibility, of course, is to the president. But I feel I also have a responsibility to Congress and the American public to ensure that the office of the presidency is occupied by a person who's up to the job."

"You're not telling me you're thinking of going public with this? Because if you are ...."

"No, no. I couldn't do that. There's the matter of physician-patient confidentiality. But I think the president should disclose his illness."

Matt waited for a group of joggers, two men and a woman, to pass before he asked, "When?"

"Immediately."

"Why?"

"Because he's already been dangerously distracted since the death of the First Lady. Hell, everybody sees it. In fact, I wonder if he isn't showing the symptoms of a profound depression. And now, with the leukemia, he's bound to be even further distracted. Matt, I'm really frightened. I don't know what he might do. I'm no psychiatrist and he won't see one, but Matt, he's a danger to the country!"

"Are you talking about the future or the present? Is it immediately impinging on his ability to carry out the duties of the presidency?" Matt asked formally, knowing what the answer would be.

"No, I don't think so. Not yet."

"So there's no problem yet?"

"Come on, Matt, you know damn well there's a problem. Things will only get worse. There will be a succession. Doesn't he owe it to the country to ensure that it's orderly?"

Orderly. How less orderly could it get if he and the president go through with their plan? "Jim, you've got to trust the president on this one. He's already involving the vice president more fully in affairs. In fact, he's about to tell her of the leukemia so she can prepare herself." Matt knew this not to be true, at least not yet. He sensed that it was the first of many deceptions, involving many people, he would have to commit before this was all over—a series of deceptions that ultimately could spin completely out of control.

"That's comforting to hear," said Stockton.

"And don't worry about your position," said Matt. "Nobody's going to blame you for respecting the president's wishes for privacy about his health."

"Oh, that's where you're wrong, Matt," laughed Stockton. "There are senators and representatives who will rake me over the coals on this. But it doesn't matter. My days in this job end with the president. The vice president will want to select her own personal physician and I'm certain that will be a woman." He paused, then asked, "Will you at least talk with him about disclosure, Matt?"

"I'll talk with him," said Matt. It was another lie. He paused, then asked, "Weren't there signs earlier? Did this thing just come up?"

"There were signs, but they were masking signs."

"What do you mean?"

"The early signs of this disease—fever, shortness of breath, easy bruising or bleeding, tiredness—can be signs of lots of things, and if one of those things is staring you in the face, the symptoms can suck you in, lead you to the diagnosis you expect. It's something we call 'confirmation bias.' Most doctors are guilty of it on occasion."

"Something was staring you in the face?"

"The symptoms I mentioned are also signs of excessive drinking. It took the pathology results to rule that out as the cause."

Matt stared at the man for a moment, nodded. "I see."

After he and Stockton parted, Matt returned home. Now that he had decided to go along with the president's plan, he turned his mind to figuring out the how of it. And here, the president had given him several obvious clues—a bank transfer from Karl Zacher to this Billy Scroggs that would act as the catalyst sending Scroggs into action. He knew the idea of a bank transfer had occurred to Baxter only because Marcie was the Vice President of Operations at a bank where Zacher had an account, something they knew from a year-old news story.

The president hadn't specifically asked Matt to involve Marcie. Indeed, he had cautioned Matt about telling anyone about their plans. However, his implication couldn't have been clearer: Matt could enlist Marcie's help without letting her in on the entire plan. The question now was: Did Matt dare ask Marcie for help? Of course, he knew that she hated people like Haskins and Zacher, but would she be willing to do something illegal to help bring them down? Everybody had a line between expediency and ethics, between realpolitik and honor, between which ends justified distasteful means and which didn't. Where did Marcie draw the line?

He would find out that night over pizza and wine. And, it occurred to him, he would learn something about their relationship and Marcie's sense of honor.

And his own sense of honor.

Chapter 10—The Truman Balcony; Mahler

Senator Haskins was worried. He knew what kind of man Karl Zacher could be and it disgusted him. However, the man, with his numerous networked contacts, both legitimate and shady, was useful to him. He was one of the few people that Facebook cut off at five thousand friends.

Haskins had never known anybody who could get things done so quickly and without fuss. Besides, the man was a big contributor and no politician can afford to ignore deep pockets. All the same, he wondered if he'd been unwise to let Zacher have such a free hand where President Baxter was concerned. With his violent past and his uncompromising hatred of Baxter, there was no telling what the man would do. And now, Haskins' doubts about Zacher had grown since the conversation with Ken Nesbitt at the French Embassy. What if Zacher had renewed his affiliation with this M-4 militia group? The last thing he needed was some idiot gunning after the president again.

If that happened, he might as well give up all ideas of becoming president because Baxter, if he survived, would receive another huge bump in the polls. And if the man didn't survive, Moore-Patterson, would become a much more formidable candidate because of the sympathy factor and because of incumbency—what he called "the Johnson effect."

It occurred to him that he was thinking only of his own political future. Julia would point out that the first concern should be the life of the president and the well-being of the country and she would be right as usual. He chastised himself and resolved that it was time to question Zacher and to rein him in if necessary. When the last of his staff left the office, he dialed Zacher's number. While waiting for the connection to go through, he watched an airplane descend over the Potomac, make a sharp turn as it passed the Pentagon, and disappear into Reagan International. After a few rings, Zacher answered. "Karl, it's Wayne."

"Good evening, Senator."

"Come on over for a few drinks. I have something I want to talk to you about."

"Tonight?"

"Yes, tonight. Is that a problem?"

"Ah, no …. I—"

"—Good. I'm in my office."

"I'll be right over."

If a pair of lovers had been strolling, arm-in-arm, near the Ellipse around midnight they might have heard the music of Mahler being pumped out from the White House at full volume. And if it were not night and they had binoculars, they might have seen, some distance away, President Baxter—wearing the camouflage Snuggie his grandchildren gave him as commander-in-chief—sitting alone on the Truman Balcony with his dog Beatrice curled in his lap, and the one lover might have said, "Poor man, he seems so lonely."

"In the blogosphere it's said he's losing it," the other lover might have replied. "That's all we need: a president gone over the edge!"

Certainly the heavily armed, black-dressed agents on the roof above him must have been assaulted by the music, but they gave no indication of discomfort, standing silently alert, dressed in black against the black sky to the north. Daily, they had the opportunity to witness the president's behavior.

But if they observed anything strange, they didn't discuss it except perhaps among themselves or with their spouses. Their job was to protect the person of the president, not to protect the presidency, or the country.

Below them, Baxter gazed to the south at the gibbous moon suspended over the Washington Monument. Shredded clouds drifted past the face of the moon, giving a special significance to the music coming from a pair of powerful Steinway Lyngdorf speakers he'd had installed in the Yellow Oval Room after Grace Baxter died. On this balmy night he left the door to the balcony open to better hear the music. It was Mahler's 2nd Symphony, the "Resurrection," Baxter's favorite. The fourth movement, "Urlicht" was being sung by Jesse Norman. And the words that passed through his awestruck brain were his own instant translation from the German:

> *"Mankind lies in greatest need!*
> *Mankind lies in greatest pain!*
> *Oh, how I would rather be in heaven."*

Uhrlicht. The primal light. The light of the beginning of time. The light before all existence. The primordial fireball from which all life emerged. The light of the moon through shredded clouds. And the shredded clouds formed phantasmal shapes of living things for which he had no name.

He took a long sip of the single malt scotch and placed the glass back on the table. His mind was flooded with shifting images: curling, crashing waves across a limitless ocean; numberless galaxies whirling in the furthest reaches of an unfathomable universe.

The symphony burst explosively into the monumental, half-hour long, 5th movement. Baxter sat transfixed, keeping time with his left foot, causing Beatrice to bounce in his lap, occasionally lifting the glass of scotch to his lips. Then the moment that always brought tears to his eyes: the hushed entrance of the huge chorus introduced mainly by the off-stage trumpets and on-stage woodwinds:

> *"You will rise again, yes, rise again after brief repose*
> *He who called you will grant you immortal life ..."*

In a soft voice, he sang with the chorus, even able to hit the B-flat below the bass clef, the lowest voiced note in the classical repertoire. As he sang, he regretted not continuing with the music lessons he's started as a youth all those many years ago. And now the music gave birth to images in his mind:

"The seed of your being was sown to bloom again ... "

He saw again, on Baxter Island, the crocuses resurrecting themselves from a thawed earth: white, purple, golden. A carpet of yellow daffodils. He remembered how, as a child, he would check every morning so he could be the first to announce their arrival. And he remembered watching bald eagles carrying branches to build nests; seeing ospreys diving for fish; listening to the complicated song of a robin.

"Nothing will be lost to you ... "

Nothing except everything that touches the senses, everything the senses savor: the foot-feel of wet sand; the scent of salt air; the sounds of seagulls and the sounds of halyards slapping masts and the sounds of laughter from grandchildren ....

"All that is born must die ... "

Lost is everything that touches the senses and that the senses savor. A radiant sunset; a cleansing moonrise; the breach of a whale; the taste of succulent fruit on the tongue; the rhythmic clang of a bell buoy.

"What dies must rise again ... "

Baxter paused for a very long time, mouth open, breathing hard, gaping at the moon as if in a trance before finally shaking his head "No," and letting the whisky glass slide from his hand. The final thundering bars of the symphony masked the crash of the glass as it shattered on the tiled floor of the balcony.

Startled, Beatrice leapt from Baxter's lap.

A half-hour after receiving Haskins' call, Zacher appeared in his office. Haskins greeted him, poured each of them a scotch, and got right to the point. "I've heard from the Attorney General that the M-4 militia group is back in business. Do you know anything about that?"

"Wayne, you asked me before if I had any contacts with them and I said I'd broken off all contacts with militia groups. Nothing's changed. So the answer is no, I know nothing about it."

Haskins stared into Zacher's eyes looking for any hint of deception. He saw none. "Okay, I'll accept that. Please keep it that way unless I ask you otherwise."

"Why would you ask me otherwise? I thought you wanted nothing to do with militia groups."

"Because if anything comes of what the Attorney General told me about, I may want you to work some back channels to put a stop to it. I can't afford to have somebody going after the president's life. I can't afford it, and the nation can't afford it. Understand?"

Zacher spread his arms. "I'm at your service whenever you need me." He laughed. "But that's not to say I wouldn't mind seeing the end of Baxter."

An angry red blush suffused Haskins' face. "I'll not have any talk like that in my office, even if it's in jest which, with you, I'm never sure about."

Zacher raised his hands, palms out. "Okay, okay. Just kidding."

Haskins held out his empty glass. "Another?"

"Sure."

As Haskins poured two more drinks, he asked, "Now about this guy, the one in the pathology lab at Bethesda, are you certain you have him under control?"

"I told you before; he won't be a problem."

"How can you be so sure?"

"Because I have him scared silly he'll lose his wife if I reveal what I have on him."

"What the hell do you have on him?" Haskins wasn't sure he really wanted to know.

Zacher gazed at Haskins for a few moments before saying, "Perhaps it's time I tell you about my troupe of boys and girls. You may find what I get from them useful to you sometime and you'll, ah, reward me accordingly when you're president."

"Reward? Meaning an ambassadorship of some kind?"

Zacher smiled. "I've always loved Switzerland. And I can speak German."

"Consider it done ... if I become president." Privately, Haskins figured Liechtenstein would be more like it. "Now, what about this troupe?"

"Right. It's about a dozen very attractive young men and women in my employ. I pay them generous salaries and they work things like conventions for me."

"What do you mean, work?"

"Simple. They're hookers. Only, the people they hop into bed with don't pay them, I pay them."

"Why the hell would you do that?"

"My people always take the target to their rooms where they have hidden cameras set up."

"Jesus Christ! You're blackmailing people?"

"Call it that if you want. I find It's a very strong motivation. I have an enormous file of photographs and videos of a great many people in this city. Powerful people. People with access. It becomes very useful."

Haskins shook his head in wonderment. "What kind of people?"

"I usually do political conventions."

"Both parties?"

Zacher smiled, gave Haskins a meaningful look. "Both parties." He paused to let that settle in, then said, "I scan the attendance list before any convention, figure out who might be useful sometime in the future, and give my boys and girls their assignments. Since my people aren't asking for money, the targets think it's all based on attraction. They're flattered. And given that, you'd be surprised at how high the hit rate is."

Haskins strode to the other end of the room. He gazed at a photograph of his wife in a stand-up frame in the bookcase. He turned and asked, "So what does this have to do with our pathology guy?"

"That was a lucky accident. There were two small conventions at this hotel and I ended up getting both lists by chance. I scanned the list of pathologists just for the hell of it, noticed that this guy was at Bethesda, put two and two together and figured that was where all pathology tests for the First Family were done. Maybe I could get some inside information that would prove useful down the road. It was pure speculation, but I said what the hell, I'm paying my people anyway and business was light that night, might as well get something on the guy."

"So you just build these files of photos on … speculation?"

"Photos and videos. Yes, that's about it. In the case of my pathologist friend, it's already proved useful in getting early information about Grace Baxter's disease I was able to use to tip off the media. This was before they moved her to George Washington Hospital,."

Haskins frowned. "It was you? I always knew you were a jerk, but this …. What possible use was information about the First Lady's health to you?"

"Oh, none to me. Not directly. But for certain individuals in the media it was manor from heaven. It allowed me to do a favor, earn some chips that I may want to cash in some day. Media types can be very useful."

"To dig up mud on people? That's what's wrong with the way politics is done these days."

"Look, don't be so fucking high and mighty—sorry, freaking high and mighty; you use the media whenever you can."

"You're the kind of person who soils everything that goes on in this town."

Zacher smiled. "Be careful what you say. I may have you in those files."

"I know that's an empty threat, because I wouldn't fall that easily into your goddamned trap." All the same, Haskins had to wonder how long Zacher had had this scheme going. It had been more than a decade before, but he still hadn't forgotten that delegate Evelyn from Oregon. Now he wondered if she'd been a delegate after all.

Shortly after six-thirty, Marcie appeared at the door carrying a bottle of Chianti in a brown paper bag. Matt was relieved to see her. After having come to his decision, he wanted desperately to be with her, to feel less like the freak he'd started to feel like, to feel normal once again, if only for a brief time. Marcie hugged him. She leaned back to search his eyes. "Well, how are you doing with your little problem?"

"I think I've figured out what to do," he replied. "But now it's a matter of how to do it."

Marcie gave him a suspicious look. "Does that mean that our hypothetical conversation this morning is going to turn real?"

"Something like that."

"I was afraid of that." She went to the kitchen counter, pulled the liter of wine out of the bag, and started to open it. She struggled with the corkscrew for a moment before finally extracting the cork. "I think I'd like a drink before we start talking. I have a funny feeling I'm going to need it." She filled two glasses and handed one to Matt. "What say we order pizza right away and hold off talking until I've had at least two glasses?"

Matt laughed. "You got it." He picked up the phone, peered at a magnetic card stuck to the refrigerator, and dialed the number. After ordering the pizza, he took a sip of wine and went into the living room to put a CD into the player. The Moody Blues, "Nights in White Satin."

"Good choice," Marcie said. "I used to smoke dope to this music. It made everything seem so unreal. Now, even without the dope, I have a feeling that's the way things are going to feel."

Twenty minutes later, the pizza was delivered and they ate and drank in silence, listening to music of the sixties and seventies—Joe Cocker, The Who, The Rolling Stones. "Wild Horses" was playing when Matt took a deep breath and said, "I spent a lot of time figuring out just what it was I could tell you about this thing because if I'm going to ask your help, it certainly wouldn't be fair if you didn't know at least something of what I ... we, the president and me ... are up to."

"My help? As in non-hypothetical?"

"Yes."

"Damn," Marcie said, pouring herself another glass of wine.

Matt said, "I can't tell you all of it, so you'll have to trust me and the president. The idea is to bring down Karl Zacher and, in the process compromise Senator Haskins."

"Hell, I'm all for that. Zacher is a dangerous creep. And Haskins? Well, I can't think of anybody in office I'd rather help bring down after what he did to the education bill."

Matt nodded. "I figured you would say that. But, as you know very well from living with me, politics isn't pretty. The ends often justify the means even if, on occasion, the means are, well, illegal."

"Really illegal? Not hypothetical?"

"Not hypothetical."

She gazed at him for a moment, then nodded. "You want me to transfer money from somebody's account."

"How did you—?"

"—That was your hypothetical question this morning," she replied. "Zacher's account?"

He nodded. "We know he has an account there because you're the one who signed him up."

"Don't remind me," she said. "But why do want me to do this?"

"It's sort of a sting operation," replied Matt. "We have very good intelligence that the group that tried to assassinate Baxter is back in operation."

"Oh, no."

"And ... and Zacher is behind it. We're confident of that."

"He'd pay somebody to assassinate the president?" Marcie asked.

"You doubt it? We're pretty sure he had something to do with the last attempt." He didn't have to tell her what the assassination attempt had meant to them personally, to their dreams of having children.

Marcie gazed at him. "It's hard to believe, even about Zacher. I thought it took somebody who had totally flipped out. But then again, he is a piece of lowlife. Maybe he would do something like that."

"Only problem was nothing could be traced to him. If he transferred money to this Scroggs guy, he did it in a way that was invisible."

"And you want me to make it visible this time," Marcie said.

"I always said you'd make a good politician."

"I'm not sure that's such a compliment." Marcie said, draining her glass. "Whew, This is pretty high-stakes stuff."

"The highest. If we can show Zacher for what he is, if we can make the connection to the M-4 militia group, we can, number one, prevent another assassination attempt and, number two, neutralize Haskins." Matt paused a moment. ... *Prevent another assassination attempt.* How quickly the lies piled up, he thought.

He continued. "With his connection to Zacher, he would have to be completely scrupulous about taking advantage of the situation in order to stave off suspicion ... no dirty ads because they'd backfire ... no wild rhetoric. We bring Zacher down; we eliminate a possible threat to the president's life; and we completely de-fang Haskins in the process."

"Oh, man!"

"Marcie, I hate to ask you this, but I think you can see why we can't involve a single person we don't have complete trust in. As it stands, only you, the president, and I are aware of this and we want to keep it that way."

"Count me in."

"What? No argument?"

"Hell, no! If it means saving the president's life and, in the process screwing both Haskins and Zacher, I'm all for it. After what he did to you … to us …." She drained her glass. "I'm on top of it, Baby. I'm willing to take the risk. Besides, with my knowledge of the bank's computer system, there's really not that much risk … if I do things right."

Matt embraced her. "You're really something special, do you know that, Marcie?"

"You better believe it." She kissed him full on the lips, thrusting her tongue into his mouth. "And you know what?" she murmured.

"What?"

"I had no idea what a turn-on this intrigue stuff could be."

They made love on the living room floor. It was satisfying, but, as always, dry and un-generative. When it was over, they showered together and went to bed. Marcie fell asleep almost instantly. But Matt remained awake for more than an hour staring up at the rotating ceiling fan. In the darkness of the room, it flared like a repeating beacon with the reflections of street lights.

He wondered if he would tell Marcie what the real purpose of her efforts was when it was all over.

Meeting with Wayne Haskins had reminded Karl Zacher of Evelyn. She'd been one of the best women he ever employed for his troupe and he wondered what she was doing now. Probably married with a pack of kids and living in some suburb and driving an SUV with one hand while holding a cell phone to her ear with the other. He wondered if, some night after a couple bottles of wine, she'd ever confessed to her husband that she had once screwed powerful men for the cameras—still and video.

He rummaged through his video cabinet looking for the DVD of her and Wayne Haskins. It took him nearly five minutes—there were so many DVDs—but at last he found it and inserted it into the player.

As the machine sucked it into its play slot, he poured himself a drink, and sat down to watch.

The images were not as good as those he got from the latest digital cameras, but they were certainly good enough, especially since it was Evelyn who'd orchestrated the encounter. She'd been good, one of the best. In addition to her pretty, girl-next-door-that-anybody-could-love looks and the way it contrasted delightfully with her sexual abandon which was always tinged with a hint of shyness, she'd always been aware, like a good porn star, of where the camera was and there were many frames in which Haskins could be clearly identified. And what Zacher saw on the screen was the face of a completely smitten man; a look that Haskins' wife probably hadn't seen in twenty or thirty years ... if ever.

Watching the tape excited Zacher. It reminded him of his own time with the exquisitely skilled, shy-bold, Evelyn—the way she teased, the way her short blond hair bounced up and down with her head like prairie grass in a soft wind. Even the clean, freshly shampooed smell of her hair came back to him.

Zacher smiled. Lately, Haskins seemed to be having doubts about him. And he knew the senator well. The man wouldn't hesitate to hang him out to dry if anything went wrong with this Baxter thing. Haskins would cut himself loose from his friend and chief contributor without a moment's thought. And if it ever came down to facing charges of some kind, Zacher knew very well he would be standing alone. You just can't trust these politicians.

When the video was finished, he slipped it back into its case and placed it in the cabinet where he could find it again quickly.

Near midnight, Matt Cannon passed through the East Gate of the White House and made his way to the Oval Office. He walked quickly, trying to persuade himself of a resolve he didn't really feel, trying to commit himself to action before he backed away. He was acutely aware that once he spoke to the president, there would be one less opportunity to turn back; things would be set in motion that would lead inexorably to the final execution of the president's bizarre plan.

He wished that he hadn't thought of that word—execution.

The Oval Office anteroom was deserted. He gave his signature rap on the Oval Office door and the president responded immediately. "Come in, Matt."

Baxter was sitting at his desk, his chin propped on his steepled hands. It was a characteristic pose, one the president always used when deep in thought. Again, he was wearing eyeglasses and Matt had difficulty seeing his eyes because of the moving reflections of the rotating crystal balls of the anniversary clock. "I've interrupted something," Matt said.

"No, not at all. I was just running over my plan one more time, trying to see if I've truly thought it all the way through."

"Do I sense some hesitation?" asked Matt, feeling a slight surge of hope.

"I don't mind telling you, it's a bit scary," the president said. "Would I be human if I didn't have some doubts about this?"

"No, I suppose not. So, what's the verdict?"

Baxter sighed deeply. "I still can't get away from the logic of it. I keep looking for some other way, anything, but I keep coming back to the same place. As far as I can see, it's the only way to prevent Haskins from becoming the next president. And if that happens ... well, we might as well have not done a damned thing. Even my executive orders would be reversed."

"So, you're sure about this?"

For a long while, the president didn't respond. He got up, walked to the window, and gazed out in the direction of the Washington monument. Finally, he said, "I wish I could talk to Grace. She sometimes saw a side of things I didn't see. I'm afraid you and I are too grounded in logic to see things clearly."

"But you and I both know there's nobody we can ask to bring a different perspective to this," said Matt.

Baxter nodded. "Nobody."

"So I repeat: are you sure about this?"

"Look, Matt, if I could wish Jim's diagnosis away; if I even had a sliver of hope for some kind of miraculous recovery, I wouldn't have the strength to see this through." He paused. "But there's absolutely no hope. It sucks, but there it is."

Matt nodded his understanding. "I've also spent a lot of time trying to find a way of believing that Jim was just wrong; that he blew the diagnosis. I guess it's a form of denial. They say people go through that ... and anger ... before they come to acceptance."

Baxter nodded. "I'm familiar with all that from Grace's last months. So where are you with it now?"

"Hell, I'm still at the angry stage."

"It took me a couple of weeks to get past that. And even now, I find myself slipping back every once in a while."

"It'll probably keep going like that."

Baxter shook his head. "For a while, perhaps. But I remember with Grace ... you eventually get to a point where total acceptance sets in. And it's not even resignation, it's just ... acceptance. Part of being human, I guess."

"Did Grace go through those phases? Denial, anger?"

"Sure. Nobody wants to die. But she got peaceful with it long before I did. I guess there's a difference between those who are going and those who are staying."

"Which is why you're ahead of me on this one?"

"Something like that. But I still have relapses. Last night I sat on the Truman Balcony listening to Mahler's 'Resurrection' Symphony, always one of my favorites. But I tried listening differently."

"How do you mean?"

"I used it to rethink my ideas about life after death. I think Mahler was trying to persuade himself that it existed; I thought maybe he could persuade me."

"Did he?"

Baxter shook his head "No." He strolled to the desk, gazed at his father's Congressional Medal of Honor for a moment, then said, "There's something else I've been agonizing over. I hate myself for putting you in this predicament, for asking you to help me out with this. I hope you understand that it's not only because you're the man I most trust in this world, but because ... I care for you."

Matt nodded, but said nothing.

"So, now it's come down to the moment of truth," Baxter said. "Matt, my dear friend. I have to ask you—"

"—I'll do it." Matt felt that if he hesitated for one moment, he would change his mind.

The president took a deep breath and said, "Eyuh. Good."

"But as long as we're being frank, Angus, I have to tell you how I feel about it."

"I think I can guess."

"No, hear me out. In some ways, it feels like I'll be the one pulling the trigger. But that's just something I'll have to live with."

"Matt, maybe we ought to just call it off. I can't bear the thought of you—"

Matt raised his hand. "—Please, Angus. You're right. The logic of it is unassailable. If we get cold feet now, we'll just keep coming back to it and torturing ourselves and in the end we'll only find ourselves in the same place. It's because we're goddamned slaves to logic and move-countermove; that's how the hell you got here in the first place. We've sacrificed sentiment on the altar of logic and I don't know if men like us can ever backtrack. Sure as hell if we did, guys like Haskins would have us for lunch. The alternative to your plan is to let events rule us, let the disease run its course and respond passively when the time comes. But we're just not built like that."

Baxter chuckled. "No, I suppose not. We've always grabbed the bull by the balls."

"I think it's supposed to be 'by the horns.'"

"Yuh."

"But I have one big problem with your plan."

"What's that?"

"What if this Billy Scroggs decides to use, say, a bomb instead of a gun? Others would get hurt."

"I thought of that. Two things: We know he has a family, a wife and daughter. As that Lake woman said, he'll want to get away. Second, he's known to have a gun collection. It's hard to imagine him using anything else. If you're an aficionado of guitars, you don't accompany your song with a piano."

"I guess that makes sense," said Matt. "There's something else. In a funny way that I can't explain, this has something to do with your father saving my grandfather's life on Omaha Beach. I don't know what it is, but I just feel that way."

Baxter nodded, but said nothing. They remained silent for a few moments, Finally, Matt said, "What about your family, Angus? I know you can't say anything to them about your plan, but don't you think they have a right to know about the leukemia?"

"I've thought long and hard about that, Matt. We're going to be taking a sailing vacation. Maybe I'll tell them then. On the other hand, I don't want to put them through the kind of long-term suffering that we all went through watching Grace die. Maybe confronting them with something sudden would be best, especially since it's going to happen anyway."

Matt gazed at his friend, debating whether to bring up the next point. Finally, he asked, "I really hate to bring this up, Angus, but have you given any thought about the autopsy?"

The president seemed taken aback. "Autopsy?"

"With the assassination of a president, there's bound to be an autopsy. I'm no doctor, but my guess is they'll find evidence of the leukemia."

"No, I hadn't thought of that. Let me mull it over. Maybe we'll have to bring Jim into this, although that's something I hate to do."

"Or else make it happen before more severe symptoms show up so Jim can argue that the leukemia was pre-symptomatic."

Baxter stared at him for a very long time. Finally, he said in a soft voice, "I'll be speaking at the Lincoln Memorial on August twenty-eight."

"I see," said Matt. After another long pause he said, "One final thing, I'll need to be away from the White House for a while. Even though I'm not officially part of the administration, people see it that way. I'll need some kind of cover."

"I thought of that. Do you have any objection to a claim of exhaustion requiring a couple of months sabbatical?"

"Objection? Hell no! It's the goddamned truth."

They both laughed.

"But one thing," said Matt. "Please invite me back. Once things are … ah, set up … I want back in. I want to spend as much time with you as possible. Know what I mean?"

Baxter gave a sad smile. "Yes." He took a deep breath. "And don't worry, you'll still be the man I go to. There are going to be tons of things to do; I'll want you by my side." He paused, then said, "You know, there's one advantage to knowing what we know. We can throw caution to the winds. We can push things harder than we would ever have dared in the past."

"Because there'll be no more campaigns?"

Baxter nodded. "Because there'll be no more campaigns."

Part 3

July—August, 3rd Year of the
Baxter Administration

'Tis pride that pulls the country down.
—William Shakespeare, Othello, ii, III

Chapter 11—Bass Run, ME

Matt Cannon pulled off the Maine Turnpike at Bangor and headed west on Route 15 in an old, battered Ford Taurus. His scalp itched from having shaved off all his hair, but the discomfort he felt now was nothing compared to the pain of getting his right forearm tattooed with a skull crossed by an M4 carbine, and the two weeks of itching that followed. Though the tattoo artist used a new kind of ink called "infinitink," that is more easily removed than traditional inks, he warned Matt that the removal of the tattoo would be more painful than its application. But Matt would worry about that later.

Though it was only late afternoon, the day had darkened considerably. Ahead, the sky was bruised, a dark gray-yellow band of clouds, like a broad nicotine stain, spread from north to south just above the serrated ridge of a low mountain. He recognized it as a squall line from old sailing cruises with the president. If the weather turned bad, he might not make Bass Run that evening. But that didn't upset him; he wasn't looking forward to meeting up with Billy Scroggs.

He gripped the wheel hard. The muscles in his forearms tensed, giving a slight distorted shape to the new tattoo. He dug his fingernails into the imitation leather of the steering wheel. They were ragged after he'd let them grow before deliberately biting them unevenly.

Anything to disguise the D. C. lawyer in him.

He was acutely aware that everything he'd done to change his appearance brought him a step closer to a personal kind of Sophie's Choice, a hideous decision he was being forced to make.

More than once, he'd cursed the president for plunging him into this situation. Selfishly, he'd at first bemoaned what following through with the president's plan would do to him, how it would change him forever, how he would have to live with this dark secret, this tumor on his conscience, never able to seek forgiveness, not even from Marcie. To obtain her forgiveness, he would have to confide in her, and that would amount to telling her that she, also, had had a hand in the assassination of the president, that they had used her. Persuading her to transfer funds from Zacher's account to Billy Scroggs had been bad enough.

He also suspected his days in the White House, and, indeed, in politics were nearly at an end. He couldn't begin to imagine how he would be able to work with Katherine Moore-Paterson or anybody else, knowing what he knew. And then, beyond his own selfish concerns, he wondered what this act would do to Baxter's family. He shuddered as he imagined himself trying to console them at the president's funeral, all the while unable to tell them that it was what the president had wanted.

Not for the first time he pondered the power of one lie, like a small wavelet in the deep ocean, to become a tsunami of lies as it reached shallow water.

And he started to think about the country as a whole. He remembered how devastated people had been at the deaths of JFK, Martin Luther King, and Bobby Kennedy, how it had changed lives. Even though he was a teenager at the time, he, too, had been deeply moved. How many hundreds of thousands of people across the country would be affected in the same way when Angus Baxter, the first president ever to have the courage to select a black woman as his running mate, was assassinated?

And then he surprised himself by thinking of Wayne Haskins. How fair was it to this man who, although a political enemy, was a good and decent man? How fair was it to implicate him, however indirectly through Zacher, in this dirty business. Didn't it amount to a slander that would forever cloud the man's reputation, the very kind of political trick he and the president professed to hate? How often had he and Baxter condemned what they called the Lee Atwater brand of politics or the politics of sleaze that had soiled Washington lately?

He wondered if the president was having similar misgivings. Once more, he cursed his friend. But each time he cursed the president, his anger was tempered by the knowledge that, for the president, the choice was far more cruel. He knew the man well. Baxter was the kind of person who would agonize over his true motives, who would proceed because he thought it was the right thing to do, but who would be tormented by doubts. It took a special kind of courage to plow ahead in the face of grave doubts because you sensed that the greater crime would be to passively allow events to shape the outcome. And when he thought this, he cursed the fates for allowing this monstrous cancer to happen to such a good man as Angus Baxter.

He was so consumed by these thoughts that the first hailstone on the windshield was like a gun going off. Images of the day when he was shot flashed through his mind. He looked up at the sky. It had become darker still, a weight of boiling cloud that seemed to press down on the land. A flash of lightening ripped the sky, followed, seconds later, by a rumble of thunder. Several more hailstones, the size of grapes, bounced off the windshield and the hood—a drumming rat-a-tat-tat like the gunshots he heard when he lay on the wet ground outside the hospital.

He switched on the headlights and the wipers and leaned forward over the steering wheel. Easing his foot off the accelerator, he squinted to make out the road ahead of him. Earlier, he'd seen a moose by the side of the road and the last thing he wanted now was to run into one of those beasts; it would be like hitting a truck. He realized he had no idea if animals would be out roaming in such a storm, but he wasn't about to take chances. Once again, he bemoaned the fact that so many years with Baxter on campaign trails and in hotels and in the halls of Congress and the White House had left him pitifully out of touch with the real world.

He came round a bend and saw blinking red lights in the distance— hazard lights reminding him of the flashing lights of the president's motorcade the day he was shot. Someone had pulled to the side of the road and he wondered if the person was in some kind of trouble or just trying to wait out the storm. Slowing down, he pulled onto the shoulder, coming to a stop behind a red pickup truck. The hail was coming down much harder now, an incessant clatter tattooing the roof of the car. It was like being inside an empty oil drum. He opened the door and stepped out into the weather.

He hiked his shirt over his head and dashed for the truck. A hailstone struck him painfully on the forearm.

A young woman rolled the driver's side window down. "Are you all right?" he shouted into the wind.

The woman reached to turn down the radio. "Yuh, we're all right. The kids just got scared." She nodded to two young boys huddled together in the passenger seat. "Thought we'd wait it out."

Matt jumped when a bolt of lightning and a deafening thunderclap appeared nearly simultaneously. Then there was a second loud report and he turned to see a huge tree branch crash to the road and splinter into several pieces. The two boys cried out. The woman paused for a moment, as if to consider the wisdom of what she was doing, then motioned to the half door behind her. "Get in," she said. "It's too dangerous out there."

He opened the door and slid into the narrow seat in the back of the cab, arranging himself lengthwise along the seat, the only position that would accommodate his legs, and said, "I haven't seen a storm like this in a long time. It's quite something."

"Ain't but a squall. Be over in no time." She turned and surveyed him. "You ain't from around here."

"What makes you say that?"

"The way you speak like you're from down to Boston or somewhere."

His speech. It wasn't something he'd thought about much in his planning. It didn't go much beyond remembering to say "ain't" instead of "isn't.

"Just vacationing," he replied. He made a note to listen to her speech patterns closely, maybe visit a bar or two before seeing Billy Scroggs.

She smiled. Her teeth were uneven and nicotine-stained. "Most folks vacationing in Maine go to the seashore, Down East somewhere where I come from. Maybe down to Bar Harbor or somewhere." She pronounced it Bah Habah. "You sure you ain't lost?"

Matt laughed. "No. I just thought I'd like to see the interior of Maine, the forests, the lakes …."

"Ain't nothing here but a bunch of poor people and hunters. Plus some yuppie types shootin' the rapids."

He smiled. "Speaking of rapids, how far is Bass Run?"

"Up the road a ways. Maybe fifty miles. Somewhere near Indian Pond."

"Is there someplace I can stay for the night between here and there? A motel? I don't want to drive another fifty miles in this."

"Covered Bridge Motel in Guilford. Maybe five or six miles up the road. You goin' fishin' for smallmouth bass?"

"No, why do you ask?"

"Lots of folks go to Indian Pond for that. Supposed to be real good. Say, you mind if I turn the radio up. Wanna hear what's happenin' with this heah storm."

"No, of course not. Go right ahead."

But instead of the weather, a news program was on the radio. A male voice with a slight Maine accent was saying " ... the vote is scheduled to take place tomorrow in the Senate. On another matter, the president announced today at his regular news conference that Vice President Moore-Paterson would represent him at the funeral of the president of Finland, Paavo Voutilainen."

Matt noted how the man mispronounced Voutilainen's name, placing the accent on the first rather than the third syllable. He smiled to himself, thinking of the scene that must have occurred in the Oval Office when Baxter asked Katherine to go to Finland. He could almost see her dark eyes glaring at the president, could almost hear her cursing and saying how she agreed to be Baxter's running mate only because he promised she wasn't going to be a ceremonial vice president who did little else but attend funerals.

The woman in the front seat gave a snort. "Wonder what them yellow-haired Finns will think when a nigger woman shows up?" Her comment jarred him. He said nothing. The woman continued. "I mean, I don't much care for that Baxter fellah, but I pray to the Lord, Jesus Christ, my savior, that he don't get himself killed or somethin'. It would wreck the country to have a nigger bitch as president. Can you even imagine that?"

Matt said, "I see what you mean." He was relieved the storm was letting up.

The woman leaned forward and spun the radio dial. A cacophony of whines and static came from the speakers, interrupted briefly with some intelligible words: "... and now to the farm report; ... two runs in the bottom of the ninth inning; ... an open house at the garden center." Finally, she found a station talking about the weather. It promised clear, but hot and humid conditions for the following day with a chance of late afternoon thundershowers. "Sounds like the front is passing us," the woman said. "It's lettin' up already." The clatter of hailstones had changed to the hiss of a steady rain.

"Sounds like it," Matt said. He opened the door. "Listen, thanks for letting me in out of that hail. I'm going to head off now."

"See yah," she replied. "Give the small mouth bass a try."

"Maybe I will."

Moments later, Matt was again driving along Route 15, filled with a new anxiety. He was assailed with doubts about his ability, despite his physical disguise, to pull off the impersonation of a militia type. Besides the fact that he'd completely forgotten about his speech, there was the matter of having to talk convincingly with the kind of fear and hatred the woman had manifested. He wasn't sure he could manage it with enough conviction that a Billy Scroggs would be taken in.

He wondered if Guilford had a library where he could get access to the internet. It occurred to him he had better review the militia web sites he'd looked at a week before to remind himself of the language they used. And even if there was a library in Guilford, what was he going to do to make himself sound less like the east coast intellectual he was?

Katherine Moore-Paterson entered the Oval Office, eyes flaring. Even though Baxter still had a pair of advisors in the office with him, she launched right into her diatribe. "Mister President, I want you to know that I don't appreciate going to state funerals in Finland ... or anywhere else for that matter. I serve at your pleasure and, of course I will do what you wish, but I just thought you ought to know what my position is."

Baxter tried, unsuccessfully, to suppress a smile. "Good morning, Katherine," he said. "Did you have a good flight?"

"Good morning, Mister President. The flight was fine. It's good to be back," replied the vice president. "So, what's it to be? Funerals or a real, contributing vice presidency?"

"I'll send the Secretary of State the next time."

"Good, he'll enjoy it."

"I doubt that," laughed Baxter. "But we'll spread the misery." He nodded to his two advisors and they quietly left the Oval Office. He turned back to Katherine Moore-Paterson. "In fact, I wanted to talk to you this morning about the very thing that has you bugged. I think you should increase your presence at National Security briefings and in Cabinet meetings. In fact, I think it might be a good idea if you ran them occasionally."

Moore-Paterson knitted her forehead. She gazed at Baxter for a moment, then said, "Something's wrong."

Baxter chuckled. "I've always thought you were the most perceptive person I ever met."

"I hope it's not your health," she said.

Baxter extended an arm, suggesting that she sit in the sofa near the fireplace. He sat beside her. For a moment he watched the rotating crystal balls of the anniversary clock. Their reflections, magnified, swept across the ceiling. He leaned toward her to speak. But before he could say anything, she said, "Oh God, it is, isn't it? Please tell me it's not serious."

"I wish I could, Katherine, but I'm afraid it is."

She placed a hand over his. "What? Tell me."

Leaving out some of the particulars, he told her about Jim Stockton's diagnosis.

She squeezed her eyes tightly closed. "Oh my God, Mister President …." She gripped his hand.

"Jim is hopeful that, with regular blood transfusions to increase the red blood cell count and with antibiotics to control infection, he can mitigate the symptoms and I can serve out a full two terms." What he didn't tell her, of course, was that it was a bold-faced lie. Stockton had no such hope. And, in any event, he, Baxter, had refused any further treatment that would reduce his energy and effectiveness. As it stood, she knew just enough to prepare herself without knowing so much that she would inadvertently make an impending succession obvious to everybody in the White House.

"This is too cruel so soon after Grace died," said Moore-Patterson. "I can't imagine how terrible you must feel."

Baxter stood, walked to his desk, and gazed at the photograph of his wife. "Actually, I feel remarkably well. In the end, I don't think there's going to be a major problem, but it makes sense that we begin to prepare you. Just in case."

"Of course."

"But you do understand, Katherine, it would be seriously disruptive on a number of fronts if we made it too obvious?"

"That goes without saying."

"I'm disclosing this to you because you have a right to know. It's only fair. As it stands, there are only four people in the world who know: the two of us, Jim Stockton, and Matt Cannon. And I want it to stay that way. No one else in the White House or on the NSC or in the Cabinet or, God forbid, in Congress. No one is to know about this."

"You can count on me."

"I know that," replied Baxter. "Now, we're going to have to be subtle about this. We can't do anything abruptly or we'll raise suspicions."

"What's your game plan?"

"I'll announce your increased involvement and I'll say it had been our intention all along. However, your special duties in straightening out some of the problems at NASA and in slimming down the bureaucracy of the executive branch had deprived you of the necessary time. And now that those problems are largely solved, we're returning to our original plan."

"Sounds good to me."

"And as far as internal White House operations are concerned, I'm going on a sailing vacation with my family in a few weeks. That'll be an ideal and natural time for you to assume more visibility with the inside staff."

Moore-Patterson nodded.

"Of course, while we're sailing, the Secret Service will be shadowing us in several pretty hefty cabin cruisers or something and, naturally, there'll be a Coast Guard cutter for a communications center and a traveling White House ...." He chuckled. "I guess I presented them with quite a challenge with my late announcement. They're probably cursing me every which way to Sunday behind my back."

The vice president laughed. "Why should they? They get to go on a cruise for heaven's sake."

"I suppose so. At any rate, my military aides will also be on the cutter and, of course, they'll be carrying the 'football.' But back here, the normal operations of the White House will continue with you essentially in charge. I'll make that clear to the Chief of Staff."

"You and I both know the real action will be where you are," said Moore-Patterson, "but at least it'll serve to increase my visibility around here."

"Which is exactly the point. No more foreign funerals for you. You're too valuable back here in Washington."

"I appreciate your confidence in me, Mister President, and I assure you I'll be fully prepared if, God forbid, the need arises."

"I know you will be, Katherine," replied Baxter. And to himself, he added, You'd better be.

Matt Cannon was startled from his sleep by the sudden roar of a motorcycle in the motel parking lot. Sleepily, he crawled out of bed, parted the Venetian blinds, and peered out. The cold front had passed in the night and on the other side of it the weather was clear and brisk, a Canadian high-pressure system. He wondered what happened to the hot, humid forecast. Puddles, lingering in the low spots, glinted with the risen sun.

He opened the door to the limit of the chain lock and inhaled the fresh, pine-scented air. It helped dispel the cobwebs of sleep. And with a cleared mind, the purpose of his being in this place seeped into his consciousness. *Billy Scroggs.*

He decided not to shave, but to leave a two-day growth of stubble. More convincing. Allowing time for a quick breakfast, he could be in Bass Run by mid morning. That would give him time to scout around, listen closely to some of the locals speaking, and prepare himself for a possible meeting with Scroggs. The previous night he'd strolled back and forth in his small room practicing a less cultivated grammar and found it coming surprisingly easy to him. He was forced to wonder if the language of his childhood was, indeed, his natural way of speaking and the educated speech was nothing but a thin veneer. He found the thought disquieting. And as far as the accent was concerned, he figured that would be no problem. He wasn't trying to pass himself off as a native in the first place; he had planned to tell Scroggs, or anyone else who asked, that he was from a militia group in California.

After dressing, he entered the motel's restaurant and took a table next to one occupied by four men, one older, three younger, who, he assumed—given their unshaven appearance and the coveralls they wore—must be locals. A waitress came to take his order.

"Gimme two eggs, up, and some toast," he said.

"Bacon?"

"Nah, I ain't got the appetite. But you can bring me some of that orange juice there," he said, nodding toward a metal cart containing several plastic decanters. "And some coffee."

When the waitress left to fetch the coffee and orange juice, he listened to the conversation at the next table while pretending to read a newspaper. Since they were talking about the next steps in a concrete foundation, he assumed they were construction workers of some kind. Their language was much like that of the woman he'd met the previous night during the hail storm.

While eating breakfast, he turned his attention to the *Bangor Daily News*. The president was mentioned in only one article headlined, "President Plans Sailing Vacation." He scanned the paper for more White House news but there was none. He assumed not much was happening back in Washington, at least as far as the *Bangor Daily News* was concerned.

Fifteen minutes later, he had checked out and was on the road toward Bass Run, his stomach upset either from the breakfast or from anxiety as he approached a possible meeting with Billy Scroggs.

There was still a chance to pull out, to tell Baxter he just couldn't do it, and he knew his friend would understand. Indeed, the president, himself, had confessed a level of uncertainty about the whole thing. The temptation to turn passive and let events run their course was almost overwhelming. At least it would absolve them of responsibility. It would be so easy to leave it to fate, not to be forced to make choices. But all their political lives, both he and the president had acted aggressively to shape and control events as much as humanly possible. They tried never to let chance determine the outcome of something that was important to them, and what could be more important than the succession and the president's legacy?

He turned his mind to thinking how he would make contact with Billy Scroggs. The ATF agent, Alexandra Lake, had mentioned a place called Bob's Bar and he thought this would be a good place to start, which reminded him of another serious problem that had been plaguing him—he knew there was a strong probability the Lake woman would be lurking around the place. The president may have nixed an outright raid, but that didn't stop people from keeping an eye on Scroggs. Indeed, he instructed Ms. Lake to do as much. Undoubtedly, ATF and the Secret Service had already placed the man on their watch list. They would make certain they knew where Scroggs was at all times.

Because they had already met in the Oval Office, Matt thought there was a chance Lake would recognize him despite the disguise. But there was nothing Matt could do about it. Obviously he couldn't go to the Secret Service or ATF and coordinate activities with them, so he would just have to take his chances. He was reasonably sure the disguise would work. Hell, he didn't think even Marcie would have recognized him, and Lake had seen him for only a few minutes when her attention was naturally focused exclusively on the president; that's what being in the Oval Office for the first time did to people.

As he was engaged with these thoughts, he rounded a bend in the road and came to a sign that read:

BASS RUN, MAINE
HOME OF WORLD CLASS SMALLMOUTH BASS FISHING

He chuckled to himself. He was there to see if he could hook his own version of a smallmouth bass.

Chapter 12—A Proposition for Scroggs

David Ruskin, the Director of the Secret Service, along with Harold Haines of the Presidential Protective Detail, and Margaret Chapleu of the White House Advance Office, filed into the Oval Office together. President Baxter greeted them warmly and ushered them to a sofa. He sat in an armchair at one end of a long, low coffee table.

The Chief of Staff, Delores Northcote already occupied a chair at the other end of the table. "Something tells me this is about my sailing vacation," Baxter said with a smile.

"Yes sir, Mister President," said Ruskin. "It's just that we're all agreed your selection of sailing area presents some very sticky problems."

"You don't like Martha's Vineyard and Nantucket Sound? The Vineyard seemed fine for Presidents Clinton and Obama."

"It's not that, sir," said Margaret Chapleu. "It's a wonderful area, to be sure. But they stayed on the island, not in a sailboat off the island."

"And the difference?"

Ruskin leaned forward. "Anytime you're moving around, Mister President, it produces additional complications. In essence, we have to organize a fleet to protect you, to be with you at all times, and then we have to have a second fleet for advance people to precede you to whatever harbor or port you decide to sail into."

"And as I've already told Harold, I plan to let the wind direction and the weather in general determine where we go," said the president. "Is that your problem?"

"Exactly, sir," said Ruskin.

Baxter smiled. "Then all you have to do is make sure the Navy gives me good weather reports and I can then reveal my plans a day or two ahead of time."

"But Mister President—"

"—I don't know if any of you have ever sailed," Baxter said, "but let me tell you something about it. It's a very pure kind of thing. Sort of a dance with the wind, if you don't mind a little poetry, in which neither you nor the wind really has the lead. Unless you have a specific place you need to be, you can afford to give up a certain amount of control and just go where the wind blows. Now that, for a president of the United States, is a true vacation because no responsible president could possibly afford such luxury in the day-to-day business of governing."

"I see your point, Mister President," said Ruskin. "That's why we're not here to try to dissuade you from sailing. We just wonder if you wouldn't consider a different location. Say the Downeast coast of Maine."

"Near the Downeast White House? Why there?"

"Much less traffic, much easier to patrol."

The president shook his head. "Too much chance of fog. Obviously, I've sailed there."

Harold Haines leaned forward as he unfolded a chart. "May I, sir?"

Baxter nodded. "Go ahead."

Haines spread the chart across the coffee table, right side up to the president. He took out a telescoping pointer, extended it, and tapped the chart. "There's regular ferry service from here at Woods Hole to Edgartown and from here at Hyannis to Nantucket."

"I'm well aware of that."

"Well, the problem, sir, is that represents only a small amount of the traffic. Nantucket Sound and Vineyard Sound are swarming with boats of all kinds this time of year. And the place is only about three and a half miles wide in some places. Also, we were thinking of bringing in the *Leyte*

Gulf, a five-hundred-and-sixty-seven foot *Ticonderoga* class cruiser, but there's simply not enough water in Vineyard and Nantucket Sounds."

"A cruiser? Isn't that overkill?"

Instead of answering the president directly, Haines said, "So the Secret Service guys will be on two eighty-seven foot Coast Guard patrol boats. And we'll also have a medium endurance Coast Guard cutter, the *Seneca*, because we can keep an HH-65 Dolphin helicopter aboard her. That's a lot of floating assets."

Baxter turned to his Chief of Staff. "Delores, What does Admiral Konarska say about this?" He was referring to the Commandant of the Coast Guard.

"He said it would be no problem, sir, as long as you avoided some of the major ports like Edgartown and Vineyard Haven. They would establish a perimeter around you and the cruiser. At the speed you would be sailing, it wouldn't pose a problem to patrol that perimeter."

The three people on the sofa glanced at each other. Haines leaned forward and started to pick up the chart.

"No, leave it there," said the president. "May I borrow your pointer?" Haines handed him the pointer. "What I can do to make your job easier," said Baxter, "is do just as the admiral advises—stay away from the bigger ports where most of the tourists congregate. Instead, I'll pull into places like Tarpaulin Cove here on Naushon." He tapped the chart. "And Cuttyhunk, here." Another tap. "I'd love to pull into Hadley's Harbor, but you'd only be able to get a patrol boat in there and the cutter wouldn't be able to stand off in Woods Hole because that's a narrow channel with a lot of traffic. She'd have to wait at her dock."

"Actually, Mister President," said Haines. "Hadley's Harbor wouldn't be so bad. It's a narrow entrance. We could easily check out every boat that goes in there. After all, the place will only hold a dozen or so boats anyway."

"What about helicopter evacuation if necessary?" asked Ruskin.

"There'll be helicopters at the Woods Hole Coast Guard Station just a mile or so away. HH-65 Dolphins."

Baxter rose from his seat. "Well, then, there you go. And don't worry. Given what we've discussed, you'll be dealing with a hundred times fewer people than when Presidents Clinton and Obama visited Martha's Vineyard." He smiled. "Why, it will be a relaxing vacation for every one of us!"

Matt Cannon spent the afternoon wandering around the small town of Bass Run. All the buildings he saw were in some form of decay: an abandoned textile mill in which every window was either broken or covered over with plywood; houses that hadn't seen a coat of paint in years and with overgrown patches of weeds in their front yards; shops along what he assumed was the main street all boarded up. The sidewalk had weeds growing from the cracks between slabs. A small boy, swaying, rode a bicycle whose training wheels alternately lifted clear of the ground or locked and skidded along the pavement. Matt stepped aside to let the child pass.

The one motel in town reeked of cheap cleaning fluid and its chairs were mostly covered in cracked and torn vinyl.

What he saw before him was not some fine point of debate on the second amendment or the New World Order; not a philosophical or ethical dispute about when an embryo becomes a human being or whether cloning stem cells destroys life; but simple, abject poverty.

Something had done these people in, whether it was their own government, their God, themselves, Wall Street, or some nameless, hidden enemy. Everything he saw cried out for some score-settling, some form of retribution.

The poverty before him was not the same thing that was discussed in white-shirted Washington—a concept, a number. Instead, it was real—it looked real, it felt real, it smelled real. Should he wonder that such conditions would give rise to militia groups bent on lashing out at anything and everything that oppressed them? Wasn't that the same kind of assertive action against the randomness of things, the unfairness of life, that both he and the president prided themselves in? Wasn't it the same kind of real poverty, tinged with thoughts of revenge, that oiled conflict in the Middle East and so many other places?

In the early evening, feeling depressed, he found Bob's Bar on the outskirts of town and ventured inside. Only two or three men sat at the bar. Otherwise, the place was deserted. He'd noticed a sign by the door that advertised BLTs so he went up to the bar and ordered one along with a beer. He reminded himself to order Budweiser, not Amstel Light which was ordinarily his preference. They probably didn't even carry Amstel Light. While he waited for the sandwich and beer, he noticed some words (Greek?) carved into the surface of the bar.

μολὼν λαβέ

He had no idea what they meant but he cautioned himself not to ask for fear that it was some kind of slogan that anyone in a militia group would know.

Moments later, the bartender brought him the beer and sandwich. "You ain't from around here," the man said. Not a question, but a statement.

Matt shook his head. "California. You Bob?"

The bartender shook his head. "Name's Zeke. Bought the bar from Bob some twenty years ago. What brings you all the way out here?"

Matt took a bite of the sandwich. It was cold and the bacon was dried out, shriveled up. It was slathered with far too much mayonnaise. "Wanna see a man," he mumbled as he chewed.

"What man?"

"A man, that's all."

Zeke stared at him while he took another bite of the BLT then said, "Lot's of men here." He pronounced it heah. "Maybe I can help you find him if you tell me his name."

"Billy Scroggs. You know him?"

"Sure I know him. What do you want with him?"

"Got business between him an' me. That's all."

"Good business?"

"He ain't got a problem, if that's what you mean."

"Well, that's good to hear, 'cause Billy, he's got a lot o' friends in this town. Know what I mean?"

Matt feigned indifference. "Uhm hmm." He took another bite of the sandwich and chased it with a swig of beer.

Zeke regarded him for another moment, shrugged, and went to turn on the TV. Some woman was giving a weather report for coastal Maine and the inland areas. Matt saw Zeke lean close to one of the patrons, a grizzled old man dressed in denim, and say something to him in a low voice. The man leaned back to look at Matt but quickly averted his eyes when he saw that Matt was looking at him. A news reporter came on the TV. He talked mainly of a three-car accident on Route 15 near Bangor and then of a house fire nearby that claimed the life of an old man.

"Dumb fuck probably burned his own house down for the insurance and forgot to get out," the denim-clad old man said. He placed an emphasis on the "in" in "insurance."

The others laughed.

A different newscaster came on the TV. He said, "In national news, it's been learned that President Baxter will be taking his family on a yachting vacation this month near Cape Cod in Massachusetts."

"Yachting vacation," said one of the patrons, adding a special note of derision to the word 'yachting'. "That fucking rich asshole."

Privately, Matt grimaced. He wondered if it was some idiot in the White House Communications Office or if it was the media who'd decided to use the phrase "yachting vacation" instead of "sailing vacation."

The old man in denim looked at Matt. "You hear that? Baxter's goin' yachting." He pronounced it yahwwting. "Maybe we should go with him. Whatcha think?"

"Don't mean shit to me," Matt answered, repeating exactly what he'd heard one of the men at breakfast say.

The old man shrugged.

No one spoke to Matt the rest of the evening. At one point he realized that the old man had left. He kept waiting for someone to walk in whom the people would greet as Billy. But of the men who were greeted by name, none of them was Billy. After about two hours, he got up and paid his tab. "You tell Billy Scroggs that if he wants to meet with me, I got a proposition for him from one of the California militias. I'm in room six at the motel."

By the time he made it back to the motel, it had become dark. Several letters on the neon motel sign were missing, leaving:

B SS R N MO EL

although the missing 'A' and 'U' flickered hopefully.

The parking spot facing the door to room six was beside a large dumpster. He pulled into the spot and got out of the car. Fumbling for his key, he went to the door. Just as he inserted the key, he was startled by a voice.

"I hear you're looking for me."

He turned in the direction of the voice. At first, he saw nobody. Then, a shadowy figure emerged from behind the dumpster.

He held a gun.

It was pointed at Matt.

Alexandra Lake was vaguely troubled when she saw the man walk out of Bob's Bar. It was dark and she couldn't be sure, but she'd been trained to recognize people despite disguises—by their walk, by the way they carried themselves—and the man she'd seen instantly put her in mind of Matt Cannon, the man she saw at the White House. What would he be doing in Bass Run obviously trying to disguise himself? Fishing? Were friends of presidents so well known that they had to go around in disguise when vacationing on their own? Unlikely, she told herself. But then what? Is it possible the president so distrusts ATF that he would send his own man to keep an eye on Billy Scroggs? Strange as it sounded, she could think of no other reason.

When she'd seen Cannon—if that's who it was—she had stepped back into the shadows and watched as the man got into a car and drove off. She'd waited until the car turned a corner, signal light blinking, before continuing toward Bob's Bar. She'd been sitting at a corner table for only a few minutes, enduring the salacious glances of men, when Billy Scroggs walked in, talked briefly with the bartender, then left.

Thinking it unlikely Scroggs would be back, Alexandra finished her beer and walked out. It was a fifteen minute drive to the small farm where she rented a room and she was happy to have an early night. As she drove, she wondered if she should report seeing Cannon to people higher up in ATF. The last thing she wanted was to get involved in administration warfare.

Matt stared at the gun and tried to collect himself. Though his heart was racing, he realized he needed to act calm and tough if there was any chance of Scroggs accepting him for the man he was pretending to be. "Put the gun away," he said, trying to sound dismissive.

"No. First, you tell me who you are." The man stepped out of the shadows. A flood of light fell on his face.

Matt experienced a shock of recognition. "Ain't gonna do that," he replied. He realized that in the split second he had seen the assassin's face two years earlier, he'd lodged it in his memory. Now he was looking at nearly the same face again. It sent chills through him.

"You ain't gonna tell me your name? Why?"

"You don't need to know."

"I'll check the motel register."

"Are you so stupid to think I'd use my real name?" Matt saw the man flinch. It gave him encouragement.

Scroggs was silent for a moment. He appeared to be evaluating Matt. Finally, he said, "You don't look like a fed."

Matt laughed. "Now, that would be a joke." He paused, feigning hesitation, then spoke. "Listen, I ain't gonna tell you my fucking name and you'll understand why in a minute. But I will tell you what I told the bartender: I'm from a militia group in California."

"What are you doin' out here?"

"I came to make you a proposition."

"What kinda proposition?"

"A money one. You interested?"

"Go on."

Matt shook his head. "Not here, and sure as hell not while you're holding that."

Scroggs lowered the gun.

"That's better," said Matt. "Come on inside."

Now it was Scroggs who shook his head. "No. You come out to my place."

Matt thought for a moment. The mention of money had obviously piqued the man's interest. He figured it would be safe. "Your place it is."

"Can I use your phone?"

"Room has no phone."

"In the fuckin' lobby, then."

Matt shrugged. He followed Scroggs into the lobby and waited while Scroggs asked the clerk, whom he obviously knew, to use the desk phone. Matt stood close enough to listen in. Despite the cool air outside, it was stuffy in the lobby and the clerk, a small balding man, had set a tiny fan on the counter aimed at himself. Despite that, the man was sweating and the few wisps of hair he possessed waved stiff and wet in the breeze. "Home?" he asked Scroggs.

Scroggs nodded.

The clerk dialed the number from memory and handed the receiver to Scroggs. Scroggs leaned over the counter, held the phone to his ear, waited a moment, then said, "Honey, it's me. I'll be home in fifteen. And I'm bringin' company."

There was a brief pause before he said, "I don't know. Some guy from California. It's okay."

Another brief pause, then, in a lowered voice, "Yuh, me too."

Scroggs handed the phone back to the clerk and turned to Matt. "Okay, let's go. My truck is around the corner. Follow me. And, listen, I got a daughter so watch your fuckin' language. Got it?"

"Got it."

Moments later, Matt pulled his car in behind the truck. Once outside of town, the road was pitch black. Matt had to focus on the taillights of the truck to stay on the road. One of them flickered every so often, a loose connection. He sensed, but could not see, trees looming over him. Finally, they pulled off the road into a rutted driveway. Scroggs parked the truck off to the side and Matt eased the Ford Taurus in close to the rear bumper. When Matt got out of the car, Scroggs said, "Come on in. And remember what I said about language." As they walked to the house, Scroggs asked, "What do I tell my wife your name is?"

Matt thought quickly. "Bob Jones."

Scroggs laughed. "Okay, so it's Bob Jones. Careful of the stairs." Several of the stairs leading up to the porch were broken. Matt grabbed the banister to support himself, but it swayed under his weight. Only one of the two porch lights was working. A pair of moths flitted around it. Beyond the house,

Matt heard the high-pitched chirps of what must have been millions of cicadae. "I gotta fix them stairs before my daughter gets hurt."

A girl appeared at the door. She yanked the screen door open and threw herself into Scroggs' arms. "Daddy!" she cried.

Scroggs hoisted her off the ground and spun her around. "Hey yah, Sweetie Pie." He turned to Matt. "This here's my daughter, Annie."

Matt nodded. "Hi, Annie."

"And this here's my wife, Mary-Ann."

Matt turned to see a blond woman with tired eyes looking at him. "Evening, Mrs. Scroggs," he said.

Scroggs kissed his wife on the cheek, then motioned for Matt to follow him into the house.

As it was when he'd walked about the town, everything he saw screamed poverty and desperation. There were curtains in the windows, but they were tattered, though clean. The sink was filled with unwashed dishes, but they were covered by sudsy water. The linoleum floor was cracked in many places and curling up at the corners. A spider scampered across and disappeared under the table. "We were just about to have supper," said Mary-Ann Scroggs. "Fried bologna sandwiches. Can I make you one?"

Matt had never even heard of a fried bologna sandwich but he figured he'd better accept. "Sure, sounds good." He glanced at the stove where a frying pan sizzled with curling slices of bologna.

Scroggs pulled several beers from the refrigerator and placed them on the table. "Have a seat," he said. Matt, Scroggs, and Annie sat down. Mary-Ann Scroggs placed plastic containers of ketchup and mustard on the table before returning to the stove. Scroggs opened the beer bottles and handed one to Matt. He placed another across from him, presumably where his wife would sit, and took a long swig from his. "You just arrive today?" he asked.

"Yuh," replied Matt.

"Fly?"

Matt shook his head. "Drove." What he didn't tell Scroggs, of course, was that he'd flown to California, bought a used car, had a friend register it so he'd have California plates, then drove east, giving him time to settle into his new identity.

"How long's it take to get here from California drivin'?"

"Four, five days if you push it."

Scroggs was just about to ask another question when his wife appeared with a platter of sandwiches. She placed it in the middle of the table and took her seat.

"Help yourself, Mister Jones," she said. She lifted her beer to her lips and drained half the bottle.

While they ate, Scroggs and his wife quizzed him about where he'd said he come from. Mrs. Scroggs asked, "So, what's it like in California?"

Matt guessed they'd never been to California, probably never traveled outside of Maine, so he felt free to invent. He tapped his memory of the bus trip through California during the Baxter campaign to come up with details about the countryside. As he talked, he found that the bologna sandwich was surprisingly tasty. He told himself he'd have to make some for himself and Marcie when he returned, a prospect that seemed far distant from him at the moment.

After they ate, Scroggs invited Matt to join him in the cellar to see his gun collection. They descended a flight of dark, rickety stairs into a dirt-floored cellar that reeked of mold and a mixture of other smells Matt couldn't place. He guessed the place must have once been a farmhouse and the cellar had been used to store things like potatoes and fruits of various kinds.

Scroggs pulled a cord and a naked light bulb went on over a bench filled with at least a dozen firearms. The light bulb, swaying like a pendulum, cast traveling highlights across the array of guns, glinting along their barrels. It was obvious to Matt that Scroggs, however poor he might be, had spent much of his money on the collection. "Half of this belonged to my brother," Scroggs said.

"Donnie?"

"You knew him?"

"One of the guys from my militia was at the memorial service you held for him."

Scroggs gazed at Matt, visibly pleased. He lifted a nasty looking automatic rifle, long, with a pistol grip and a large magazine. "M4 Assault Carbine. It was Donnie's favorite. Here, feel how light it is." He handed the weapon to Matt.

Matt hefted it. He couldn't remember ever having held such a gun before. "Impressive," he said.

"She can fire up to a thousand rounds a minute," said Scroggs with visible pride.

"Also can be fitted with an M203 grenade launcher," said Matt, recalling details he'd memorized in the few weeks it took for his disguise, especially the tattoo, to settle in.

"Yuh. Sure like to get me one of them someday," Scroggs replied.

For an instant, Matt had a horrifying image of Scroggs using such a thing on the president. He was consoled only by the knowledge that there was no way the man could get something like that past the Secret Service. He looked at Scroggs. Light from the swaying bulb swept across the man's face. "You interested in hearing about my proposition?"

"Sure."

"Like I said, one of my boys was out here for your brother's memorial service. Said he heard you speak. You said something about taking up where your brother left off." Matt was glad to have had the complete report from Alexandra Lake.

"Is that what this is all about?"

Matt nodded. "I work for some high mucky-muck. He's authorized me to offer you money to finish the job."

"Who's that?"

"There you go again, wanting names," said Matt. "Something like this, no names are involved until you agree to do the job. Got it?"

"Yah, sure." Scroggs hesitated a moment then asked, "How do I know this is on the up and up?"

"If you tell me it's a go, you'll know when the money shows up in your bank account. That's also when you'll know the name and you'll see it's somebody who wants Baxter out of the way."

Matt reached into his pocket and pulled out a wad of bills. He counted out ten one hundred dollar notes. "Here's a thousand bucks down payment. Deposit it tomorrow while I wait outside the bank then give me the slip with your account number on it and in a few days there'll be a lot more in there."

Scroggs took the money and stared at it. "Jesus," he muttered. He glanced up at Matt. "How much more?"

"Two hundred and fifty grand."

Scroggs was speechless. Matt guessed the man had never imagined that kind of money before, at least not since he'd lost his job. A tiny flicker of hesitation appeared in Scroggs' eyes. "What makes you think I want to do the job? I got a family, you know. There's little Annie to think about."

"From what I heard, you'd do the job for free. We're just giving you the means and the encouragement. Also, there's another two-fifty when the job is done."

Scroggs took a deep breath. "Half a million?"

"That's the deal."

"Jesus. Do I get to think about it?"

Matt shook his head. He reached for the thousand dollars. "If you don't want to do it, we'll find somebody else." He hoped the man would back down, refuse the job. After having met Scroggs' family, Matt wanted no part of this business. It was easy when Scroggs had been a faceless person, but when Scroggs had warned him about foul language, and when little Annie had leapt into the man's arms at the screen door, everything had changed for Matt. He would just tell the president he couldn't go through with it and that would be that.

Scroggs hesitated. "How do I know this ain't some kind of frame-up?"

"With that kind of money you can change your identity, move your family. There's nobody to frame. Also, your sponsor's name will be on the transaction slip. Why would he do that if it was a setup? Why would he expose himself like that?"

"I need to think about it."

Matt nodded. He was happy to see the hesitation in the man. "Let me know tomorrow. I'll be at the motel."

That night, Matt's sleep was punctuated by dreams of violence. Shortly after seven he was lying in bed, arms behind his head, staring at the ceiling, when a sharp knock came at the door. "In a minute," he called. Heart racing, he threw some clothes on and shuffled bare-footed to the door. He prayed that Scroggs would refuse the offer and he could go back to Washington and Marci. He opened the door. "Well?" he asked.

"I'll do it," Scroggs said.

Matt's heart sank. He could see no way now of withdrawing the offer. He forced himself to nod and say, "Okay, then it's done. When the money appears in your account, begin your planning. We have a man inside the White House. We'll be able to get word to you about Baxter's schedule and when a good opportunity comes up."

"You got a man inside the fuckin' White House?"

Matt nodded. "We don't screw around."

Scroggs shook his head in amazement.

Later that morning, Matt, in the Ford Taurus, followed Scroggs into Guilford where the man deposited the thousand dollars and emerged to hand Matt a slip of paper with the account number written on it.

Matt wrote the number down then said, "Check your account in a few days."

After Scroggs left for Bass Run, Matt returned to the Covered Bridge Motel. He felt sick to his stomach and silently cursed the president for getting him into this. He had to force himself to remember everything that was at stake—Baxter's programs which he was convinced were what the country needed; possible peace in the Middle East; the danger of Senator Haskins getting his hands on foreign policy; and, of course, the presidency itself. Then he thought of his own revenge for the dreams of a family that he and Marci had lost. Later that evening, he called Marcie on a pay phone and gave her the account number.

For the first time in a long time, Matt Cannon got himself blind drunk. After talking with Marcie, he'd tuned to CNN. But when news came on about the president's forthcoming sailing vacation, he'd switched the TV off and gone into the restaurant where he ordered a steak dinner and a bottle of wine. He knew his friend well enough to know what Angus Baxter's intentions during the vacation were, and a fog of sadness had descended on him.

In addition, the previous day's encounter with Billy Scroggs and his family had left him feeling profoundly depressed. He felt he was now going to be responsible for the killing of two men, one his lifelong friend and the other, a man whose politics and potential for violence repelled him, but who had a daughter named Annie whom he obviously loved and who loved him in return.

He needed to wash away the memory of it, to wash the blood from his hands like Lady Macbeth. Except, in his case, the blood hadn't yet been shed and the cleaning agent would not be water, but alcohol. For, even if nothing had yet happened, he felt that with the call to Marcie he'd set something in motion that would run its inexorable course, almost impossible to stop. Until then, he'd only talked about the plan with Scroggs. If the money never appeared in Scroggs' account, it was unlikely the man would act; he would sense there had been some kind of betrayal and he would think it far too risky to go ahead.

And, of course, there had been a betrayal. But it was not Scroggs who'd been betrayed. It was the president who had betrayed their friendship by asking him to do this in the first place. And it was he who had betrayed Marcie into thinking this was nothing more than a simple sting operation. And he had betrayed himself. He'd acted against his best instincts, the idealism he had harbored in his breast ever since the early days of his work with Baxter.

Of course, his experience in the White House had shown him that his idealism was, more likely than not, misplaced. Politics, he'd learned, was shaped more by Lee Atwater's ads than by the Robert Kennedy speeches he'd studied so avidly. And who knew if RFK was as good as he appeared anyway? After all, hadn't he been considered by many to be ruthless and consumed with ambition? Now, Matt knew close hand what ruthless ambition was. He knew his friend, the president.

And he knew himself.

A cascade of betrayals.

After dinner, he'd found a bar in a neighboring town and ordered a scotch. The one scotch was followed by another until, by midnight, he could scarcely find his way back to the motel. At last inside his room, he rummaged his confused mind for some way to stop what he'd already set in motion. Seizing on a vague idea, he started to call Marcie. Maybe he could stop her. Later, he would explain to Baxter why he couldn't go through with it. But something pierced the fog of his mind and told him it wasn't a good idea to call Marcie from anything other than a pay phone. He slammed the receiver down, threw himself onto the bed, and passed out.

Marcie Gaudet was far more nervous than she'd expected to be. When she and Matt had discussed it, it seemed so easy—a simple sting operation to bring Karl Zacher down. Now she wondered what it was she'd gotten herself into.

For the first time in their relationship, a trickle of distrust seeped into her mind about Matt. He'd seemed terribly upset on the phone. She could sense he was struggling with himself and was on the verge of calling the whole thing off, whatever it was. But he'd gone ahead and given her the bank account number anyway. Now it was up to her. She knocked on the glass doors of the bank and the night guard came to let her in. "Working late, Ms. Gaudet?" he asked.

"I just remembered a report that's due first thing in the morning," she replied. "If I don't have it on the old man's desk when he comes in, all hell will break loose."

He smiled. "That's why I'm not some big shot. I get to work regular hours."

She went into her office, got a key to the main operations room, walked down the darkened corridor, unlocked the door, and let herself in. She found a terminal that had not been shut off, its screen saver creating surreal patterns in the semi-darkness. She sat down, took a deep breath, and nudged the mouse along the mouse pad. The screen brightened, revealing a cluster of icons. Its glow deepened the creases in her forehead. She placed the sheet on which she'd written the bank account number by the monitor and began to click her way through menus.

She heard the tired voice of Lorraine, the cleaning lady, singing in the corridor. "Damn!" she whispered. She rose from her seat, hurried to the door, opened it, stepped out into the corridor, and said, "Oh, hello Lorraine."

"Ms. Gaudet. What you be doin' here so late in t'night?"

"Some extra work. Boss wants it in the morning."

Lorraine shook her head. "You young folk. Don't know when to quit." She continued down the corridor with her mop and bucket.

Marcie made a show of going back to her office as if to retrieve something then returned to the operations room. Lorraine had passed around the corner. Marcie sat at the computer again and, working quickly, pulled up Zacher's account. Her fingers flew over the keyboard as she entered the data to effect the transfer. When she finished, she studied the screen for several moments, her right index finger poised over the "ENTER" key. Then with a shuddering breath, she tapped the key.

Chapter 13—"Hope you have Triple A."

Billy Scroggs couldn't believe his eyes when he looked at the piece of paper the teller at the Dexter Regional Federal Credit Union had slid across the counter to him. He looked up at the young woman who was regarding him with a frown and turned to walk out of the bank. Once in the street he could scarcely contain an impulse to run; he felt as though he had just robbed the bank, and from the way the teller had looked at him, she probably thought the same thing.

All the previous night he had worried about the arrangement. He couldn't get it out of his head that it was some kind of setup. But it was a lot of money, an opportunity to provide Annie the things that, until now, had been impossible. He especially wanted to put aside money for her education, a way of helping her lift herself out of the poverty he and Mary-Ann had been living with. In the end, he decided it was worth the risk. He would go along with it and trust himself to smell out anything that appeared suspicious. If his experience in Iraq taught him anything, it was that he knew how to evade trouble, to disguise his actions. He would simply apply those skills to go underground so deeply that even if it was a setup they wouldn't be able to nail him. He kept reminding himself it was all for Annie.

Forcing himself to remain calm, he walked slowly to his truck which was parked around the corner on School Street. He averted his eyes as a police cruiser drove slowly by. When it didn't stop, he breathed more freely. Looking over his shoulder at the cruiser disappearing around a corner, he climbed into the truck and started back for Bass Run. But he'd traveled no more than a mile when, on an impulse, he turned and headed for Bangor. It would take him several hours to make the round trip and he'd be late arriving back home, but he was determined to buy something for Mary-Ann and Annie. He couldn't remember the last time he'd had enough money to buy them gifts. He cautioned himself to make it something small, knowing that spending money extravagantly would be the surest way to raise suspicions.

At a large mall on the outskirts of Bangor, he shopped first for Annie and found a bright red bicycle he knew she would love. He told them to install a bell while he did some other shopping, then spent ten minutes strolling the mall corridors and looking into display windows. He entered a women's store and, after looking around for a long time, settled on a leather handbag for Mary-Ann. The sales clerk assured him it was the latest Italian design and that his wife would be thrilled. He was heading back to the bicycle shop when he saw a barbecue grill in a window. It was something Mary-Ann had always wanted, so he went in and bought it. Finally, he stored his purchases inside the truck and drove around back to the loading dock of the bicycle shop where he loaded the bike and set off again for Bass Run.

He resisted the temptation to buy himself a gun. That would be too much spending for one day. Besides, though he had kept an eye out, he'd seen no gun shops in the mall.

It was early evening when he arrived home. He was excited and couldn't wait to show Mary-Ann and Annie their gifts. He skidded the truck to a stop and, even before the engine stopped knocking, he called out to them. "Mary-Ann, Annie, come on outside."

The screen door burst open and Annie came hurtling down the porch steps and into his arms. "Daddy! You're late. We were worried."

Mary-Ann appeared at the door, wiping her hands on her apron. She wore an amused expression. "What're you doing, Billy? You're as excited as a little boy."

"I got something for you both. Come here."

He led Annie by the hand to the back of the truck where he hauled out the bike and set it down before her. "This is yours, Sweetheart."

Annie was speechless. Her jaw dropped. She reached out tentatively and touched the handle bars.

"Billy?" said Mary-Ann. "What...?" Then she saw the barbecue grill standing in the bed of the truck. She shook her head in wonderment. "Billy, have you gone nuts?"

"How about a cookout, tonight?" he asked. "I got the charcoal and stuff. Even got some hot dogs and rolls."

She gave a bemused laugh. "Well, sure, but—"

"—And I got somethin' else for you." He went around to the passenger door, reached in, and returned with the leather handbag.

Mary-Ann gasped and raised a hand to her mouth. Annie gave a delighted giggle. "Mommy, look. It's for you."

Mary-Ann gazed at her husband, her eyes narrowed with suspicion. "I don't understand."

"I'm tired of seein' you in church with your crummy old handbag while the other women strut around with new ones."

"How could you afford this?"

Annie tugged at his sleeve. "Daddy, can I ride my bike now?"

"Just for a few minutes, Sweetheart," said Scroggs. It's getting dark. But first thing in the mornin' we'll give it a real workout, okay?" He turned to Mary-Ann. "I came into some money for a job I'm gonna do."

"What kind of job?"

"I'll tell you later," he said, watching with delight as Annie scooted back and forth along the rutted driveway.

"Billy, it's not—"

"—Later."

"But I want to know. Billy...?"

He placed his hands on her shoulders, nodded toward Annie, who had pulled to a stop in front of him, and said, "Later, Honey." Then he mouthed the words, "When she's in bed." He turned to Annie. "Come on Sweetheart, help Daddy set up the barbecue while Mommy gets the stuff ready."

Later that night, after Annie went to bed, Scroggs and Mary-Ann sat out on the porch. Moths fluttered around the single light and threw themselves against the screen door. Mary-Ann asked if the job was related to the man from California who'd been out to their place several nights before. He nodded, telling her about the conversation and the transfer of funds.

"Remember I told you God would send somebody my way when it was time? Well, He did."

"Oh God, Billy! I don't like this," Mary-Ann said.

"You know it's somethin' I needed to do ever since Donnie got himself killed."

"I know, I know," she replied with deep resignation. "But what if you get killed?"

"I ain't gonna. I'll figure some way of doin' it without getting blown away in the process."

"But how can you? Donnie didn't want to die either."

"Now that's where you're wrong, Mary-Ann. You don't go walkin' up to the goddamned president, and pull a handgun, without expectin' to get yourself killed. It was somethin' real brave that he did, or real wacko, but he could afford to do it because he didn't have no wife and kid."

"And because you do, that means they won't get you?"

He shook his head. "No. It's because I'll figure a way of doin' the job without getting' caught. Elsewise, I won't do it."

"But you still could get caught. Do you think givin' Annie a bike will make up for her losin' her daddy?"

"Of course not."

"Or me? No handbag is worth you riskin' your life."

"I tell you, Mary-Ann," Scroggs said, "I ain't gonna take no unnecessary chances."

"But somethin' can go wrong. It always does."

"Ain't nothin' gonna go wrong. Believe me, I'm good. You know what I done in Iraq."

"Yes, but I still think—"

"—God protected me there, and He'll protect me now. Remember what it says in the Bible: 'Therefore saith the Lord, I will avenge me of mine enemies.' Well, Baxter is an enemy of God. He favors abortion;

he favors killin' the unborn for research; when he was a senator, he voted to kill Terri Schiavo. God will avenge him and He's chosen me as the instrument of that revenge."

"But, Billy...."

"I can't go against the will of God, Mary-Ann. I just can't."

They fell silent for a while, surrounded by the high-pitched, electric buzz of cicadae. Somewhere in the distance, an owl hooted. Finally, Scroggs leaned forward, looked into Mary-Ann's eyes, "Look, this is our big chance to get ourselves out of this hell hole. I gotta do it."

"I know, Billy, but I can't help worrying."

He smiled. "You don't need to worry 'bout me. It's Baxter you need to worry 'bout."

Matt Cannon couldn't wait to get out of Bass Run. For the second night in a row he had drunk himself into a stupor trying to forget why he was in this place. And now that he had set things in motion, it was time to return to Washington and wait. Having checked out earlier, he stuffed all his belongings haphazardly into his backpack, threw it over his shoulder, and went out into the parking lot. The sun was just rising above the serrated ridge to the east, giving him a long, distorted shadow as he hurried toward his car.

Minutes later, he was speeding along a two-lane road away from Bass Run when he noticed, in the rear-view mirror, a truck keeping pace with him, though he was already well above the speed limit. He furrowed his brow and accelerated to eighty. He went round a turn and the car skidded, almost ending up in the ditch. Finally, heart racing, he regained control and eased his foot off the accelerator. He checked the mirror. The truck was closer still.

"What the fuck?" he muttered. He tried to remember what Billy Scroggs' truck looked like. Could this be him? Had something gone wrong with the bank transfer?

Another glance at the mirror told him the truck was nearer still. After what happened in that last turn, he didn't dare go any faster. What if this was Scroggs after him with a gun? How would he defend himself?

Up ahead, Matt saw a widening of the road where a small building sat boarded up. An abandoned roadside stand. Should he pull over and hope the truck would pass? But before he could even consider an answer, the truck came roaring by on his left, cut across the road, almost colliding with him, and forced him, skidding, into the dirt lot. The truck also skidded into the lot and made a full one-eighty turn, sending up a cloud of dust.

As the dust settled, Matt steeled himself for a confrontation. There seemed no option except to take the offensive and hope that Scroggs, or whoever it was, would back down. He climbed out of the car and advanced toward the truck. The passenger side door swung open.

Cautiously, he approached. He looked in. Alexandra Lake!

"Get in. We need to talk," Lake said.

After a moment's hesitation, Matt climbed into the truck. "What the hell is this? What are you doing here?" he asked.

"Oh, man, is that ever the wrong question," she replied. "What are *you* doing here? Did you think your disguise would fool me? You still look like a Washington lawyer, only more disreputable if that's possible."

"Look, Ms. Lake, I—"

"—Why go to a bank with Scroggs?"

"You're tailing me?"

"I'm tailing Scroggs. It's my job. Remember? What the fuck is going on?"

"Ms. Lake, you don't need to know."

"Bullshit! Something's going down involving my target. And you might as well call me Alex because we're about to have a knock-down-drag-out fight until you tell me what's up."

"I can't tell you anything."

"Really?" Alexandra leaned toward Matt, reached into the glove box, and pulled out a Sig Sauer 229 handgun. She held the gun inches from Matt's nose, aimed out the window, and squeezed the trigger. BAM! The left front tire on Matt's car hissed flat.

"What the fuck?" Matt cried.

"Hope you have Triple A."

"You're crazy!"

"There's a tire company twenty miles up the road. I'll give you a lift when you talk. Otherwise, you walk."

"Shit!"

"Listen, Dude, the president calls me to the White House. I show up and there's nobody from Homeland Security, nobody from Justice, the Secret Service, ATF. Just you and the president."

"It's complicated," said Matt.

"No, it's not."

"What do you mean?"

"Not in the least complicated. So who's the target of your sting operation?"

"What makes you think—"

"—Oh, come on!," Alexandra replied. "What do you take me for, some innocent, pretty little girl? I'm a fucking federal agent! I can smell shit from a mile away. You show up here looking for the guy who wants to kill the president then you take him to a bank. Now why would he do that, I ask myself."

Matt gave a short laugh. "You're not the shy person I met before."

"That was in the Oval Office. It's fucking intimidating. But you're in my territory now. So, why the bank? Who's the target?"

"You certainly aren't innocent, but you are pretty."

"I know. And you're stalling. Who's the target? And don't tell me it's Scroggs; he's too small for this kind of operation. You're going after someone bigger and you need to tell me because you're getting in my way."

"Alex, I ...." Matt paused. Finally, he asked, "Do you think Donnie Scroggs acted alone?"

"No. He was even poorer than his brother, yet we learned he stayed at an Arlington hotel for a week. Somebody funded him."

"Who?"

"We couldn't get anything, but you have a good idea who was behind it and that's why you're doing this."

"Do you know who Karl Zacher is?" Matt asked.

"Of course. A number one scumbag with his little troupe of hookers."

"Troupe of hookers?"

"Boy and girl hookers Zacher pays to screw targets for blackmail. Videos, et cetera. You'd be surprised at how much a guy will spill to somebody who'd just given him a loving blow job, or a bored wife will say to a stud who just fucked her brains out."

Matt shook his head in amazement. "Justice knows that much about Zacher?"

"No. I do."

"How?"

"I'll tell you, but first, is Zacher your target?"

"Yes."

"Are you guys insane? Jesus, if that's the kind of thinking that goes on at the White House, I swear to God I'm moving to Canada! Do you have any idea how dangerous the game you're playing is? Scroggs is no pussycat. He's a whole lot more put together than his brother was and you're thinking of setting him loose just to get Zacher? What if you can't stop him? Have you thought of that?"

Matt stared at her. Several possible answers came to him but none was appropriate. The only true answer was: Yes, that's the whole idea.

When Matt didn't answer her, Alexandra continued. "By the way, you look like shit. I saw you come out of the liquor store last night. I think you put on a world class drunk, like a man who's not too happy with what he's doing."

"How do you know about Zacher's troupe?" Matt asked.

"Heather."

"Heather?"

"My roommate at Georgetown. She was one of his girls. Tuition money. She worked for several years then got married and quit. A year or so later he tried to get her to come back but she refused. He threatened to send her husband a video of her with a client. She didn't believe he'd do it. He did. She drove herself into a bridge abutment."

"Jesus!" said Matt.

"Yuh, spare me. So where do we go from here?"

"What do you intend to do?"

"Exactly what I'm doing. Keep tabs on Scroggs. Except now I have the additional problem of trying to screw up your insane plans. And you know what? I'm thinking you'd be happy if I threw a wrench into things. I think that's why you drank yourself silly last night. You don't want it to play out. You're like the guy who uses lipstick to write, 'stop me before I kill again' on the mirror."

"I don't use lipstick."

"Funny. Let's buy you a new tire."

A week later, dressed for vacation, the First Family stood near the missile launcher on the deck of the Guided Missile Frigate, *USS Robert G. Bradley*. Among the many people surrounding them were a dozen Secret Service men, a half dozen officers of the ship, the president's personal physician, Jim Stockton, who always traveled with him, and his military aide, made conspicuous by the locked briefcase, called the "football," that he gripped in his right hand. Sitting on the deck near the boarding ladder was a pile of personal gear bags and numerous boxes of food and other supplies.

The frigate had slowed to a crawl in the deep waters a mile or so off Great Point Light at the northern tip of Nantucket. Ahead, astern, and on both sides of them, three Secret Service cabin cruisers, four high-speed power boats, and two U. S. Coast Guard "Island" class patrol boats cruised a wide circle around the frigate, maintaining a secure perimeter.

A half mile ahead, a large sailboat sat on its wavy reflection, riding a gentle swell. It was a brand new Sou'wester 70 loaned to the presidential party by the Hinkley Company from Southwest Harbor on Mount Desert Island, Maine. They had the reputation of being some of the finest yachts built in the world. When the White House had contacted them about the possibility of a loan, the Hinkley people checked with the owners for whom the boat had been built but not yet delivered. The owners agreed happily, even asking if it would be appropriate to name the boat *Grace*.

When he was approached with this suggestion by his advance staff, the president, deeply moved, agreed immediately and assigned his staff to finding a suitable gift for both Hinkley and the prospective owners.

Baxter had made two concessions to the Secret Service. First, he'd agreed to board the yacht at sea rather than at some port. Accordingly, it was a crew of experienced Secret Service agents plus a few people from Hinkley who had sailed the boat down from Maine and now stood on her deck ready to transfer control to the president. In the meantime, the president and his family had been flown out to the *USS Robert G. Bradley* aboard *Marine One*.

Since every presidential departure or arrival in a public place, including just getting in and out of the limousine, is considered a security threat requiring advance work and special arrangements, the Secret Service was saved a great deal of effort and worry by the president's acquiescence to this transfer at sea.

The second concession he'd made, this time with a great deal more reluctance, was to permit an agent to be on board the sailboat with the family. However, he'd exacted a solemn promise that the man would absolutely respect the privacy of the First Family whenever they gathered to talk, for he had planned to use this vacation to reacquaint himself with his children and grandchildren. Of course, he didn't tell anyone about the heavy weight of knowledge in his chest that this would be the last time he would enjoy such extended time with them.

As the frigate drew to within a few hundred yards of *Grace*, the president and his family, along with several sailors, descended the boarding ladder to a waiting motor launch. The family's gear and supplies had already been transferred to the launch, so as soon as they were aboard, the launch's engines rumbled to life and they were soon crossing over to *Grace*.

The president was dressed in T-shirt, shorts, and boating moccasins. With the sunglasses perched on his nose he gave the appearance of an older John Kennedy about which his son and daughter had teased him aboard the helicopter. He watched the huge, white "49" that identified the frigate grow smaller, then turned to gaze at the lovely sailboat he was about to command for more than a week. She was slightly more than seventy feet long, her topsides painted a dark blue and framed by a brilliant white waterline and a thin gold boot top ending at the bow and stern with the Hinkley logo. This version of the yacht was ketch-rigged, its after mast—the mizzen—rising to a height equal to about the third set of spreaders on the main mast.

They approached the boat from astern and Baxter saw the letters *GRACE* in gold adorning the transom. Her homeport was identified as "Southwest Harbor, Maine." The president's eyes welled. He remembered the time, as newlyweds, that he and Grace toured the Maine coast and ended up in Southwest Harbor. They'd poked around the Hinkley yard and he'd developed an abiding love for these boats. He looked forward to the coming days with his family.

The time would be interrupted only twice for meetings that he deemed of supreme importance to the country … and to his legacy. On the following Monday he planned to meet with leaders of the House and Senate to push forward on the Grace Baxter Education Bill, and, two days later, a critical meeting with the Secretary of State in preparation for a peace conference with the Palestinian leader, Ahmad Bakhit, and the Israeli prime minister, Jehu Golani. Both meetings would take place aboard the *Robert G. Bradley*.

Spitting mist from its exhaust, the motor launch pulled up alongside *Grace*. Sailors threw lines up to the men on board and as soon as the launch was secured to *Grace*, a Secret Service man attached an aluminum boarding ladder to its brackets and opened the life-line gate. One by one, the president and his family boarded *Grace*. Once they were aboard, a man came forward and said, "Good morning, Mister President. I'm Jack Emory from Hinkley. Welcome aboard."

Baxter shook the man's hand, pumping vigorously. "Mister Emory, you don't know how much this means to me and my family. Thank you very much. Also thank the fine folks for whom you built this boat. I plan to have you all over to the White House soon."

"Our pleasure, sir," Emory replied. "May I show you around while they stow your gear?"

"Please do."

With Emory leading the way, they descended the companionway into a lush, cherry-trimmed interior. On the starboard side of the main cabin was a large, U-shaped seat, big as a sofa, before a fiddled table. Opposite, on the port side, was another seat, L-shaped. Further aft on the port side was a well-equipped galley with a stove, oven, and a double sink. After having all his meals cooked for him at the White House, Baxter was looking forward to treating his family to his own cooking. He planned buttermilk pancakes for the following morning.

Beyond the chart table, a door opened into the aft cabin. Jack Emory said, "It's not exactly the Lincoln Bedroom, Mister President, but this is your cabin. We've installed a direct line to the Bradley so you can have total privacy if necessary."

Baxter surveyed the cabin with its private head and said, "It'll do quite nicely, Mister Emory. You folks build handsome boats."

"Thank you, sir."

They moved to the part of the boat forward of the main cabin. Next came two cabins, one to starboard and one to port. Emory opened the door of the port cabin. "Each of these is identical with a double berth and a private head, Mister President. We figure your son and daughter with their spouses would like to use these."

"Fine by me," said Maxwell. "Looks pretty plush if you ask me."

Emory opened a door mounted on the centerline of the boat. "And this is the forward cabin. Four berths, two upper and two lower. Just right for the grandchildren and the agent we understand will be sailing with you."

The president turned to smile at the agent, Mickey Weekes, a man who had crewed on several Newport-to-Bermuda races. "Don't worry, Mickey, you'll love bunking up with the kids."

Mickey smiled good-naturedly. "I'm sure I will, Mister President."

Once they had explored below decks, Emory gave the president a tour topside pointing out special features such as how the sails automatically furled into the masts with the push of a button, and how the dodger—the canvass cover over the companionway—was raised and lowered. Then he wished the family good sailing and lowered himself into the motor launch along with the others who had helped deliver the boat from Maine.

Baxter watched the launch recede, then turned and said, "Well, folks, I say it's time for some lunch before we shove off. I've got the makings for cold cuts—ham, turkey, chicken, roast beef—with all the trimmings. And ..." he squatted to address the grandchildren, "...peanut butter and jelly. So what will it be?"

Hesitantly at first, because nobody was used to this, they gave him their orders. All except, Mickey Weekes.

"What about you, Mickey?"

"Oh, that's all right, Mister President. I'll make my own when you're all finished."

"Nonsense. While you're on this boat, you're part of the family and the penalty is you've got to eat my cooking."

Blushing, Weekes said, "If you insist, Mister President. I'll...I'll have a peanut butter and jelly sandwich."

Baxter smiled. "You see, you do belong in the forward cabin with the children."

Weekes gave a shy smile, "Yes, sir."

Baxter told them to sort their things in their cabins while he prepared lunch. Then he went into the galley and began to work. He closed his eyes tightly. Yes, he said to himself, this would be a wonderful place for him to say the goodbyes that only he knew he would be saying.

Later that evening, the president went into his cabin and emerged with a large duffel bag that he hauled on deck, announcing he had gifts for everyone. He pulled out dark blue baseball caps with the boat's name, *Grace*, embroidered on the front and passed them around. Then he pulled out sailing shirts and, examining the labels to make sure the sizes matched the individualized shirts, handed each person his or her own shirt. Embroidered discreetly on the front of each shirt was the legend "USS Grace." Each person's name was embroidered over the pocket.

"I figured because we no longer have a presidential yacht after that skinflint, Jimmy Carter, sold the *Sequoia*," he said, "then I will, by executive order, declare Grace the presidential yacht for as long as we are aboard her." He examined another shirt and handed it to Mickey Weekes.

Weekes was visibly moved. "I get one too, Mister President?"

"I told you, while you're aboard this boat, you're part of the family. It's something to show your grandchildren."

Before going to bed that first night aboard *Grace*, Baxter told everybody he wanted them up two hours before dawn to be underway. They protested mildly but relented when he said that he had something to show them that would remind them of their mother.

He awoke only two or three times in the night. Unlike at the White House where he could wander corridors, he was confined to his cabin lest he wake the others and this probably helped him sleep better than most nights. That, and the gentle rocking of the boat on the waves. When he awoke at 4:00 am to the alarm on his digital wristwatch, he dressed and went into the main cabin where he started coffee brewing.

He gently knocked on the doors of the starboard and port cabins until Maxwell and Kyla answered. Telling them that coffee was on and to wake the others, he mounted the companionway steps. He emerged on deck into a star-strewn morning. Cassiopeia was sitting low on the northern horizon, tilted and balanced on the right-hand point of her "W." He measured three fingers above the easternmost star of Cassiopeia, and found Ursa Minor, the Little Dipper. Looking to the west, he saw the full moon just where he expected it to be, fat and low and approaching the horizon. He checked the red glow of the digital wind instruments and learned they had a fifteen knot breeze out of the south-southwest—perfect for what he had in mind. The USS *Robert G. Bradley* loomed several hundred yards to the east, its lights burning brightly. Beyond her, a faint rim of blood red was beginning to show on the eastern horizon.

He went below. Mickey Weekes and Kyla were already pouring coffee and he could hear stirrings from the others. "Morning, folks," he said.

"Good morning, Mister President."

"Morning, Dad."

"It's a perfect day for what I plan to show you," Baxter said. "Absolutely clear and a good breeze from the south, south-west."

"So what is it you have in mind, Dad?" asked Maxwell who had just emerged from his cabin.

"Only the most miraculous sail you could imagine. You'll see." He sat at the navigation table, turned the radio dial to channel 16—used only for distress calls and to initiate contact—lifted the mike from its bracket, pressed the send button, and said, "Bradley, come in please. This is *Grace*. Over."

Instantly, the reply came. "*Grace ... Bradley* here. Good morning Mister President. Over."

"Good morning. Switch to channel 49, please. Over." Special crystals had been installed on *Grace* and the USS *Robert G. Bradley* radio sets to ensure secure communications.

"Switching channel 49, sir. Over."

The president spun the dial, pressed the send button again, and said, "*Bradley*, this is *Grace* on channel 49. Over."

"*Grace ... Bradley* here. This is Commander Lawton. Over."

"Good to see you up so bright and early, Commander. Lovely day. I plan to shove off in half an hour. I'll be heading on a course of two-eight-zero and I request that you take up station abeam of us to the north. You have a hell of a lot of lights that would ruin the effect of the rising sun. I would like there to be no lights to the east or the west of us. Over."

"Copy that, sir. Two-eight-zero degrees; abeam to the north on *Grace's* starboard side. Will do. Over."

"Thank you, Commander. And you folks pay attention to what happens when the sun comes up. Look to both the east and west. Over."

"Will do, sir. I think I know what you're doing; sounds to me like you checked the almanac. Will that be all, sir? Over."

"Yes, thank you. *Grace* switching back to channel 16. Over and out."

"*Bradley* to 16. Good sailing, sir. Over and out."

When everyone was on deck, they raised the sails and set a course for Woods Hole some thirty nautical miles away. Soon, they were making a solid nine knots. *Grace* leaned slightly to port on a starboard beam reach in seas of one foot— ideal sailing conditions. Baxter was at the wheel with little Petey in his lap. Petey's hands, gripping the wheel, were covered by Baxter's who was guiding him.

"Slightly to port, Petey," said the president. "Watch the jib luff. If it starts to break, bear off to port until it fills with wind again." Baxter closed his eyes to concentrate on the feel of wind in his hair. It reminded him of the many sailing cruises he and Grace had taken alone.

He checked his watch. 5:02. He looked to the east. The horizon was now burnished gold, the sky above it a deep cobalt blue. On Grace's port side, the intermittent flash of a lighthouse told him they were just passing close by Cape Poge on Martha's Vineyard. Because there would not be much sea room to the south for the next ten or fifteen minutes, the Coast Guard Patrol Boat that had been guarding their port side drew back into their wake. It continued to cross Grace's wake and take up station on her starboard quarter because the president had insisted he wanted a clear view astern, unmarred by running lights. Baxter knew that as soon as they passed the cape, the patrol boat would resume its station because it was here that the water opened up into the yawning mouth of Edgartown Harbor.

"Okay, everybody, listen up," the president said. "The sun will be up in six or seven minutes and then you're going to see something that will blow your minds. Your mother and I saw it once and she wrote a poem about it." He looked straight ahead of them to see the moon nearly at the western horizon. He smiled.

At 5:09 the rim of the sun peeked above the horizon. Baxter glanced at it then turned to study the faces of his family. They were enraptured, all bathed in a golden light. No one spoke. The only sounds were the foamy hiss of salt water along the swiftly moving hull and, in the distance to starboard, the faint rumble of the frigate's engines. He looked at Kyla who smiled at him. Above Kyla's head, the moon sat full and fat and Kyla's wind-whipped hair seemed to brush its surface. As each year passed, Kyla looked more and more like her mother, he thought. He looked over his shoulder. The sun was three-quarters up. "Now look forward," he called out.

They all turned. He heard Maxwell gasp and it sent a surge of joy through him. He looked to starboard and saw that dozens of men were standing on the bridge and the deck of the frigate, apparently watching the play of moon and sun. Again, he looked over his shoulder. The lower rim of the sun was just lifting free of the horizon. He looked forward. The full moon sat heavily on the western horizon.

In a soft, reverent voice, he recited, " ... and the harvest moon made itself heavy in the west to seesaw the sun from Haleakala's kiln ...."

Kyla gazed at him, smiling. "Mother's poem?"

Baxter nodded.

Maxwell said, "It's like we're on a wire vibrating between the sun and the moon."

"Your mother said almost exactly the same thing."

It didn't last long. Like a human life, Baxter thought. Soon, the moon sank below the horizon and the moment was over. But he'd shown it to the people he loved and from their reaction, he knew they would never forget it. All their lives, when they saw the same stunning confluence, they would think of him ... and their mother.

And then he shivered to think he would never again see such beauty.

It was at that moment that Petey called out, "Grandpa, look. There's a boat coming toward us."

Baxter looked to port. A powerboat, throwing scarves of spray from its bow, was speeding toward them out of Edgartown Harbor.

Mickey Weekes drew his gun.

"Oh, no," Baxter muttered to himself. "Not so soon. Please God, not so soon. Not with my family present."

Chapter 14—Adam Krasinsky

Though she'd visited Bob's Bar each day for a week at the time Billy Scroggs usually dropped in, Alexandra Lake had seen no sign of the man. And that left her worried. Toward the middle of the week she'd even taken to cruising around Bass Run as inconspicuously as possible hoping to catch sight of Scroggs. It was inconceivable that in all that time the man wouldn't have an errand to run—some grocery shopping with his wife and kid, a fill-up at the gas station, a cigarette run. But there was nothing. It was as if the man had disappeared from the face of the earth. And there had also been no sign of Mary-Ann Scroggs.

She thought, perhaps, Scroggs might have come down with something and she would see Mary-Ann Scroggs dropping into the drugstore for some medications. But she, too, never appeared.

She couldn't believe she'd lost her man. She debated whether to alert her higher-ups, or Matt Cannon, but decided first she would risk going out to the Scroggs' place to see if there were any signs of life. She waited until dusk before making the five-mile drive along the lonely, rutted road leading to where Scroggs lived.

About a half mile from the place, she pulled deep into an old logging road that branched off to the right, parked the car behind a stand of trees, and got out to walk the rest of the way. She knew the logging road continued further into the woods for a distance, turned left to parallel the main road, then connected with it again about fifty yards from Scroggs' house. She was confident she'd be able to see the house without going out onto the main road. Otherwise, there was too great a risk that Scroggs, if he was there, would see her and the game would be up. The department would have to repeat the long and difficult task of planting somebody new in Bass Run and by that time, it might be too late.

Her nerves were taut as she trudged along the rutted dirt road. Several times she jumped at the sudden sound of an animal in the undergrowth. Once, she caught sight of a coyote some fifty yards ahead of her. Both she and the animal stopped and stared at each other for several seconds before the coyote bounded into the woods. Another time, a deer bolted across the road from her left to her right no more than twenty yards ahead of her. It took a few minutes for Alexandra's heart to stop beating furiously.

At last, she saw a brightening up ahead and guessed it was where the logging road rejoined the main road. She approached cautiously, looking for a spot to her right where she might be able to see Scroggs' house. She came to a small, grassy clearing bordered by a thin line of trees. Here, she felt Scroggs' presence because there were spent cartridges strewn across the ground. *Practice?*

Moving as quietly as possible, Alexandra advanced toward the line of pine trees. At first, she saw the roof of the house, then, as she took a few more steps, the rest of the house came into view. She scanned the front yard and the driveway. Scroggs' truck wasn't there. Though it was dusk, there were no lights in the windows. Nothing. No sign of life.

She was sure of it now—she'd lost her man.

The Secret Service people must have seen the speeding power boat at the same moment Baxter and Weekes did. Past his starboard quarter he saw the bow of the Coast Guard Patrol Boat lift like a raring stallion, throwing out sheets of seawater, and hurtle through *Grace's* wake toward the power boat. At the same time, he heard the whap-whap-whap of helicopter blades and turned to see an HH-65 Dolphin lift off from the Coast Guard cutter. "Kids, get below decks now!" he cried to the grandchildren. "Everybody else, too!"

"I'm afraid that includes you, too, Mister President," said Mickey Weekes.

Baxter looked at the man, then back at the onrushing powerboat. He felt a tremble pass through his body. He shook his head. "Go below, Mickey."

"Begging your pardon, sir, but not without you."

"Mickey, I—" Baxter started to say, but his words were drowned out by the roar of the helicopter passing overhead. He looked to port and saw the powerboat still coming on, full speed. To his left, the patrol boat was bearing down on them, leaping the waves, spitting foaming seawater from its bow. It appeared to Baxter that the patrol boat and the powerboat were on a collision course. But there was still a good hundred yards separating them. The point of collision would be almost exactly where *Grace* would be if she maintained her current speed.

Could he have been so wrong about Scroggs?

"Mickey, loose the jib sheets," Baxter called as he himself reached for the mainsheet. "We've got to spill wind from these sails." His first thought when he saw the powerboat was that there could be a rifleman aboard. And though it was far too early, he found himself surprisingly prepared for it—perhaps because it all happened so suddenly. But then a sickening thought came to him. What if it wasn't a rifleman? What if the boat was rigged with a bomb? Is it possible this could be a suicide attempt like all those car bombs in Iraq and Afghanistan, like the 9/11 terrorists?

He thought of his children and grandchildren and tried desperately to slow *Grace* down in hopes of giving the patrol boat a few extra seconds to close the gap.

Maxwell and Kyla appeared in the companionway. "I don't know what's going on," Maxwell said, "but I intend to help."

"Me, too," said Kyla.

"For God's sake make sure the kids stay below," Baxter said.

"They will."

"Maxwell ... Kyla, help Mickey take in the sails while I fire the engine up," said Baxter as he lunged for the wheel and the engine controls. He fumbled at the controls. Perhaps if he could put on a burst of reverse speed .... Within seconds the diesel engine roared to life and he jammed the transmission into reverse even before the mainsail was completely down. For a few seconds the engine and the wind-filled sail fought each other, one trying to drive *Grace* forward, the other back. Finally, the mainsail cascaded down in folds, burying the occupants of *Grace's* cockpit.

For a moment, Baxter lost sight of what was happening to port of *Grace*, but the growing sounds of engines made it clear that a collision was imminent.

He struggled from under the heavy weight of the mainsail. When he looked, the powerboat was still coming full bore at *Grace*. His slowing tactics appeared to have failed.

The patrol boat also was still coming at breakneck speed. It appeared all three boats would meet in a massive collision.

Baxter struggled to slam the transmission into forward, hoping to turn away from the boat. But just at the last moment, the powerboat swerved to its port and decelerated abruptly to avoid the patrol boat. It fell off its bow wave, digging its bow into the sea, and the occupants, now clearly visible, lurched forward.

One of them, a woman, stumbled and was prevented from being thrown overboard only when one of the men grabbed her by the legs. The patrol boat also slowed rapidly, its engines screaming in reverse. Its steep bow wave, still hurtling forward, nearly swamped the powerboat which no longer had forward momentum. It rocked violently in the bow wave pushed forward by the patrol boat. One of the men in the powerboat shouted, "What the hell's goin' on? Jesus Christ!" His words were slurred.

A coastguardsman, holding an electric bullhorn, said, "Put your hands where we can see them."

"Shit man, we ain't carrying no drugs."

"Put your hands where we can see them and stay put. We're coming aboard."

"Aw, man! Whaz this all about?"

Maxwell came up to the president. "Who are they?" he asked.

"Not who I ... we ... thought they were," replied Baxter. "They're just a bunch of drunks out for a wild ride. There's no danger. But I still want the kids to stay below."

"Why?"

"Because those two women are butt naked, that's why. Guess they really were having a good time. I'll bet the men on that patrol boat are fighting over who gets to board them."

Matt Cannon dawdled on his way back to Washington. He spent a lot of time thinking about Alexandra Lake. There was no denying she was a brilliant woman; she'd figured out what he was doing in no time. He let out an ironic chuckle when he remembered how appalled she had been at the dangerous game they were playing. She'd made it clear that once Scroggs was funded and pointed in the president's direction, he would be difficult to stop.

What she didn't know, however, was that that was the point.

"That's the whole fucking point!" he shouted to himself as he pulled into a rest area to settle his nerves.

Given his appearance and his state of agitation, Matt wasn't eager to see Marcie. His emotions were so raw, he was feeling so fragile, that if he took her out to a nice restaurant for a good meal and few drinks—something he desperately wanted to do—he was afraid he'd blurt everything to her. So he decided to lay over in Boston for a few days to give his troubled mind some time to settle down and to strip himself of as much of his disguise as possible. Though it would take some time for his hair to grow back, he could at least get rid of the mustache and give his fingernails something approaching a decent trim. Later, he would face the painful sessions to remove the tattoo.

After checking himself in at the Commonwealth Hotel in Kenmore Square—why not treat himself, he thought—he took a long shower and shaved. Having bought a package of emery boards at the hotel's gift store, he set to work on his nails while he half-watched and listened to CNN.

Somewhat later, he took a nap and, feeling refreshed when he awoke, decided to visit the Museum of Fine Arts.

He realized that he was not being subtle at all about trying to ease his way back into some semblance of civilization and culture, but he allowed himself to go with it. He remembered going to the museum with his old ethics professor at Harvard Law, Adam Krasinski and he had the sudden urge to talk with the man. Using his cell phone, he called information, got the main number for Harvard, and, after a few tries, reached the professor.

"Matt Cannon!" said Krasinski. "What a pleasure to hear from you after all this time. How is your friend, the president?"

Matt paused for a moment before answering, "He's fine, Professor." He asked Krasinski if he might be free for dinner.

"Ah, unfortunately I have an engagement tonight. However, I'm free for lunch tomorrow if that suits you."

"That would be perfect," Matt said. "I'm in Boston for a few days." They made arrangements about where and when to meet, then hung up.

That night, Matt went to a Red Sox game at Fenway Park. Though there were no tickets available at the box office, he managed to scalp a box seat behind the first base dugout for three times the face value. All through the game he was reminded of the stories Angus Baxter had told him about performing on this same field as a rookie and by the end of the game, he knew why it was he had called Adam Krasinski. He was impatient to meet with the man the following day.

As eager as he was to get on with it, Billy Scroggs thought it was far too soon to go into action. There were things to check out first, things to plan. Careful, methodical—those were the key words. No stupid, sudden rush at the president.

He was happy he'd decided to take Mary-Ann and Annie for a vacation the previous week. They'd gone to Camden and took a week-long windjammer cruise along the coast of Maine. All that idle time had given him a chance to work out a detailed plan and now he was ready to put it into motion. He was even reminded of his mission when, on the third day of the cruise, they passed close by Baxter Island.

Now, he sat in a slant of sunlight before a computer terminal at the library. He pulled up an internet search engine, and typed in "Karl Zacher."

After a moment, the computer returned eleven references to Zacher. He started to peruse them. Most talked about fund raising and Senator Haskins. But one was a newspaper account mentioning, among other things, that Zacher had a daughter, Linda, attending Harvard University. It was the kind of information Scroggs was looking for. He entered "Linda Zacher" in the search field. Two references came up. One listed a field of finishers for a road race in Boston where she'd finished twelfth among the women.

The second was a Harvard University site listing her as an editor for the student newspaper. Having thus confirmed Zacher's daughter was, indeed, at Harvard, Scroggs smiled.

Insurance.

Matt Cannon and Adam Krasinski entered a small restaurant on Newbury Street in Boston. They took a table by a window looking out on the busy street crowded with passers-by, many of them summer students at nearby Berklee College of Music, judging by the instrument cases they carried.

After ordering cheeseburgers and sodas, they talked for a while about Marcie Gaudet and about Krasinski's family, then Matt said, "In all my years at Harvard, your course in ethics is the one that made the most impression on me."

"I'm flattered," said Professor Krasinski. "But I'm guessing you didn't bring that up idly. You have a real-world question of ethics and you're hoping I can offer you some help. I can see by your face that something's troubling you."

"Yuh, something like that. I can only talk in generalities. I can't tell you what the real issue is."

"I see. This sounds like one of those 'I have a friend' questions. Except, in your case, I believe you do have a friend and I suspect I know who it is." He gazed at Matt over the rims of eyeglasses that sat propped on the tip of his nose.

"You'd probably be right."

Krasinski glanced to his right and left, leaned forward, and in a soft voice said, "Yes, well, it either makes me feel good, or it makes me feel nervous, that someone so close to the president is asking questions about ethics. The problem is, I don't know which."

"I don't know, either."

"That bad, huh?" In the street, a police cruiser sped past, siren blaring, its blue and white strobe lights flashing. They reflected momentarily in Krasinski's glasses. "Well, I'm afraid you won't like my answer."

"Why not?" Matt asked, watching the police cruiser and remembering the assassination attempt—the hot feel of bullets slamming into his body.

"Because I think you've done or are contemplating doing something, probably acting for the president, and you think by engaging me in a classroom discussion of such subjects as, say, the deontologists who judge moral actions on the basis of rules like Kant's categorical imperative—if the action were to become a general rule and bad things would result, then it is immoral; or, perhaps, the consequentialists, who believe that if the consequences of an action are good, then the action is moral, as if all possible consequences could ever be known; or the Christian thinkers who hold that ends never justify means and God is the only arbiter of moral action and we must obey His laws; or—"

"—Professor Krasinski, I didn't expect—"

"—or we could delve further and discuss all the permutations and variations of these general ethical theories; we could certainly discuss old Immanuel Kant and David Hume and Confucius and Aquinas and, of course, we mustn't forget the pragmatists, John Stuart Mill and Jeremy Bentham. We could explore the subtleties of each of their doctrines, but in the end—in the end, Matt—it would just be a bunch of scribbling on the classroom board because the answer to your question can't be found there. Hell, completely satisfactory answers to ethical questions haven't been found despite thousands of years of heavy thinking by some minds far more brilliant than ours."

"Professor Krasinski," said Matt. "That's not what I was looking for."

"Good. I made that recitation as a way of demonstrating to you that classroom ethical theory won't solve your problem. And, of course, to impress you," Krasinski said with a teasing smile. "So what are you looking for?"

"I don't know. I—"

"—You're looking for me to offer philosophical or scholarly forgiveness for something you've done or are planning to do."

Matt shrugged. "I suppose I was just trying to figure it out for myself."

"Well you won't find the answer by looking outside yourself. It doesn't exist in textbooks or on blackboards or, for that matter, in old academics like me; it exists within yourself."

"But what if I'm wrong?"

Krasinski waited for the waitress to finish delivering the cheeseburgers and leave the table. "Then you'll suffer the consequences." He paused, leaned toward Matt, and said, "All that aside, maybe there is something I can offer. If the president is, say, planning to initiate a war …" He glanced to his left and right again. "…or assassinate some foreign leader because he truly believes a greater good would come of it, you have to ask yourself if you would be willing to make that sort of thing standard practice for everybody. In other words, ask yourself: would you be willing to accept it as a universal principle?

"That's our old friend, Kant speaking. The problem is, there are lots of true believers in this world and they don't all believe what you believe. For example, some of them truly believe, to the roots of their souls, that it would be the greater good for humanity to rid the world of American power. And if you act as if the principle applies to you but not to them, then your argument is reduced to pure power—might makes right."

"It seems that's the only rule we go by in the end anyway."

"And maybe it has to be."

"What do you mean?"

"It's possible that presidents can't afford the luxury of being moral beings, or even Christians. It's possible they can't afford to worry about the niceties of ethical theory."

"How so?"

"It seems to me a president is obligated to be so concerned about the safety of the nation and the welfare of its people that he can't afford to worry about the finer points of means."

"That's not very heartening."

"Perhaps not, but the game is defined by those willing to use the most evil means, because they are usually the most effective. If a president is to honor his oath, he must respond in kind. You can dress up your actions, put nice clothes on them—for example, you can try to minimize what those damned Pentagon people call 'collateral damage'—but in the end, innocent people die and you are back to the means-justifying-ends question."

"For which you say there is no answer."

"No, no, I'm not saying that. There may be an answer; you need to consider your audience, your witnesses. Much of what we do is done before an audience—either God, if you're a believer, or society. And in your case, you also have a certain sector of society that we call the electorate. I dearly hope the president isn't making moral judgments based on what he thinks the reaction of these audiences—especially the last—will be. And, Dear God, certainly not the first; we've had enough people making lethal choices because they thought it would please their god. No, those aren't the right audiences because there's always another audience, another witness. Put it this way: when the audience has left and the lights are off and you're alone on the stage, that's when we call what you do, whether it's good or bad, character. *You* are the audience."

"So if we believe in our hearts that whatever we do will have positive results for the country; and if we do everything possible to mitigate the bad effects of bad means; then there's a good chance it's a moral action?"

Krasinski shrugged. "That assumes you know all the consequences. Can you?"

"No," said Matt, shaking his head. "And if we've figured wrong and the results aren't what we'd hoped for, or the means turn out to have unpredictable, nasty consequences?"

"Then you've condemned yourself before yourself."

The mood aboard *Grace* that night was somber. Everyone was still disturbed by the incident with the speedboat and the possibilities it had raised. While the others were belowdecks in their cabins seeing that the grandchildren were safely tucked away for the night, Baxter sat behind the helm nursing a scotch and studying the night sky. Mickey Weekes sat seventy feet away gripping the forestay and dangling his legs over the bow.

When he'd first seen the speedboat hurtling out of the morning light, Baxter had been seized with fear. He'd realized in an instant how easily his scheme could go horribly wrong. Although he and Matt had set the thing in motion, they had no control over how it would turn out. In this regard, he was powerless.

He recalled Eisenhower's dictum that no battle plan survives contact with the enemy. What if Scroggs wasn't as devoted to guns as they had assumed? What if the man decided to use a bomb instead? All this time Baxter had thought of the deed as a surgical thing—one bullet, one man—and he would be the only target. But now the specter of a mass murder designed to take him out by killing him and everyone around him presented itself, like the bloody assassination of Anwar Sadat. He worried that he'd inadvertently, and through blind selfishness, put others in danger, especially the people he most loved in the world. It would be unforgivable, but he knew of no way to stop it short of ordering a massive manhunt and revealing why he—not the ATF, or the FBI, or the Department of Homeland Security—why he, alone, thought it was necessary. Not without revealing how monstrously he had intended to violate the trust of the American people … and of his children and grandchildren.

And he'd also, that morning, been seized with fear for his own life. When he saw what he thought was the moment of his death approaching, full speed, he realized he wasn't ready. Now he had to ask himself if he would ever be ready. Would he, in the end, be able to go through with it? And if not, how could he avoid it without barricading himself inside the White House which, of course, was impossible?

Kyla, followed by Maxwell and the others, appeared in the companionway and joined him on deck. They had drinks of their own. "They're already asleep," said Kyla. "I think it's this sea air."

Baxter smiled. "Beautiful night. I don't know if I've ever seen Orion so bright." He gestured to the sky.

Kyla glanced at the stars. She turned to him and said, "Dad, we've been talking. It probably won't do any good but we thought we should have a word with you."

He raised his eyebrows, took a sip of the scotch, and said, "Of course. What do you have in mind?"

"That boat this morning," Kyla began, "it may have been innocent but it couldn't help but remind us of the very real possibility that we, that you, live with every day."

"It comes with the territory. We've always known that."

"Maybe, but we put it out of our minds until something happens like this morning."

Maxwell put a hand on his father's knee. "What Kyla wants to say— what we all want to say—is we think you should give some thought to resigning."

"Just because some drunks in a speedboat scared the hell out of us?"

"No, of course not. Not them. But there're always other people out there, fanatics. Hell, they already tried to get you once. Do you have any idea how we suffered through that, especially with Mother dying on the same day?"

Baxter stared at his son but remained silent, a swirl of emotions running through his head.

"Dad, we understand how terribly difficult and painful it would be, but the other thing is you haven't been yourself since Mother…."

The American flag, fixed to a staff angled out over the stern, lifted to a new breeze. It brushed Baxter's elbow. "Wind coming up," he said. "Let's hope it stays through tomorrow."

"We understand how much you planned to do great things. Hell, anyone who runs for president does."

"From the southwest. Could be beautiful sailing tomorrow."

"Dad, please listen to us!" said Kyla. "It wouldn't mean you'd have to give up everything. You could strike a deal with Moore-Paterson. She could appoint you special envoy to the Middle East. You could be the person who finally brings peace to that place."

"It was Mother's dream," said Maxwell. "You'd be honoring her memory."

Baxter turned away. He stared at the overspreading stars in silence. His eyes misted.

"The American people would love you for it. They'd understand, what with Mother's death, the assassination attempt …."

He turned back to fix them with a harsh stare. "The American people would understand that they elected me to office because they trusted that I would accomplish what they, what the country, needed. They would understand that I had betrayed that trust."

"No, I think you're wrong," said Maxwell.

"That trust is sacred."

"Dad," said Kyla, "the people may think you're a great man with the capacity to accomplish great things. But they also know you're a human being. Maxwell's right, they'd understand."

Once again, Baxter turned away from them. Pretending to be gazing at the stars, he closed his eyes tightly. For a long time, the only sounds were the flutter of the flag, the lazy clink of a wire halyard in the hollow of the metal mast, and the trickle of water being expelled by the bilge pump. Finally, Kyla said, "It may be selfish, but we're also asking for us Dad.

After Mother died … well, I don't know if we could take it if something happened to you."

He turned to them and held out his glass. "Would you please pour me another?"

"Sure," said Maxwell. "Look, we can talk about this another time."

Baxter nodded.

Another time.

Marcie Gaudet was shocked when she saw Matt. Though he was clean-shaven and neatly dressed, his head was nearly bald except for a stubble of new growth and there were dark bags of skin under his eyes. "My God, Matt," she cried. "What's happened to you?"

"I've been on the road all day. I just drove down from Boston." He held her tightly.

"But your head … your eyes."

"It'll grow back," replied Matt. "Please, Marcie, don't ask me to explain. Not yet, at least."

"When?"

"I don't know," he said. "God, I'm so tired."

She studied him for a long moment. Finally, she said, "C'mon, You'll feel better after a shower."

"I need a bath," he murmured.

She gazed at him. She couldn't remember ever having seen him take a bath. "Okay, a bath it is, then. I'll run some water while you get out of your clothes."

As he sat in the bathtub, resting his head against the tiled wall and staring blankly at the ceiling, Marcie brewed some coffee and brought him a cup. She balanced it on the flat edge of the tub, pulled the stool out from under the sink, and sat down. After he had drunk half of the coffee, she said, "You must tell me what happened. I've never seen you like this."

"Maybe later."

"Here, lean forward and I'll wash your back." She soaped up a long-handled brush and began scrubbing his back from the shoulders down to the tail bone. She took great care to be gentle around the puckered scar of the bullet wound in his side.

"It used to be that everything was either right or wrong," he said. "It was all clear to me. That's why I've made such a hotshot lawyer—I only took cases I believed in one hundred percent, then worked my ass off. I knew damn well what was right and what was wrong." He paused, sighed, and said, "Now I just don't know anymore."

"It's this thing the president asked you to do …."

He nodded. "It's changed everything." He gave a bitter laugh. "You know, the reason I was happy to work on the campaign and even to oversee the transition but I didn't want any part of the administration was because I could see things coming up that I would have no desire to be part of."

"What kind of things?"

"Things where I would have to compromise myself, where I would have to smudge up the distinction between right and wrong…."

"And Baxter has sucked you into it? This thing with Zacher?"

He laughed. "In a big way. Now I'm afraid we've come to a place where there is no right, only varying degrees of wrong. And it makes me sick; I just want to escape somewhere but …."

"But whatever this is, it's happened or is going to happen and you can't stop it?"

"Something like that."

Three men stood around the saw table in Vernon Ludlow's woodworking shed. They were Ludlow, Huey Figg, and the man who had called the meeting, Billy Scroggs. A hanging fluorescent fixture, one of its bulbs loose, cast an eerie, green-gray, flickering light on their faces. In the far corner, its aerator bubbling, sat an elaborately designed aquarium that Ludlow had built to satisfy his hobby of collecting tropical fish.

Scroggs picked the two men because they had the qualifications he needed for his plan. They were single, without serious relationships, had been active members of the M-4 militia group, and were professionals when it came to guns. And, most important, they hated Baxter and the current government of the United States with its global leanings every bit as much as he did. In short, they were men who knew that a new American Revolution was needed and were eager to be part of it.

As a bonus, Vernon Ludlow was a master handyman who was proficient in working with both wood and metal. He had, indeed, hand-crafted some of his own guns. And Huey Figg had a brother-in-law who was a printer and who would serve their printing needs, no questions asked, for a small fee. "I brought you guys in on this because I trust you and because I know you want to finish the job my brother started," said Scroggs.

"You got that right," said Huey Figg.

Vernon Ludlow nodded.

"Now, there were two problems with what Donnie did. First, smart as he was, he didn't think the way most of us think and as a result he wasn't too professional about it. He just rushed at the president like the guy who tried to get Reagan or what's-her-name who tried to get Ford. That ain't the way to do it. I aim to make this as professional a job as possible, more on the order of Lee Harvey Oswald or, to use a better example, the Jackal. You guys see that movie?"

They both nodded.

"Then you know what I mean. We go completely underground, new identities, everything," said Scroggs. "That's where your brother-in-law comes in handy, Huey, if you think we can trust him."

"Don't worry about him," replied Huey. "He can be trusted."

"Good."

"What was the second thing your brother did wrong?" asked Vernon Ludlow.

"He thought too small. If you're gonna stir up militia groups across the country, you gotta do somethin' impressive. Just takin' out the president ain't enough." He paused, then said, "You guys know what the succession is?"

"You mean who follows the president if he's killed?" asked Huey Figg.

"Yeah. What is it?"

"It's the vice president, of course. That nigger woman."

"And then?"

Ludlow and Figg looked at each other and shrugged their shoulders.

"Next in line is the Speaker of the House. That's George Olcott, the same man who wants to outlaw guns altogether."

"Fuckin' prick!"

"Right," said Scroggs. "Now who comes after that?"

"Secretary of State?" asked Vernon Ludlow.

Scroggs smiled, shook his head. "No, he's fourth."

"Hell, then, I don't know."

"It's the President pro tem of the Senate. Senator Haskins."

"So what's your point?" asked Huey Figg.

"My point's this: we don't accomplish a damn thing if all we do is take out the president. Hell, that Moore-Paterson broad is just as bad, maybe worse. Same goes for Olcott."

"You ain't tellin' us you want to waste all three of 'em?" asked Vernon Ludlow.

"That's exactly what I'm tellin' you," said Scroggs. "And all three of 'em at precisely the same time."

"Jesus, Billy!" said Huey Figg.

Vernon Ludlow said, "I don't know, Billy ...."

"C'mon you two, just think about it for a goddamned minute, for Christ's sake. All three get taken down at exactly the same time, people know it's a real coordinated thing. The federal government is thrown into a tizzy. Haskins becomes president, but because of his right-wing base, he ain't able to move fast to crack down on things. That gives our brothers in the militia movement some breathing room to follow through on the example we set. That's why it has to be coordinated and real professional. Let 'em know it can be done."

Huey Figg shook his head in amazement. "You always was a good thinker, Billy. A lot smarter'n your brother."

Billy tested Vernon's saw blade, pricked his finger, and a small droplet of blood formed. "I ain't finished yet." He sucked the blood into his mouth. "We're probably on the Secret Service watch list, especially me. So I figure we go under cover a while till they lose track of us. It'll mean traveling around."

"I don't have no problem with that."

"Me neither."

"Good. And we might as well make use of our time, so I figure we can visit some of the militia groups, tell 'em something big is goin' down without sayin' what it is. Let 'em know if they was plannin' something, late August would be a good time."

"Is that when you're figurin' we'll do it?"

Scroggs nodded. "Yeah."

"Why late August?"

"There's gonna be a ceremony honorin' Martin Luther King on August twenty-eighth. That's the anniversary of his 'I have a dream …' speech. I'm bettin' all three of our targets will be there, all on stage together."

"So what about the other militia groups."

"We tell 'em to plan anything they want, so long's it's not in Washington, D.C. We tell 'em to be ready by late August, but we don't tell 'em the date. That's to keep what we plan absolutely secret. All we tell 'em is a coded message will go out on the internet to all militia groups a little ahead of time announcin' the date and time for action."

"Just like in that movie The Longest Day," said Figg. "When they was about to invade Normandy, they sent a coded message to the resistance people in France."

"Then, when we hit," said Ludlow. "Kaboom! Shit happens all across the country."

Scroggs nodded. "And we want to get a group to hit the UN building. Together with everything else, that'll send a real clear message."

"Fuck, Billy, that would start a revolution!"

"That's the idea."

Chapter 15—Zacher's Accountant

The motor launch carrying Baxter and Mickey Weekes back to *Grace* from the *USS Robert G. Bradley*, which was anchored in the deeper waters of Vineyard Sound, eased into Tarpaulin Cove. As it slowed, its bow, which had been riding high on its own wave, settled heavily into the water causing all the passengers to lurch forward slightly. Baxter was returning to his vacation after spending much of the day reviewing documents and meeting with the Secretary of State and a number of aides aboard the frigate, proving once again that a president can never truly vacation.

Under ordinary circumstances, the meetings aboard the *Bradley* would have left Baxter happy and filled with hope. Secretary of State Monteson had reported excellent progress toward a peace conference at Camp David between Ahmad Bakhit and Jehu Golani that could lead to a breakthrough in the Middle East conflict.

The recent, near-simultaneous emergence of the two men as leaders on the Israeli and Palestinian sides, both of them far more moderate than their predecessors, had presented a unique opportunity for hammering out a new, American-brokered, peace accord that promised to be comprehensive, lasting, and final. If concluded, the breadth and depth of commitment from both sides meant that it would far surpass Wye, Oslo, and the first Camp David. Furthermore, Monteson had said, both Bakhit and Golani were prepared to meet with absolutely no pre-conditions save one: that President Baxter was personally and intimately involved. On this, both sides were in total agreement. As the secretary said, it represented a chance for Baxter to go down in history as the president who finally won peace in the Middle East—enough to ensure any man's legacy.

While Baxter was aboard the *Bradley*, he was handed a cryptic message from Matt Cannon. It read, simply, "Mission accomplished. A good guess is late August." He knew what the message meant. Never would he be more exposed than on August 28th.

After receiving that message, he instructed the Secretary of State to make arrangements for a Middle East summit meeting in late August. He knew the conference would last at least a week. He also told the secretary to involve Vice President Moore-Paterson in the preliminary arrangements.

He sat on the starboard rail of the motor launch, watching the way sunlight suffused the spray thrown up by the bow as they approached the cove where *Grace* squatted comfortably on her reflection.

He stared at the inverted, opalescent image of the boat made up of countless flashes of varicolored radiance that seemed to appear and die in nearly the same instant. He thought, on the scale of the universe, a human life has no more duration than one of those brilliant flashes—here, then gone almost in the same instant.

He was awash in a sense of his own mortality. Most men are hit with it when their fathers die. It's as though death were a schoolyard bully who will take on all comers, one at a time, and the father is in line ahead of the son. When the father falls, the son is suddenly face to face with the bully. But for Baxter, it hadn't worked out that way. His father died when he was much too young to interpret the meaning of death. Rather, it was a sequence of other events that had now brought Baxter eyeball-to-eyeball with death. First, his mother, substituting in this case for his father, died during Baxter's campaign for the presidency. Then, a few years after that, his wife died on the same day that an assassin tried to put a bullet into him. And, last, his doctor had come like a messenger from Death with a stupefying diagnosis.

So it was with a profound resignation to his mortality, sharpened by the opportunity for a near miraculous swan song presented him by the

Secretary of State, that President Baxter stepped from the motor launch onto the deck of *Grace*.

Tarpaulin Cove is on the east side of Naushon Island, one of the Elizabeth Islands that extend southwestward from Woods Hole at the flabby underarm of Cape Cod. The island itself is deserted, containing only a few abandoned buildings and an old, derelict lighthouse. It is populated only by sheep, deer, and ducks—thus making it, from the point of view of the Secret Service, an ideal place for the president to spend some time as long as he didn't wander too far inland where there was a danger of deer ticks carrying Lyme disease. He'd almost laughed aloud when that latter concern was expressed.

As the launch pulled alongside *Grace*, the president found only Kyla aboard. The others had gone ashore in the rubber dinghy to lounge on the soft sand beach and to explore the abandoned lighthouse. "Dad, you look like your favorite dog died," said Kyla as Baxter sat and stretched his legs out along the cockpit cushions. "Was it a bad meeting?"

"No, on the contrary, it was excellent news," he replied. "It looks like there's a real chance for peace between the Israelis and the Palestinians at long last."

"That's wonderful, Dad. So why the long face?"

He searched for an answer. He waited until Mickey Weekes disappeared forward, then he said, "It just occurred to me, I guess, that your mother would have enjoyed this news. Next to the education bill, it had been her greatest hope for our administration."

Kyla gave him an empathetic smile, passed her open hand softly along his cheek. "How about I mix you a scotch and soda? You could use a drink."

"Sure, Make it a very weak one. One of the many annoyances of the job is a president can't get drunk. That damned briefcase that Commander Headley has is like a teetotaling aunt wagging her finger at me." For years he had hidden his heavy drinking from his children and he wasn't about to stop now.

Kyla laughed and went below to fix his drink.

Baxter ached to tell his children about his illness. He may have been the president of the United States, but in the end he was just an ordinary human being confronting imminent death and he longed for the support and comfort they could give him. But he couldn't tell them because, if he did, they would naturally expect him to resign and would be bewildered when he didn't. And, of course, he couldn't tell them of his alternate plan; they would be hurt and confused beyond imagining, knowing it was, in the end, a political trick. He didn't want that to cloud their memory of him. So he was looking at the prospect of suffering his final months alone with no one to talk with about his fears and sadness except Matt Cannon and Jim Stockton.

And, now, he had a date.

The death of his wife; the diagnosis of leukemia; his decision to die by bullet instead—they all acted as a solvent to dissolve the assumptions that held his world view together, those poses and artifices by which he had so long construed himself. Through those veneers of illusion, his reality had been defined by the press and pull of abstract power, by the balance of political forces, by the generalized statistical message of surveys.

Now, increasingly, his reality was defined by the feel of a sea breeze through his hair or by the cool bite of salt spray, or by the warmth of sunlight on his brow. Once again he was becoming the man he'd been before politics, fervidly alive to the most basic of sensations. The world had become more achingly beautiful to him—the colors more intense; the smells more pungent; the feel of things sharper; the sounds, especially of his grandchildren, more melodious; the taste of scotch and of wine almost heavenly. And with this change, his legacy—which, before, was everything to him, the very validation of his life—began to seem less important, at least in the rarefied political sense. The very thing that had caused him to launch his diabolical plan was weakening.

What was this obsession with legacy after all, except a bid for a certain kind of immortality? What gave him the right, above others, to taste this fruit? And what did it matter, he now wondered, what an abstract posterity thought of him anyway? What he cared about was what his real posterity thought— Maxwell and Kyla and his grandchildren Natalie and Jeremy and Petey.

Even his eyes changed. They took on a new, thousand-mile stare.

He didn't want to die.

But this essential urge, so strong and vibrant in every cell in his body, seemed frail against the crushing inexorability of external forces, some of which he, himself, had set in motion—forces that he, the most powerful individual in the world, was powerless to stop.

He reached into a canvas bag for one of the several books he had brought along to read on the boat—Steinbeck's *East of Eden*, which he had always meant to read but had somehow never found the time. Five minutes later, he closed the book, having found himself reading and rereading the same paragraphs without absorbing them. Instead, he pulled out of the bag a collection of Robert Frost poetry. But with this, too, he found him unable to concentrate. Why read a book to feed a mind that will soon be dead? Why memorize a poem? Why lay down watermarks of memory on the mind for later appreciation, when there won't be a later time; when his brain will have passed from the pulsating world to the inert world; when it became rock-solid dead?

He remembered when he had first fallen in love with his own brain, with all brains. It had come to him one day, while warming up in the bullpen at Fenway Park, reflecting on how his brain processed input from his optic nerve to precisely locate a spot in space sixty feet, six inches away; how it instructed his fingers to grip the ball with just the right amount of pressure; how the brain sent out a complex, precisely ordered string of commands to dozens of muscles in order to set his body in motion—the lifting of his left leg, the spring-like cocking of his right arm, the extension of his left arm for balance, the pivoting of weight on his right leg, the tensioning of his leg muscles to build up an explosive force— imagining how proprioceptors fired messages back to his brain, letting it know the precise position in space of every limb and joint—and then how his brain, measuring time in thousands of a second, calculated the perfect instant for his coordinated muscles to release the ball with force and energy to that exactly triangulated spot and then rewarding itself with a chemical wash of pleasure at the thwap of the ball in the catcher's glove.

Was it possible, through the infinite possibilities of evolution through eons of time from the initial explosion, that such a brain could emerge, one precise enough to paint the outside corner of the plate with a fastball, time after time, as he had done in his one year with the Red Sox before a ruptured tendon launched him on a political career? Or does such a brain require a creator, a designer?

Long ago, he had decided against the idea of a god. Both a god and the logic of evolution could explain the healthy human brain, but evolution also easily explained the malformed brains among us. It was far more difficult to accept a divine designer who would bring about diseased brains, or babies born without limbs, or babies born with three and four limbs, or twins conjoined at the chest. In short, he saw in the world much evidence of design, but precious little of intelligence or, at least, mercy. Once he had come to that conclusion, it had been an easy matter to feign religiosity for political purposes because he was not betraying anything; nothing was at stake.

But now, how he wished he could believe, believe that such a wondrous thing as his mind would not become inert sludge, but would merely slip gently into a newer form.

Would the assassin's bullet slam into his brain?

He looked toward the beach where he saw his three grandchildren chasing each other across the sand and playing in the surf. Their cries of delight came faintly to him over the water. He watched them jump back from a wave that flopped on the shore, then chase the same wave as it back-scurried through pebbles. He smiled to himself, a bittersweet smile. How quickly he had come to feel like an interloper in a world in which he no longer belonged, the very world that, a few weeks before, had lain at his feet.

Kyla came back on deck with two drinks. She handed one to Baxter. "You've been feeling mother's absence a lot lately," she said.

"Yes, I suppose."

She nodded. "All of us do."

"It's given me a sense of my own mortality," he ventured to say. Perhaps this was a way to talk about it without disclosing to his children the fact that his death was rapidly approaching.

"Oh, Dad, don't even talk like that."

He shrugged. "A man my age has to face reality."

"You have years and years left," replied Kyla. "And after you serve out your two terms, you're going to sit back and watch your grandchildren grow and you're going to write your memoirs."

He closed his eyes tightly. It was almost too much to bear. Two traitorous tears slipped from the corners of his eyes and slid down his cheeks.

"Dad, you really *are* upset!" said Kyla. She rushed to him and embraced him.

He said nothing. He held her tightly.

"Now no more of this mortality stuff, Dad," Kyla said. "It's too soon for another goodbye."

He embraced her more tightly still. Tears flooded his eyes. And through his tears, the scene on the beach—the children laughing and playing; the crescent stretch of sand; the lighthouse in the background—became distorted as though seen at a distance through a misshapen lens.

Billy Scroggs told his visitors to keep their voices low. He didn't want to disturb Annie who was sleeping in the next room. "And watch your fuckin' language," he whispered. "I don't want Annie hearin' no bad words if she wakes up."

Vernon Ludlow and Huey Figg sat beside each other at the kitchen table opposite Scroggs. Spread out between them on the plastic, checkered table-cloth were three newly printed birth certificates. Scroggs stood, lifted one of the certificates, and held it under the naked light bulb which swayed almost imperceptibly with a breeze filtering through the screen door. Scroggs' nostrils twitched as he sampled the different smell to the air that signaled a passing front. Ever since Ieaq his senses were constantly alert to the least change in his surroundings. "These look real good," he said.

"I told you," said Huey Figg, "my brother-in-law ain't no slouch. He knows how to print these things so there ain't no way you can tell the difference between it and the real thing."

"Except for how new they look," replied Scroggs. He looked to where his wife was stirring a large pot on the stove. "How's it comin', Mary-Ann?"

"Just about ready," she answered. There was a slight quaver to her voice betraying her nervousness. "Come see what you think of the color."

Scroggs went up to her and peered over her shoulder. With a perforated ladle, she removed a dozen or so tea bags from the boiling water, which had a deep amber tint to it, and plopped them wetly into the trash. Vernon Ludlow and Huey Figg came to the stove to examine the tea-tinted water. "Looks good." said Scroggs. "Let's try it."

Mary-Ann turned the burner off and shifted the pot to another, cold, burner. She gathered up a half dozen white flyers that the men had brought and dropped them into the water, using the ladle to ensure they were totally immersed. She turned to her husband. "Tell me when a minute has passed."

They all stared at the submerged paper, waiting for the minute to elapse. When it did, Mary-Ann used a pair of tongs to remove one of the sheets. Scroggs counted off another minute after which Mary-Ann removed the second flyer, arranging it on the counter alongside the first. They continued in this way until all six flyers were arrayed along the counter in ascending order of how long they had been submerged.

"Looks like the three-minute one to me," said Figg.

Scroggs nodded. "I suppose. Can't tell much difference, though."

"Wait till they dry," said Mary-Ann. "You ain't gonna submit the birth certificates all wet like that."

Scroggs laughed. "She's right, you know," he said to the others. "C'mon, let me show you what you're gonna do with them." He went back to the table and sat. Ludlow and Figg followed. Scroggs began writing on a piece of paper. The others remained silent as the pencil scratched quickly along the paper. When he was finished, he said, "Okay, here's a list of the IDs and other documents each of us needs to get. First, we use the birth certificates with the different names we've chosen to get drivers' licenses. Each license should be from a different state, none of them from Maine."

"Why different states?"

"Because even though we're gonna be workin' together, there ain't no way the feds are gonna know that if there ain't no connections between us. That way, even if they get one of us, the others will be able to do the job."

Both Ludlow and Figg nodded. "Makes sense," said Ludlow.

"Damn right," replied Scroggs. "And the same goes with the rest of the stuff—social security cards, library cards, credit cards, membership cards …."

"Membership cards?"

Scroggs gave them a broad smile. "That's one of the beauties of my plan, and the only time there'll be a connection between us. We're all gonna become members of Mothers Against Drunk Driving and that other organization—what do they call it?—Citizens For Sane Gun Control."

"What the hell are you talking about? MADD is for broads."

"They let men in," replied Scroggs. "What do you think some cop's gonna say when he looks in your wallet and sees a membership card to MADD or the gun control thing?"

Huey Figg laughed. "He's gonna think he's got some soft queer on his hands whose against booze an' guns."

"Exactly. He sure as hell ain't gonna say I got me here a potential assassin. Especially, when your brother-in-law prints up the signs I'm gonna design."

"What signs?"

"The signs that'll hide the weapons."

Vernon Ludlow shook his head. "You're way ahead of us Billy. What do you have in mind?"

"Hang on, I'll show you." He went out on the porch and returned with a one- by-three piece of pine, five feet long. "Can you bore a hole down the center of this thing?" he asked Ludlow.

"What sort of hole?"

"One to slip a rifle barrel in."

Ludlow shook his head. "Needs to be thicker to take a rifle barrel."

"Okay," said Scroggs with obvious annoyance, "let's say you mill out a piece like this except thicker. Can you do it then?"

"Sure, no problem."

"Good. Then we take the protest signs and fold them over the top to hide the muzzle. Like this." He took a double page from a newspaper, folded it over the top of the pole, lowered the pole to horizontal, pointed it at Figg, and said, "Bang. You're dead."

"Ain't gonna work," said Vernon Ludlow. "If I get what you're headin' at, they'll find the gun with metal detectors."

"Not if it ain't metal. You know that plant down by Bangor, the Performance Composites Company?"

"Yuh."

"They make carbon fiber tubes for ski poles and bicycle parts and things like that. Stuff's stronger than any metal. You figure if we got us some of that tubing you could rifle out some gun barrels?"

"I guess. Maybe. I ain't sure what the stuff is like to work with, whether it takes tooling the way metal does. Then, we gotta figure out some kind of firing pin and trigger mechanism that also could be hidden in the wood."

"Well, there's only one way to figure all that out, and that's to do it."

"I'm with you there," said Ludlow. "I'm willin' to give it a try. You figure we just go on up to Bangor and buy some of that tubing?"

"Not buy. They can always trace the transaction," said Scroggs. "We're gonna have to steal it."

"Billy …." said Mary-Ann, her voice edged with concern.

"Don't be such a worry wart. We ain't gonna get caught. The security on stuff for ski poles can't be that tight."

Mary-Ann started to protest more, but Scroggs cut her off by saying the whole point of getting the carbon fiber tubes was so he could do the job and still come back to her and Annie. "I'm not leavin' anything to chance," he said, "because I plan to come back to the two of you. We're gonna have some plannin' to do to figure out how to spend that money."

For the next half-hour, the three men discussed how they would steal the carbon fiber tubes and, once that was done, how they would manufacture the weapons.

By the time they finished, the samples that had been soaked in tea water were dry. They examined them carefully and settled on the one that had been in for only a minute; it looked aged without looking doctored. Mary-Ann took the three birth certificates and submerged them in the fresh tea water that she'd been preparing. A minute later, she removed them and placed them on the counter to dry.

"We're on our way," said Scroggs. "I hope Baxter's enjoying his vacation, because he hasn't got much time left."

Harry Ulanowski—short, balding, fat—was Karl Zacher's personal accountant. As he reviewed his client's bank accounts late at night in his small, cluttered office in Crystal City, he came to a money transfer that caused him great consternation. He was accustomed to having his client forget to record or tell him about certain transactions, and in those cases he just shook his head, groaned, and made the necessary adjustments. But never had he encountered anything as large as a quarter million dollars without first being forewarned by Zacher. Not even remotely.

Furthermore, the transfer was to an account in a bank somewhere in Maine and Ulanowski, who knew more details about Zacher's business dealings than Zacher, himself, was unaware of anything his client was doing in Maine. If Zacher had started a new venture Ulanowski would have been aware of it. Indeed, Zacher never entered an arrangement without seeking the advice of his accountant.

Ulanowski frowned. Something was suspicious here. He started to reach for the phone to call Zacher but then realized how late it was. He decided he would contact his client in the morning and get to the bottom of this.

Baxter woke early on the last day of his vacation. After starting the coffee, he went out on deck. He remembered vaguely hearing in his half-sleep a thunderstorm pass in the early morning hours and now he saw that a front had, indeed, swept over them. The weather had changed completely. The clear, dry air mass that had been with them for more than a week had given way to hot, humid conditions. Beads of moisture sweated every surface of *Grace*. When he went to the compass to check the set of the current, he had to wipe the globe with his shirt sleeve in order to see the card. The sun, so clear and sharp each morning of the previous week, now rose as a refracted, diffuse light in the east.

Across the sound, Martha's Vineyard was invisible behind a scrim of light-suffused fog. A movement, seen in the corner of his eye, made him turn his gaze to the hill behind Tarpaulin Cove. Two deer stood looking out at *Grace* and the other boats in the tiny harbor. As soon as he fixed his gaze on them, they disappeared. For some reason, that brief encounter filled him with an unspeakable sadness. He had a sense of time accelerating at breakneck speed and of him being swept up in its headlong rush, unable to slow it down or to help himself in any way. Never in his adult life had he felt so powerless. He wondered if his father had experienced a similar feeling of being in the jaws of something greater than himself on Omaha Beach with shells whistling by on all sides, with explosions hurling sand and flesh and bone and blood into the air, with helpless men crying for help all around him. It must have been a very similar feeling of being only a single, small player in a drama bigger than the human race.

The forces accelerating Baxter's drama may have been less violent, but they were no less powerful and against their impetus he was like a twig in a torrent. It left him with unspeakable sadness—time hurtling down a steep slope. One hour from now ... one day from now ... this time next week. Eight short weeks to the event he knew would present an assassin with the best possible chance—the King ceremony.

He had no idea why he was so certain that would be the day. Perhaps it just made sense because the ceremony would take place outdoors in a difficult area to secure. Also, it would be his first significant public appearance in a long time.

He was sure of it. His day would be August 28th. And time was hurling him toward that date with dizzying speed.

Matt Cannon tossed the Sunday paper on the coffee table and said, "As soon as this is over, I'm finished with politics."

"As soon as what is over?" asked Marcie.

He looked at her. Of course she didn't know what he was talking about. She couldn't know that he meant as soon as Angus Baxter was dead. He had used her in the same way the president had used him, and confiding in her now was out of the question. If she learned she'd been tricked by the man she loved into helping to arrange a presidential assassination, their relationship would be over. As it should be, he thought, given what he'd done. Reflecting morosely that it always seemed to take a lie to preserve a lie, he said, "As soon as Angus serves out his full two terms."

She laughed. "Well, that's a good long way off. You'll feel differently by then."

"I don't think so." He closed his eyes. An image of Billy Scroggs standing before the president, gun in hand, came to him. He could see the gun going off, Angus Baxter's head exploding in blood. Where would he, himself, be when it happened? Would he be standing near his friend like the last time, close enough to plant a kiss of betrayal? Would he be sitting where he was now, watching endless replays from a safe CNN distance? Would Mary-Ann Scroggs and Annie also be watching on television? Would they see the husband and father they loved gunned down by the Secret Service all because Matt Cannon had been unable to refuse a friend's unbalanced request?

Marcie dropped the book she was reading to her lap. "You really are wound up. Is it this sting operation or whatever you call it that you and the president are pulling on Karl Zacher?"

"Something like that, I guess," he replied.

"Well, I can't say I'm too thrilled about my role in it," said Marcie. "It's been causing me nightmares."

And she only knew a small part of it, he thought. Then another thought occurred to him. Shouldn't he tell Maxwell and Kyla not to watch television that day and especially—dear God, especially!—tell them not to allow the president's grandchildren to watch television?

But how could he do that without raising suspicions?

Karl Zacher stared incredulously across his huge, kidney-shaped desk at his accountant, Harry Ulanowski. "I made no such authorization," he said. "A quarter million dollars? That's ridiculous. You know I'd tell you if I did something like that."

"That's what I said to myself," said Ulanowski. "Something isn't right here and we need to figure out what it is before it happens again."

"Have you traced where the money went?"

Ulanowski nodded. "That's another thing. It was so simple that I'm suspicious about it."

"What do you mean?"

"I mean the money was transferred to a bank in Maine and there was no effort to disguise the account or anything like that. What that tells me is the man who received the money really thinks you transferred it to him. He's not the culprit."

"You mean whoever did this wants the man to think I sent him the money?"

"Exactly."

"What's the man's name, the one who has the account?"

"William Scroggs."

Zacher closed his eyes tightly. "Oh, shit!" he murmured.

"You know the man?" asked Ulanowski.

Zacher rose from his chair and stood facing the cherry-paneled wall on which two dozen photographs of him with celebrities, mostly politicians, hung. "Doesn't the name Scroggs mean anything to you?" he asked. Hands behind his back, he scanned the photographs one by one, wondering if the clue to who was behind this appeared in the pictures.

"Can't say that it does."

"Try Donnie Scroggs."

Ulanowski paused a moment, then said, "Oh yes ... wasn't that the flake who tried to assassinate Baxter?"

Zacher nodded. "This William Scroggs is his brother."

Harry Ulanowski knitted his brow, shook his head. "I don't understand what the hell is—"

"—I'm being set up," said Zacher.

"What do you mean, set up?"

"Someone wants to make it look like I'm bankrolling an assassination. That's why they've made the thing so damned traceable."

"Who the hell would want to do that? Why?"

Zacher scanned the two dozen photographs on the paneled wall. "Who wouldn't want to bring me down? The real question is how the hell do we stop this?"

"Come right out and say what happened," replied Ulanowski. "Expose it. I'd certainly back you up on that."

Zacher gave a sardonic laugh. "That's why you're an accountant and not a politician, Harry. The problem is, I've funded militia groups in the past and my views on Baxter are well known. That doesn't give me much of what the politicians call plausible deniability, now, does it?"

"No, I suppose not. So, what are you going to do?"

Zacher didn't answer the man at first. He paced back and forth in front of his desk for a few moments, hands behind his back, head bent. Finally, he said, "Well, the first thing is, I better have a meeting with Wayne Haskins. If somebody is out to get me, it may be an indirect way of getting him."

"I understand that," said Ulanowski. "And you need to do that right away so he's alerted. But what if—"

"—What if this Scroggs guy has already gone into motion?"

"Yes, precisely."

"Then I need to stop him. I need to put some of my men on it and they need to take him out if necessary."

Billy Scroggs and his friends thought they had picked the perfect night to hit the Performance Composites Company. A heavy cloud cover

obscured the moon and a light drizzle was falling, keeping people inside the only building within sight of the small factory, a roadside restaurant specializing in barbecued chicken and spare ribs. Scroggs parked his truck in a cleared field behind the factory. He'd been hoping that stocks of carbon fiber tubing would be stored in the field, but it was empty except for a large dumpster that was overflowing with unusable scrap. The field was bounded on all sides by the low, sprawling, single-story factory building and by woods.

The three men followed the bloom of a heavy-duty flashlight, carried by Huey Figg, to the back of the building. There they found an elevated shipping dock and a pair of padlocked steel doors. They climbed up on the shipping dock and Vernon Ludlow went to work on the padlock with a pair of bolt cutters. Within moments, he had cut through the U-shaped bar of the padlock and it fell with a clatter to the wooden dock.

A snarl came from the other side of the doors. It was followed by a loud bark, then another.

"Hell," said Figg. "They have a fuckin' watchdog."

"You ain't scared of no dog are you?" asked Scroggs with a laugh.

"Damn right I am. It's probably a pit bull or somethin' like that."

"Don't worry, I'll take care of him for you," said Scroggs, drawing a pistol he had tucked in his pants. It had a silencer projecting from the barrel.

The dog must have heard them talking, for it started to bark furiously—deep throated barks that signaled a large animal.

"Fuck, he's gonna wake up the whole state of Maine," said Ludlow.

"I'll shut him up," said Scroggs. He stood back and held the pistol at arm's length, steadying his gun hand with his other hand. "Open the doors real sudden like."

Figg and Ludlow each took a door and, on a nod from Scroggs, flung them open. The dog, a German Sheppard, bounded out onto the dock with a snarl. Almost in the same instant, Scroggs squeezed the trigger. The gun fired with a muffled phfft. The dog let out a shrill cry and fell muzzle first to the dock. His momentum carried him over the edge and he landed with a thud in the gravel. Ludlow pointed the flashlight at the dog. "Jesus, Billy, you got him right between the fuckin' eyes."

"Practicing for Baxter," Scroggs replied.

The three men slipped inside the building. As they'd expected, they found themselves in a storage room. Stacks of open shelves towered above them, each containing tubes of differing lengths and diameters. Each shelf was neatly labeled. Working quickly, they located a section reserved for carbon fiber tubes and filled their arms with a wide variety of sizes. Ludlow had said he wanted a large selection because he couldn't be sure at the outset which sizes would work and which would not. Within moments, the men had loaded the tubes into the back of Scroggs' pickup truck and covered them with a tarpaulin. They piled into the truck and Scroggs eased out of the narrow road on the eastern side of the building with the headlights off. He came within sight of the road and stopped, waiting for several cars to pass. Finally, when there was no bloom of headlights in either direction, he pulled out onto the road and headed west for Bass Run. As soon as they were out of view of the roadside restaurant, he flicked the headlights on, leaned back in the seat, and said, "Fuck, man, that was easy!"

"Yuh," said Ludlow. "But now comes the hard part."

"Aw, come on," said Scroggs. "You ain't got enough confidence in yourself. You'll be able to make the guns alright."

"I ain't talkin' about that. There was only the one dog at that place. That's a whole lot different than a couple dozen armed Secret Service agents."

Unable to sleep, Baxter rose from his bed in the family quarters of the White House at three in the morning and dressed. Sometime in the middle of the night he'd conceived the idea of visiting all one hundred and thirty-two rooms in the executive mansion—all, that is, except for the ones occupied by his family and by the permanent domestic staff on the third floor. Shortly after 3:00 a.m. he descended in the elevator to the ground floor and found his way into the library. He was met immediately by two men from the Uniformed Division of the Secret Service, a small part of the several hundred officers who guarded the outer, middle, and inner perimeters of the White House in round-the-clock shifts. "Mister President, is something wrong?" asked one of the men.

"No. I just decided I'd like to see this place," Baxter replied. "You know, I've been living here for several years and I don't think I've seen all the rooms. Isn't that strange?"

The men exchanged glances. The second agent asked, "Shall we call the chief usher, sir? Perhaps he or the curator can walk through with you."

"At this hour of the morning? Don't be silly. I'll find my own way around." He leaned toward them in a feigned conspiratorial manner. "It's something I've always wanted to do, you know."

"Yes, sir," they said simultaneously.

"You may want to alert the others that I'll be poking around." He knew he didn't have to say that. One of their functions was to know where the president was at all times, and he knew that as soon as he was out of hearing distance, they would call the Secret Service Command Post, located directly under the Oval Office. The men there would monitor his progress through the White House by means of the many electronic locator boxes that kept tabs on protectees. It was part of the reason he could never feel completely at home in the White House.

He crossed the hall from the library to the Vermeil Room and then to the China Room, with its light colors and china cabinets. This opened up to the Diplomatic Reception Room. So far, he was in familiar territory. He'd often greeted foreign dignitaries in this room. After finishing his exploration of the ground floor, he moved up to the first floor and the oval-shaped Blue Room. The chief usher, looking disheveled, greeted him. "Mister President, I'd be honored to guide you through the place if you'd permit me," the man said, adjusting the knot in his necktie.

"I told them not to disturb you, Arnold."

"Oh, it's no problem, sir."

Baxter frowned. "Let me ask you this, Arnold. When you're at home are you permitted to wander about without dozens of people keeping tabs on you?" There was a clear note of annoyance in the president's voice.

"This is my home, sir. I live here."

"Oh, yes, of course."

"But I get your point, Mister President. If you'd prefer, I'll return to my quarters and leave you to explore at your leisure."

"I would prefer, Arnold."

"Very well, sir." The man turned and hurried out of the room, nearly bumping into two uniformed agents. The three men exchanged perplexed glances.

Baxter continued to explore, ending up in the State Dining Room with its bare tables sitting idle under a massive chandelier. In its silence, it appeared vastly different from the other times he'd been in the room. It had always been buzzing with conversation and the clinking of glasses. He remembered how it was Grace who'd always brightened these occasions and how, during the few state dinners he'd held since her death, the room itself had seemed subdued to him.

This was, supposedly, his home. But it was hard for him to see it that way. Each room, each wall, each carpet, each guard, constituted a barrier interposed between the man he projected as president and the man—the true man—he'd been aboard the yacht Grace, shorn of all pretense and free to carry on a direct, sensual relationship with the world around him. And he was once again filled with regret at how each layer of ambition and artifice wedged him further and further away from the unassuming boy he'd been before the experience of politics and obligation had entrapped him.

He crossed into the Red Room. Let the guards wonder about his wanderings. He caught a glimpse of two of them in the corridor; they were shadowing him. He chuckled sardonically to himself. His house, indeed! He was only a temporary visitor. But wasn't his life like that also, his to live for a time, a very brief time? And then all the sunrises and all the moonsets; all the sea breezes and the gulls; all the perfumes of roses and all the sounds of grandchildren passed on to others to experience. Such a brief time. And as each day passed, his time was becoming briefer still. For he knew that somewhere out there, beyond the walls of the White House, a man was planning his final moment in exacting detail.

When the last of Senator Haskins' aides left his office, he signaled to Karl Zacher to come in. Zacher entered a darkened room, lit only by a desk lamp that deepened the creases in the senator's face, making him look at least ten years older, and a lot meaner. Haskins was wearing his eyeglasses and when he looked up at Zacher, the reflection of the desk lamp in each lens masked his pupils, giving the senator a possessed look.

It was not calculated to put Zacher at ease. Zacher found his way to a chair, took a deep breath, and said, "We have a big problem."

"That's what you said over the phone." Haskins' voice was cold and unmistakably hostile.

Zacher told the senator about the money transfer his accountant had discovered but which he, Zacher, had never made.

Haskins' eyes grew round; a flush came to his neck. But he said nothing. He continued to stare at Zacher.

Nervously, Zacher said, "I think this could be big time trouble."

This time, Haskins responded. His face grew even redder. "Son of a bitch!" He stood, leaned over his desk, bracing himself with his arms, and shouted, "I told you that you're goddamned support of those militia groups was going to create trouble. Goddamn it, I told you!" His arm bumped against the desk lamp and the switch chain clicked against the brass base several times.

"But I told you: I didn't make this transfer. It's a setup."

"You wouldn't have been vulnerable to a setup if there hadn't been a record," Haskins snapped.

"All right, all right … You made your point," Zacher said, his voice also rising. "But that's water over the dam. What's important now is somebody is trying to set up the appearance of an assassination and trying to pin it on me."

"The *appearance* of an assassination? A guy who's already said he would finish what his brother tried gets a quarter million bucks and you call it the *appearance* of an assassination?" Haskins shook his head. "No, my friend. Whoever it is, they mean to kill Baxter. *That's* what they're trying to pin on you. And if they succeed, they'll also manage to raise just enough doubts about my friendship with you to destroy me politically. That's what you're goddamned idiocy has gotten us into." The senator reached into his desk drawer and pulled out a cigarette.

"I didn't know you smoke," said Zacher. Haskins had been one of the leaders in the second round of fights with the tobacco industry.

Haskins ignored him. "Who is doing this? Any ideas?"

Zacher said nothing. He shifted nervously in his chair.

Haskins frowned at him. "There's something you're not telling me."

Zacher shook his head. "It's just too crazy. Impossible."

"What's too crazy?"

"I spent hours trying to figure out who it could be. I kept asking myself: who would benefit most if you and I were destroyed? And I kept coming back to the same answer …." He hesitated.

"Well?"

"Baxter."

Haskins stared at him incredulously. "Baxter? You are not trying to tell me the president would arrange to pay somebody to try to assassinate him?"

"As incredible as it seems, it's possible."

Haskins gave a loud, derisive laugh. "Bullshit! What guarantee would he have that they could stop this Scroggs fellow in time. That would be playing with fire in a way that is damned near inconceivable—a kind of Russian roulette where, if he's lucky, he survives and we take the fall."

"What if he didn't want to stop the man?"

"You mean, what if he wanted to be killed?"

Zacher nodded.

Haskins gave him a bewildered look. "Am I living some kind of nightmare here, some kind of theater of the absurd?" His voice rose to a shout. "Am I hearing what I think I'm hearing?"

"I know it sounds stupid, but—"

"—What the hell would make him want that? I know he's depressed after his wife died, but that's ridiculous." Haskins walked to the other end of the office, parted the curtains, and gazed out into the street.

"What if he thought he was going to die anyway?"

"What do you mean?" Haskins whirled to face Zacher. "I'm suddenly getting a very sick feeling that you have something to tell me that I don't want to hear."

"The medical records …."

"Baxter's? About the state of his mental health?"

Zacher nodded. "The reason you wanted me to get my hands on that report was so you could persuade him to resign by letting him know the report would be released if he didn't."

"That was the idea," Haskins replied tentatively.

"Well, I didn't think it would work. I figured he'd stonewall it."

Haskins closed his eyes as though to shut out a sight he didn't want to see. "So you did something different. You took it upon yourself to improve the plan."

"Baxter had had a regular exam by his physician…."

"And?"

Zacher took a deep breath. "And I had my man, the pathologist, alter the results. In fact, he built a program to insert certain values each time the president's physician ordered a test."

"Jesus Christ! You falsified medical records?"

"I wanted to be sure the man resigned."

Haskins glared at Zacher. "I'm almost afraid to ask…."

"The president thinks he's dying from an incurable, untreatable form of leukemia."

"But he isn't?"

Zacher shook his head. "No. It's all made up."

Inside a large shed at the abandoned saw mill where the memorial event for Donnie Scroggs had been held, Vernon Ludlow pulled a number of items from a large duffel bag and spread them across a table of planks supported by sawhorses. "Basically, I had two problems, both involving the silencer. First, it was tough getting the threading on this mandrel exactly right to accept the silencer." He held out one of the carbon fiber tubes, the last two inches of which tapered to a smaller diameter. The two-inch projection was threaded to accept the silencer, a Brugger & Thomet model imported from Switzerland, which Figg now screwed onto the mandrel. Then he handed the assembled rifle barrel to Billy Scroggs.

Scroggs hefted it, twisted the silencer to test the fit, and said, "Good work. I guess you solved that problem."

"Wait a minute," said Huey Figg. "The silencer's made of metal. It'll never get past the detectors."

"Don't worry. This is only the one I used as a model," Ludlow said. He reached into the bag and removed a silencer that appeared identical in every way except that it was made of carbon fiber. "I copied it exactly. Man, that wasn't an easy thing to do either."

"Genius," said Scroggs.

Ludlow beamed. "The second problem is pretty obvious if you look at it." He lifted a long, thin length of wood, and held it out to them. "As you can see, the barrel will fit nicely into the bore, but the silencer is too big. Of course, I could have just started with a larger piece of pine, but then it would look like we was carrying signs on four-by-fours. Bound to raise suspicion."

"So what did you do?" asked Huey Figg.

Ludlow smiled. He slid his hands from the other end of the length of wood to reveal a tapered thickening in the wood. "A little like a baseball bat," he said, "except not round." He slid the rifle barrel, narrow end first into the bored-out shaft in the center of the wood and demonstrated how the thickened part of the wood, with its internal bore, perfectly housed the silencer. Then he reached for a large square of cardboard and folded it over the top, hiding the muzzle of the silencer. "The sign covers it up so nobody will notice how the wood gets thicker," he said, a huge smile on his face.

Scroggs nodded his satisfaction. "You're a goddamned genius, Vernon. I always said that."

"Wait, that ain't all." He turned the wooden shaft around and showed them the butt end at the bottom. He tapped the side of the wood several times to loosen a wooden plug which he then removed. It revealed a round cavity in which a plastic button was lodged. "The plug has just enough play so that if you push it, it bumps against the button. The button, in turn, is spring loaded and it releases the firing pin. That, my boys, is our trigger mechanism."

Ludlow passed out the components for three copies of the weapon and showed the others how to assemble them. Then they went outside and set up tin cans atop the bed of the old log saw. "This one's Baxter," said Scroggs, arranging one of the cans. "He's all mine."

"It's all made up?" Senator Haskins shouted. He stared at Zacher for a long time, a look of unalloyed hatred in his eyes. "You, Zacher, are the most foul human being I've ever met. I've had enough of you. Take your filthy money and get out of here. I never want to see you again." He paused, then said, "And if you have a video of me with one of your bimbos, go ahead and release it, you slime ball. I don't give a damn!"

"Wayne, I—"

"—Get the hell out of here!" Haskins jerked the door open and shouted into his anteroom, "Get this lowlife out of here and make sure he never steps foot in this place again."

A half dozen aides stared in astonishment at the senator. His chief of staff came over and said, "Senator, are you sure—"

"—Get him out of here before I kill him!"

Nobody had to help Zacher out of the office. Without glancing at any of them, he hurried out into the corridor and disappeared.

Haskins' chief of staff, his forehead deeply creased, started to ask, "Senator, what—"

But Haskins interrupted him. "Don't ask. That man is so low he can look up a snake's ass and think it's the North Star! I'm going home." He grabbed his suit jacket and hurried out of the office.

"Do you want a driver?" somebody called after him.

"No. I'll drive myself."

A half-hour later, he drove up to his house in McLean. Even before he emerged from the car, his wife, Julia, was hurrying down the steps to the driveway. "Wayne," she cried. "You look so agitated. What happened?"

"I'll tell you inside," he replied. "I need a drink."

"But it's still the afternoon."

"I don't care. Are the children here?"

"No, Jimmy's taken them to the Air and Space Museum."

After Julia made him a tall scotch and soda, they sat in the living room and he told her what Zacher had done.

"Oh, my God! What an unconscionable thing to do."

"I can't believe how cruel the man is," said Haskins. "I told him I never want to see him again."

"I should say not!"

When Haskins told Julia about the money transfer and how Zacher thinks it may be the president who, assured he was going to die anyway, had ordered his own assassination, he asked, "Do you think it's even remotely possible?"

She didn't answer at first. She seemed to be trying to absorb everything he had told her. Finally, she said, "If you had asked me that back in the old days, I would have thought you mad. But ever since the nineties, ever since Gingrich and Clinton and all that, politics has become so foul. And, given Grace Baxter's death and the president's apparent depression … well, it no longer seems wildly impossible to me. The man has always had a great deal of courage, but this?"

He nodded. "That's what I was thinking as I drove home. You take a man like Baxter who has a deeply imbedded sense of his own legacy, add a serious depression because his wife died, then tell him he's only got months to live …. Well, he just might do something like this to ensure that Moore-Patterson is elected."

"You do know what you have to do, don't you, Wayne?"

He nodded. "I have to see Baxter myself. I have to tell him."

"Do you think he'll still have time, if it is him, to stop this assassin?"

"God, I hope so."

Chapter 16—Camp David

When he finished arranging the empty beer cans on the table of the rusted saw mill, Ludlow turned to Scroggs and asked, "What distance?"

Scroggs said, "We should be able to get pretty close. Do you remember that controversy a while back where the Secret Service said it wouldn't allow itself to be used politically? That was when campaign folks wanted them to keep protesters away from the candidates but the Secret Service guys said they were in the business of protecting the candidates from physical harm, not legitimate protest. Ever since then, people with signs, especially like ones against drunk driving or for world peace, are allowed pretty close. I figure we can get within fifty yards after we pass through metal detectors and physical checks."

"Hell, man," said Ludlow. "I could put a bullet right into Baxter's ear hole at that distance."

"That's the idea," said Scroggs, "because it'll probably be a side shot. There'll be invited guests in chairs in front of the podium most likely."

"Ain't nothin' wrong with that. A side shot gives you the whole temple area and the back of the head."

Scroggs said, "Okay, Vernon, show us the goods."

Ludlow raised the shaft in both hands, held it in front of his eyes, and pushed the wooden plug. There was a soft *phfft* and one of the cans leaped from the bed of the old saw machine.

"Good shot," said Scroggs. "But you're a dead man."

"What do you mean?"

"I mean, I'm a Secret Service guy and I saw you aiming the goddamn sign. It looks mighty peculiar to me, especially when I notice the president's head exploding at just about the same time."

"Well, how the hell would you do it?"

"In a way that maximizes my chances of seeing my little Annie and Mary-Ann again." He lowered the shaft to hip level, steadied it, and pressed the wooden plug. Phfft. One of the remaining tin cans went spinning into the air.

"Jesus Christ!" said Huey Figg.

Scroggs smiled. "You're a dead man, Angus Baxter," he said.

Wayne Haskins sat nervously by the phone in the living room of his McLean, Virginia home. He'd been told the president would return his call by 10:00 a.m. and it was now ten minutes after ten. Political games? Keep the other man waiting? "Do you think he'll call?" asked Julia Haskins.

The senator shrugged.

"What will you do if he doesn't?"

Haskins was about to answer when the phone rang. He picked it up on the second ring, listened for a moment, glanced at Julia, and said, "Thank you for calling, Mister President." They exchanged pleasantries for a few minutes. Finally, Haskins said, "I need to meet with you … without aides."

"It's not something we can talk about over the phone?" Baxter asked.

"No. It needs to be in person…and private."

"I see," said Baxter. "Well, listen, "I'm going to be spending the weekend at Camp David with my family. Why don't you and Julia come out and join us?"

"We wouldn't want to intrude, Mister President. Both Julia and I know how valuable and rare family time is in our business."

"No intrusion. Most of my staff won't be there, and only a skeleton Camp David crew. So I'll have plenty of time to be with Maxwell, Kyla, and the grandchildren. I imagine I can spare an hour or two for something important. Maybe when they're napping."

"It *is* important."

"It must be. You wouldn't call for a private meeting, without aides, if it wasn't. And I must admit, Wayne, it has me intrigued."

"Then, we'd be delighted to come to Camp David," replied Haskins, glancing at his wife and nodding.

"Good. Drive up to the main gate and a marine will guide you to your cabin."

After he hung the phone up, Haskins turned to Julia. "Well, it's done. We'll meet at Camp David."

"Do you think I should be in the room when you tell him about Zacher?"

"I think it would help persuade him of my sincerity."

Julia nodded. "Perhaps you're right."

Haskins gave a deep sigh. "This is not something I look forward to."

Early in the evening on a mid August day, Billy Scroggs dropped his large, army-issue duffle bag on the kitchen floor near the screen door. Huey Figg and Vernon Ludlow were waiting patiently on the porch. Smoke from their cigarettes drifted in through the screen. Scroggs was a half-hour late because earlier he'd noticed a tear in the screen and he'd taken the time to fix it so Mary-Ann wouldn't have to deal with it while he was gone. He'd been happy for the extra time because he wasn't looking forward to being away from Mary-Ann and, especially, Annie, for so long. But now the time for delay was over. If they were going to pick up the van in Bangor that night, they had to hurry before the rental office closed.

Scroggs bent over to pick Annie up and hold her close to him. He felt how hot her skin was. "I have to go now, Sweetheart. I want you to behave yourself while I'm gone." He turned to Mary-Ann. "Promise you'll take her to see a doctor. I don't like the way she looks. It feels like she has a fever."

"I'll take her first thing tomorrow."

"When will you be back, Daddy?" asked Annie.

"As soon as I can. Then you, Mommy, and me will go away somewhere. Maybe Disney World." When he had told her, several days before, that he and his friends were going out of state to work on a construction job, she'd accepted it in stride. But now that the time for leaving had arrived, her eyes were filled with tears. Scroggs leaned back and wiped the tears gently with his forefinger. "Now be a brave girl for your daddy. Okay? I won't be gone long."

"Okay."

"That's my girl." He hugged her tightly then lowered her to the floor, tickling her in the ribs as he did so. She giggled. "There, that's better," he said. "Now listen to Mrs. Preston when she tells you to go to bed."

"I will."

"When you wake up in the mornin', Mommy will be here. Then, before you know it, I'll be back, too."

"Okay."

Scroggs' turned to his neighbor, Mrs. Preston. "Thanks again for watchin' her. Mary-Ann should be back in three or four hours."

He opened the screen door. Several moths flew past him into the kitchen. He handed his duffel bag to Huey Figg who threw it into the back of the pickup truck and climbed in after it. Vernon Ludlow joined him. Mary-Ann, who would be driving the truck back, got into the passenger seat. Scroggs climbed into the driver's seat, started the truck, rolled down the window, leaned out to kiss Annie who was standing on her toes, then drove off.

He hated leaving her again, especially for so long. He remembered how badly he felt earlier that month when he and his companions made a quick two-day trip to Washington where they reconnoitered the area in front of the Lincoln Memorial, where the King ceremony would be, then found a storage company in Arlington to stash the placards and the homemade guns. Scroggs didn't want them to be traveling around with that kind of suspicious equipment until they were needed.

It took them more than an hour and a half to get to Bangor. They arrived with only ten minutes to spare. There were no customers in the Budget rental office and the sole employee was in the process of closing up. Just as well. She would be the only one who would see them.

After handing the woman his new driver's license with its fake name and filling out the necessary papers, Scroggs and his companions transferred their gear to a blue Chevy van. Within fifteen minutes they were ready to leave. Scroggs turned to his wife. "I'm sorry I won't be able to call you often, but they can trace phone calls."

"Even cell phones?"

"Now they can, yes. That's the kind of government Baxter and the others have given us. And now cell phone traces are more valuable to them than pay phones because they become like homing beacons; they travel with you as you move. That's why I'll call only when I can find a pay phone. There are still a few left."

"It'll be hard not hearing from you every day."

"I know. And I'll miss talkin' to you, and to Annie. But that's the way it's gotta be. We gotta go completely underground."

"I'll worry like crazy until you're back safely."

Scroggs hugged Mary-Ann. "Yuh, but it's somethin' we gotta do. It's all so Annie can have a better world—a chance to be somethin' in life. Remember that. They're takin' everything away from us. By the time Annie grows up there'll be nothin' left. It'll all be owned by Jews, niggers, and foreigners." He held her at arm's length and looked into her tear-filled eyes. "I love you, Mary-Ann."

"I love you, too."

"When I get back, everything will be better." He climbed into the van and rolled down the driver's window. "We'll spend money like we never done before. You, me, and Annie will finally have things."

"Be careful, Billy."

He laughed. "Don't worry about Billy Scroggs. He knows how to handle himself. I made it through Iraq, didn't I."

"Yes, Billy, you made it through Iraq."

"And I'll make it through again." He started the engine, shoved the van in gear, and rolled out of the parking lot. In the rear-view mirror, he saw Mary-Ann standing beside the pickup, watching them.

Wayne Haskins and his wife drove northwest toward Frederick, Maryland. They rode mostly in silence. Haskins was rehearsing what he would say to Angus Baxter, and Julia seemed absorbed in her own thoughts. At Frederick, they picked up US 15 towards Thurmont. At Thurmont they would turn west toward Hagerstown, then right at the Catoctin Mountain Park visitor's center where they would begin a steep climb on a narrow, tree-lined road towards Camp David.

Sunlight filtered through the trees creating a chiaroscuro effect on the road. Several times, Haskins slowed to let squirrels scamper safely across. He was a man who hated to kill anything. Julia was frequently, and pleasantly, amused by the effort he would make to usher a bee or a hornet out of the house by trapping it in a drinking glass pressed against a window, sliding a piece of paper between glass and window, and rushing outdoors where he would let the creature free. More than once she asked him what he would do as president if he ever had to send troops into combat and the only thing he would say was, "It'd be the hardest thing I'd ever have to do in my life." Then he would add, "But sometimes having great power and responsibility means compromising with your most basic instincts. It's a price we pay—sometimes a horrific price."

A high metal gate, with several marines stationed behind it, guarded the grounds of Camp David. One of the marines came to the driver's side of Haskins' car. "Senator Haskins, we've been expecting you. The president has asked that we take you and Mrs. Haskins to the Birch cabin. It's where Menahem Begin stayed during the peace talks with President Carter and Anwar Sadat." The marine made a signal and the huge gate swung open.

"Hop in back and show us the way," Haskins said.

"Yes, sir. My pleasure, sir," the marine said. He climbed into the rear seat.

They drove along narrow tree-lined roads until they pulled up in front of a rustic cabin with a sign over the door reading "Birch." The marine helped them carry their luggage inside, told them how to contact the camp staff should they have any needs, then left.

The cabin had two bedrooms, a large living room opening out to a patio, vaulted ceilings, and a huge stone fireplace.

"It's charming," Julia Haskins said.

"Yes. I only wish we could be here under different circumstances."

They had no sooner unpacked when a knock came on the door. Julia answered it. Angus Baxter stood grinning at her. "Welcome to Camp David, Julia. It's good to see you."

"Good morning Mister President. Thank you for inviting us."

"Not at all. Is everything to your liking?"

Haskins came forward and extended his hand. "It's perfect." He studied the president's face, trying to detect something, though unsure exactly what it was he was looking for. He saw only Baxter's familiar, friendly expression.

"Good to see you, Wayne," said the president, grasping the man's hand. "Now before we get down to whatever it is you want to talk about, how about some skeet shooting? We can talk over lunch. And remember, Wayne, clay targets are not living things," he said with a laugh. "You can shoot them with a clear conscience."

The skeet range was in a large clearing near the boundary of the camp grounds that also served as a heliport. For the next hour, Baxter and his guests, along with Maxwell and Kyla and their spouses, shot at clay targets launched by a marine.

Wayne Haskins, preoccupied with thoughts of his up-coming meeting with Baxter, performed poorly. He spent the whole time studying the president, trying to detect signs of Baxter's disposition. Here was a man who thought he was within weeks or months of death. He seemed less jovial than usual and every once in a while he didn't hear something somebody said and had to ask the person to repeat it—signs of distraction.

But they were subtle signs, easily associated with the depression into which everybody thought the president had slipped since the death of his wife. Given what the senator knew about the president's health—or at least what the president thought his health was—and given his suspicion about what Baxter may have planned as a result, Haskins had expected to see a more troubled countenance.

He concluded that Baxter was holding it all inside himself and he shuddered to think what turmoil must be in the man's mind.

"You're not concentrating, Wayne," said Baxter.

"I never was a good shot, Mister President. Don't much like guns."

"Don't let the NRA hear you say that," Baxter said with a laugh. "You'll lose their support."

Haskins smiled but said nothing.

Baxter glanced at his watch. "Well, what say you, Julia, and I head over to Aspen for lunch. It should be just about ready. It's a pleasant walk. Then, after lunch, we can have our talk."

They strolled along tree-shaded paths, dappled with sunlight, and came to a stone-lined pond fed by water cascading down a spillway over rocks. The gentle splash and burble of the water gave Haskins a momentary illusion of peace. But it was quickly overwhelmed by the knowledge of the confession he was soon to make.

Baxter, chatting amiably with Julia about grandchildren, led them up to the Aspen Lodge. The primary meeting place at Camp David, it had a large sun porch, a dining room, a fireplace-dominated sitting room, several bedrooms, the presidential office, and, for summer use, a large flagstone patio. It was to this patio that Baxter now led his guests. They took seats at a table set for lunch.

Baxter drew their attention to stone flower boxes resting against the outer wall of the lodge. "They were added by Nancy Reagan," he said. "I think they add a nice soft touch, don't you?"

"Yes, they do," replied Julia Haskins.

Senator Haskins nodded absently. All through lunch, which consisted of several courses, he remained silent, letting Julia carry the conversation with Baxter. Occasionally he would nod his agreement or make a curt comment or two. His mind was already in the more serious conversation they would have as soon as lunch was finished.

When Billy Scroggs and his companions crossed from Maine into New Hampshire, he glanced at his watch. "We're making good time," he said. "We should be in Boston in about an hour or so."

A New Hampshire state trooper passed them in the left lane. "Fuck! Those guys make me nervous," said Vernon Ludlow.

"Better get used to it," Scroggs replied. "From now on every cop we see we're gonna figure is after us."

"Why?" asked Huey Figg. "They have no way of knowing what we're up to."

Scroggs turned to look at him. "You don't think the government had people watching us at Donnie's memorial service? You don't think they probably had somebody in Bass Run keepin' tabs on me all this time?"

"You think so?"

"Take that Alexandra Lake broad, for example. I'm not sure she's the real thing."

"She seemed convincin' to me," said Ludlow. "Damned pretty, too. I bet if you got her in bed she'd seem like the real thing."

"All I'm sayin' is never assume the enemy is dumb," Scroggs said. "If I'm right, it won't be long before they figure out that we're no longer in Bass Run, then they'll probably start searchin' everywhere. When they see our cars are still there, they'll start checkin' out bus stations and airports. Eventually, they'll get to the rental agency."

"So that's why you're so hell bent on getting' rid of this van."

"You better believe it. I aim to stay at least one step ahead of them the whole time."

"How're we gonna to do that, Billy?"

"You'll see. I just need you guys to stay sharp. We're goin' for a long drive."

"Washington?"

Scroggs frowned at the man. "Are you crazy? We ain't showin' up there until it's time."

"Then where are we goin'?"

"Midwest. I figure we need to stay on the move, so we might as well make good use of the time. We're gonna get the gears in motion for a revolution." The cars in front of them suddenly slowed. "It's the goddamned Durham tolls," Scroggs said.

"We just passed a sign that said the tolls were still two miles away."

"Then we just got ourselves into a lousy two mile backup. We don't need this shit!"

During lunch, Baxter saw that Wayne Haskins was distracted, indeed nervous. It honed his curiosity. What was it the man wanted to talk about? For Haskins to call for a private meeting without aides and then to be acting this way, whatever he had to talk about must be something very weighty. Baxter couldn't even begin to imagine what it was. So when they had finished the cherry pie and coffee was served, he slid his chair back and said, "Well, now, let's go inside and have comfortable seats in the lounge and have a nice talk."

Coffee cups in hand, they moved through the patio doors into a room dominated by a massive stone fireplace with the presidential seal centered above the mantle. Exposed wooden rafters and cross-beams interrupted the white ceiling at regular intervals, giving the room a warm, rustic feeling. A grouping of easy chairs surrounded a coffee table on three sides in front of the fireplace. Baxter guided Wayne and Julia Haskins to chairs and took one on the opposite side of the coffee table. He leaned forward, placed his coffee cup on the table, and said, "So, Wayne, what is it you have in mind? It must be important to meet privately like this." Baxter took note of the worried glances his guests exchanged.

"Mister President—"

"—Please, 'Angus' ... we're alone here."

Haskins gave a half smile. "Angus, all the way out here I tried to figure out a good way to say what I have to say and I could come up with nothing. So I guess the only thing is to come right out with it. I'm ashamed to confess I arranged with Karl Zacher to get access to your medical records."

Baxter felt a fluttering in his chest. His expression darkened. "My medical records? Those are confidential. How the hell ...?"

"Zacher's pretty resourceful—"

"—And not a little unethical."

Haskins visibly flinched. "If you're applying that judgment to me, Angus, you have every right to. All I can do is apologize."

"Why?"

"I'm sure it hasn't escaped your attention that people have been worried about ... about your capacity to continue in office considering—"

"—Considering?"

"Considering your reaction to Grace's death. Many people feel you're depressed to the point of debilitation."

No mention of leukemia. Perhaps they didn't know. "And?"

"My idea was to confront you with the medical records ... well, actually, have people close to you confront you with them and try to persuade you to resign."

Baxter felt a welling of anger at this invasion of his privacy. He wondered how they'd managed it. He had complete confidence in his physician, at least, he thought he did. "Did Jim Stockton—"

Haskins held up a hand. "No, no. Jim Stockton had nothing to do with it. Zacher blackmailed a technician at Bethesda. Stockton knows nothing about it. In fact, he even tried to disguise your records by giving them a false name but this technician caught on to it."

"Jim needs to hear this. I'll get him here," said Baxter.

"I thought he'd be here already. Isn't he supposed to be always at your side?"

"There are several physicians in the White House Medical Office. Jim needs an occasional break." Baxter rose and walked to the fireplace. He turned and glared at Haskins for a long moment then said, "Wayne, I have to confess I'm surprised and somewhat disappointed. I know we've engaged in cheap political tricks from time to time, but this ...."

A shadow of anger crossed Haskins' face. Julia reached out to hold his hand. "Fair enough, Angus. I'll accept full responsibility. Zacher was my man."

"Was?"

"I got rid of him."

"Why, if you put him up to it?"

"Because, Angus, he didn't just gain access to your medical records. He took it upon himself, without my knowledge, to go a step further."

"How so?"

Haskins glanced at his wife then fixed his gaze on Baxter's eyes. "Angus ... you are not dying of leukemia."

Baxter stared at the man. He walked back to his chair and sat heavily. His mind was spinning. He shook his head from side to side in disbelief.

Haskins continued. "Zacher had this technician alter the records."

Baxter looked at Julia Haskins, searching for confirmation. She returned his stare with an expression of deep compassion. Without taking his gaze from Julia's eyes, he said, "I don't believe it."

"It's true," said Haskins.

Julia nodded.

For long moments they sat in silence while Baxter tried to absorb the full impact of what he'd just been told. Finally, he rose and walked to a sideboard where a telephone sat. He lifted the phone. After a moment, he said, "Please find Matt Cannon. Have him call me immediately. Also, Jim Stockton. And make sure *Marine One* is waiting for them at the White House." He replaced the receiver in the cradle and turned to Haskins. "Are you certain about this?"

"Absolutely certain."

Julia said, "I can't think of anything more cruel. I can only imagine what you must have been going through. But please don't blame Wayne for this. It was entirely Karl Zacher's idea. Wayne knew nothing about it and when he found out he was as angry as I've ever seen him."

Baxter could find no words. His mind was still swimming with the implications of what he'd learned. It was too much to take in. "How did you find out about this? I hope you're not trying to tell me Zacher just walked into your office one day and said, 'Oh, by the way, guess what I did.' Because I would find that utterly unbelievable."

"No," replied Haskins. "He came to me because he was frightened."

"Of what?"

But before Haskins could answer, the phone rang. Baxter crossed to the sideboard and lifted the receiver. "Yes? Okay, patch him through." He glanced from Haskins to Julia and back to Haskins as he waited. "Matt?...I need you out here immediately...within the hour. And bring Jim Stockton." He paused, then said, "I'll tell you when you get here. And, listen Matt, see if that Lake woman is in D.C. If she is, bring her along." He slammed the receiver into the cradle. He turned to Haskins. "Zacher was frightened of what?" He had a sinking feeling he knew the answer.

"He thought he was being set up."

"In what way?"

"To be linked to your assassination."

Baxter said nothing. He tried to fix his expression, to hide what he was feeling.

Haskins, a strange mixture of anger and empathy written on his face, leaned forward. "Now that we're admitting to political tricks, Angus, I'm forced to ask you something ...." He told Baxter of the transfer of funds from Zacher's account to one held by Billy Scroggs; of the reports he received from the attorney general concerning Baxter's curious indifference when told of a possible assassination attempt; of a report he'd received that Matt Cannon had been sighted in Bass Run where Billy Scroggs lived; plus the fact that Marcie Gaudet is a vice president at the bank from which the funds transfer was made. "Angus, I put all these things together and I'm forced to ask: Do you hate me so much that you would actually plot your own assassination to defeat me? Is that possible? Please tell me it isn't. Please, God, tell me I have it all wrong!"

Baxter said nothing. He lowered his head to his hands.

"Oh, Christ!" muttered Haskins.

Julia rose from her chair and sat next to the president. "Angus … why?"

"I didn't want the children to suffer through another wasting illness, not after Grace," he replied. "And I didn't want to suffer."

"And you saw an opportunity to destroy me," said Haskins. He rose and started to pace back and forth. "Jesus Christ!"

"It was Zacher we were after."

"But his association with me was a tidy convenience you weren't about to overlook. Do you hate me that much?"

"No, Wayne, I don't hate you."

"Then what? Because I'm having a great deal of difficulty understanding all this."

Baxter lifted his head from his hands. He looked from Haskins to Julia and back again. "When I found out I was dying of leukemia … when I *thought* I was dying of leukemia … all I could think of was Maxwell, Kyla, and the grandchildren. Grace's death was so hard on them, so very hard … I didn't want another …."

"You all must have suffered so much," said Julia, reaching for his hand.

"Bullshit!" said Haskins. "That wasn't all you thought about."

Baxter shot him an angry look. "Yes, I admit it: I'm a political animal … like you. I thought I saw a way, by rousing sympathy through crisis, to help Moore-Paterson … to get Bakhit and Golani to find a breakthrough … and also Grace's education bill …."

"To ensure your legacy."

Baxter nodded. "To ensure my legacy."

Haskins shook his head sadly. "Wow!"

Baxter gave a sardonic laugh. "Once a man steps inside the White House, this legacy business becomes an unbelievable obsession. It's as if you have to do something great to justify all the effort, all the suffering, to get there. You have to make it worthwhile … giving up your family … all that time. And all the while you have pictures or statues of Lincoln and Washington,

Roosevelt and Jefferson watching you to see how you're doing." He rose, walked slowly to the sideboard. "I'm going to have a drink. Can I have them bring you two something?"

"Under the circumstances, Angus," said Julia, "I think we should all have a drink. Wayne and I enjoy martinis."

Baxter lifted the phone. After a pause, he said, "We'd like three martinis. And, yes, a Jack Daniels for Matt Cannon and a Diet Coke for Jim Stockton." He lowered the phone, chuckled, and said, "Jim doesn't drink, although this may start him."

Haskins and Julia laughed. It was a release of tension.

Baxter returned to his chair. The three maintained an uncomfortable silence for many moments before Baxter leaned forward, locked his gaze on Haskins, and said, "Wayne, I can't tell you how sorry I am. I guess we get carried away with ourselves."

"Pardon me if I say I don't find you totally convincing."

Baxter glared at Haskins, but before he could say anything, a knock came on the door. Baxter called, "Come in," and a steward entered with a tray of glasses, a couple of cans of Diet Coke, and a pitcher of martinis. He placed them on the sideboard. "Leave them there, Robert," said Baxter. "I'll serve."

When the steward left, Baxter poured martinis for Julia, Haskins, and himself. They drank in an uncomfortable, frosty silence until Baxter finally said, "Listen, I think we could all use a break. What say I show you around the lodge until Matt and Jim Stockton arrive? We'll take our drinks with us.

By the time they finished the tour and Baxter poured fresh drinks, Matt, Alexandra Lake and Jim Stockton appeared. They were dressed in casual clothes and wore bewildered expressions. Matt was unshaven. He appeared startled to see Wayne Haskins and Julia in the room and greeted them warily. Alexandra Lake looked even more bemused than she did that one time in the Oval Office.

Baxter handed Matt a glass of Jack Daniels and gave a can of Diet Coke to Jim Stockton. "It's a stiff one, Matt. You'll need it." He looked at Alexandra. "What will you have, Ms. Lake?"

"The same, sir. Neat."

As he poured Alexandra's drink he said to Stockton, "Are you sure you won't have something with a little more kick?"

"No, Mister President; I'm fine with the Coke. Though I have to say, sir, I suspect I may regret that choice in a few minutes."

Baxter smiled. "That's a guarantee, Jim. Have a seat, gentlemen; we have two things to discuss. First, there's the matter of my health. Then, Jim, I'm sorry but I'm going to ask you to leave while we continue the discussion. First question, Jim: Is it possible my medical records could be falsified without you knowing it?"

Stockton frowned. "I ... I suppose it's possible. But—"

"—Please, Angus, let me explain. It's my responsibility." He turned to Stockton and explained in full what Karl Zacher had done.

"My God," Stockton whispered. "I saw the slides."

"Somebody else's slides. They were switched."

"I ran the tests three times."

"There was a computer program designed to watch for your test orders and generate falsified results. You could have re-tested a dozen times."

"But how...?"

Haskins explained about Zacher and the technician at Bethesda Naval Hospital.

Stockton shook his head, incredulous. "I don't know what to say."

"Do you want that drink now?" asked Baxter.

Stockton shook his head, said nothing.

"But what about the symptoms," asked Matt Cannon. "You pointed out once that the president's headaches, shortness of breath, and tiredness were all associated with the leukemia."

"Yes, those plus a generally pale complexion and anemia," replied Stockton. "The problem is they can be masking symptoms. In other words, they can stem from something else entirely."

"Such as?" Matt remembered that Stockton had explained this to him before, but he wanted the doctor to say it again in front of everyone. It was a kind of knee-jerk revenge on Baxter.

Stocking glanced from Matt to Baxter.

"Go ahead, Jim. My drinking is hardly a secret," said Baxter.

"Yes, sir." Stockton turned to the others. "All those symptoms can be attributed equally to heavy alcohol consumption. That's the reason I relied for my diagnosis mostly on the blood tests and other tests like bone marrow aspirates, and biopsy; cytogenetic studies to determine chromosonal changes; flow cytometry ... other things."

"None of which I understand," said Matt. "But I'm assuming they all can be falsified,"

Stockton nodded. "If someone had access to the computer records which would require my password—"

"—Easily obtained by a hacker who knew how," said Matt.

"And if they substituted someone else's slides. I examined them myself to be sure."

"Again, easily done by someone in the know."

"Perhaps we need more tests," said Baxter.

"Yes, Mister President. Absolutely."

"Can we avoid the goddamned bone marrow tests?"

"Given what Senator Haskins has told us, I think we can get away with a simple blood test."

"Good," said Baxter with a small laugh. "Now, Jim, I'm sorry, but I'm going to have to ask you to leave. Go let them make you some lunch. And, of course, all this stays absolutely confidential."

"Of course, Mister President," Stockton replied. "I regard this, unusual as it is, still to fall under physician-patient confidentiality." He rose and left quickly.

Baxter turned to Matt. "Now, Senator Haskins and Mrs. Haskins know about our project. And, Ms. Lake, Matt tells me you figured it out. So there's nothing to hide. Here's what we need to know: How far along is it?"

Matt closed his eyes. "Oh, God," he whispered. He gave Baxter a look filled with anger.

"That doesn't sound good."

"Sir, Scroggs has disappeared," said Alexandra. "I'm afraid I lost him. He's gone underground."

To Wayne and Julia Haskins, Baxter said, "Ms. Lake is an ATF agent who was keeping an eye on Scroggs." He turned to Matt. "Do *you* think he's already gone underground as Ms. Lake says?"

Matt nodded. "Until the twenty-eighth."

Baxter turned to Wayne and Julia Haskins. "That's the day I give a speech at the Lincoln Memorial for that King event."

"You gave the man a date?" cried Haskins. "An appointment?"

Matt gave a futile shrug of his shoulders.

"In other words," said Haskins, dripping sarcasm, "the damn thing's already in motion and you have no idea how to stop it?"

Matt said, "I could contact his wife, tell her to tell him the whole thing's off if she hears from him. The problem is, he's probably too smart to call her."

Haskins expelled a long breath. He looked at Baxter. "You're just going to have to avoid public appearances until he's found."

"You'd like that, Wayne. Wouldn't you?"

"What choice do you have?"

"You know I can't do that. No president can afford not to be front and center. That's what they pay us for, Wayne."

"But you can claim some infirmity or something."

Baxter shook his head again. "No. We're just going to have to find him; that's all we can do—and before August twenty-eighth."

"Angus," said Julia, "you've been living with a … a specific execution date? My God, Angus, you can't appear at that dedication."

"And expose Katherine Moore-Paterson to assassination? What if he's determined to make a hit and I'm not there. Don't you think it's possible he'll take it out on Katherine? I can't do that."

Matt stood. "May I speak frankly?"

"You have something you want to get off your chest," said Baxter. "And I think you have the right. Go ahead, say what's on your mind."

"Well, it seems to me you two have been plotting things with a view only to the tactics and strategies of it," he said, his voice unsteady. "You, Mister President, asked your best friend to arrange for someone to kill you. Well, I did that and I'll never be the same again. If it happens, I'll never be able to live with myself. Have you thought of that?"

"Matt, I wrestled with it for—"

"—You wrestled with it, but in the end, it all came down to expediency. No consideration for the human beings involved." He turned to Haskins. "And you, Senator, did pretty much the same thing. You had to suspect Zacher would elaborate on your scheme. You knew there were some good indications he was indirectly involved with the last assassination attempt and—"

"—Now, hold on, Matt."

"No, you hold on. I'm not saying you knew anything about it and certainly not that you'd have approved it. But you chose to turn a blind eye to Zacher when you knew what kind of man he was."

"I've broken off all contact with him."

"Pardon me, sir, but your timing sucks," Matt said. He walked to the door and opened it. Turning, he said, "Mister President, Alex and I will do everything in our power to stop this train. Whether we can or not is an open question. What isn't a question, however, is that when this is all over, I can no longer serve at your pleasure."

He started out the door, but stopped and turned again. "And just to make sure the accounting is complete about the lives you two have been playing with, you should know that Billy Scroggs may be a bigoted man, he may be filled with hate, and he may be a killer. But he thinks he's right. And, more important, he has a wife and a daughter both of whom he loves. He's not just a goddamned instrument of policy. Think about that, both of you—if you can get beyond your arrogance, that is." He slammed the door.

Baxter and Haskins looked at one another. "We deserved that," said Baxter.

Haskins nodded. "That we did. Arrogance. Do you think that's what it is?"

"What do you think?" asked Julia with unaccustomed bitterness.

Alexandra caught up with Matt outside the Aspen Lodge. "Let me ask you something," she said. "When the hell are we gonna have a woman president so we don't have to put up with this kind of shit?"

"Unless we find Scroggs, it may be sooner than you think," replied Matt.

"I swear to God; I'm gonna move to Canada!"

The day after arriving in the Boston area the three men in the blue van pulled into Logan Airport. They took the exit for Terminal B and came to a stop at American Airlines where Huey Figg stepped out of the van. Carrying a suitcase, he went through the revolving doors and turned left. Following a previously discussed plan, he walked through the long corridor into Terminal C where he took the escalator down to the baggage claim area and the rental car desks. There, he completed the necessary paperwork at Hertz, and emerged onto the terminal road where he waited for a Hertz bus to take him to the van he'd just rented.

Meanwhile, Billy Scroggs and Vernon Ludlow drove the blue van to the Budget lot, turned it in, and took the shuttle to the Airport subway station. They took a blue line train into downtown Boston, changed to a red line train and rode it to Kendall Square in Cambridge. Scroggs and Ludlow entered the Marriott Hotel, took the elevator to the room they'd rented the night before under their assumed names, and retrieved their gear. They took it down to the garage and waited for Huey Figg to show up with the new van.

A half-hour later, they had packed the gear into the red Ford Aerostar, pulled out of the garage and headed for the Massachusetts Turnpike.

"Guys," Scroggs said, "we are now going underground."

Part 4

*Tis too much proved—that with devotion's visage
And pious action we do sugar o'er
The devil himself.*
—William Shakespeare, Hamlet, III, I, 46

Chapter 17—Mary-Ann Scroggs

Having read the letter she held in her unsteady hand, Alexandra Lake couldn't quite believe it. She was sitting on the Oval Office couch, Matt Cannon at her side. Behind his large desk, Angus Baxter, chin resting on his steepled hands, stared at her. The globes of the anniversary clock rotated slowly, every few seconds sending a flash of light toward Alexandra like a lighthouse.

Senator Haskins sat sullenly in an armchair to Alexandra's right, also staring at her. Everyone was silent. Alexandra glanced at the president and the senator and read the letter once more.

Printed on White House stationary, it read:

To whom it may concern,

You are hereby requested to render assistance in any form requested by special agent Alexandra Lake of the Bureau of Alcohol, Tobacco, and Firearms and to the President's Special Advisor Mathew Cannon. You are further requested not to discuss any aspect of this communication, or any assistance requested and rendered thereby, in any manner or form whatsoever, with any other person, including superiors. If you require confirmation of this letter, Ms. Lake and Mr. Cannon are authorized to place a call to me and, upon reaching me, to hand you the phone. I will then personally confirm the contents of this letter.—Angus Baxter, President of the United States

When Alexandra at last looked up at President Baxter, the president said, "The part about not telling a soul about this applies to you and Matt also. Is that understood? We can't afford to bring the regular authorities into this. I'm sure you understand why."

"Yes, sir, Mister President."

"That includes your superiors at ATF and at Justice."

"Yes, sir." Alexandra's head was swimming.

"Matt will brief you on what this is all about, but I want to say it is of the utmost importance to me and to the country."

"And my mere presence here," said Senator Haskins, "should persuade you that the president and I, though for very different reasons, are in total agreement on this one."

"Yes, sir. It does persuade me. Absolutely, sir."

Baxter laughed. "Good. Now I believe you have a flight to catch. You have just enough time to pack."

Alexandra gave the president a quizzical look then turned to Matt Cannon who waved a pair of airline tickets. "Come on, I'll drive you," said Matt. "We'll talk on the way." They rose and walked to the door.

"And, good luck," said Baxter.

"That goes for me, too," said Haskins.

Billy Scroggs turned the van from Boston's Storrow Drive onto the Southeast Expressway. He accelerated to ten miles an hour above the speed limit—fast enough to keep up with most of the traffic, but not so fast that he'd draw attention from the cops. It had always amazed him how people trying to evade the law got themselves caught because of some stupid traffic violation. That's what happened to Timothy McVeigh; it had nothing to do with the bombing of the Federal office building. He was pulled over because he was driving a car without a license plate. *Incredibly stupid!* Scroggs was determined not to make the same kind of mistake and he insisted that Huey Figg and Vernon Ludlow do likewise. "I'll come down hard on the first one of you who pull's a bonehead play. This is going to be a real professional operation, not like McVeigh or my brother."

He'd carefully planned the trip on which they were now embarked. While working to encourage other militia groups to swing into action in late August, he and his friends would stay on the move, going deeper and deeper underground. Furthermore, his schedule would get them back to Boston approximately when Zacher's daughter was due to return from one of Harvard's summer programs abroad. It hadn't been difficult to find her itinerary, and he knew just when to meet her flight at Logan Airport. Moreover, from a photograph he downloaded off the internet, he figured he'd have no trouble identifying her.

He saw it as insurance.

For the first time since his tour in Iraq, Scroggs felt a sense of purpose larger than himself. At last he was doing something not only about his own family's miserable life, but also about the disgusting situation into which bleeding-heart politicians and soulless corporations had dragged his county. They were ruining the democracy. As he saw it, there were only two kinds of people in the country. Either you were a member of the rich people's club and you owned most of America, and your stocks kept turning out dividends, and you kept getting obscene bonuses, and you kept getting richer … or you were one of the millions of poor people who only kept getting poorer.

If you were one of the fat cats, all you needed was connections and no soul. But if you were on the other side, you needed courage and cunning … and you needed faith. You needed to listen to the voice of God.

Muttering, "Amen," to himself, Scroggs slid the van carefully into the right lane where it disappeared into a long tunnel.

Matt and Alexandra flew from Washington to Boston where they transferred to a flight for Bangor and soon were on the road toward Bass Run. Matt was even more worried than the last time he'd driven along this road. Back then, he'd had no idea what to expect and his fears were all about the unknown.

But now he had an uncomfortable notion that he knew exactly what was coming, and it filled him with even greater fear. "Well," he said, turning to Alexandra, "We'll soon know what we're up against."

"I only have one question," she said from the passenger seat. "The president said we can't bring anybody in on this—not Justice, not the Secret Service, nobody. And if we use local police, it's only for narrow specific needs; they're not to get any idea of the whole picture. So my question is why? Wouldn't we have a much better chance of stopping Scroggs if we initiated a nationwide hunt?"

"Two reasons. If we bring everybody in and they get Scroggs, he'll go on trial for threatening to assassinate the president. Once that train leaves the station there's no way we'd be able to stop it."

Alexandra nodded. "He'll try to save his ass. Zacher will be the first domino to fall and it wouldn't be long before the president and Haskins fall."

"You got it. He talks and this whole thing unravels. Baxter and Senator Haskins are destroyed. And oh, by the way, I go to prison. Probably the president, too. It's a federal offense to plan an assassination. I'm not sure what the law says about plotting your own assassination, and I sure as hell don't want a reason to find out."

Alexandra shook her head in amazement. "I still can't believe you guys came up with this crazy plan. I feel like Alice; Washington sure feels like a rabbit hole. And the second reason?"

"We lose all negotiating power with Scroggs. We're the only ones who can bury this and let him walk free so long as he doesn't talk. We involve Justice and it's out of our hands."

"So the whole thing's on us."

"You got it."

They fell silent for a while. Finally, Matt asked, "Think there's any chance Scroggs will still be there?"

"No chance," Alexandra replied. "No chance in hell."

"Maybe he's changed his mind."

Alexandra shot him a skeptical look.

Matt gave a rueful smile. "No, I suppose not."

"We can only hope his wife is still there," said Alexandra. "She's our avenue to him."

"If we can get her to talk."

"Right. But that's a mighty big if."

When, following Alexandra's directions, Matt pulled the car into Scroggs' driveway, they saw no lights on in the house and no truck in the driveway. "Damn," Matt said. "We may be too late."

Alexandra frowned. "He wouldn't take his wife and kid with him. Let's try again in the morning. If they're still not here, we'll have to ask around."

As they drove back to the Covered Bridge Motel in Guilford where they had already booked separate rooms, Alexandra said, "I'm disappointed in you. You didn't tell me the idea was for Scroggs to really pull it off."

Matt said nothing.

"And you thought this was a friend helping a friend die with you playing the role of Doctor Kevorkian? Jesus!"

Matt remained silent. Alexandra continued. "I read an FBI study that said over ten percent of the time some suffering fool is killed by a cop in L.A., it's actually suicide-by-cop. It's a real phenomenon, but you guys have put a whole new twist on it with the president playing the suffering fool and Scroggs playing the cop. I swear to God, I'm gonna move to Canada!"

"Look, this is my responsibility," said Matt. "Why are you here?"

"You need me."

"Why?"

"If the only way to stop Scroggs is to shoot him, could you do it? It's not like filing a fucking brief, you know. You squeeze the trigger with the flesh of your finger."

Some six hours after leaving Boston, Scroggs and his friends found a motel near Niagara Falls that had a blinking green neon sign advertising VACANCY. "Looks like that's our home for the night," said Scroggs, surveying the mold on the green aluminum siding. It was just the kind of nondescript place he wanted.

"Then we head out for Michigan tomorrow?" asked Huey Figg.

"No, we're here for a couple of nights."

"I thought you said one night."

"In this motel, yes. Then we find another place in the area. I don't plan on us stayin' in the same place more than one night."

"But why not move on to Michigan?"

"Because I intend to meet with some militia guys outside of Rochester back there a few miles. Plenty of time to get to Michigan and all the other places we're goin' before our appointment in Washington."

"What other places?"

"You'll see when we get there."

They piled out of the van and entered the small lobby where a lone clerk was thumbing indifferently through a magazine. A strong smell of disinfectant leeched from the carpet and the shabby sofa. After checking in, Scroggs told the others he was going out to fill the gas tank. Although there was a gas station directly across the street from the motel, he drove down the road a mile west until he came to another gas station where he filled the van's fuel tank. Inside the attached convenience store, he paid for the gas and asked the clerk how long before he crossed into Canada.

"Only a few miles up the road."

"Good, I gotta get to Toronto before nightfall."

"You oughta make it. You got another hour and a half, two hours to go, depending on traffic and customs."

He chatted with the clerk for several minutes, hoping the man would remember him, then went outside, pulled the van up to a bank of pay phones and called Mary-Ann.

"Where are you?" Mary-Ann asked.

"You know I can't tell you that. Did you take Annie to the doctor?"

"Billy, I wish you could tell me where you are so I wouldn't have to worry."

"Damn it, Mary-Ann, I can't," Scroggs snapped. "Now I only have a few more seconds before I have to hang up. Did you take Annie to the doctor?"

"Yuh. He said we should watch her for a few days. I'll take her back tomorrow."

"Did he say what it is?"

"No. They took some blood and—"

"—How's she feelin' now?"

"I think better. She's sleeping now."

"Okay. Listen, Honey, I gotta go." He hung up before she had a chance to protest. He didn't think there had been enough time for somebody to trace the call and, even if they had, it would take them to a gas station where the clerk would say, "Yuh, I remember the guy. Headed for Toronto."

Before returning to the van, he went back into the store and bought a soda. As he paid for it, he said, "Had to call the wife back in Maine. She worries all the time."

He pulled out of the station and headed west toward the Canadian border. But as soon as the gas station was out of sight, he turned into a road on his right and, navigating small streets, eventually found his way back to the main road east of the motel. When he got back to the room, Vernon Ludlow was sitting on a bed watching TV. "Where's Huey?" asked Scroggs.

"This place has a bar off the lobby. He went for a beer."

"Goddamn it! Didn't I tell you guys we gotta stay sharp?"

"Yuh, Billy, I told him. But what was I gonna do? Tie him to a chair?"

"Fuckin' right!" shouted Scroggs as he stormed out of the room, slamming the door behind him.

When he found Huey Figg sitting with a stranger, four beer bottles on the table between them, he clenched his fists. Gathering himself because he couldn't afford to make a scene, he casually strolled to the table and sat down. The wooden table was covered with varnished-over cigarette burns left over from the days when smoking was permitted.

"Billy," said Huey, "say 'Hi' to Johnny Waters, here."

Scroggs extended his hand, but said nothing.

Huey lowered his voice. "Johnny's a militia guy. He's plannin' to hook up with the same guys we are."

"That so?" asked Scroggs, looking at the man. "When?"

"Tomorrow."

"You alone?" Scroggs glanced at the one other person in the dimly lit room—the bartender, who was focused on counting bottles and jotting figures in a small notebook.

"Yes."

"Then why don't you come out with us in the mornin'? We'll meet for breakfast."

"Sure, why not?"

"Good," said Scroggs. "Say seven o'clock." He turned to Figg and said, "Now I'm afraid I have to tear you away from this gentleman. There are some things we need to talk about back in the room."

They said goodnight to Johnny Waters and walked up to the corridor leading to their room. But when Scroggs strode purposefully past their door, Figg said, "Wait a minute. The room's right here."

"This way," Scroggs replied as he headed to a side door. He opened the door and checked outside to see nothing but an empty dirt lot with a dumpster where, he guessed, delivery trucks pulled up. The dumpster overflowed with garbage. A startled cat shot from behind it, scurried across the lot, and disappeared into the bordering woods. "Here," said Scroggs.

"What's up?"

Scroggs closed the door, grabbed Figg by the shoulder, and pushed him behind the dumpster. "What the fuck?" Figg cried.

Speaking in a strained voice through clenched teeth, Scroggs said, "You stupid son-of-a-bitch! Didn't I tell you no fuckin' drinkin'?" He struck Figg hard across the cheek with the back of his hand. "Didn't I?"

"Jesus, Billy …." Figg stumbled backwards, lost his balance, and fell to the ground. As he pulled himself to his feet, he raised a hand to his cheek. "C'mon, Billy, I didn't mean to—"

"—And then you meet up with this turkey and who the hell knows what you told him?"

"I didn't tell him nothin'."

"You told him my name, you idiot!"

"But he seems okay. He's a militia guy, for Chrissake."

"You do this kind of thing again and you're a dead man. This is no fuckin' game we're playing."

"Okay, okay. It won't happen again."

"It better not."

"Besides," Figg said, "even you figured the guy was okay. You invited him to have breakfast with us."

"Not for the reason you think."

"Then why?"

"Did you notice how much the guy looks like you—the same height and weight, the same hair colorin'? Christ, even the same eye color."

"He doesn't look like me."

"In all the important ways he does," replied Scroggs with an enigmatic smile. "Why, hell, I think he was sent to us by God."

"What do you mean?"

"You'll see." Scroggs bent down to pick something off the ground. "You lost this when you fell." He started to hand it to Figg, but stopped. "What the hell's this?"

"What's what?"

"It's your driver's license. Your real one! Where's the phony license?"

"It's in my wallet."

"Then what the hell are you carryin' this around for? I told both you guys to get rid of anything that could identify you."

"I guess I forgot."

"You fuckin' forgot? Jesus Christ, you've got to be the dumbest prick in the whole world!" Scroggs pocketed the card. "Get your ass in the room and empty all your pockets and your bag."

They returned to the room where Scroggs told Vernon Ludlow also to show him every piece of paper or card he was carrying. When at last he was satisfied that Figg's old driver's license was the only incriminating document, he looked at the man and said, "I promise you, any more fuck-ups like this and I'll personally kill you. I'm not gonna let you mess up the whole operation, because I intend to return to my wife and daughter when this is over and if either one of you gets in the way of that, I'll take you out. I don't care if it means we only get Baxter."

"Don't worry, Billy, there won't be any more fuck-ups," said Ludlow. "I'll keep an eye on him."

"We both will. And I'll keep an eye on you, too."

"You should get rid of his license. Burn it."

"I will, but not here."

When Mary-Ann Scroggs saw, through her kitchen window, the strange car pull into the driveway, she thought something bad had happened to Billy. She glanced at the room where Annie was sleeping, dropped the dish towel to the counter, and raised her hand to her mouth. She bit into the knuckle of her forefinger hard enough to leave marks. Her finger tasted of dishwashing detergent.

Two people emerged from the car, looked at the house for a moment, then made their way onto the porch. She recognized the woman who had asked her questions at Donnie's memorial event and it made her worry all the more. The man—the way he walked—also struck a chord of recognition, but she couldn't place him. They knocked on the screen door. Mary-Ann sucked in a breath.

She went to Annie's room and, after checking that Annie was still asleep, quietly closed the bedroom door. Another knock came. She hesitated, not knowing what to do and realizing that they knew she was there because the house was open except for the screen door which wasn't locked. She couldn't call for help because the telephone rested on a table adjacent to the door. They would see her and stop her before she could finish punching in the number even if she could think of a number to call. She had to let them in. Knees shaking, she went to the door. "Yes?"

"Mrs. Scroggs, do you remember me?" asked the woman.

"You were at Donnie's memorial."

"That's right, but I have to tell you that I lied. I pretended I was there out of respect for your brother-in-law but I'm really with the Department of Justice. My job was to keep an eye on your husband."

"Oh, God."

"I'm sorry, I know it comes as a shock, but you must hear us out. We know what Billy's up to. You have to persuade him to call it off."

"You don't know nothin'."

"We stopped by last night, but you weren't here. We were worried because it's very, very urgent."

"I was visitin' Mrs. Preston," she said. "Besides, that's none of your business because you don't know nothin'."

Matt stepped forward. "But we do know, Mrs. Scroggs," he said in a voice that was vaguely familiar to her. "We know because I'm the man who put him up to it. I was in disguise. I had dinner here. You served bologna sandwiches. Billy and I went downstairs so he could show me his gun collection."

"I ... I don't understand."

"The whole thing was an elaborate scheme, a foolish, elaborate scheme, and your husband was being set up so that some people could bring down another man. He's being used as a pawn by certain powers in Washington."

"I don't believe you."

"You have to believe us. It's not too late for Billy. If he calls this thing off now, he can walk away and you can keep the money. There's no point to it anymore."

From the bedroom Annie called, "Mommy?"

Mary-Ann glanced at the bedroom door, then back at Matt and Alexandra.

"Go to her," said the woman. "We can wait."

She went into Annie's room and closed the door behind her. She was glad of the interruption to have some time to think. "What is it, Sweetheart?"

"I feel hot," Annie said. "Can I have a glass of water?"

Mary-Ann felt the girl's forehead, patted her hair. "Sure. I'll be right back."

"Who are you talking to?"

"They're just some friends of Daddy's. They came to say he's doin' real good," Mary-Ann replied. "I'll get your water." She stepped from the bedroom into the kitchen and went to the sink. "She wants some water," she said, an apologetic tone to her voice.

They smiled and nodded.

She brought the water to Annie, stayed with her while she drank it, then returned to the kitchen. "I'm sorry, whoever you are, but you gotta go and leave us alone."

"My name's Matt Cannon. You already know Alexandra Lake and I'm afraid we can't go until you hear us out. It's too important. Lives are at stake … including Billy's."

Her heart began to race. She shook her head, incredulous. How did they know so much? "Please leave my house," she said. "I'll call the cops." She reached for the phone.

Alexandra placed a restraining hand on her wrist. "Believe me, for Billy's sake, you don't want to involve the police. We have the power, power in very high places, to put this thing to bed without Billy getting hurt. But if the police become involved, we'll start to lose control of the situation."

Mary-Ann stared at Alexandra. Slowly, she removed her hand from the phone. Her eyes filled with tears. "What can I do?" she asked, half to herself. "Jesus Christ, what can I do?"

"Tell Billy it's off. Tell him to come home. Tell him the money is his so long as not a word of this gets out."

"But I don't know where he is."

Matt glanced at Annie's bedroom door and said, "I suspect he'll call. I was here. I saw how much he loves your daughter."

She hesitated for a long moment, glancing around the kitchen, looking for something but not knowing what it was she was looking for. She saw the dishcloth, the glasses waiting to be dried. She had an overwhelming urge to go back to them, to make everything normal again. Finally, she shook her head slowly. "No. You're lyin' to me. Now, please leave."

"Okay, we'll leave," said Matt. "I think you need time to think this over. But we'll be back tomorrow morning. That should give you plenty of time to think about it. In the meantime, I'm going to see if I can arrange a phone call for you. It's one I'd like you to take."

"What for? Who ...?" Her voice was full of alarm.

"Someone very special," he replied, looking at her phone and jotting the phone number down.

The moon was full and fat over the Washington Monument in the hour before dawn. It was like a great white eye looking down at Angus Baxter as he stood at the window of the Oval Office. Reflections from the rotating balls of the anniversary clock slid across the window pane like vaguely seen planets in deep space.

Baxter's eyes were bleary from wandering the White House corridors most of the night causing bemused messages to crackle over Secret Service two-way radios. With each day that passed, with each hour swept into eternity by the clock's hands, he felt his self-appointed death approaching. He had put himself into an impossible position, and only Matt Cannon and Alexandra Lake could get him out of it. So he waited eagerly for a call from them. For days, he'd been waiting for the call that never came, the call that would tell him the hunt was over, the call that he would be allowed to live.

Of course he could bring in the ATF, the FBI, others, tell them about Scroggs, but that would heap even greater dishonor onto the office he held in trust because he would have to explain why he, not they, came by the information. And if he tried to concoct a different story, Haskins would be all over him and it would become public knowledge anyway.

There was also a part of him that didn't want to hear from Matt because of the agony he had caused his friend and because of the shame he felt. Given that he was responsible for what was happening, he had adopted a new sense of obligation to see to it that others would not be hurt, especially his children and grandchildren.

It was one thing when he thought he would die from leukemia. Then, it was fated; there wasn't a thing he could do about it and the children and grandchildren would simply have had to cope just as they would with any sudden death. But he had changed the equation. Now, he had to do everything possible to stay alive, and he had to do it in a way that preserved the dignity of the presidency. Even though it was important for the president not to appear afraid, he would ask the Secret Service for extra protection. He could always say it was a delayed reaction to the wake-up call of the first assassination attempt. And at least he could protect Moore-Paterson from his foolishness.

He waited for her to appear in the Oval Office.

As always since he'd been away, Scroggs had gone to bed thinking of Mary-Ann and Annie. He knew he shouldn't use the phone again, but he thought maybe he'd risk calling them before breakfast. Mary-Ann would be up—she was an early riser—and he hoped Annie would be awake, too. He hated himself for being away from them but it was something that had to be done. He consoled himself with the certainty that there were things, right things, that a man of courage and sacrifice—a man of God, had to do, And this was one of them.

Doing something about this guy, Johnny Waters, was another.

Scroggs had passed a fitful night, his restless mind endlessly reviewing plans and contingencies. Unlike what happened with his brother, this operation was going to be as thoroughly planned as he could make it.

But he also realized you had to adjust your plans when unexpected opportunities presented themselves—gifts from God. And, if he was lucky, just such a thing might occur at breakfast. Part of the secret was recognizing these unexpected opportunities and acting on them.

Like when you found yourself alone with a shit-for-brains officer.

Like Iraq.

Matt and Alexandra returned early the next morning. Though Annie's fever worried her, Mary-Ann was relieved that it caused her daughter to sleep; she didn't want her to see the visitors. First stopping to make sure Annie's door was closed, she went to the screen door. "Nothing's changed since yesterday," she said as she opened the door. "I still think this is some kind of trick."

Alexandra said, "We hope to convince you otherwise."

"May I use your phone to initiate the call I mentioned yesterday?" asked Matt.

"Go ahead, but it ain't gonna change nothin'."

"We'll see."

Matt picked up the phone, punched in some numbers, and waited. After a moment he said, "It's Matt. Please tell him we're ready when he has a moment." He hung up the phone and turned to Mary-Ann. "It'll be a few moments."

"While we're waiting," said Alexandra, "we brought along some muffins and donuts for you and Annie." She held out a Dunkin' Donuts box.

"She's asleep."

"Save some for her. In the meantime, feel free. We also have some coffee. I left it in the car. I'll go get it."

When she returned, Mary-Ann allowed Alexandra to pour her a cup from the large thermos and reached for a donut. "That's a mighty big thermos of coffee. You two planning to stay long?" She said it with a resigned cynicism.

"As long as it takes," said Matt. "Or until you kick us out."

Mary-Ann was just finishing her donut when the phone rang. Matt picked it up, listened for a moment, and said, "Yes, sir, here she is." He handed the phone to her.

She hesitated before taking it. "Hello?" she said, her voice tentative.

"Mrs. Scroggs, this is Angus Baxter."

She looked at her two visitors with an incredulous expression. She said nothing.

"Mrs. Scroggs, are you there?"

After a long pause, she said, weakly, "Yes."

"Surely, you must recognize my ugly voice."

She did. A current of anxiety ran through her. She brushed her hand across her lips, wiping the remains of sugar from the donut. "Yes … I do."

"Good. How is Annie doing?"

She was caught off balance. "Fine … I mean, no, she has a fever."

"Yes, I heard. I hope she gets well soon. I remember how Grace and I worried every time Kyla or Maxwell came down with something. It's one of those difficult things parents like us have to deal with. Neither Matt nor Alexandra have children, so they wouldn't know."

"Yes … thank you, Mister President."

"Listen, Mrs. Scroggs, I'm calling to tell you that everything Matt and Alexandra have told you is true. I'm asking you to listen to them. It's for your husband's own good … and Annie's. I'm sure she misses her father."

Mary-Ann paused a long while before saying, "I … I don't know whether to believe you."

The president gave a short laugh. "I can certainly understand that. We politicians don't have a sterling reputation where the truth is concerned. But I can tell you that in things that really matter, I have never lied. And this really matters. I can't give you all the details but I can tell you that your husband was set up. He needs to call this thing off. You have my word that if he does, nothing will happen to him."

She thought of Billy, everything he'd said—his speeches to militia groups; his conversations with Huey Figg and Vernon Ludlow; the things he said to her in the darkness of their bedroom. Summoning courage from somewhere deep in her gut, she said, with a quaver to her voice, "You're an evil man."

"Believe me, Mrs. Scroggs, I've heard that before. Hell, half of Congress would agree with you, perhaps, half the nation."

"I'll tell people you called. I'll tell them what you said."

"Do you truly think anyone would believe you? Think for a moment how absurd that would sound."

"I ... I just don't know."

Annie's bedroom door opened. Annie, rubbing sleep from her eyes, emerged. "Mommy?"

"I'm sorry," Mary-Ann said into the phone. "My daughter just woke up and is calling for me. I have to go."

"Of course. But please think about what I've said. And, listen, if there's anything at all Matt and Alexandra can do for you—run to the drugstore for some medicine, anything—just ask."

She hung up the phone and went to Annie. She gathered her daughter in her arms. "Sweetheart, how are you feelin'?"

Annie looked at the two visitors, leaned her head against Mary-Ann's shoulder, and said, "Mommy, when's Daddy coming home? I miss him."

"Soon, Sweetheart. Soon." She sighed deeply. Turning to Matt and Alexandra, she said, "That really was the president, wasn't it?"

"It was."

"And he knows about Billy."

"He does."

"Billy has just a few friends, but the president, he has the whole damned government—the FBI, the CIA, the Army ...."

Matt and Alexandra remained silent.

A tear formed in the corner of Mary-Ann's eye. Sighing once again, she asked. "What is it you want to know?"

Chapter 18—Johnny Waters

When they showed up for breakfast in the small restaurant, Johnny Waters was waiting for them. A brown paper bag sat on the table in front of him—a table that bore the same kind of glazed-over cigarette burns as the one in the bar the previous night. Scroggs and his two companions said "Good morning," sat at the table, and turned their coffee cups right-side up. A waitress came by and filled the cups. She dropped small containers of cream and packets of sugar into a basket and said she'd be back to take their orders.

"What's in the bag?" asked Scroggs. A slant off sunlight glinted off the polished table, causing him to squint.

"Huey said you was a gun collector, so I thought you'd like to see this." He glanced around the restaurant, surrounded the bag with one arm to hide it from view, and slipped a handgun from it. The gun gleamed black in the band of sunlight. "It's a Tokarev TT-33. I took it off a dead Shiite guy."

"So you were in Iraq?" Scroggs asked.

"Yuh, I was a lieutenant."

Scroggs gave an enigmatic smile. "You have ammo for it?"

"Thing's loaded right now."

Scroggs nodded, still showing the enigmatic smile. "Never know what might come up."

"Exactly."

Two men dressed in jeans and dirty T-shirts came through the door. They took a table at the far side of the room. Scroggs waited until the waitress approached their table with coffee before turning to Waters. "So you're goin' out to see these militia guys? They know you're comin'?"

"Nah. I'm comin' up from Jim Claxton's outfit in Gary, Indiana."

"Looks like a rented van you're drivin'."

"Yuh, rented it in Gary. Lousy bank repossessed my car."

"Perfect."

Huey Figg and Vernon Ludlow gave Scroggs an inquisitive look. As the waitress approached the table, Waters quickly slipped the gun back into the bag. The waitress took their orders and went off to the kitchen.

"You have family back in Gary?" Scroggs asked.

Waters shook his head. "Got fed up. Walked out on my wife and kids more than a year ago. Haven't heard from 'em since."

"A job?"

"Got laid off six months ago."

"So no one knows you're here?"

"Nope. Came up on a whim."

"Perfect."

Waters furrowed his brow.

The waitress returned with their breakfasts and they began eating, mostly in silence. When they finished, Scroggs said, "Why don't you come out to Rochester with us? No point in makin' that drive alone."

"Sounds great. I'll be ready as soon as I check out." Waters rose and started for the lobby.

Scroggs smiled.

Matt watched Mary-Ann Scroggs cradle Annie in her arms and rock back and forth against the creaking slats of her chair, comforting the girl. Behind her, the counter was piled with dirty dishes. He felt a lingering heat emanating from the stove immediately to his right. On one of the burners, a frying pan sat cooling. An aroma of bacon permeated the air.

He felt sorry for the woman, regretted what they were putting her through. But he could see that she fully understood the situation and was about to do whatever she could to save her husband's life. If Billy Scroggs went through with his plan—with the plan that he, Matt, had suckered him into—there was almost no chance he would survive. He might be able to assassinate Angus Baxter, because it was next to impossible to protect the president against a determined and clever assassin. But given the security around the president since the last assassination attempt, Scroggs wouldn't stand a chance of escaping. He would either be killed or caught. And if caught, it would be an almost automatic death sentence. Whichever way it went, Scroggs would lose.

And Mary-Ann and Annie would lose, too. He could see from her expression that Mary-Ann knew this; she knew the powers that were arrayed against her and Scroggs. And she knew the only way out was to cooperate with him and Alexandra, to give them the information they needed to stop Scroggs before he got to the president. All this, he thought he saw in her troubled face. "First, we need to know … does Billy call you?" he asked.

"He called yesterday but he said he couldn't call often."

Matt wrote his cell phone number on a piece of paper. "If he calls again, please give him this number. Tell him the deal's off and if he calls me I'll explain."

"You don't know him. It won't be that easy."

"Please try," Matt said. "Now we need you to tell us everything you know, starting with where Billy is now."

"I have no idea where they are. All he said was they was goin' underground until it was time to … to …."

"*They?* What do you mean, *they?*" asked Alexandra.

"Huey Figg and Vernon Ludlow are with him."

Alexandra wrote the names down in her notebook. "I know them," she said to Matt. "They hang out at Bob's Bar a lot."

It surprised Matt that Scroggs would take two others into the plot with him. He knew the man to be clever and careful and he expected he would operate alone because there would be less chance of a slip up. "Why did he take these two guys with him?" he asked Mary-Ann.

She closed her eyes and hugged Annie closer to her. When she opened her eyes, it was to look at the ceiling, at the sink, at the screen door where a moth was beating its head against the wire mash—anywhere but at Matt and Alexandra. "Annie," she said. "Don't you want to go outside and ride your bike?" As soon as Annie left, she turned to the other two.

"Mrs. Scroggs, why did he take them with him?" Matt repeated, a bubble of fear swelling in his chest.

Mary-Ann turned her gaze to him. Her eyes were pleading. She shook her head slowly, but said nothing.

"Mrs. Scroggs, we need to know."

"He's not the only one," she finally said.

"Who? Who's not the only one? Billy?"

"No. The president."

The bubble of fear in Matt's chest burst. "Oh no, please God … don't tell me … Who else?"

"The vice president … and the, what do you call it … the speaker."

Matt turned to Alexandra. "Jesus Christ! He's planning to assassinate the whole succession down to Haskins." He turned back to Mary-Ann. "Why?"

She told him how Billy believed the only way to get the United States out of the U.N. was to get Haskins in office. She said Billy figured they would all be at the Martin Luther King event and each of the men—Billy, Huey Figg, and Vernon Ludlow—would have a target. Billy, of course, would have the president. She said they were all traveling under false IDs and they were in disguise.

"Do you know the IDs they're using?"

"No. I helped them make birth certificates—we dipped them in tea water to make them look old—but I can't remember the names."

"You've got to remember."

"I … I can't."

"You've got to."

"I DON'T REMEMBER!"

Annie looked up, startled.

Mary-Ann stroked her daughter's hair. "I'm sorry, Sweetheart. I didn't mean to yell."

"Do you have any idea where they're headed?"

"I already told you I don't know where he is now, never mind where he's goin'. All I know is he planned to meet up with some militia groups."

"Why?"

"To talk them into doin' some kind of action at the same time he ... he ... you know ...."

"You mean to coordinate things?"

"He thinks he can start a grass roots revolution."

"Damn!" Matt said, looking at Alexandra. "God save us from disillusioned fanatics."

"I'll place some calls," said Alexandra. "I have a number of friends who are planted with some of the most violent of the militia groups. I think I can get them to quietly give us a call if three guys suddenly show up."

"Without going up the chain at ATF?"

Alexandra nodded. "They're good friends. We trained together."

Matt turned back to Mary-Ann Scroggs. "Is there anything more you can tell us? Anything? For example, how are they traveling?"

"They rented a van at the Bangor Airport. I drove them there. It was Budget."

"We need to get to Bangor and check it out right away," Matt said to Alexandra. Then, turning to Mary-Ann, he asked, "Anything else?"

"Not that I can think of."

"For instance, do you know how they plan to do it?"

"No, they didn't let me in on that. After the business with the I.D.s, Billy wouldn't tell me anything; he said it was for my own good."

Matt turned to Alexandra. "They must be planning on guns. Why else would it take three men if they expected all the targets to be together?"

Alexandra nodded. "Mrs. Scroggs," she said, "did Billy do anything at all unusual before he left? Anything out of the ordinary?"

The woman thought for a moment. "No ... nothing unusual."

"Nothing at all? No errands you weren't expecting, no purchases that were unusual?"

"No."

Matt looked at Alexandra as if to ask where they could go from here. Alexandra shook her head. She couldn't think of anything further to ask. They'd struck out. "What about a computer?" Alexandra asked. "I'm assuming he has one. Did he take it with him?"

"He doesn't have a computer."

"But wasn't he a software person?"

"Yuh. We had a computer, but the hard drive crashed and we couldn't afford to get it fixed."

"Even after all the money Billy received?" Matt asked.

"He just never got around to it. Instead, he used the computer at the library."

Matt felt a glimmer of hope. "Recently?"

"Yuh, just last week."

"Did he say why?"

"No, but he was there a long time."

Matt smiled at Alexandra and turned back to Mary-Ann. "Mrs. Scroggs, you may have given us what we need to stop this thing."

"We need to get to the library right away," said Alexandra. "And we need to get a computer forensics expert."

After getting Mary-Ann to promise to call them if she heard from Billy, they left the house and drove into town. They stopped first at the police station and, after showing the letter from the president asking for cooperation, got a policeman to accompany them to the library.

After they checked out of the motel, the four men piled into the van and set out toward Rochester. They were mostly silent until Scroggs took an exit off Route 290.

Huey Figg, who had a road map unfolded in his lap, said, "Hey, ain't we supposed to hook up with Route 90? What are you doin', Billy?"

"Don't you guys want to do some sightseeing? I thought we'd go north first before turnin' east for Rochester. We'll get to see Lake Ontario."

"But ain't we supposed to meet the militia guys at their shootin' range in a couple 'o hours?"

"What's the hurry? They'll be there all day."

The men glanced at each other and shrugged. About an hour later, they came to the southern shore of Lake Ontario where Scroggs turned east on a road skirting the lake. They drove another fifteen minutes before Scroggs suddenly braked and pulled to the right.

"What's up, Billy?" Vernon Ludlow asked.

Scroggs didn't answer. Instead, he made a U-turn and drove west for a hundred yards before turning onto a dirt road they had just passed.

"Where are you goin'?" asked Huey Figg.

"I'd like to give Johnny's gun a try," Scroggs replied. "Never fired a Tokarev."

"But we're goin' to a firing range. You can try it there."

"Can't wait."

The library was a small, white, wooden building with a handicap ramp leading to the front door. A sign stuck to the door with duct tape, peeling at the edges, gave notice that the library would be closed weekends until further notice due to budget constraints. Next to it was a poster advertising a bean supper by the friends of the library to raise funds for the purchase of books. A woman behind the checkout counter sent Matt and Alexandra to the reference desk where the library director was doubling as a reference librarian. She was an older woman, slender, with gray-streaked white hair. Matt asked her if she knew Billy Scroggs.

"Yes, of course," she replied. "He was in here a little while ago."

"Did he use the computer?"

"Yes. I remember he was annoyed because we only have one computer for patrons and somebody was already using it to play computer games. Why do you want to know?"

"But he did use it eventually?"

She hesitated. "Yes." She glanced at the policeman and asked again, "Why do you want to know?"

"Believe me, it's very important. We need to figure out what he was doing on the computer."

"I'm sorry, Mr. Cannon, but that sounds like a Patriot Act issue to me. The Town Council has voted that they must approve all requests for library use information."

"We don't have time for the Town Council to meet," Matt replied harshly.

"Then I'm afraid there's nothing I can do for you."

Alexandra stepped forward. "Listen, if you're familiar with the Patriot Act you know that in a case of national security we don't need your permission. We can simply confiscate the computer. But if you let us have a computer forensics expert work with it for a while, you get to keep the computer, and there will be very little interruption."

The librarian looked at the policeman who nodded his confirmation. "Well, in that case, what choice do I have?" she asked frostily.

"Good," said Matt. "We've already called for an expert. She's on her way from Portsmouth, New Hampshire. In the meantime, did he say anything to you that would give you an idea why he wanted to use the computer?"

Again, she hesitated before answering, "He asked how he could get driving directions from one place to another. I told him Mapquest."

Matt turned to Alexandra. "He doesn't know it, but he's probably told us where he's going."

Scroggs drove on until they were well off the main road. He came to a clearing on the left where he parked the van in a small copse of trees. The men climbed out of the car. Huey Figg and Johnny Waters went over to the edge of the trees to urinate. A hawk circled low overhead, its shadow gliding across the clearing.

Scroggs went round to the passenger side, leaned into the van, and pulled a pair of latex gloves from the glove compartment. He snapped them on like a surgeon about to perform an operation.

"What are the gloves for, Billy?" Vernon Ludlow asked.

Scroggs didn't answer. Instead, he walked over to Johnny Waters and asked, "Mind if I give your gun a try?"

"No, feel free," Waters replied, wrinkling his brow at the surgical gloves. He went back to the van, retrieved the gun, and handed it to Scroggs.

"She loaded?" Scroggs asked. The day was oppressive with mosquitoes, the trees, the ground, the air all exhaling humidity. It blistered sweat beads on his upper lip.

"Yuh," Waters replied.

Scroggs nodded. A small animal scurried through the underbrush creating a dead scritch of last year's leaves. Scroggs hefted the gun, aiming it to the right and the left. He picked out a slender birch sapling, aimed, and fired. A flock of crows rose from the trees cawing frantically. "Nice action," Scroggs said. The woods fell still as the echo of the gunshot throbbed to silence. Scroggs walked back to Johnny Waters and, holding the gun by the barrel, offered it back to him. But as soon as Waters had the gun in his hand, Scroggs grabbed his wrist with one hand and, with the other, forced the man's finger onto the trigger.

"What the fuck...?" cried Waters. "Ow! That hurts." He struggled to free his hand, but Scroggs was too strong. "What the fuck's going on?" Waters cried.

"You're gonna shoot yourself."

"Are you crazy?"

Scroggs bent the man's arm at the elbow and forced him to point the gun at his own temple.

"Jesus!"

"Go ahead," said Scroggs in a soft voice. "Do it."

Crickets started to chirp again. From the corner of his eye, Scroggs saw a squirrel scamper across the clearing.

"You're fuckin' crazy!" cried Waters.

"Go ahead, squeeze the trigger. What do you have to live for, anyway?"

"Please ... please stop this." Waters called to the others. "Make him fuckin' stop."

Scroggs said, "Man, you walked out on your wife and kids. You don't deserve to live."

"Please ... please, God, don't! I'm a Christian!"

"Then you should be happy. You're part of God's plan, an instrument of His will."

"Billy, what the fuck are you doin'?" asked Vernon Ludlow urgently.

Scroggs ignored him. "Go ahead, a nice gentle squeeze."

"Billy?" asked Huey Figg.

"For Christ's sake, Billy," Ludlow said, "leave the man—"

Scroggs slipped his gloved finger over Water's and pressed. The gun exploded. A shard of bone leaped from Water's skull. Once again, crows lifted from the trees in a flurry of wings and cries. Waters crumbled to the ground, landing on his back, eyes staring widely at the sky.

"What the fuck did you do that for?" asked Vernon Ludlow.

"He was too good to pass up. God dropped him into our hands so we had a van they could never trace to us." Scroggs reached into his pocket and pulled out Huey Figg's driver's license, the one he confiscated from the man the previous night. He handed it to Figg. "Take his I.D. papers and put this in his pocket. You are now known as Johnny Waters. Huey Figg is dead."

After some hesitation, Figg did as he was ordered in silence. Vernon Ludlow stood shaking his head.

"What's with you guys?" Scroggs asked. "Considerin' what we're plannin' to do, you'd think this would mean nothin' to you."

"Yuh, Billy, but—"

"—But nothin'! Now let's get goin'. We're goin' back to get his van then we're gonna bring ours back here. We'll still have plenty of time to make it to the firing range." He reached into the van and retrieved another pair of gloves. "Here, wear these when we pick up his van. From now on, none of us drives without gloves."

During the time it took to drive back to Niagara Falls, get the other van, and return to the dirt road, very little was said. Huey Figg never spoke, and Vernon Ludlow only asked, "Where'd you get the gloves?"

"I come prepared."

"Jesus!" Ludlow said, shaking his head. "The president ain't got a fuckin' chance!"

Chapter 19—Katherine Moore-Paterson

They were driving to Bangor Airport when Alexandra said, "I don't know. "Something doesn't add up about this." They were making use of the time while waiting for the computer forensics expert who said it would take her five or six hours to arrive in Bass Run from New Hampshire.

"What do you mean?"

"He made it pretty damned obvious what he was doing. First he makes a scene about the computer being in use, then he asks the librarian about Mapquest. Doesn't sound like a man trying to hide his intention. Don't forget, he was a computer software guy before he got laid off. He should have known about Mapquest."

Matt thought for a moment. "No, I think you're giving him too much credit. He had no reason to believe we would be turned onto the library."

"All the same ...."

At the rental agency, after some heavy persuasion and the use of the presidential letter, they were shown all the van rental documents. There were only four and they were quickly able—with the help of the rental agent on duty when Mary-Ann said she'd dropped them off—to narrow it down to the one van that was rented by three men. They initiated a trace on it, then returned to Bass Run.

Two hours later, the computer expert arrived. She was a woman in her twenties with a small silver ring piercing the corner of her lower lip. "No sweat," she said when Matt told her they wanted to recover the data from a Mapquest session on the date and at the time the librarian had given them.

An hour later, she had the answer. "He got a route from Bass Run to Toronto, Canada. A little over thirteen hours. It took him south through Massachusetts then west on 90 and up through Niagara Falls."

"That's his first mistake," said Matt. "We can get him at customs."

"But why Toronto?" asked Alexandra.

"He figures there might be a nation-wide search. He's laying low out of the country until it's time to head for Washington. When he does that, we get him at customs. In fact, if they broke the trip up and stayed overnight somewhere, we might get them on their way *into* Canada."

Back at Scroggs' house Matt asked Mary-Ann, "Does Billy have any relatives or friends in Toronto?"

"Canada? No, not that I know of."

Matt turned to Alexandra. "We should get our asses to Niagara Falls so we'll be there when the customs people get him."

"What if they re-enter through Detroit?"

"Then they'll get him at the border there and we'll be that much closer."

Matt's cell phone chirped. He answered it, listened for a while, and when he finished turned to Alexandra. "The van was turned in at Logan Airport in Boston."

"Then they're flying to Toronto?"

"But why would they get driving instructions? Scroggs is smart enough to know that boarding a plane makes him easier to track. I think what they did is switch cars to keep us off balance. We need to get to Boston."

After getting permission from Mary-Ann to put a tap on her phone, Matt said, "You have my cell phone number. Please call me the moment he calls."

"Nothing gets traced back to me," said Karl Zacher. "Understand? Nothing."

"Don't worry, Mister Zacher, we know what we're doing," said Ralph Stanley who had the good looks of a gigolo.

"We'll call when we have her," said Donna Quinn who was equally attractive.

They left Zacher's office in the Watergate complex, closing the door behind them.

Zacher sat back in his plush leather chair, hands behind his head, and smiled with satisfaction. Stanley and Quinn were costing him a pretty penny, but he had learned long ago that when things start to go wrong, the important thing was not to sit still but to act.

After meeting with the militia group near Rochester, Billy Scroggs was pissed off. He couldn't get them to agree to any action because they said they were laying low for a while. "They've turned into a fuckin' gun club," Scroggs said to his companions. "Unless some of the other groups decide to move, we'll have to start this thing ourselves with Baxter and the others. Maybe then these guys will wake up and take some action."

That evening, he lay on his bed wrestling with the temptation to call Mary-Ann. He knew he shouldn't, but he had to find out how Annie was doing. A flickering neon light from the motel sign cast reflections on the telephone. He started to reach for it, then decided that, yes, he would place the call, but not from his room. He left the motel and drove several miles east until he found a gas station with a pay phone. Parking so that the van was between the phone bank and the station attendants, he picked up the receiver, deposited a number of quarters, and punched in his home number. The phone rang several times before Mary-Ann picked it up. "It's me," he said. "How's Annie doin'?"

"Billy!"

"How's Annie doin'? Is the fever gone?"

"She's doin' better. Billy, the man who put you up to this was here with that Alexandra Lake woman. They want you to call the whole thing off. Please, Billy, come home."

Scroggs gripped the receiver. "Damn it, Mary-Ann, did you tell them anything?"

She said something, but he couldn't hear because a truck sped past the gas station at that moment. The bloom from its headlights swept across his face. When the truck disappeared down the road, he repeated, "Did you tell them anything?"

"Billy, I only want to get you back. They said you could keep the money."

"Goddamn, Mary-Ann!" He slammed the phone down. There was a good chance they'd already put a trace on the phone line. He jumped into the van and spun wheels leaving the gas station. It was going on eight o'clock by the time he got back to the motel. He found Huey Figg and Vernon Ludlow in the room. "Let's go, we're gettin' out of here," he said.

"What the hell, Billy? We're just settlin' in," said Huey Figg.

"No arguments. We're movin'." He wasn't going to tell them how he'd risked a phone call that could lead the cops to them. He started to throw his clothes into his bag. Reluctantly, the others followed. Within fifteen minutes, they were in the van and traveling down the highway.

Wayne Haskins hadn't heard from Karl Zacher in more than two weeks. There was no telling what the bastard was up to, and all Haskins could do was worry and wait for the shoe to drop. He thought of the video he suspected Zacher had, the one of him screwing the lovely, presumed delegate, Evelyn with joyful abandon. If that got out, it could destroy his marriage. Julia was an understanding and a most forgiving woman, but this ....

He looked at Julia who had fallen asleep in her reading chair, a book sprawled in her lap. The fall of light from the reading lamp softened her features. She had always been beautiful, he thought, and seldom more so than when she was sleeping. He loved her deeply and she was good to him. He felt a knot of nausea rising in his stomach at the thought of hurting her. A shudder passed through his body.

And then there were the grandchildren. He closed his eyes and felt a tear slide down his cheek. If Zacher threatened to release the video to some news organization or post it on the internet, so be it. He would have to deal with it and hope Julia—and his children and grandchildren—could forgive him. As horrible as it would be, it would be far better than the disgrace that would befall him if it got out about falsifying the president's medical records, a disgrace almost as great as Angus Baxter would feel if his insane self-assassination plot were exposed.

"We're headed for Gary, Indiana, by way of Cleveland," Scroggs said. He showed them the map on which he'd highlighted the route. "One of you guys drive; I'm gonna spread out in the back seat and try to get some sleep."

"Why Gary?"

"Because we're gonna return this van. Water's rental papers say it's due back the day after tomorrow. We don't need no rental car company placin' a trace on it. We'll return it a day early."

"But why go through Cleveland? Wouldn't it be faster to go through Detroit?" Figg asked.

"And go through U.S. and Canadian customs here, and again in Detroit? What, are you fuckin' crazy? Head for Cleveland."

After they settled onto Route 190 South, Scroggs stretched out in the back seat of the van, exhausted. The hum of the tires lulled him into a semi-conscious state halfway between wakefulness and sleep and he was only vaguely aware of the sporadic conversation between Huey Figg and Vernon Ludlow. His unformulated thoughts turned to Mary-Ann and Annie. He saw them in the kitchen of their rundown house and imagined what it would be like once they could renovate the place—lay down a new floor, buy new appliances. His eyelids grew heavy and he drifted slowly into a sporadic, troubled, dream-filled sleep. Once, he heard Vernon Ludlow utter a phrase that should have woken him like an alarm clock:

"… so fast…"

But it didn't come through loudly enough to register. He didn't know how long he'd been asleep, but he gradually became aware of the van slowing to a stop. When, at last, his eyes fluttered open, he bolted upright. "What the hell's goin' on?" he asked, panic edging his voice. The inside of the van was strobed by alternating blue and white lights. He turned to see a police cruiser pulling to a stop behind them. "Jesus Christ! What's happenin'?"

Vernon Ludlow spoke. "I told him to slow down. The son-of-a-bitch was doin' eighty."

"Huey, you fuckin' jerk!" Scroggs muttered. He stared at the back of Figg's head as the trooper came up to the van.

"License and registration," the trooper said.

Huey Figg, glancing at Scroggs, fumbled for the driver's license that had Johnny Waters' name and picture on it. He handed it to the man who examined it in the beam of a flashlight. He then shone the light on Figg's face and asked, "Is this your picture."

"Ah … yuh. Yuh, it's my picture."

The trooper frowned.

Scroggs leaned forward. "I was with him when he had it taken, Officer. It was several years ago and he's put on a lota weight since. Too much pizza and too many beers, I guess." He gave a chuckle and punched Figg on the shoulder, a little harder than necessary.

The trooper gazed at Scroggs for a moment before saying, "Registration."

Vernon Ludlow, meanwhile, had opened the glove compartment and pulled out the rental contract. He handed it across to Figg who gave it to the trooper.

"You headed back to Gary, now?"

"Ah, yuh."

"Wait here." The trooper went back to the cruiser and got in.

Scroggs stared straight ahead, saying nothing. Figg turned to him and said, "Jesus, Billy, I'm sorry. I guess I didn't know how fast I was driving."

"I told you we were goin' eighty, you idiot," said Vernon Ludlow.

Scroggs said nothing. In the flashing lights of the police cruiser, the two men could see his cheek muscles quiver. Five minutes later, the trooper returned and handed Figg a speeding ticket. "Go easy on the speed and get yourself a new picture taken."

Figg nodded, put the van in gear, and slowly pulled back onto the highway. Once they were out of sight of the cruiser, Scroggs said, "Pull over. Vernon's gonna drive."

Figg slowed and pulled the van into the breakdown lane. As he climbed out of the driver's seat, he said, "Aw, Christ, Billy, I ain't gonna do nothin' like that again."

"That, Huey, you can take to the bank."

Less than three hours later, they entered the outskirts of Cleveland. After stopping for gas, they pulled onto Route 90 West, headed for Gary, almost five hours away.

When they arrived at the Enterprise location on Grant Street in Gary at 6:00 a.m. the morning of the 22nd, they found the place wouldn't be open until 7:30. Figg and Ludlow wanted to find a place for breakfast, but Scroggs said he wasn't about to be driving all around Gary and risk raising suspicion, so they sat sullenly in the car with little conversation. Figg was especially nervous. Several times he tried to get Scroggs to say he was forgiven for the run-in with the state trooper, but Scroggs remained silent.

At last, they saw a woman unlock the door of the agency and walk in. Scroggs waited five minutes before sending Figg in to return the car.

When Figg returned, he asked, "Where to now, Billy?"

Scroggs said, "We're layin' low here for a day. Stay off the roads. I got something to work out."

"What do you need to work out?"

"Somethin'. "

At Logan Airport, with the help of the president's To Whom it May Concern Letter, Matt and Alexandra were able to visit all the car rental agencies and compare names with airline passenger lists. For the day the original van was dropped off, they found only five people who had rented a car without first flying into Boston and four of those cars had already been returned. Even more persuasive was that the fifth rental was a van. "That's got to be them," Matt said.

"I agree," said Alexandra. "What do you say we put out an APB on the van?"

"Go for it."

An hour later, as they were leaving Logan Airport, Matt's cell phone chirped. It was Mary-Ann Scroggs. Her voice was strained. "I told him to come home but he just swore at me and hung up."

"He called? When?"

"Last night."

"Last night?" Matt repeated with annoyance.

"I'm sorry I didn't call right away; I'm still not sure—"

"—Did he say anything? Do you have any idea where he is?"

"No," she answered. "Mr. Cannon, you have to find him. Please."

"We will," he replied. "We think we know the van they're driving."

"Annie is sick; she needs him. She misses him."

Matt felt a pang of empathy. From the day he and Marcie decided they wanted a baby, he'd looked at children in a very different way, especially Annie. He imagined what it would be like to have a child like her—reading books at bedtime, going to the zoo, playing games on the living room floor, hearing her speak her first words. Mommy … Daddy … book … toy … water. And along with the empathy came a flood of anger, even jealousy. He thought: "Sure, Mary-Ann, but let's not forget it was your brother-in-law— a man your husband is trying to emulate—who robbed me and Marcie of the opportunity to have a child like Annie, so don't give me this crap about your daughter needing her father. My un-conceived child needed a father, too." He thought it, but he didn't say it. Instead, he said, "Try not to worry, Mrs. Scroggs. We're working very hard to track your husband down. And when we find him, we won't harm him. That's a promise. We'll bring him back to you and Annie."

Angus Baxter, sitting with his secretaries in the cabinet room, no longer knew what was right and what was wrong. Until now, he had always depended on logic, and logic had always carried him through. But now he questioned the very reliability of logic. Clearly, it had led him into a blind alley. And blind was the right word. He wondered where and when he'd lost the touchstone of compassion and feeling that might have made his calculating mind less toxic. He summoned an image of his father's Medal of Honor that sat on his desk several doors away. A devotee of pop psychology might say the emotional side of him had become calloused when, as a child, he lost his father. But he didn't believe in pop psychology; leave that to television talk shows. Perhaps if he had been a religious man he might have found an answer, but his religion was just a pretense, a necessary sham in order to get elected and the more he faked it, the more remote he became from any kind of true religious feeling.

He was a withered man. Had he instinctively known this about himself— that he was an incomplete being, as sterile in his soul as Matt was in his body? Had he known all along he needed somebody to provide that dimension of character for him? Was that the role Grace had played in his life? Until now, Grace had always been there with her understanding and her consolation and her counsel.

Grace.

"Mister President?" asked the secretary of State.

Baxter looked up to see the cabinet secretaries and their staffs staring at him. The vice president, especially, had a worried look on her face. "Yes, John," Baxter said. "You were saying?"

"I was saying, sir, that you apparently established a solid foundation with Bakhit and Golani aboard the *Bradley*. Amazingly, they've both agreed to another summit with no pre-conditions. What's more, the Knesset and the Palestinian authority are on board. This is certainly without doubt the most promising opportunity ever. Even the Al-Aqsa Martyrs Brigade and Hamas have agreed, in principle, to lay low during the talks. That's something we've never had before."

Baxter gazed at the Secretary of State for a long moment. In the corner of his eye he saw the other secretaries shifting nervously in their chairs. He knew what it was that worried them and he realized he had to demonstrate his presence. Yes, his presence, he thought. He asked, "And what about the Islamic Jihadists?"

"We haven't heard from them yet, but there's every reason to believe they'll go along. I'm telling you, sir, the climate is unlike anything we've ever seen before and it's largely due to your meeting aboard the *Bradley*."

"Perhaps, but it's like an asymptotic curve. Getting that last one percent done is far more difficult than the first ninety-nine percent. So, what are the next steps?" *It was something to hang on to—a geometric reference; orderly progress; one step following another; the logic of sequence; cause preceding effect; effect following cause; simple equations.*

He was in control of his mind.

"Select a neutral site."

"Where?" *Pinpointing a location on earth; exquisite logic of longitude and latitude; the earth rotating precisely on its axis; spinning in its orbit in the regularity of the universe; strict periodicity; determined location.* He struggled to focus his mind. "Where?" he asked again, interrupting the secretary who had already begun to answer.

"Yes … As I was saying, I think we need to be careful about negative associations. Oslo, Camp David, Wye, are definitely out; they represent failure. Also, it has to be in some country that has no association—real or imagined—with one side or the other. A location without a history of anti-Semitism or anti-Islamic sentiment."

The Defense Secretary, Erwin Scobel, gave a wry chuckle. "Well, that just about eliminates any place on earth."

"Tonga," said the Secretary of State.

"Tonga?" several people asked with bemused expressions.

"It's capital, Nuku'alofa. There are some good resorts that would provide an appropriate ambiance for peace talks; the airport has an eight-thousand-seven-hundred-foot runway, enough for *Air Force One* and other large planes; the only significant religion is the Free Wesleyan Church which, as far as I know, hasn't much of a history of anti-Islamic or anti-Jewish conflict. Also, they have excellent bilateral relations with Japan who has very little anti-Semitism and very few Muslims. There are only a couple dozen mosques in all of Japan. It may be a great opportunity to engage the Japanese in some kind of peacemaking role."

"But for Christ's sake, John, Tonga is nowhere! Thousands of miles from any of the participants."

"Exactly."

Baxter sensed he had a question, but he had trouble formulating it. He kept his silence.

"We're listening, John," said the Defense Secretary.

Baxter scribbled something on the notepad in front of him.

"Get them far from their daily lives of bombings and retaliations. An entirely different environment. Sunsets and palm trees instead of guns and smoke clouds. Get them to feel …."

Eight thousand seven hundred feet. Baxter marveled at the sound, seven syllables infiltrating the tympanic cavity, vibrating the eardrum and sending sound waves into the cochlea where they are converted into impulses that translate into a concept, a distance. Baxter's pencil scratched out: Eight-thousand-seven-hundred … 8,700 … 5,280 feet to a mile … 1.6 miles. Or, to be more precise …. Laboriously, filling up the paper, he did the calculations. 1.6477 miles. All that from microscopic nerve cells in the cerebral cortex that become little more than inert cat food upon death.

Vice President Moore-Paterson, sitting next to the president, took a sip of coffee then unobtrusively slid her coffee cup in front of the president's notepad. She disguised the move by spreading several memos in the space where the coffee cup had been. Turning to the row of seats against the wall, she motioned for an aide to approach her. She handed the aide a quickly scribbled note and the aide stepped from the cabinet room.

The Secretary of State was still talking. "I've already sounded out the Tongolese government. They were thrilled at the prospect of drawing all that attention to Tonga. The media coverage alone, with the special location features they like to do, would encourage a big increase in tourism."

"Plus, I'll bet they've never had a visit from a sitting president," said the Commerce Secretary. "Wherever *Air Force One* touches down, it brings instant prestige."

Baxter said, "Your mention of Japan reminds me of something I learned the other day when I was meeting their ambassador. He told me that even skilled Japanese translators—especially those who do simultaneous translation like at the U.N.—have a very difficult time going from English to Japanese for the word 'you.' It's because we only have one word but the Japanese have several words that correspond to 'you' depending on a person's social rank relative to the person who is speaking. For example, if you are speaking to a person of very low status, the word is 'omae;' but if the person is a subordinate or, say, a girlfriend, the word is 'kimi.' Then if a person is on your same level, it's 'anata,' and if you want to acknowledge a person as being esteemed, you attach the suffix –'sama' to his name. The Japanese can insult someone by intentionally using a word for 'you' that is beneath that person's actual status. Can you imagine the diplomatic furor if the translator got it wrong?"

And to himself, he thought: Which of the versions of "you" would a Japanese assassin use to his target? One of respect which elevates the importance of the assassination and hence, in the assassin's eyes, his own importance; or one of disrespect, born of the hatred that is the motive for the assassination, which diminishes the act. Nobody would derive satisfaction from assassinating a low level flunky.

"That's very interesting, Mister President," said Katherine Moore-Paterson, "but I think we should return to the question of Tonga." Without waiting for a reply, she turned to the Under Secretary of State for Political Affairs—the ranking career diplomat at State, and a man famous for not being shy about disagreeing with his boss—and asked, "What do you think, Arthur?"

"I totally agree with Secretary Monteson," he replied.

Other cabinet officials offered their opinions, mostly in favor of Tonga. The conversation was just about to turn to dates when the president's secretary entered the room. "Mister President, General Gillespie needs you and the vice president right away in the situation room."

"I see," said Baxter. Turning to the others and rising, he said, "If the Tongolese agree, I'm in favor of approaching the Palestinians and Israelis about it. Let's see if we can get a date in the near future." As they left the room, Moore-Paterson handed him his notepad. "You'll need this, sir."

Matt and Alexandra were approaching Niagara Falls when her cell phone chirped. She listened for a while, asked a few questions, then said, "We're probably an hour or so away. Give me your phone number and we'll call as we get closer. You can guide us in." She flipped the cover on the phone and turned to Matt. "They found the van. A couple of kids were hiking in the woods near Rochester and came across it. There was a dead body. Shot in the head. Apparent suicide."

"Any I.D.?"

"Huey Figg," Alexandra replied.

"Damn! How do we get there?"

"I'm looking now," Alexandra said as she unfolded a map.

By the time they arrived, several police cruisers were pulled over on the side near a dirt road leading into the woods. They stopped and showed a policeman their I.D.s. "Are you the people who called in an APB on the van?"

"That's us," said Alexandra.

"What the hell's ATF got to do with this? You figure the guy was a smuggler or something?"

"Something like that."

"Yuh. Well, drive on in. It's about a quarter mile. The crime scene folks are there."

They drove slowly along the rutted road until they came to a clearing where yellow crime scene tape was strung between trees at the periphery of a clearing. The tape fluttered and twisted in a stiff wind. A cluster of people were gathered around a blue van. Matt and Alexandra stepped from the car, ducked under the tape, and approached the investigators. One of them, a white-haired man in his fifties, asked, "Who are you two?"

Alexandra showed him her I.D.

"Feds, huh? I'm Detective Ryan. We don't often see you folks around here." He turned to Matt. "You with ATF, too?"

"No."

"Then who are you with?"

"Nobody. I'm a private citizen."

"In that case, you don't belong here. This is official business."

Matt reached into his jacket and pulled out the presidential letter. "Here, Detective Ryan, you might want to read this."

The man frowned, unfolded the sheet of paper, and read. His frown deepened. "You gotta be kidding me. I don't suppose you can tell me what this is about."

"Afraid not," said Alexandra.

"Didn't think so," said Ryan. "But you're telling me the president's interested in this?"

"Depends on who that guy is," Matt replied, nodding to the body laying face up beside the van.

"Name on the driver's license says Huey Figg."

"That's not Huey Figg," said Alexandra flatly. "I can tell even from this distance that's not him."

"What do you mean? You know this guy?"

"I know Huey Figg," said Alexandra. "I don't know this guy."

"Did he have any other papers?" asked Matt.

Ryan shook his head. "Just the license. You wanna come into Niagara Falls with me?"

"Why Niagara Falls?" Alexandra asked.

Ryan handed her a book of matches. "Found this on the victim's body."

Alexandra looked at the book of matches then handed it to Matt. On the cover was written "Niagara Falls Motel."

As they followed Ryan to Niagara Falls, Alexandra said, "That may not have been Huey Figg, but sure as hell Figg was here."

Matt nodded. "Along with Scroggs and Vernon Ludlow is my guess. And I have a pretty good idea why they would take that guy out, whoever he was."

"That's not hard to figure," replied Alexandra. "They switched cars."

"Which means we have no idea what they're driving now."

"Not unless the cops find a match on the guy's fingerprints or they get a missing person report that allows them to identify the sucker."

"Or we get lucky at the motel."

"I hope so," said Alexandra, "because we can't afford to wait around while they try to figure out who the victim is, but I'm fresh out of ideas about where to start looking."

Matt said, "What gets me is why they would deliberately plant Figg's license on the poor bastard."

"To persuade us that the Toronto thing is real. A line extended from Bass Run through where the van was found brings you to Toronto."

"So you're saying the Mapquest directions and the license were deliberate screw-ups to get us off track?"

"I told you back in Bass Run that Scroggs was too smart to leave such an obvious clue as the Mapquest directions."

Matt frowned. "Yuh, I guess you were right after all. So where do you think they could be going?

"Change their route only slightly and you come to Michigan."

"You think Michigan? Why?"

"There's an especially militant group in the northern part of the state," Alexandra said. "I have a friend embedded with them. I think it's time I give Jack a call."

"Makes sense," Matt said. "But to get to Michigan, they'll still have to pass through Canadian Customs."

"Then maybe we can get them there."

At the Niagara Falls Motel Detective Ryan showed the desk clerk his cell phone with a digital image of the victim. "Oh, God!" said the clerk.

"Know him?" Ryan asked.

"Yuh. He checked in two nights ago."

"Well, you can mark him checked out now. Show us the registration card, please."

The clerk searched through a rack until he found the card. He handed it to Ryan who turned to Matt and Alexandra and said, "Name's John Waters."

Alexandra asked the clerk, "Is his car still here?"

"No."

"It was rented from Gary, Indiana," said Ryan. "I'll put a trace on it."

After Ryan left and Matt and Alexandra had returned to their car, Matt said, "You know, something else has occurred to me."

"What's that?"

"Our plan was to call Scroggs off by promising to keep everything quiet so it doesn't blow up in the president's and Senator Haskins' faces. I didn't have too much of a problem with that because it amounted to ignoring something Scroggs was only planning to do."

"And now?"

"Now it means we have to keep an actual murder quiet."

"I thought of that. Can we do it?"

"I don't know. All I know is this whole thing is beginning to stink a whole lot more than before."

"Yuh," Alexandra said. "But right now we need to stop for gas." As she pulled into a service station, Matt's phone chirped. "You get that," Alexandra said. "I'll pump the gas."

As she was filling the tank, she couldn't help but overhear Matt's end of the conversation through the open window. He listened for a long time, finally saying, "That bad?" Then another long pause followed by, "Okay, thanks. I don't blame you for being frightened. Just hang in there."

Alexandra climbed into the passenger seat. "White House?" she asked. "Yuh."

"Look, it's getting late," said Alexandra. "What do you say to getting a place in Niagara Falls and treating ourselves to a nice dinner? We can discuss our next steps over drinks."

"Sounds like a plan to me. Why don't you call the Sheraton-On-The-Falls and see if they have rooms?"

"You know the place?"

"I stayed there before. It's got a great restaurant with a nice view."

"Honeymoon?"

Matt laughed. "No. I met some clients for a round of golf."

318 Norman G. Gautreau

As they talked, Alexandra pulled up the hotels app on her phone, located the Sheraton-On-The-Falls hotel, found the reservations number and called it. Moments later, she said, "Hi, I'm calling to see if you have any rooms available for two people." She cupped her hand over the phone, turned to Matt, and asked, "Who's paying?"

"The president, eventually."

She returned to the phone, listened for a moment, and said, "Good. We'll take one of the presidential corner suites. The name is Matt Cannon and we'll be there within the hour.

"The presidential suite?" said Matt. "I assumed you'd get two rooms."

"It has a fireplace and a Jacuzzi."

"How many bedrooms?"

"One. What's the matter? Afraid of me?"

"Well, I ...."

"Relax, there's a sofa. We'd only have to wrestle about who gets the sofa and who gets the king size bed," Alexandra said. "And don't forget, I went through rigorous physical training for the ATF."

Chapter 20—The Rabbit Hole; Huey Figg

Entering the Oval Office, Vice President Moore-Paterson said, "I hope you'll forgive me, sir, but I had to get you out of there."

"No General Gillespie?"

The vice president nodded. "Only a ruse."

"What's going on?"

"You were drifting in there. You were in another world. You were making some kind of mathematical notes, and what's with the Japanese words for 'you'?"

Baxter walked to the window and gazed out at the White House lawn. "I was bored."

"You were bored by a possible Middle East breakthrough with all the importance you attach to that? Excuse me, sir, but you were not bored; you were losing focus. Badly. And it was becoming apparent to everybody."

"So what of it?"

"You can't be serious, Mister President," Moore-Paterson said. She gestured toward the cabinet room. "They may all be your appointees, but you have enemies in there. That's a price you have to pay to have a bi-partisan administration."

"Oh come on, Katherine, I trust every one of them."

"And I think you can trust them … as long as they have confidence in your ability to lead the administration. But once they lose that confidence, it's every man for himself."

"Do you think I've lost the ability to function?"

"I think you should talk to Jim Stockton. It could be that the treatments you're getting for leukemia are affecting your concentration."

Baxter stared at her. He'd chosen not to tell her the leukemia wasn't real because she wasn't the kind of person who would let it go at that. She would probe. She would want to know how Jim Stockton could make such a mistake and eventually, she would learn the truth. With that, everything else would begin to unravel and if that happened, she just might chose to resign herself rather than be part of his administration. It would be a good political move. All she would have to do is leak the scheme and when everything came out, she would be praised for having the integrity to resign and she would have eliminated Senator Haskins, her major obstacle after Baxter himself, to the White House. And he knew she burned with a passion to occupy the Oval Office.

"I'll talk to Jim," he finally said. "And, Katherine, can you return later this evening? I have something very important to discuss with you. Say, about nine o'clock when most everybody else will be gone?"

Moore-Paterson gave him a quizzical look. "Of course, Angus. I'll be here."

"You're staring at me," said Matt.

Alexandra smiled. "Payback."

They sat across from each other at a table set against a wall of windows in the Fallsview Restaurant on the penthouse level of the Sheraton.

Earlier, they'd spent an hour in the fitness center where Matt enjoyed ogling Alexandra's legs as she worked out energetically on the elliptical machine in front of him, admiring the way the muscles of her calves and thighs moved under the taut skin of her trim legs and feeling himself become aroused.

"What do you mean, payback?"

"The windows in the fitness center give a good reflection. I saw you staring at my butt and legs."

"You have lovely legs. Sorry about staring," said Matt with a laugh.

"Don't be. I'm flattered. But what about my butt?"

"You have a great butt, too."

"I know," Alexandra said. "I'm sorry Marcie left you. That sucks." She continued to stare at him while holding a glass of wine in front of her that she swirled with subtle movements of her wrist. Reflections from the table candle flickered in the belly of the glass and on the silver bracelet that moved with her wrist.

"I asked her to commit a crime."

"She could have said no," Alexandra answered. "You don't think he's sane, do you?"

"Are you gonna have dessert?"

"The cherry pie. That's what the call from the White House was about. He's getting worse, isn't he?"

"The cherry pie sounds good," Matt said.

"Matt, I need to know." She glared at him as he remained silent. "I'm just trying to figure out who you are. If I'm Alice, you must be the White Rabbit."

"Why the White Rabbit?"

"Because I'm following you down this hole where nothing makes sense," Alexandra replied. "Matt, I need to know if you're serious about stopping Scroggs."

"Do you want whipped cream with the pie?"

"Damn it, Matt! Listen to me!" She slammed her fist on the table, spilling some of the wine from her glass. She mopped it up with a napkin. "Listen, if you're planning to save the country from your lunatic friend, you better come up with a better way. I'm getting Scroggs. Don't screw with me."

The waiter appeared. "May I get you dessert?"

"Bring us each a slice of cherry pie, please," said Matt.

Alexandra waited for the waiter to leave before continuing. "Or maybe it's Scroggs. Things would be easier if he kicked puppies and burned kittens instead of hugging his daughter. You want things to be black and white, but they never are."

"Damn!" Matt said. "I forgot to ask for whipped cream."

"Forget the pie. Let's fuck."

Matt stared at her for a long moment before saying, "What? Just like that?"

"You need a way out of the rabbit hole and I get horny when I drink."

Again, Matt paused before asking, "Why did you leave your husband?"

"What husband?"

"It's faded now, but you had a ring of lighter skin where a wedding band was."

"Don't need it anymore."

"What? The marriage?"

She shook her head. "The tan line."

"I'm confused."

"Why am I not surprised? It was cover, back story for the benefit of the M4 yokels. Did it in a tanning booth."

"Christ!"

"Pay the bill. I'll be in the room."

She rose and walked toward the exit. He watched her hips move.

Baxter and Katherine Moore-Paterson sat alone in the Oval Office. A bright moon spilled in through the West Wing windows, shimmering on the presidential seal in the middle of the carpet and igniting the rotating globes of the anniversary clock. Shadows of branches from the crab apple trees in the Rose Garden shivered on the floor and on the polished surface of the desk, giving the appearance of fingering the Congressional Medal of Honor.

The vice president held her glass of scotch in a shaft of moonlight and studied the amber liquid. The president stood, walked to the sideboard, dropped an ice cube into his crystal glass with a clink that seemed to fill the room, and poured another two fingers of the single malt. He gestured to Moore-Paterson, silently asking if she, too, wanted her drink freshened; she smiled and shook her head. Baxter returned to his armchair, leaned forward, and asked, "Well, what do you think?"

She sighed. "I think you're offering me a great honor. I only wish it didn't have to conflict with the King event."

"Yes, that's unfortunate, but it can't be helped. This snag with the peace talks came up suddenly and these were the only dates that both Bakhit and Golani would agree to." What he didn't tell her was how much back-channel pressure he had put on them to accept the dates that included the 28th. He paused, swirled his glass, passed it under his nose, and inhaled deeply. "Look at it this way, Katherine. If King himself were here and he knew you were being asked to go to Jerusalem and Ramallah to get the Tonga Conference back on track, what would he say?"

"He'd say, 'Go.' "

"Exactly. It's an opportunity to lay a more solid groundwork for the peace conference. You wanted more meaty assignments, so here it is. It's a far cry from a state funeral."

"I know that, sir. And, believe me, I'm deeply grateful …."

"But you had your heart set on the ceremony."

"I'm an African-American vice president. It's Martin Luther King."

"We could always reschedule the ceremony …." Baxter startled himself with this instinctive eruption of faintheartedness. Even if she had no possible way of knowing that his blurted idea was a sign of fear for his own safety, he wished he could withdraw the comment.

"Reschedule the ceremony?" she asked in a voice inflecting to falsetto. "Impossible! It has to be done on the anniversary of his 'I have a Dream' speech. Nothing else makes sense from a symbolic point-of-view."

"Yes. Of course, you're right." Even as he berated himself for his earlier fearfulness, he was at least consoled in the knowledge that he had, in all probability, just saved the vice president's life. Furthermore, he was convinced that, by meeting with Bakhit and Golani, she will have made it possible for him achieve something every modern day president had tried and failed—a lasting peace in the Middle East.

He only hoped he would survive to see it.

The penthouse presidential suite had two stories. On the first floor was a living room with fireplace, a large plasma television, floor-to-ceiling windows, and a large balcony that overlooked both the Horseshoe Falls and the American Falls; and on the second floor was a bedroom with a king size bed and a bathroom with an oversize Jacuzzi bathtub.

Alexandra started to fill the Jacuzzi while Matt waited on the first level for the wine to be delivered. He wrote out a hasty note for the room service person asking that the wine be left on the coffee table and placed it on the floor by the door which he left ajar with a rolled up magazine. He put a five dollar bill down beside the note, then went into the first floor bathroom and took a quick shower. By the time he finished and donned a hotel bathrobe, the wine was sitting on the coffee table along with two clean glasses. He gathered them up and climbed the stairs.

Alexandra was reclining in the Jacuzzi, her breasts and knees emerging from the water. "Why, it's Mister White Rabbit," she said.

As he filled the two glasses and handed her one, he said, "Alex, please stop it with the White Rabbit thing."

She frowned. "Why?"

"If I remember the story, he was always late. 'I'm late! I'm late! For a very important date!' Well, I'm late too, and the date is the twenty-eighth. I don't need to be reminded."

"I'm sorry, I'll stop. But, Matt, there's nothing we can do about it tonight. We'll go full steam ahead in the morning." She smiled, gestured toward his bathrobe. "Now get rid of that and show me what you've got for me."

He dropped the robe.

"My! My!" she said, raising her eyebrows. "Come on in. Let me make you feel better about things."

Matt climbed into the Jacuzzi and sat facing her. She moved a foot between his legs and teased him with her toes. "Tell me things about you I don't know. For example, what's your favorite thing to do—besides screwing me, I mean, which is about to become your favorite?"

He laughed. "Well, I'm guessing anything else would come in a poor second, but I suppose I like sailing more than anything else."

She gave a delighted cry. "Me, too! See the things we learn about each other?"

They talked for a while about boats, learning that they both had raced in college and that they both had chartered in the Caribbean with friends.

Still teasing him with her foot, Alexandra asked, "What about music? What do you like?"

He felt himself becoming increasingly aroused. "Mostly classical. Mahler, Shostakovich."

"Old fogy!"

"Also, rock: the Beatles, especially John Lennon; Eric Clapton ...." He leaned back, letting the jets palpate the small of his back.

"Still an old fogy!"

"I suppose you like all the contemporary groups, rap, that sort of thing?"

"No."

"What, then?" He tried to focus on her eyes, but his gaze fell on her breasts.

"Classical," she replied with a smile. "I studied the cello. You're staring at my tits."

"Sorry."

"Don't be."

"They're lovely. Why the cello?"

"I like the way it vibrates between my thighs," she answered with a cherubic smile.

They talked on like this, with Alexandra taking the lead, about movies, books, sports, music again.

"What are your favorite pieces to play on the cello?"

"Bach's Cello Suites, especially the D Minor. The minuet gave me loads of trouble but I finally got it. I suppose that's why it's my favorite."

"You can really feel the vibrations of the cello in your thighs?"

"Sure, if I squeeze them against the waist, near the F holes."

"I've never see a cellist do that."

"You haven't seen me play the cello."

"I guess you must really like the feeling."

"What woman wouldn't want Johann Sebastian vibrating between her legs?"

Matt laughed. "I can think of many."

"Boorish louts!"

When they finally finished the wine, they climbed out of the Jacuzzi, toweled each other off, slipped into bathrobes, and moved to the bedroom, leaving wet spots on the carpet. As they kissed, Matt lifted the robe from her shoulders and let it cascade to the floor. She did the same with his robe. They climbed onto the bed and spent a long time fondling and caressing each other before finally making love.

When she heard the car approaching the house, Mary-Ann Scroggs rushed to close the door to Annie's room. Even though the fever had broken and Annie appeared to be recovering, she was tired and needed her sleep. Mary-Ann returned to the kitchen, surveyed the sink piled with dirty dishes and shrugged.

They would just have to see the place as it was; she'd been far too occupied with concern for Annie and for her husband to keep up with the housework.

She went to the window and pulled back the curtain, expecting to see Matt Cannon and Alexandra Lake. Instead, Ralph Stanley and Donna Quinn stepped out of the car and approached the kitchen door. She let the curtain fall back and rushed to the door to lock it. But they were already on the porch and pushing through the door. Mary-Ann jumped back. "Who are you? What do you want?" she asked in a quavering voice.

Ralph Stanley asked, "Are you Mrs. Scroggs?"

"Who are you?" she asked again as she started to sidle toward Annie's room.

"Never mind that. You and your daughter are coming with us."

"Are you from the government?"

Donna Quinn laughed. Stanley said, "Just get your daughter."

"No. Leave us alone."

Stanley said, "She's probably in that room. Get her."

Mary-Ann made a move to step in front of the door, but Stanley grabbed her roughly by the wrist and held her back. Quinn opened the door to Annie's room. Mary-Ann heard Annie call out "Mommy?"

"Leave her alone!" Mary-Ann shouted, struggling to break free from the Stanley's grasp but it was useless. Quinn appeared, carrying Annie who was flailing her legs and arms, and hustled her out the door to the waiting car. Stanley pushed Mary-Ann after them.

Within minutes, they were speeding along the dirt road leaving whirling dust clouds in their wake.

Matt sat on the balcony gazing at the falls as he waited for Alexandra to finish getting ready. He was eager to continue their search for Billy Scroggs.

A short time later, Alexandra came up behind him and put her arms around his neck. "The falls, they're spectacular, aren't they," she said. "I've been watching you. You seem lost in thought."

He put his hands over hers. "The falls are like all of the good intentions of the Baxter Administration cascading off the cliff. I don't see how he can continue. What he did is an impeachable offense and I don't think he should get away with it."

"You're angry for what he did to you."

"Yes, that's true. And I'm angry at myself for going along with it, and also for getting Marcie involved."

"She's a grown woman. She could have said no."

"I could have, too. But I didn't."

"Well, it's done. Let's go on to the next thing. We need to make some calls."

When several calls to U.S. and Canadian customs turned up nothing, Matt said, "That doesn't mean anything. We know they're using different and we have no idea what they're driving."

Alexandra shook her head. "But we do know that in all likelihood they're driving together and it's only the three of them. I asked the border agents on both sides to check out every car, van, or truck carrying three men in their forties. My guess is they'd be carrying stuff with them—probably guns of some sort—that the guards would find. They're pretty good at that since nine-eleven." She paused, then said, "No, I don't think they went through Canada. What's more, I don't think Scroggs ever intended to go through Canada. It's just another one of his deliberately obvious moves calculated to throw us off."

"Okay, so where the hell do we go from here?"

"Back to the Rochester Police. See if they turned up anything on that dead body."

"That doesn't sound very promising."

"Do you have any other ideas?"

Matt shook his head. "Guess not. Let's go."

Twenty minutes later, Detective Ryan said, "As you know, Waters rented a blue Ford Aerostar, but the car he was found beside was green—a Plymouth Voyager.

"Were you able to trace the Plymouth?"

"Uhhuh. Rented at Logan Airport in Boston."

"I knew it!" said Alexandra. "What name?"

"Timothy Cain."

"Great, thanks," Alexandra said as she scribbled the name in her notebook. "Just one more thing—I assume you asked the Gary police to watch for somebody returning a blue Ford Aerostar to Enterprise."

"Not necessary. The car's already been turned in."

"Damn!" Matt said. He turned to Alexandra. "Let's get our asses to Gary."

"Not so fast," said Ryan. "I got a corpse turning in a rented car many hours after he's dead, and I got another rented car that the corpse was laying beside except he didn't rent it because somebody named Timothy Cain rented it and I don't know who the hell this Timothy Cain is. I've got all that, but what I don't have is whatever it is you ain't telling me."

Matt and Alexandra exchanged glances. Matt said, "Look, we don't know anything you don't know except …."

"Except?"

"Except what we can't tell you."

"Involving the president," Ryan said with a sardonic nod. "And what if this mission of yours is related somehow to my corpse?"

"If we find that it is, we won't hide it from you."

"You're asking me to trust you on this?"

Matt nodded. "Yes, we are. Believe me, we wouldn't ask if it didn't involve national security."

"Shit," muttered Ryan.

After they left the police station and climbed into the car, Matt inserted the key in the ignition and said, "Okay, Alex, plot me a course to Gary."

Scroggs and the others took a taxi to the Gary Regional Airport where they walked up to the Hertz counter. Using his fake driver's license and credit card, Scroggs rented a Chevrolet Impala. After the clerk, a heavy set, middle-aged man, filled out the paperwork, Scroggs asked for directions to Harrisburg, Illinois. "That's Harrisburg, Illinois. Not Harrisburg, Pennsylvania."

"Wait," Figg said. "I thought we—"

"—Shut up," Scroggs snapped. He turned back to the clerk. "You got that? Harrisburg, Illinois. Not Harrisburg, Pennsylvania."

"Yuh, yuh. I got it."

"Good."

"For a little extra money, I can rent you a car with GPS."

"Just print the directions."

"Whatever." The clerk printed out the driving directions and handed them to Scroggs along with the car keys and rental agreement. Ten minutes later, Scroggs turned onto I-80 West.

"Why a sedan?" asked Vernon Ludlow. "We've been renting vans all along. That trunk is pretty stuffed."

"Don't want to establish a pattern. We've seen our last van."

They rode in silence until Scroggs turned south on I-57. "Hey," said Figg. "You're takin' us south. Where the hell we goin'?"

"You'll see," Scroggs replied. "You'll like where you're goin'."

Vernon Ludlow, consulting the map spread across his lap, said, "Harrisburg is almost in Kentucky. Ain't we goin' the wrong way?"

"Nope. It's tough luck, but this is the only way to go."

Figg asked, "What do you mean by that?" But Scroggs remained silent.

They drove on for a while until Scroggs suddenly crossed two lanes of traffic to take an exit.

"Where are we goin' now?" Ludlow asked.

"Gotta find some gas."

Ludlow leaned across the front seat and peered at the fuel gauge. "We got almost half a tank."

"Might as well keep it full. Besides, I wouldn't mind a cup of coffee."

"We passed a rest area a few miles back. Why didn't you stop there?"

Scroggs said nothing. He drove for a few miles until he came to a side road in an unpopulated area where he pulled to a stop.

"What now?" asked Figg.

"Get out of the car."

"What do you mean? Why?"

Scroggs opened the driver's door, stepped from the car, then opened the left, rear door. "Out," he said.

Figg climbed out of the car. "C'mon, Billy, tell us what the fuck's goin' on."

"Kneel."

"What? Are you crazy?"

"Kneel." When Figg didn't move, Scroggs placed a hand on Figg's shoulder and forced the smaller man down to his knees. "Kneel. You're gonna apologize."

Figg looked wide-eyed at Ludlow. "Vern, stop him! Please! I don't know what the fuck is goin' on!"

"C'mon, Billy," Ludlow said, "Cut the crap."

"Billy?" Figg said, his voice pleading.

"Shut up!"

"Billy, for Christ's sake," Ludlow said, approaching the two men. "We ain't—"

In one quick motion, Scroggs pulled out Johnny Waters' gun, pressed it against the back of Figg's skull, and pulled the trigger. Figg's head exploded and a jet of blood shot toward Ludlow who jumped back, mouth agape, in shocked silence.

"Sorry, Huey," Scroggs said. "But you were becomin' a problem." He turned to Ludlow and said, "Nobody's gonna keep me from returning to Mary-Ann and Annie. Nobody! I can't afford screw-ups like him." He bent down, fished through Figg's pockets, and pulled out the fake I.D. he'd had when they left Bass Run.

Ludlow stared at him. He looked at the sleeve of his shirt where a splash of Figg's blood stained it. "He was a friend of ours, Billy! He was a fuckin' friend of ours!"

"A friend's one thing, family's another. Ain't nobody gonna deprive Annie of her father. Got that? Now give me your camera."

Ludlow stared at him in stunned silence, gave him the camera. Scroggs took a snapshot of Figg, focussing on the man's head.

"Nobody's gonna deprive Annie of her father. You got that, Vernon?" Billy shouted.

"Yuh. Yuh, Billy, I got that."

"Good. Now let's get to Michigan."

Karl Zacher sat behind his kidney-shaped desk in the Watergate waiting for the call he was expecting at any moment. He had just finished watching the video of Wayne Haskins and Evelyn, backing it up and replaying parts of it in slow motion.

On his desk, The Washington Post was open to an inside story about the apparent suicide of a young technician in the pathology lab at Bethesda Naval Hospital named Roger Anderson. It said how he left a wife and a newborn baby. Neighbors and friends reported that he was a friendly man who had seemed mostly happy except for the last few months. No one could offer an explanation for his recent troubled appearance and certainly nobody could fathom a reason for him taking his own life. His wife was devastated and was being treated for shock while Anderson's parents watched over the infant.

"Loser," muttered Zacher, shaking his head. "He was in the clear and had nothing to worry about."

The phone rang. Zacher answered it before the second ring. "Hello?"

"We got her."

"Good," replied Zacher. He hung up the phone, then lifted it again and punched in Gary Molesworth's number in Traverse City, Michigan. When Molesworth answered, Zacher said only, "It's your benefactor. I have a request."

"Yes, sir. You name it."

"You know Billy Scroggs?"

"Sure do. From Maine."

"He might be showing up there."

"Here? Why?"

"I can't get into that. But if he does make an appearance, I want you to give him a message without mentioning my name."

"What's the message?"

"Tell him the operation is off. He's not to go through with it if he wants to see his wife and kid again."

After executing Huey Figg, Scroggs thought it best to stay off the roads for a day. Also, he thought Vernon Ludlow needed some time to get over the shock of Figg's death. Scroggs hated to lose the day and a half because it meant he'd only have time to visit the Michigan militia guys before heading back to Washington for the 28th, but that was far better than jeopardizing the entire operation. So he'd continued south into Kentucky where they passed the rest of the 23rd and all of the 24th in a motel room watching television in sullen silence. There was mention on the news of the discovery of the body of a man shot execution style, but, Scroggs was pleased to note, there were no leads.

At mid morning on the 25th, they at last set out for Michigan. Driving the entire distance himself, because he no longer trusted even Ludlow, Scroggs made it to Traverse City in just under seven hours. Throughout the trip, Ludlow sat morosely in the passenger seat, occasionally weeping.

It disgusted Scroggs; the sniffling sounds were like miniature rasps running up and down his spine, and he'd already had to put up with a day and a half of it. Didn't Ludlow understand that Huey Figg had been his friend, too? But the thing is, nobody with any balls can allow friendship to stand in the way of things that have to be done. He had been friendly with one or two junior officers in Iraq, but that didn't stop him from fragging them when they put the whole unit in jeopardy because of their weakness and incompetence.

Such weakness, such incompetence, simply could not be tolerated. It hurt Scroggs deeply when he realized his own brother had gotten himself killed by acting so much like a loser.

And now Ludlow was beginning to show signs of weakness. Scroggs was beginning to think he would have to dump the man and go it alone. But for now, Ludlow was useful. It wouldn't make much of an impression on Molesworth and the others if Scroggs showed up by himself. One lone man on a mission could be written off as crazy, but with two you had at least the beginning of a coordinated action. You had the start of a combat unit.

When they came to a gas station on the outskirts of Traverse City, Scroggs slowed and pulled into a spot beside the bank of telephones that stood in the far corner of the lot near an undeveloped, wooded area. It was mostly hidden from the road and the gas station office. Vernon Ludlow tensed and eyed Scroggs suspiciously.

Scroggs smiled and said, "Wait here. I'll call Molesworth." He stepped out of the car, walked to the furthest phone, glanced at a slip of paper with Molesworth's cell phone number, and dialed.

As he waited for the connection, he stared through the windshield at Ludlow who kept averting his eyes.

Finally, after five rings, a man answered. "Yuh?"

"Gary?"

"Who wants to know?"

"It's Billy Scroggs from Maine. I want to come by and talk."

"What do you want to talk about."

"Tell me where to meet you and we'll talk."

"Where are you now?"

Scroggs read him the name on the gas station sign.

"You're only a few miles away," Molesworth said. "There's a Little League field about three miles up the road. It's tucked away in a grove of trees and nobody's there because a game just ended. My kid hit a home run."

"Congratulations."

"Yuh. Anyway, there ain't another game. I'm here tending the field. Look for a road on the right a hundred yards or so after a narrow bridge."

"I'll be right there," Scroggs said and hung up the phone.

Ten minutes later, Scroggs realized too late that he was passing the road Molesworth had described. He pulled onto the shoulder to make a U-turn. Ludlow sucked in his breath and looked nervously at Scroggs who said, "Jesus, Vernon, don't be so jumpy. You ain't done nothin' wrong." He laughed, skidded a U-turn, and drove back to the road, now a left turn. A hundred yards down the road, he pulled in alongside a pickup truck parked behind the backstop. When he stepped from the car, his ears were assaulted by the electric din of millions of cicadae. The smell of an approaching thunderstorm was in the air. Molesworth, rake in hand, was smoothing out the dirt around the batter's box. Another man was smoothing out the pitcher's mound.

"Who's he?" Scroggs asked as he came around the backstop.

"Andy McBride. He's my right hand man."

"He okay?"

"I told you, he's my right hand man."

Scroggs smiled. "Fair enough." Gesturing toward the rake, he asked, "You do this all the time?"

"I'm coach, groundskeeper, and cheering father."

Scroggs turned to Ludlow and said, "Now that's what I call a good father. Not like that Waters asshole." Turning back to Molesworth, he said, "You bake apple pies, too?"

"Funny," Molesworth said. He motioned for Andy McBride to join them. "What do you want to talk about?"

McBride came in from the pitcher's mound and shook Scroggs' hand. Scroggs gestured to Ludlow who had just come around the backstop to join them. "This is my buddy, Vernon. We got an operation going ... the twenty-eighth of this month."

"What kind of operation?" Molesworth asked.

"You know better than to ask that," Scroggs said, looking from Molesworth to McBride. "I'll only say it's real big and could ignite the revolution this country needs."

Molesworth shrugged. "Why tell us even that much?"

"Because things would change a lot quicker if people thought it was part of a widespread, coordinated movement. I want you guys to figure out some action you could pull off in the next week or so."

"In the next week? Who else have you got?"

"There are others," Scroggs said. He figured Molesworth and McBride didn't need to know about the chickenshits near Rochester or that there were no others.

Molesworth started to drag the rake across the right hand batter's box. "Funny how those kids can dig such deep holes," he said. "This'll be nothing but a mud hole if we don't smooth it out before the rain comes."

"Well, what do you say?" asked Scroggs. "You game?"

"What kinda action?"

"Somethin' big. Maybe on the lines of Oklahoma City."

Molesworth paused a long time before finally saying, "Not big enough."

"What do you mean?"

"We're already plannin' somethin' bigger. We can move the date to the twenty-eighth."

"Perfect!"

"Except, you got a problem," said Molesworth.

"What problem?"

"Zacher gave me a message for you. He said if you want to see your wife and kid again, you'll call the operation off."

Scroggs stared dumfounded at the man.

Molesworth said, "We'll get things started on this end. Go do what you gotta do. I happen to know Zacher's got a place in Maine. I'll give you the address. If you miss the twenty-eighth, we'll go ahead anyway."

Chapter 21—.44 Magnum; A Michigan Barn

Matt and Alexandra had no difficulty finding the Enterprise Car Rental office in Gary. The clerk, a young woman with glasses and long blond hair, confirmed that the blue Ford Aerostar had been returned by a John Waters.

"What did this John Waters look like?"

The clerk gave a description, with several repetitions of the word "average," that proved entirely useless.

"Did John Waters rent another car?"

"No."

"Try the name Timothy Cain," Alexandra said. "Anybody by that name rent a car?"

The young woman worked at her computer for several moments before shaking her head. "Nope. Nobody by that name."

"How about three men renting a car?" asked Matt. "Most likely a van."

"Not from me that I can remember. I'll ask my colleague. She poked her head into a small back office. "Hey, Alan, you rent a vehicle to three men in the last few days?"

Matt heard the man's answer. "No."

The blond turned to them. "Only other possibility is Dorothy. She covers some shifts. I can call her if you want."

"Yes, please."

She made the call, but Dorothy also couldn't recall three men. "Maybe some other company," the woman said. At their request, she wrote down a list of all the car rental companies in and around Gary.

Matt and Alexandra set out to check each of them. At the Gary Regional Airport, they finally found what they were looking for. "Yes, I remember them," said a middle-aged man behind the Hertz counter. He must have received his Hertz uniform before a weight gain because the shirt buttons were strained. "We rented a Chevrolet Impala to someone named Timothy Cain who was with a couple of other guys. I remember him clearly. Rude fellow."

"Why do you say rude?" asked Alexandra.

"He asked for directions to Harrisburg, Illinois and several times reminded me that he didn't mean Harrisburg, Pennsylvania. I understood him the first time, but he kept insisting. It even seemed to confuse one of the men he was with."

"Why do you say that?"

"Because the man started to say, 'But I thought we were going—' and this Cain fellow cut him off pretty abruptly. He told the guy to shut up."

"Do they plan to return the car here?" asked Matt.

The man consulted his computer screen. "Yes. There's no drop-off charges or location."

"Good," said Matt, taking a brochure from a rack and jotting down two telephone numbers in the white margin. "Here are our cell phone numbers. Please call us the instant he returns the car."

Alexandra asked the man for the registration number of the Impala which she wrote down in her notebook, and they left. They went to all the other agencies, leaving their telephone numbers in case someone named Timothy Cain—or somebody with a different name but who was with two other men—tried to rent a car. "That's becoming his M.O.," said Alexandra. "Drop one car off, pick up another one from a different company."

As they walked toward the parking lot, Matt asked, "So, do we put out an APB on the Impala?"

"I don't think so," said Alexandra. "Detective Ryan back in Rochester will probably see it and will recognize the name. He'll figure that's his murderer."

"Of course, and there's no way we can afford to have him come into the case. We've simply got to find Scroggs ourselves."

Alexandra nodded. "Which is going to make it infinitely more difficult. Unless …."

"Unless?"

"Unless you, Haskins, and the president decide it's worth the exposure in order to prevent the assassination," she replied. "That would free us up to pull out all the stops."

Matt shook his head. "I don't think Haskins or the president are ready for that yet."

"And you?"

"I helped to arrange a presidential assassination. That's a federal crime."

"Enough said."

"So let's go get him," Matt said. "What do you suppose this Harrisburg, Illinois—Harrisburg, Pennsylvania thing is all about?"

"Misdirection. Scroggs was trying his best to make certain the agent remembered Harrisburg, Illinois. It's like the Mapquest thing. I think it means he's heading in the opposite direction."

"Michigan?"

Lake nodded. "Michigan. Which means there's a good chance we'll be hearing from my friend." At that moment, her cell phone chirped.

"Speaking of your friend …." Matt said.

Alexandra flipped the phone open and looked at the caller I.D. number. "No such luck; it's a 585 area code." She answered the phone. "Hello?"

"Alexandra Lake?"

"Yes."

"Detective Sergeant Ryan here—Rochester Police. Thought you'd like to know. We ran a trace on this John Waters guy. Came up with a fresh report that there was a guy erased, execution style, in Illinois," Ryan paused, apparently waiting for a response.

"And?" Alexandra asked impatiently.

"I.D. on the body said, John Waters. Poor bastard has a habit of getting killed."

"Jesus!" Alexandra pulled a map from the glove compartment and said, "Location?" As she listened, she traced a finger along the map until she came to a small town a hundred miles or so southwest of Gary. "Got it. Thanks. I'll let you know if anything turns up."

"Yuh, you do that," Ryan said sarcastically. "And, listen, I'll give you a call if I hear about another place where our pal Johnny Waters turns up dead. Must be a damned hobby of his."

Alexandra flipped her cell phone closed and turned to Matt. "Well, it guess I was wrong; they headed south towards Harrisburg, Illinois after all." She told Matt what Ryan had reported and said, "We'd better get down there. It occurs to me it could be Scroggs, himself."

Matt nodded. "Maybe Figg and Ludlow got cold feet and decided the best way out was to eliminate him."

"Or it could be one of them."

"Only one way to find out. How long will it take us to get there?"

"I calculate about two hours."

Traffic was light and ten minutes shy of two hours, they pulled up in front of the county morgue. After displaying their I.D.s and waving the presidential letter before a stubbornly officious person, they were shown the body. They glanced at each other, then Alexandra said to the pathologist, "Thanks for taking the time, but that's not our man."

"But we got a message from the police in Rochester, New York that they also have a body named John Waters. We were hoping you could identify who this is."

"I don't know," said Alexandra. "It would be a hell of a coincidence, but it could be two unrelated guys with the same name; it's not such an unusual name. All I can say is we don't know the guy."

The pathologist tried to pump them for information about their interest, especially in light of the presidential letter, but they said nothing.

Later, as they climbed into their car, Matt said, "I could tell by your expression you knew the guy."

Alexandra nodded. "Huey Figg. I saw him a number of times at Bob's Bar in Bass Run. It appears that Scroggs' team is breaking up. I wouldn't be surprised if Vernon Ludlow turns up dead somewhere."

"Which tells me two things. One, Scroggs is willing to go it alone, meaning that if he still wants to take out the succession down to Haskins ...."

Alexandra frowned, nodded. "The possibility of a bomb, or maybe a grenade launcher, comes into play. And the second thing?"

"That's the good part: Scroggs is getting nervous," Matt replied. "He's bound to make some mistakes."

"I agree. I think we should gamble and get our butts to Michigan and hope we get a call from my friend on the way."

Matt glanced at his watch. "We wouldn't be getting to the Traverse City area until ten or eleven tonight. There's not much we could do at that hour, so we might as well stay overnight somewhere and get an early start in the morning."

"Now you're talking, you man-cello, you. I think I'll play a fugue on you tonight."

"You make it sound obscene."

"You'll see."

Scroggs, with Vernon Ludlow sitting in the passenger seat, drove rapidly back to the gas station from which he'd called Gary Molesworth. Forgetting all caution, he dialed his home number. There was no answer; only Mary-Ann's voice on the answering machine message.

He tried again in case Mary-Ann had been outside and couldn't get to the phone in time. Still, no answer. A wave of frustration swept over him. He wanted to be back in Bass Run, see if the truck was in front; run up the porch stairs and through the door into the kitchen; look for a note that Mary-Ann and Annie had gone shopping; search the upstairs rooms. But he was at least a thousand miles away. With a sense of futility, he tried a third time, listened for a few moments, then slammed the receiver into its cradle. He glared through the windshield at Vernon Ludlow sitting warily in the car and tried to figure out a plan. The thought of how long it would take him to drive through Ohio, Pennsylvania, New York, and several New England states to get to Maine sickened him. He could go the shorter way through Canada, but that would involve several border crossings, a risk he was unwilling to take even considering his anxiety about Mary-Ann and Annie. Besides, it was not that much shorter; it still would take upwards of twenty hours even with only brief rest stops.

Would he risk flying? He thought about it for several moments. Then he picked up the phone and tried to call Mary-Ann one last time. When there was still no answer, he went back to the car and said to Vernon Ludlow, "Okay, we're gonna have to drive back to Maine."

"Why not fly?"

"I thought of that. Problem is, we're carrying heat. Can't show up at the airport carrying guns."

Ludlow shrugged, but said nothing. He hadn't said much since Scroggs blew Huey away.

Scroggs had all he could do to restrain himself from speeding as they drove south on Route 131. Several times, he pulled into gas stations to try calling Mary-Ann. Each time, he got only her answering machine voice.

By the time they pulled into the parking space at the Gary Regional Airport, it was approaching midnight. The terminal was closed. "Damn," said Scroggs. "We're gonna have to go to that motel we passed and come back in the morning."

"We can't just keep this car?" asked Ludlow.

"Too risky in case they got a lead on us. We'll come back in the mornin' and rent another." Scroggs gunned the car out of the parking lot and headed for the motel.

As soon as they checked in and entered their room, Scroggs lifted the phone and tried calling his house again. Listening to it ring once, twice, three times, he begged for an answer, cursing when the answering machine kicked in. He was certain now that something was wrong. There was no way Mary-Ann would be out at this hour and if she was in bed there was no doubt she would have heard the extension phone on the nightstand inches from her ear. He turned away from Ludlow when he felt tears of frustration and worry welling in his eyes.

Ludlow said, "You ain't never called from a motel room before; you always used a pay phone at some gas station."

Scroggs sat on the edge of the far bed staring at the cheap, blue carpet. He said nothing.

Ludlow continued. "Way I see it is: you're startin' to get careless."

"Shut up. I'm thinking."

Matt felt Alexandra lean over and trace her tongue around the pucker of his bullet wound. They were naked on the king size bed. "What's it like?" she asked.

"What?"

"Being on the receiving end of a bullet."

Matt thought a moment. "It's hurtful. Makes you want to hurt someone back."

Alexandra nodded. "It always gave me comfort that training targets don't feel anything." At that moment her phone chirped. She glanced at the caller I.D. and sat up quickly, suddenly alert. As she lifted the smart phone to her ear, she said to Matt, " My Michigan contact." Into the phone she said, "Hi, Andy. Got something for me?"

Matt watched her expression change to one of alarm. "Jesus!" she whispered. She gave Matt a worried look as she continued to listen for several long moments. Finally, she said, No, Andy, don't. We can't call anybody else in on this. Trust me; I'll explain later. Where can we meet you?" She grabbed a pad of notepaper from the night table and began to write. "Okay, got it. We'll leave immediately … Who? …. a Washington lawyer; it's a long story. By the way, he's gonna need a weapon …. Good. I'll call as soon as I figure out how long it will take us to get there." She hit 'END' on her phone.

"What's up?" asked Matt. "What's this about a weapon?"

"Two things. We're not alone; Zacher's also trying to stop Scroggs. It looks like he nabbed Mary-Ann and Annie. Scroggs took off in a panic."

"Sounds like we're heading back to Maine," Matt said.

"Yes, but not yet. Andy needs our help. His targets are rigging a truck bomb for U.N. headquarters coordinated with Scroggs' action. I asked Andy not to call in help because any post-action debriefing might easily blow the lid on everything; his targets would be asked what it was they were coordinating with and it would just go from there. Eventually it would lead to Scroggs, then Zacher, then Haskins, then the president, then—"

"—Then me."

"You got it."

"Where are we going?"

"About a hundred miles north of Detroit."

"Let's get going, then."

"I figure it will take us about six hours. We'll be there at first light," said Alexandra. "And listen: I'm going to have to let Andy in on what's going down."

"No way, Alex," said Matt. "You know what the president said."

"I know what the president said," she replied. "But I also know what his intentions were: Specifically, that none of this gets out. The only way Andy won't call in reinforcements is if he has a clear picture of the consequences. If he calls in help, everything starts to unravel. So, as you drive, I'm gonna call him and tell him everything."

"What makes you think everything starts to unravel?"

"Zacher called Molesworth to stop Scroggs. That means he has the guy's telephone number; that means there's a connection between them; that probably means Zacher supports Molesworth and his gang. Are you getting the picture?" she asked. "If anybody but us questions Molesworth, Zacher is likely to come up. Then they go after Zacher. We talked about this before: If that happens Zacher squeals to protect himself. Make sense?"

Matt nodded.

"I'm calling Andy. If you have a problem with that, try to stop me."

Matt stared at her. He had no answer.

Scroggs spent a sleepless night. He was already feeling exhausted as they set out toward Toledo with a new car by 8:00 a.m. He couldn't imagine how he was going to get through the next twenty or twenty-four hours going through Michigan, Ohio, Pennsylvania, New York, Massachusetts, and New Hampshire before finally arriving in Maine. But the knowledge that Mary-Ann and Annie had probably been kidnapped drove him on. He would have to keep going for a couple of days straight if he was going to find them, get them to a safe place, and get to Washington in time to complete his mission.

After a long trip during which they took turns driving, Matt and Alexandra pulled into a parking lot near the Fort Gratiot Lighthouse, in Port Huron, Michigan, where Andy McBride said they should meet. Fog hovered over Lake Huron. The lighthouse's green light flashed every six seconds; it swept reflections across the windshield.

They climbed out of the car and stretched their legs. Somewhere out on the lake, unseen ships sounded their foghorns, warning each other of their presence.

"No problems finding the place?"

Matt and Alexandra turned to see Andy McBride approaching them. Alexandra gave him a hug. "Andy! It's so good to see you again. This is Matt Cannon."

McBride shook hands with Matt. "You do know that you and Baxter are fucking crazy, don't you?"

"Leave it be, Andy," said Alexandra. "I've already come down hard on him. Did you bring him a weapon?"

"Sure did," McBride replied as he reached into the back of his car and retrieved a revolver. He handed it to Alexandra.

Alexandra looked at the gun and smiled at Matt. "Andy didn't exactly bring you a beginner's gun. This is a forty-four magnum. You feeling as strong as Dirty Harry?"

"That was his gun?"

"Yuh. It'll take down a goddamned buffalo." She handed him the gun. "Try it out; it's not loaded. Hold it with both hands. Tight. Like squeezing a tennis ball."

Matt raised the gun, pointed out at the lake, and squeezed. Click. "Seems easy enough," he said.

"You ever fire a gun before?" McBride asked Matt.

"No."

"Yuh, well you oughta get a kick out of it." He turned to Alexandra. "There's an abandoned dairy farm that borders the place where Molesworth and his guys are meeting. A cowshed provides good cover where we can watch them."

Karl Zacher was just about to step from his office when the phone rang. He rushed to his gleaming desk, glanced at the digital window where caller I.D.s appeared, and was relieved to recognize his daughter's cell phone number. He picked up the phone. "Linda!"

"Hi, Dad. I just flew in from Rio last night. I'm in Miami and I have a flight to Boston later."

"Welcome back, Honey. I was expecting your call. Did you have a good time?" He listened while his daughter told him about her trip. When she finished, he said, "Listen, why don't I grab a flight to Boston and take you out to dinner?"

"You don't have to do that, Dad."

"It's no big deal. I have to go there on business anyway. I'll be there to meet you when your plane arrives." They talked for a little while longer then Zacher hung up the phone and smiled. The part about having business in Boston wasn't a complete lie. After seeing his daughter and buying her a nice dinner, he figured he'd rent a car the following morning and drive up to Maine where he truly did have business. With a quick phone call, he booked an American flight that got into Boston that afternoon.

Matt and Alexandra, their headlights off, picked their way along a dirt road as they followed McBride's truck. Soon, McBride pulled up to an abandoned cowshed and climbed out of the truck. Matt and Alexandra rolled to a stop behind the truck and also got out.

McBride pulled an M4 assault rifle, with an M203 grenade launcher, from the back of his truck. "Follow me," he said, as he entered the cowshed. He led them across the room to the opposite wall where he leaned his M4 next to a small window. He looked out the window. "They're there already," he said.

Matt looked out a second window. About two hundred yards away, four men milled about a furniture truck which was parked at the open door of a barn. "There's Greek lettering on the wall," Matt said. "It's the same as is carved into the counter at Bob's bar. Any idea what it means?"

Alexandra nodded. "*Molon labé.* Come and take them. It's what the Spartan king said to the Persians who demanded they surrender their weapons. Like Charlton Heston's 'from my cold, dead hands.' Hand me your gun; we're gonna accept their invitation."

Matt handed her the .44 magnum. Expertly using a speed loader, she dropped six rounds into the cylinder. "Remember: Two hands, like squeezing a tennis ball."

McBride nodded toward the truck. "That baby is packed with ammonium nitrate and fuel oil."

"They'll never get it close to the U. N. building," said Alexandra.

"Wrong. They have somebody on the inside at the shipping dock. They were just waiting for the right time. That's where Scroggs came in."

"No, you're wrong, Andy," said Alexandra. "Now that we're here, this is as close as they get to the U. N." She snapped a magazine into her Sig Sauer 229 handgun.

"I'll be right back," said McBride as he made for the door. "I've got more ammo in the truck."

While he was gone, Matt asked, "What do you intend to do?"

"It's Andy's district; it's his call, or at least his chain-of-command's call."

"But what if he decides to bust it up and Molesworth and his gang start talking?"

"As long as they talk only to you, me and Andy, we could probably control how it's written up."

McBride returned with several boxes of ammunition. "The team from Detroit will be here in an hour or two," he said. "We'll move then."

"What?" cried Matt.

"Or maybe we *can't* control how it's written up," said Alexandra.

"You called them?" demanded Matt. "I thought you agreed not to bring in reinforcements."

"That was before I knew they had four guys. Those aren't great odds, considering we're effectively outnumbered two to one because you've never fired a gun. Also, we've only seen four guys. How do we know there aren't more that we can't see? Maybe a couple more guys inside the truck packing things away."

Matt turned to Alexandra. "Alex, tell him he's got to call the guys from Detroit off. We have direct orders from the president."

"*You* have direct orders from the president," said McBride. "I don't."

By the time they passed a sign saying Cleveland was fifty miles up the road, Scroggs had revised his plan. He was nearly certain that Karl Zacher, somehow having got cold feet, had Mary-Ann and Annie, and planned on using them to force him to show his hand.

What he needed, Scroggs thought, was a counter argument of similar weight.

So he decided they would make a short detour to Boston to meet Linda Zacher's flight.

Matt was still angry at Andy McBride. He realized that unless he did something, and soon, everything could fall apart. But what? What could he do to prevent the Detroit office of BATF from getting access to Molesworth and his comrades? And then there was the other question: Did it really matter? According to McBride, Molesworth knew nothing about the true nature of Scroggs' mission, nor of Zacher's connection to it; and he certainly knew nothing of President Baxter's role.

That may be true, he decided, but what Molesworth knew and did not know was irrelevant. The important part was the link between Molesworth and Zacher and that was something the Detroit office would undoubtedly explore. And that meant that somewhere down the line somebody—most likely Zacher—would cut a plea bargain and everything would come out.

His first instinct was right, he thought. He had to do something to make sure that didn't happen.

He started toward the door. "I'll be right back," he said to McBride and Alexandra. "I gotta take a leak."

After he walked out the door, McBride said, "Good. Maybe when the action starts he won't piss his pants."

"Why Boston?" Ludlow asked as they crossed the border between Ohio and Pennsylvania.

"Zacher has a daughter named Linda who's flying into Boston."

"So? What's that to us?"

"Jesus, Vern, you can be thick sometimes!" Scroggs said with a dismissive laugh. "Zacher's got my little girl. I need to get his and take her to Maine so we can have a prisoner swap. Otherwise, we'd have to go into his place in Maine with guns blazing and there are two things wrong with that: one, we don't know how many guys we'd be up against; he could have a whole, fuckin' army for all we know."

"Yuh. You got a point, there, Billy."

"And the second point is: Mary-Ann and Annie could be exposed to cross fire and I damn sure ain't gonna let that happen."

"I don't know, Billy. What you're talkin' about is kidnappin' and you plan to take her from Boston to Maine. That's across state lines which makes it a federal crime."

Scroggs looked across at Ludlow whose face went from light to dark as they went under an overpass. He gave a disgusted shake of his head. "Here we are about to kill the president and who knows who else, and you're worried about a little kidnapping? I don't believe you sometimes!"

McBride looked out the window and cried, "Shit! What the hell is your friend doing?"

Alexandra rushed to the window and peered out. "Damn it! He's forcing our hand before your guys get here! C'mon, we've gotta stop him before he gets himself killed." She grabbed the M-4 and its grenade launcher and started out of the cowshed with McBride on her heels.

"He's gone into that copse," McBride said. "On the other side, he'll be visible to them."

They dashed into the thicket of trees and soon emerged on the other side. They saw Matt crouching about a hundred yards from the men at the barn. Nothing was between him and them. Alexandra and McBride hunched over and scampered toward Matt. They were halfway there when a clump of grass erupted into the air in front of them in the same instant that a gunshot rang out.

Hunched over, Alexandra and McBride, scurried towards Matt who had assumed a shooting position on one knee and was aiming toward the barn. Alexandra looked to her left and saw Molesworth and two of his associates crouching behind the truck and some barrels and firing in the direction of Matt.

They must have seen her at that moment, because suddenly the ground around her was erupting with bullet hits.

"Matt, get down!" Alexandra cried.

But Matt either ignored her or didn't hear her because he aimed the Magnum and fired. The recoil knocked him on his backside.

"Spread out!" shouted McBride as he dove behind a tree and trained his weapon on Molesworth.

Alexandra threw herself behind a three-foot-high boulder. As soon as she was sprawled on her belly, several bullets blasted chips of granite from the boulder.

Alexandra saw that Matt had struggled back to an upright position and was taking aim again for Molesworth. In the same instant, she saw a man emerge from the copse of trees on the far side of Matt. She yelled, "Matt, to your right!"

Matt whirled and fired the Magnum. A sliver of bark flew from the tree to the man's left. The man darted to the right and took aim at Matt. Alexandra fired her M-4 at the man. Simultaneously, Matt fired the Magnum. The man's forehead exploded in a spray of blood and a shard of bone flew against a tree.

Alexandra called, "Good shot, Matt!" She spun around to focus on the barn again. There was no sign of Molesworth. One of his associates stood out from behind a barrel to aim at her but he was instantly dropped by a bullet from McBride who had fired from his position behind a tree. At the sound of McBride's gun, Alexandra turned and asked, "Where the hell did Molesworth go?"

"Back into the barn," McBride answered. "He may be trying to circle around like that guy you just wasted."

But as soon as he said it, Molesworth appeared again at the door of the barn and a stream of bullets starting ripping up the ground around them and Matt.

"Shit, that's an M-16 he's firing!" McBride said. "Looks like he's got a hundred round drum on it!"

Alexandra frowned. "Nothing like being out-gunned. Well, if wants to escalate ...." She armed the the M-4's grenade launcher, rolled out from behind the boulder, took quick aim, and fired. In the same instant she fired, she saw Molesworth's dog emerge from the barn and rush toward Molesworth. "Shit!" she muttered as the grenade hit the truck creating a massive explosion.

Alexandra waited several moments and when she still saw no activity near the barn, she scrambled over to Matt. "Are you okay?" she asked.

He looked at her with a stunned expression then muttered "Sorry!" before turning his back to her, bending over, and vomitting.

Alexandra smiled. She patted him on the shoulder. "It's okay. That's the way a decent man should react the first time."

Chapter 22—Vernon Ludlow; Linda Zacher

Having driven straight through—except for a number of pee stops plus gas stops in Buffalo and Albany—Scroggs and Ludlow finally arrived at Logan Airport after an exhausting seventeen hours. They hadn't even stopped for lunch, preferring instead to eat as they drove. The nearer they got to Boston, the more Ludlow complained about kidnapping Linda Zacher.

Once they arrived in Terminal B, Scroggs said, "Let's find a place to get a sandwich or something and talk. We have three hours before her plane comes in."

After checking out a few places, they settled on a corner table at Legal Sea Foods where they each ordered fried clams and a beer.

"I still don't like it, Billy," Ludlow said. "Whichever way you cut it, it's still kidnappin'."

Scroggs looked at him, expressionless. "You getting cold feet?"

Ludlow glanced around, then leaned forward and whispered, "You shouldn't have killed Huey, Billy."

"It had to be done."

"Well, maybe so, but I ain't goin' on. I'm done with this, Billy. I don't want you to think I'm chickenshit or anything. It's just that everything is getting too complicated."

Scroggs stared into the man's eyes for a long time, his cheek muscles twitching. Finally, he said, "It's okay, Vernon. I've started to think the same way, too."

Ludlow gave a surprised expression. "You serious?"

"Yuh, I'm serious. We have to call the whole thing off. I gotta get Mary-Ann and Annie back."

Ludlow's face brightened. "Man, am I glad to hear you say that."

"I thought you would be."

Matt and Alexandra settled into their seats on the American Airlines flight from Chicago. They found it frustrating, but the way the airline schedules worked the fastest way to Boston was to fly west from Detroit and connect through Chicago. Before they left the gate, Alexandra took out her tablet computer and turned it on. "Don't worry," she said to Matt, "Andy won't say a thing. We got the six shells you fired; as far as they'll know, he was alone and took them on single-handed when they opened fire on him. He won't have to explain why he violated every protocol or how it happened that he had a whole arsenal of weapons."

"In fact, they should give him a medal," Matt said as he rubbed his sore wrist.

Alexandra pressed a few keys then turned and smiled at him. "That forty-four magnum has quite a kick, huh?"

"Man, oh man!"

"Got it!" she cried. "Zacher's place is in Boothbay Harbor; it's a little over three hours from Boston."

"Check on connections from Boston."

"I should have known he'd have his dog with him."

"Would it have made a difference?"

She didn't answer. Instead, she studied the computer screen and finally said, "It'll be quicker to drive."

"What made you change your mind?" Ludlow asked as he dipped a fried clam into the dish of ketchup and brought it to his mouth.

"You did. You've always been clear thinkin' and I guess I just got caught up in the idea of givin' it back to the big guys that I ... that I was startin' to let my emotions get in the way."

"Yuh, I was sure worryin'," Ludlow said. "I mean, the way you was actin' and all ...."

"It's just become too much," Scroggs said. "After that Waters guy and Huey ... well I gotta tell you, I was just barely hangin' on. Now, with Mary-Ann and Annie being held somewhere, I just can't go through with it. Know what I mean?"

"Yuh, Billy, I sure do."

"I'm worried sick about Mary-Ann and Annie."

"What are you gonna do?"

Scroggs shook his head. "Somehow, I have to convince this Zacher fellow that I've scrapped the whole idea."

"How?"

"I don't know, Man," Scroggs replied, his voice faltering. "I just don't know. Maybe his daughter will have some ideas. I mean, hell, when she hears how her father could be trapped, she'll probably convince him to set everything back to zero like it never happened."

"Listen, Billy, I'll do whatever I can to help."

"Thanks, Vernon; you're a real friend." Scroggs paused a long while, then said, "Listen, Vernon, I'm real sorry about Huey." Again, there was a break in his voice. "I can't tell you how much ...." He shook his head sadly.

"Yuh, I know what you mean." Ludlow was silent for a long time before he said, "Would we have to kidnap her?"

"The Zacher girl?"

"Yuh. Would we have to kidnap her?"

"What do you have in mind?"

"What if we just told her the situation? Like you said, maybe she could somehow convince her father ...."

"I don't know, Vernon," replied Zacher. I just don't know."

They ate in silence for a while before Scroggs said, "Listen, we've still got plenty of time before the Zacher girl's flight comes in. What say we go into Boston, look around?"

"They have a good aquarium," Ludlow said. "Let's go there. They're supposed to have some great tropical fish."

Scroggs laughed. "You and your damned fish!"

"It's my hobby," Ludlow replied, sheepishly. "What can I say?"

"Who's been feedin' them while you're away?"

"Zeke."

"Good man. I can't wait to get back to Bass Run and have Zeke slide beers across the bar to you and me."

Ludlow laughed. "Man, does that sound good."

After making inquiries, they took an airport shuttle bus to the Blue Line station and boarded a subway car. Ten minutes later, they emerged onto Atlantic Avenue near the aquarium.

"Smell that nice sea air," Scroggs said, inhaling deeply. "It's a real relief after that long drive."

"You can say that again."

"I don't know about you," said Scroggs, "but my legs are stiff from all that drivin'. How about a little walk to stretch them out?"

"Sure, why not?"

They set off north on Atlantic Avenue, passing the Marriott Hotel and entering a tree-lined waterfront park. At this time of day, many families walked with their children. Scroggs watched a girl, about Annie's age, furiously pedaling a tricycle toward a flock of pigeons to make them scatter. An instinctive smile of delight came to him before he remembered where Annie was and his smile turned to an expression of anger. "See that little girl, Vernon," he said. "She's a lot like my Annie."

"Sure is."

"You don't have kids, so you can't know what it's like, know what I mean?"

"Yuh, I guess."

"That's why Huey had to go. You understand that, don't you? I mean, I couldn't allow anything to get in the way of me makin' it back to Annie."

"Yuh," Ludlow said. "I guess."

"Damn! I'm sick with worry about them."

"We'll find them, Billy. I'm there for you, my friend; you can count on my help."

"I promise you we won't hurt the Zacher girl."

"I know, Billy," Ludlow said. "I know how it is with you about fathers and daughters."

They walked in silence until they came to a wharf crowded with condominiums, their balconies overlooking Boston Harbor. "You have any idea what those places cost, Vernon?" Scroggs asked.

Ludlow shrugged.

"A hell of a lot more than you or me can afford," said Scroggs. "Those are the rich people who screw people like us, the people who vote for guys like Baxter."

"I guess."

They passed several more condominium wharfs before coming to yet another wharf, this one deserted. Scroggs turned to stroll along the wharf's edge and Ludlow followed him. "Soon, they'll be puttin' up more places here that people like us can't afford," Scroggs said.

Ludlow nodded. "Before you know it, we'll be surrounded. Then they'll build summer places in Bass Run for the bass fishin' and we'll be screwed again."

"Yuh," Scroggs replied. "That's why I gotta go through with it."

Ludlow stopped and gaped at Scroggs. "Wait, I thought you said you were gonna call the whole thing off."

"Yuh."

"But now you're changin' your mind again? Jesus, Billy, I just don't get you."

Scroggs said, "You know, seein' that girl on the bike back there, it's gotta make you understand why I had to get rid of Huey, don't it?"

Ludlow said nothing.

Scroggs continued. "I mean, you have to see why I can't let anything or anyone stand in the way of me makin' a better life for Annie. See what I mean?"

"You never intended to call the whole thing off, did you?" Ludlow asked.

Scroggs shook his head.

"Well, what I said back at the airport, still holds, then. I'm out."

By this time they had arrived at the end of the wharf, Scroggs peered over the edge. The slick pilings rose about fifteen feet from the water. There was no ladder. About a mile across the water, he saw a plane descend to the airport runway.

"Did you hear what I said, Billy? I'm out."

"I hear you. You'll have to get rid of those fake IDs. You still have them on you, don't you?"

"Yuh."

"Perfect," Scroggs said. "Pretty, ain't it?"

"What?"

Scroggs pointed. "The way that jumbo jet hardly seems to be movin'."

Ludlow glanced over his shoulder. As he did so, Scroggs gave him a hard shove in the middle of the back. Ludlow let out a startled cry as he plunged off the wharf's edge and hit the water. He disappeared for a long time before finally bobbing to the top, sputtering. "Billy, I can't swim!" he gasped.

"Perfect," said Scroggs. He watched as Ludlow sank and bobbed to the surface several more times. Then, after the man disappeared and two minutes passed with no sign of him, Scroggs turned and strolled down the wharf back to Atlantic Avenue. "The part about you can't swim, Vernon: I knew that," he muttered to himself. "Sorry, pal, but I can't afford somebody who's got cold feet."

Mary-Ann Scroggs held Annie close to her on the sofa of the living room in a cottage overlooking the ocean. She guessed they were somewhere on the coast of Maine because the drive from Bass Run had taken only a few hours and she could smell sea air. Throughout the drive, she had sat meekly in the back seat with Annie and now she was disgusted with herself. Why hadn't she put up more of a fight? She hated to see Annie so terrified and, gradually, through a combination of self-disgust and a sense of urgency, she felt an unaccustomed courage seep into her spirit. The two people—she had never learned their names, nor did she want to—were in the kitchen making sandwiches when the idea of making an escape came to her. She put her lips close to Annie's ear and whispered, "Annie, do you want us to get out of here?"

Annie nodded, wide eyed.

"Go very, very quietly to the front door. As soon as you see me slam the kitchen door on them, you open the front door and run as fast as you can down the driveway. At the end, go right and don't stop until you come into the town. It's only a few hundred yards from here; you can make it."

"What about you?" Annie whispered.

"Leave the door open, and I'll be right behind you."

"Okay."

"And if you see a car, wave at it; get them to stop. Understand?"

"Uhm hmm."

"Good. Now go very quietly," Mary-Ann whispered. "And don't be afraid. Mommy will be right behind you."

Annie glanced nervously at the kitchen, then carefully rose to her feet. She tiptoed to the front door and looked back at Mary-Ann with round, excited eyes.

Moving stealthily, Mary-Ann crossed the room, lifted the small chair from the writing desk in the corner and carried it to the kitchen door. Pausing for a moment to take a deep breath, she slammed the door shut. "Go, Annie!" she yelled. Hurriedly, she jammed the back of the chair under the door knob as best she could then bolted for the open front door.

Annie was already thirty yards down the driveway. Without looking back, Mary-Ann dashed after her.

Annie looked over her shoulder and tripped on a tree root that had broken the surface of the dirt driveway. Mary-Ann caught up to her and lifted her into her arms. A quick glance behind her told her that the man and woman had already broken out of the kitchen and were bursting from the house at full speed.

She turned and started to run, carrying Annie, as fast as she could toward the road. She knew she had no hope of making it into town, but if she could reach the road, maybe a car would come along before they caught up with her and Annie. Her legs screamed with agony as she ran faster than she ever had before. Already, she could feel her lungs burning. She looked back. They were gaining on her. Turning, she saw the black surface of the paved road no more than twenty yards in front of her. Desperately, she made an effort to quicken her pace. A car passed on the road and she cried, "Wait! Wait! Help us!" but the car continued on past. With a last bit of effort, she made it to the road and turned right, hoping to see another car coming toward them. The brake lights of the passing car flickered as it slowed for a curve, then it disappeared. The road ahead of them was deserted.

She looked back to see if there might be a car coming from the other direction, but there was none. Instead, the man and woman were almost upon them. Mary-Ann put Annie down and told her to run. Annie made a whimpering sound, then took off as fast as her legs would carry her. Mary-Ann turned to block their two captors. When they reached her, the man grabbed her by the shoulders. She kicked him in the shin as hard as she could.

"Ow! Fuck!" the man shouted. She kicked at him again. Still holding her by the shoulders, the man moved his lower body as far from her legs as possible. "Get the girl," he said to the woman.

Mary-Ann swung her arms wildly, catching the man squarely on the nose with her fist. "Leave my daughter alone!" she screamed.

Bringing a hand to his nose, the man loosened his grasp on her. She broke free and took off after Annie and the woman. But she had taken only a few steps before the man placed a bear hug on her from behind. At the same time, she saw that the woman had caught Annie and was carrying her back. Mary-Ann had no more strength to resist. Her shoulders sagged and she was forced to allow them to carry and shove her and Annie back up the driveway. They had gone only a short distance when she heard another car passing in the road. As she turned to look, the man clasped a hand over her mouth. All she could do was utter a frustrated sigh.

Scroggs checked his watch. There was still well over an hour before Linda Zacher's plane was due. As he headed back to the subway station he silently complimented himself on his efficiency. It was too bad that friends like Huey Figg and Vernon Ludlow had to be sacrificed, but there was a higher purpose to be fulfilled.

Back at the airport, he rented a car and drove it to a parking spot in the Central Garage. Then, returning to Terminal B, he purchased a writing pad and a blue marker. Taking them into a stall in the men's room, he printed Linda Zacher's name in big letters on the cardboard backing of the writing pad. He had no way of knowing how old the photograph he had seen of her on the internet was, so he'd decided to let her identify herself just in case.

The flight from Miami was a few minutes early. Scroggs stationed himself near the exit from the corridor leading from her arrival gate and waited, holding the sign. It turned out he'd not needed the sign; he recognized her immediately from the photograph as she approached, only the third person off the plane. "Bitch travels first class," Scroggs muttered under his breath.

She saw the sign and came up to him, an inquisitive look on her face. "I'm Linda Zacher." She was tall and lean with a healthy glow to her angular face—a woman who had the money and leisure to eat well and work out. She had the kind of beauty Mary-Ann used to have before things got rough, he thought ruefully.

"I'm Timothy Caine," Scroggs said. "Your father asked me to meet you."

"I thought Dad was meeting me here. He said he was booking an American flight to arrive just a little before mine. We're going to dinner at his hotel."

Thinking quickly, Scroggs said, "He came in early. He's already at the hotel. He asked me to pick you up and deliver you there."

"That's typical of him," Linda Zacher said with a shrug. "But I need to get my bags first."

They took an escalator to the baggage claim area in silence. While Linda Zacher watched carousel 3 for her luggage, Scroggs studied an arrival screen. There was an American flight 836 from Washington originally scheduled to arrive at 2:45 but now marked for 3:20. Scroggs guessed that was Karl Zacher's flight. He glanced at his watch. It was 3:15.

After they arrived at their gate on time at 2:47, Matt and Alexandra made their way through the baggage claim area toward the outside doors. The area was crowded and they had to weave through the people gathered around carousel 3. Finally, they emerged from the terminal and took an airport bus to the rental car area. While Alexandra went to the Hertz desk to arrange for a car, Matt stood in a corner and punched in the special telephone number that went straight through to the president's secretary. When Doris answered, Matt asked, "Does the president have any time to call me from the residence this afternoon?"

"He's going there in ten minutes for a late lunch with his family. I'll ask him to give you a call."

"Thanks, Doris. Tell him it's important."

In a whispered conversation during the flight, Matt and Alexandra had agreed to make this call because they were becoming increasingly alarmed and frustrated by their inability to locate Scroggs. Also, the deaths of Johnny Waters and Huey Figg convinced them that Scroggs would stop at nothing, especially now that his wife and daughter were somehow involved. And, finally, there was the real possibility that Zacher was making moves that might blow everything up in their faces.

While they awaited the president's call, they moved to a remote area at the end of the terminal building. One man, an airline employee, stood smoking a cigarette, but he was a good twenty yards from them—plenty of space for a private conversation with the president. At last, Matt's phone rang. He answered it. "Matt, here."

"It's Angus. What's up? How are you doing?"

"Good afternoon, Mister President. I'm afraid we're not having much luck. Alexandra and I have talked about it and we think you've got to authorize us—"

"—No."

"Please, Mister President. Hear me out. You've got to authorize us to bring others in. Scroggs is dead serious. He—"

"—I said 'no', Matt."

"But we need help."

"Matt, you know what's at stake. It has to be just you and the Lake woman."

Matt felt a flush of anger suffuse his face. He turned away from Alexandra and said in a forced whisper, "Jesus Christ, Angus, are you still thinking of your reputation, your legacy? It's your damned *life* that's at stake!"

"The ground rules remain the same. Local police only, and that only for narrow purposes. Your man knows Zacher and Zacher knows the whole story. We can't afford to let him fall into the hands of the Treasury people or anybody else. You need to get him."

"But Angus, please listen. He's—"

"—I'm sorry, Matt, but that's the way it is. Now I'm going to try to have a pleasant lunch with Maxwell, Kyla, and the grandchildren." The line went dead. Matt angrily snapped his cell phone closed.

Alexandra appeared. "No dice?"

"He's a stubborn jackass, He'd rather die than have what he did exposed."

"Or he'd just rather die," Alexandra said. "Have you thought of that?"

"Uhm. Did you get a car?"

"All out. They said to try Avis."

"Timothy Caine?"

"Didn't rent from Hertz," Alexandra replied, "so we need to go to Avis anyway."

Angus Baxter, sitting alone in his private, book-lined study, placed the phone back in its cradle. He couldn't blame Matt for being so insistent, but what his friend proposed was out of the question.

When Matt had asked him if his stubbornness was because he was still thinking of his reputation and legacy, it had stung. But for one of the rare times in the last several months, he felt he was thinking clearly and his legacy, although admittedly important, was not what kept him from ordering a broader search for Scroggs.

Rather, it was the certain knowledge of what the unraveling of his scheme would unjustly do to others. First, of course, were his children and grand-children. It's one thing to witness the death of a parent; it's another thing altogether to experience the death of one's respect for that person. It would be horribly painful for Kyla and Maxwell. But as bad as that would be, it would be even worse for Natalie, Jeremy, and Peter. In addition to their own faith in their grandfather being destroyed, they would have to endure the inevitable taunts of classmates who, like everybody else, take a special pleasure—*schadenfreude*—in seeing prominent people taken down.

Then there was Matt. My god, he thought, what have I done to my friend? If the scheme was exposed, Matt would be accused of plotting a presidential assassination. No matter how good or misguided the intentions, there would be some prosecutor in the Justice Department who, hungry for his own advancement and encouraged by Baxter's opponents, would come out snarling and would pounce on Matt as the first step in bringing the prosecution all the way to the Oval Office. And there would be nothing Baxter could do to stop it because he would already have been discredited. There would be nothing he could do to save the American people from the agony of witnessing another blot on the White House and of experiencing the distrust and apathy that would inevitably follow. All this after Baxter had taken pride in restoring credibility to the institution.

And there was Marcie Gaudet to consider. Any avenue that would culminate in the total destruction of the president of the United States would be pursued with merciless ferocity and she would be treated like insignificant collateral damage. Look what happened to some of the associates of Bill Clinton when Ken Starr, smelling blood, donned his mask of righteousness.

And these wouldn't be the only people who would suffer. Katherine Moore-Paterson was a decent and honorable woman and didn't deserve to suffer the taint-by-association fate that Al Gore experienced. Katherine would be forced to run a defensive campaign from a discredited White House. In short, she would almost certainly lose and that would be the tragic end to a brilliant career.

And, perhaps most important, there was Grace and everything she stood for. While Washington was reeling with investigation and shock, the administration would come to a grinding stop. The Education Bill would undoubtedly sink and, worse still, the potential Middle East breakthrough would die a slow and agonizing death. Thousands more innocent people would die, perhaps more.

Was all this worth his life?

He decided it was time for him to live up to his father's example. It's been said that a combat soldier's greatest fear is not that he might die, but that he might fail, he might betray his buddies and those he loves. In the last few weeks, Baxter had become convinced that notion was true and if it came to it, he would rather let the assassination happen than to continue the course of betrayal he had been on. With deep sadness, he rose wearily from his chair and went into the dining room to join his family.

At last, a loud buzzer and a blinking red light signaled that the baggage carousel was about to move. Scroggs looked at his watch again. *3:20.* He glanced at the arrival screen. Flight AA 836 was reported as having landed. He calculated it would take Zacher five to ten minutes to make it to baggage claim assuming, as he guessed, he flew first class like his daughter.

Linda Zacher, having somehow allowed people to move in front of her, now stood in the second row of people waiting for their bags. With annoyance in his voice, Scroggs asked, "What does your bag look like?"

"There are two—a matched set. They're a black suitcase and a black carryall."

Scroggs studied the bags riding past them on the carousel. "They're almost all black!" He glanced at his watch, then at the escalator by which passengers entered the area.

"They both have a Brazilian flag sticker on them—green with a yellow triangle in the middle," Linda said.

Scroggs elbowed his way to the front row and watched the bags descending the chute. Her bags appeared within two minutes, but it seemed much longer to him. "Okay, let's go. I'm in the central garage," he said, shouldering the bags and leading her to an elevator.

Minutes later, they pulled out of the garage, exited the airport, and took the Sumner Tunnel into Boston. Once out of the tunnel, Scroggs took Route 93 North over the graceful span of the Zakim Bridge.

"Where are you going?" Linda Zacher asked. "My father always stays at the Bostonian near Faneuil Hall."

Scroggs remained silent. He pressed the child-safety button that locked the windows and doors with a loud click.

She shot him a look of alarm. "Where are you taking me?"

"You'll see."

"No. Take me back to Boston," she said, her voice rising in panic. "Turn around." When he didn't answer, she said, "My father knows some powerful people. You won't get away with this." When he still didn't answer, she started to curse at him, threatening him with everything from imprisonment to death.

Scroggs said nothing until, five miles up the highway, he pulled off at an exit marked "Spot Pond." At the bottom of the exit, he parked overlooking the small pond and said, "You have a cell phone?" When she nodded, he said, "Hand it over." He took the phone, flipped the cover open and asked, "What's your father's cell phone number?"

Frustrated and angry at being late, Karl Zacher checked the arrivals screen and learned that his daughter's plane had landed long before. Assuming she would be waiting for him in baggage claim, he found the escalator and bounded down the moving steps. He checked the signs over the baggage carousels and found that her flight had used Carousel 3. But there were only a few people left at the carousel. Scanning the large room and seeing no sign of his daughter, he pulled out his cell phone and started to enter her number. As he was doing this, the phone rang. He glanced at the caller I.D. and, smiling with relief, answered. "Hello, Linda, sorry I'm late. I—"

"—Zacher, I have your daughter."

"What? Who's this?"

"You have my wife and daughter, now I have your daughter. Looks like we have an old Mexican standoff."

Zacher paused for a moment, still stunned. Finally, he said, "Look, the deal's off. In fact, there never was—"

"—No way, the deal's off. Me and my family ain't goin' back to the way it was. That's something you need to get through your head."

"But I never—"

"—Shut up and listen to me. What I'm proposin' is a different deal. Call it a rider to our contract. You tell me where my wife and kid are, then you meet me there with a whole lot of cash. The second installment has gone way up and it's become due immediately. You'll do it, or your daughter's dead."

In a wavering voice, Zacher asked, "How much?"

"A million bucks."

"A million?"

"Are you saying pretty Linda here ain't worth a million?"

"No, I'm not saying that. Of course I'll do it."

"Then tell me where my family is."

Zacher paused a long time before saying, "They're in Maine."

"Don't screw with me!" Scroggs shouted. "*Where* in Maine?" Of course, he knew the answer because Molesworth had given him the address; he was just testing Zacher.

"My summer place in Boothbay Harbor."

"Does your daughter know where it is?"

"Yes."

"Who's guardin' them?"

"Two people. A man and a woman," Zacher replied.

"Call them. Tell them I'm comin'. When I pull up and flash my lights three times, they come out, leave any weapons they have on the ground, step far away from them, and place their hands on top of their heads. I'll have a gun at the back of Linda's head. Got it?"

"Yes ... yes."

"Come alone. And don't even think about the police. I kept the transfer slip for the quarter million and I gave it to a friend with instructions to hand it over to the cops if anything happened to me. Even the threat of assassination is a damned serious crime."

"But I—"

"—Shut up, Zacher. I don't want to hear any more. I'll see you in Maine. Now, I'm gonna give Linda the phone. You tell her she's to show me how to get to your place and she's to just sit back and relax and enjoy the ride. If she behaves, everything will be alright. Okay?"

"Okay."

"Good. I'll give her the phone now. Chat with her all you want; I know how it is between fathers and daughters."

At Avis, Matt and Alexandra found no record of a Timothy Caine renting a car. However, they were able to rent a car for themselves. It was while Matt was filling out the paperwork that Alexandra got a call from one of her contacts in Washington. She answered it, spoke for a few moments, then turned to Matt. "Zacher boarded a flight for—are you ready for this?—Boston."

"Jesus! Did your man say what flight?"

"Yuh, it landed about an hour ago."

"Damn it!" He turned to the Avis clerk, showed her the letter from Baxter, and asked, "Did a man named Karl Zacher rent a car here?"

The woman checked her computer. "No. No one by that name."

Alexandra said to Matt, "Cycle back through the car rental companies again?"

"You bet!"

They re-visited three agencies before they came to Hertz again. The young man behind the counter smiled and said, "Back again?"

"This time we're looking for a different name—Karl Zacher," Matt said.

"And I suppose this is covered by that letter from the president, too?"

"You bet. Can you check your computer, please?"

"Don't need to; Mr. Zacher was here about twenty minutes ago, just after you left. I waited on him myself. He had a reservation; otherwise I could have given you the car I gave him."

Matt and Alexandra glanced at each other. Alexandra said to the clerk, "Please, we need the make, model, and color of the car and we need the plate number."

The man checked his computer and wrote down the information on a slip of paper which he handed to Alexandra.

After they left the agency, Matt asked, "Now what?"

"When was the last time you had a lobster dinner?"

"Meaning?"

"We head for his place in Boothbay Harbor."

Chapter 23—Boothbay Harbor; A Remote Cabin

Scroggs drove over the Piscataqua River Bridge in Portsmouth, New Hampshire, and on the other side entered Maine. Scroggs broke a long silence by looking at Linda Zacher, sitting slumped in the passenger seat, and saying, "I'm truly sorry for scaring you." He said it in an earnest, soft voice. "I have a daughter myself, you know."

For a long while she didn't answer, and when she did, it was to say, "Stay on this until exit forty-four."

Scroggs felt a frisson of sadness. He had nothing particular against Linda Zacher; she was probably a decent person who didn't deserve to be caught up in this. True, she had advantages that he could only dream about for Annie, but she didn't appear to be like that vulture woman in the Jaguar, or the vice president of the mortgage bank, or the various officers in Iraq. She wasn't after him or his family. When, trying to make conversation after they left Boston, he'd asked her what she'd been doing in Brazil, and she had reluctantly told him that she'd gone with an anthropological group from Harvard to work among the Yanomani people in the rainforests of northern Brazil.

"What are those people like?" he'd asked.

"They're being destroyed. There's been a gold rush and prospectors have exterminated whole villages. The government promises to help, but it doesn't."

"What were you doing?"

"Studying their culture before it disappears. Trying to help them in any way we could."

"It sounds like a dangerous place to be."

She'd only nodded, then fell silent for many miles.

He thought: These Yanomani people are a lot like him and some of the people he knew—poor victims of a kind of corporate greed, left to their own devices by a government that didn't give a crap. It sounded like everything that was wrong with America repeated in some primitive rainforest. He wondered why people like her didn't spend more of their time helping the victims of America rather than going to Brazil. All the same, he admired her for her courage and her willingness to do something.

Scroggs merged onto I-295 North toward South Portland. Still feeling a tinge of guilt at having to put Linda Zacher through this, he said, "Think of this, Linda—may I call you Linda?" When she only shrugged, he said, "I know I frighten you, but my little Annie is only seven years old. Think of how frightened she must have been when your father's people took her and my wife away."

"What's this all about between you and my father, anyway?"

"Believe me, that's something you're far better off not knowing."

After a long silence, Scroggs asked, "What's Harvard like?"

"What do you mean, what's it like?"

"I mean, what if my daughter was to go there, would she enjoy it?"

"I suppose so; I do."

An hour later, they drove over the Sagadahoc Bridge in Bath, heading for Wiscasset where they would take a right to drop dead south toward Boothbay Harbor.

For more than an hour Scroggs has been able to rest his mind from the immediate problem by imagining what he would do with the money from Zacher: a move to a new house; trips to vacation spots; later, trips to Boston to visit Annie at Harvard …. He had learned in Iraq that you stayed sharp for combat by distracting yourself from it in periods of relative calm. That's probably why so many soldiers took drugs. But now he had to focus on the matter at hand. He assumed that Zacher's people had guns—anybody in the business of kidnapping is bound to have a gun—and his first task would be to get his hands on them.

Linda said, "Turn right at the next intersection."

He asked himself if he was confident Zacher had called his people and told them to watch for the signal—would they lay their guns down as he'd instructed Zacher to tell them? He decided the answer was yes; Zacher apparently loved his daughter. The man wouldn't take the risk.

"It's the second driveway on the left."

"I don't see a house."

"It's about a hundred yards or so in, overlooking the water."

Scroggs made the turn and, peering ahead of him, finally saw the house. It was a large, contemporary, post-and-beam cottage with gray shingles squatting on a rise fifty feet above East Penobscot Bay. Several kayaks sat on racks near the separate garage.

Scroggs pulled to a stop facing the front door which was twenty yards away. He tooted the horn. When he saw a figure appear at the door, he flashed the headlights three times. While Linda Zacher was distracted by the activity at the front door, he reached behind her seat, retrieved the Tokarev TT-33 and pressed the muzzle to the back of her head. She sucked in her breath. "Don't move or do anything and you'll be fine," he said.

Ralph Stanley and Donna Quinn appeared on the stoop.

Scroggs called out. "Did Zacher call you?"

"Yes," said Stanley.

"Then you know I have a gun at the back of his daughter's head. I want to see you put your guns down on the ground then step far away from them." When they did as he instructed, he studied Stanley for a moment, feeling a hint of recognition. "What's your name?" he asked.

"Ralph Stanley."

He ran the name through his mind but it didn't register. He was sure he'd not heard that name before. Finally, he said, "Take your clothes off, both of you."

"What?" cried Stanley. At the same moment, Quinn said, "Are you crazy?"

"You heard me," Scroggs said. He turned to Linda Zacher. "Tell 'em."

"Do it," she said. "He has a gun to my head."

Hesitantly, Stanley and Quinn stripped down to their underwear.

"Okay, that's enough," said Scroggs. "I ain't lookin' for no cheap thrills. Now step away from the clothes."

Both of them backed away several steps.

"More."

They took several more steps back from the clothes.

Scroggs bolted from the car and kicked their weapons further away from them. He rifled through their clothes for additional weapons and finding none, turned to point his gun at Linda Zacher. "Out!"

Warily, she slipped out of the car.

"The tool shed over there with the padlock, you know where the key is?"

"On a hook inside the front door," replied Linda.

"Get it. Leave the door open so I can see you."

Linda mounted the two steps of the stoop, reached inside, retrieved a key, and showed it to Scroggs who said, "Unlock the shed and hand me the key."

Linda did as he instructed.

"Okay, all three of you inside," he said, waving the gun in their faces.

Stanley and the two women filed into the shed. Scroggs picked up the discarded clothes and threw them into the shed. He slammed the door closed and turned the key in the padlock. He pulled on it twice to assure himself it was locked then turned and ran for the house.

He burst into the living room to find Mary-Ann sitting on a sofa with her ankles bound together. Annie sat beside her, her arms around her mother's neck.

"Billy!"

"Daddy!"

"I thought that must have been you," Mary-Ann said.

"Are you okay?" Scroggs asked.

"Yuh, we're fine. Annie was just a little scared."

"I'm not scared anymore," said Annie.

"That's great Sweetheart," said Scroggs. "I'm gonna take you two out of here, but not just yet. I have a little more business to do."

It took all of Karl Zacher's willpower not to drive too fast along Route 27 between Wiscasset and Boothbay which was often patrolled by police. He was within ten minutes of his summer home and he couldn't wait to see if his daughter was safe. He had never loved anyone the way he loved his only child. When he divorced his wife, his only regret was that he wouldn't get to see Linda as often. Now, he wouldn't forgive himself if she were harmed because of his involvement with militia groups.

Some forty miles behind Zacher, Matt and Alexandra were approaching the turnoff from I-295 onto US-1 North near Brunswick. A voice from the navigation system said, "Prepare to exit highway on the right at Exit 28 US One, Coastal Route, Brunswick, Bath."

Zacher drove up to his summer cottage. He bounded up to the front door and opened it. He saw Scroggs, Mary-Ann and Annie sitting together on the sofa. Scroggs pointed a gun at Zacher.

"Where's my daughter?" asked Zacher.

"Don't worry; She's okay," replied Scroggs who then turned to Mary-Ann and said, "Take Annie in the kitchen and stay there."

"Why?"

"Please don't argue with me."

"But—"

"—Please, Mary-Ann," Scroggs snapped. "I don't know what I might have to do; I just don't want Annie to see it, in case."

Reluctantly, Mary-Ann shepherded Annie into the kitchen and closed the door. As soon as they were gone, Zacher said, "I want to see my daughter."

"You will," Scroggs replied. "Just as soon as you write a letter."

"What letter?"

"The letter I'm gonna dictate to you. Sit down at that computer and pull up your word processing program." He pointed to a roll-up desk on which sat a computer.

Nervously, Zacher sat, launched the word processing program, and looked over his shoulder at Scroggs.

"Okay," said Scroggs, "here's what you type: I, Karl Zacher, confess to arrangin' the failed assassination of President Baxter by Donald A. Scroggs—"

"—Now, wait a minute!"

"Type or your daughter dies."

When Zacher hesitated, Scroggs pulled out the snapshot of Figg's body. "See that?" he asked. "See how his brains spill out on the ground? I did that. And he was a friend of mine. Now, TYPE!"

Zacher started to type, then stopped and said, "This is bullshit; I didn't even know your brother."

Scroggs reached into his pocket, pulled out a photograph, and shoved in Zacher's face. "You recognize that pretty boy talkin' with my brother? Name's Ralph Stanley, right? Next sentence: I also confess to financing the second attempt."

"But I didn't; we're being set up."

"Correction: *You* were bein' set up and this letter is undoin' it, makin' it real the way it's gonna be."

"But if you go through with it, I'll be indicted, too. It could mean the death penalty."

"Now you're getting' the drift. You'll be fine as long as everything works out. We're gonna be partners, you an' me, so you better hope I get away with it. Now write what I said and put your Washington address on the bottom."

"Why my address?"

"In case I need a hangout tomorrow until it's time to go to the Lincoln Memorial."

"But—"

"—Write!" Scroggs shouted.

His hands trembling, Zacher typed the last sentence, then added his address.

"Now print it," Scroggs said.

Zacher clicked on "PRINT" and the printer kicked into action. A single sheet floated into the output tray. Scroggs grabbed the letter and placed it in front of Zacher. "Sign it."

Zacher pulled out a fountain pen and signed the letter.

"Now gimme the pen," said Scroggs.

Zacher held the pen out to him. Scroggs grabbed it and snapped it in half. He let the ink spill onto the desk then he grasped Zacher's hand and forced his thumb first into the ink, then onto the letter. "This is goin' to the same guy who's holdin' the transfer slip. If I don't make it, he'll give it to the cops." Scroggs crossed the room and opened the kitchen door. "Let's go Honey, Sweetheart, we're getting' outa here."

He motioned for Zacher to lead them out of the house.

"Where's Linda?" Zacher asked.

Scroggs handed him a key. "In the shed. Unlock it."

Zacher crossed the yard to the shed and unlocked it. He opened the door and Linda came out. She was followed by Stanley and Quinn who were both fully dressed.

Scroggs said, "Okay, Zacher, give me your car keys."

With a trembling hand, Zacher gave him the car keys. Scroggs, in turn, gave Zacher the keys to the car he had rented. "We're switchin' cars." He turned to Mary-Ann and said, "You and Annie get in the back seat." Then he motioned to Linda, "You get in the front seat."

Zacher said, "Now wait a minute!"

"She'll be fine as long as you play along," Scroggs said as he climbed into the car that Zacher had rented. He made a U-turn in the dirt driveway, rolled the window down, pointed his gun at the left front tire of the car he had rented, and fired. The tire hissed flat.

Scroggs tore out of the driveway, leaving Zacher, Stanley and Quinn gaping after him.

Matt and Alexandra skirted Boothbay Harbor along Atlantic Avenue when the GPS said, "Prepare to turn left on Lobster Cove Road in three tenths of a mile."

When they arrived at the intersection and turned left, they passed a car going in the opposite direction that seemed to be riding on a donut spare tire. The low afternoon sun caused a glare in the windshield of the car obscuring its occupants.

"This is a pretty nice area," said Alexandra. "It must be nice to be Zacher."

Before Matt could say anything, the GPS announced "Turn right in two tenths of a mile to your destination."

"Where are we goin' Billy?" asked Mary-Ann. "This ain't the way home."

"I'm takin' you and Annie somewhere safe until all this is over."

"You can't mean you're still goin' through with it after all this."

"Mary-Ann, I told you before," said Scroggs. "It's something I gotta do."

"But—"

"—That's enough, Mary-Ann!"

Cautiously, Matt and Alexandra drove up to the house. Guns drawn, they stepped out of the car and approached the front door.

"Doesn't look like there's anyone around," said Matt.

"Yuh, except the front door's slightly open. Be careful."

Matt glanced at the door and saw that it, indeed, was slightly ajar. "Shall we?" he asked.

Instead of answering him, Alexandra leaned her shoulder into the door and it swung open. "Somebody left here in a hurry," Alexandra said.

"What makes you say that?"

"Door's open; light's on; computer's on," said Alexandra. "What do you think it means?" She crossed the room and sat at the roll-top desk. She moved the mouse and the screen saver disappeared to reveal a word processing program left open. She read the letter and said, "Well, now, what have we here?" She read the letter to him.

Matt touched the spill of ink on the desk. "Still wet," he said. "By the looks of it, Scroggs must have gotten Zacher to put his fingerprint on the confession, meaning—"

"—Meaning if Scroggs knows what to do with it—and I'm betting he does—he has all he needs to force Zacher to help him," said Alexandra. "I mean, what would Zacher have to lose? If Scroggs insists on going through with the assassination, the only way Zacher gets out of it is if Scroggs succeeds and gets away. Otherwise, this confession will show up somewhere."

"Do you suppose Scroggs gave it to his wife with instructions on how to use it?" asked Matt.

"No, he probably doesn't completely trust her, knowing she's against the idea. More likely, he's given it to a friend with instructions to do nothing unless something happens to him. My guess is the friend has no idea what it is."

Matt glanced at his watch. "In a few hours, it will be the twenty-seventh. We've got little more than a day."

"We have to assume Scroggs is on his way to Washington right now, probably with Zacher."

"And that means we better get our butts to Washington, too."

President Baxter caused an unwelcome flurry of activity in the West Wing when he insisted on visiting the Lincoln Memorial that night. A Secret Service detail was quickly gathered and within twenty minutes a hastily assembled motorcade was waiting in the driveway by the Rose Garden.

Pennsylvania Avenue and 23rd Street were mostly deserted as the motorcade, lights flashing, sped past. The flags mounted above the headlights of the presidential limousine snapped as the car sped down 23rd Street. Finally, they pulled up alongside the memorial. Secret Service agents fanned out along the circular path around the memorial and on the wide steps facing the reflecting pool. When they were in place, an agent opened the president's door. Baxter unfolded his long legs to step from the limousine. He walked briskly around to the front of the building and mounted the steps where a clutch of late night tourists stood gaping behind a thin phalanx of Secret Service agents and police officers.

For a long moment, Baxter stared at the softly lit, seated statue. What was it he saw in the stone face looking back down on him—sternness, sadness, a deep, world-weary wisdom? He had never been able to figure out that look, that thousand-yard stare, that gaze out past the Reflecting Pool, past the World War II Memorial, Past the Washington Monument and the Mall, all the way to the Capitol. Perhaps the expression contained a foreknowledge of his assassination. Was that it? Did Lincoln know of the coming of his own death even as he, Baxter, another but far less worthy president, one whose words would never be embossed on a plaque or hacked out of stone, knew of his appointment with an assassin?

Baxter moved to the south chamber and read the words that always stirred him: "... that cause for which they gave the last full measure of their devotion—that we here highly resolve that they shall not have died in vain ...."

Died in vain.

He turned to look out at the reflecting pool which appeared blood red in the refracted lights. To his left, he saw the platform, lit by Klieg lights, from where he would deliver his Martin Luther King address in little more than thirty-six hours, and a vague memory was stirred in him of a novel he'd read many years before. Was it Dickens? Stendhal? Dumas? He couldn't remember. All he could recall was a scene in which a character, a prisoner, peers out from his cell to see the scaffolding being built for his execution.

Died in vain.

How appropriate that word, vain, meaning excessive pride; vain, meaning useless; vain, meaning trivial.

Died in vain.

He looked out over the Reflecting Pool. A man walking in the middle of it raised and automatic weapon. He saw the white muzzle flashes. Then they resolved into a woman dressed all in white. "The glorious lady of my mind!" he whispered to himself.

It was nearing 10:00 p.m. when Scroggs pulled off the main road and turned onto a rutted, dirt road—barely visible parallel tracks with an island of grass in the middle. After lurching and bouncing for a half-hour, he finally pulled up to an old hunting shack. He, Mary-Ann, Annie and Linda Zacher stepped out of the car carrying bags of groceries. Scroggs guided them with a large flashlight. They entered the shack which was a one-room log cabin. It had a table with four chairs, a small ice chest, a kerosene stove and two stacked, double bunk beds.

Scroggs dropped the final bag of groceries on the table and said, "This will hold you two until I get back."

"You really are going through with it, aren't you?" Mary-Ann said with an incredulous look.

He placed his hands on her shoulders. "Everything will be okay. I'll be back tomorrow night."

"It's obvious he's blackmailing Zacher," said Matt. They were driving back out toward Wiscasset and Route 1.

"Well, duh!," said Alexandra. "You might make it as an agent after all."

"Zacher's address at the bottom?"

"He's got Zacher cornered. He'll use his Georgetown place to hide out until it's time."

"Well, let's be there to greet him."

After dropping Mary-Ann and Annie off at the hunting shack deep in the woods of northeastern Maine shortly after midnight, Scroggs turned to begin the long drive to Washington with Linda Zacher. But instead of returning via the main highways, he headed southwest on back roads, working his way into New Hampshire and then south through Massachusetts. Linda Zacher slept soundly in the passenger seat. Scroggs envied her; he had been on the go for several days with little sleep. But adrenalin was keeping him going and he would have plenty of time to rest at some Caribbean resort or other in a few days.

Driving carefully so not to draw attention the way Huey Figg had done, he kept pulling over to the side to check road maps and take short rests. He was determined to avoid all major highways, especially those with toll booths, all the way to Washington. It would take them at least twice as long, but he had the time. The ceremony in front of the Lincoln Memorial wasn't scheduled to start until noon the following day.

After her husband left, Mary-Ann Scroggs was overcome by a wave of despair. They'd driven more than a half-hour along a rutted dirt road and now they were somewhere deep in the woods. She had little idea where they were. She looked around the hunting shack. It was a simple, one-room log cabin with no plumbing. In the moonlight, she saw an outhouse twenty yards away, but it frightened her to think about having to go out in the dark to use it. A large pail that Scroggs had filled with fresh drinking water sat in a corner near a table on which rested a kerosene stove. Beside it were two empty beer bottles covered with a patina of dust.

"How long will we have to stay here, Mommy?" Annie asked.

"Daddy will be back tomorrow night. Until then, we might as well get some sleep. It's way past your bedtime." She put Annie into the lower of two bunk beds, pulled heavy woolen blankets over her, and climbed into the top bunk. In moments, she heard Annie breathing deeply in sleep. But she could not sleep. She lay awake, the blankets—smelling of stale man-sweat—pulled to her chin, and stared into the darkness, trying to think what to do. She lost track of time, dozing in and out of a fitful sleep, until she heard Annie stirring below her. She opened her eyes to see a tiny spiral of dust, ignited by a slant of sunlight from the high window next to her head. It caused her to sit up with a start. She rose to her hands and knees and peered out the small, screened window. The shadows of trees told her it was already mid morning.

She was surprised Annie had slept that late until she remembered it was past midnight when her daughter had gone to bed. In a low voice, she called out, "Are you awake, Annie?"

"Yes."

"Do you have to go to the bathroom?"

"Yes."

"Okay," Mary-Ann said, climbing down from the top bunk. "I'll take you to that outhouse and wait for you."

"What about bears?" Annie asked in a frightened voice.

"I'll watch out for you. Don't worry."

As they slipped out the door and warily crossed the twenty yards to the outhouse, Annie said, "I want to go home."

"I do, too, but we have to wait for Daddy."

After taking Annie back into the cabin, Mary-Ann went by herself to the outhouse. She returned and fixed bowls of cereal for them from the groceries they'd stopped and bought on the way. All the while, she tried to figure out what to do. The thought came to her that she had Matt Cannon's cell phone number with her. If she could call him, he and the Lake woman might be able to stop Billy before it was too late.

But there was no phone in the cabin. She tried to estimate how far back it was to the town where they'd bought the groceries at a small market attached to a gas station, because she remembered seeing a telephone there. Five miles? Ten? She'd been half asleep and it had been dark.

Finally, sometime after noon, she decided it made no difference how far it was; she had to do it. She refused to entertain the thought of them spending another night in this cabin, not when there was one last chance of stopping Billy. "Annie, Sweetheart," she said, "we're gonna walk back to where we got groceries so we can go home."

"How far is it?"

"I'm not sure, but it's not that far. It will be like takin' a hike. Do you think you can manage it?"

Annie nodded.

After drinking the remainder of the milk and scooping up some candy bars, they set out down the dirt road. As they walked, Mary-Ann kept glancing to their right and left every time she heard a sound. There were lots of bears in the Maine woods and she tried to remember what you're supposed to do if you came across one of them. They'd been walking for almost two hours, taking frequent breaks so Annie could rest her young, slender legs, when they came to a fork in the road. Mary-Ann's heart sank. She couldn't remember there being a fork; it had been dark when they'd passed this way and, in any event, her eyes had probably been closed. She had no idea which road to take.

After some futile deliberation, she decided to take the one on the left. They continued on for another hour. Once or twice they heard distant gun shots. Hunters. At first, she hoped they wouldn't come across them, but then she realized they would have a car or a truck and might give her and Annie a ride back to the village, wherever it was.

Another hour and a half further on, they came to a clearing and Mary-Ann let out a cry of despair. They'd circled around and come back to the hunting cabin where they'd spent the night.

Linda Zacher screamed, "Watch out!"

At the same instant, Scroggs saw the headlights coming straight at them. He jerked the wheel to the right. The car shot across the road toward the verge just as a truck hurtled by on their left. The car's tires skidded in the soft shoulder, throwing up clods of dirt and grass. Struggling, Scroggs spun the steering wheel back to the left and they slid back onto the road. He applied the brakes, turned again to the right, and straightened the car out. His heart was thumping wildly.

"Jesus, you're falling asleep," said Linda Zacher. "You almost got us killed!"

Scroggs said nothing. He knew they were somewhere in New Jersey, or maybe Delaware, but he wasn't sure exactly. The last stretch of miles were a blank to him and he realized he had to do something to keep himself awake.

"Why don't you let me drive?" Linda Zacher said.

It was tempting, but Scroggs knew that if he turned the wheel over to her, he'd be asleep within minutes. Saying nothing, he turned the volume on the radio up so it was blasting music. He continued driving, more slowly, down the road. Seeing a sign for a rest stop, he slowed even more and drifted to the right. He pulled into the rest area, parked, turned the engine off, and stepped from the car. Only two other cars were in the parking lot.

"What are you doing?"

"I'm gonna throw water on my face," Scroggs replied. "Stay put. I've got the keys."

"I've got to pee."

"Okay, go ahead. But come right back to the car. And give me your cell phone."

She handed him her phone and they walked into the building. He watched her go into the lady's room, then he rushed into the men's room, urinated, splashed water on his face, and quickly left. He went outside to wait for Linda Zacher to emerge.

When, at last, she came out of the building, she glanced at him then started to run.

"Shit," he muttered, as he took off after her, looking over his shoulder to see if they were being watched. Within seconds, he caught her. "Get back into the car," he said with quiet authority. "I really don't want to hurt you."

She took a deep, frustrated breath, paused a moment, then meekly walked to the car. He looked back at the building. He saw no one. He got into the car, turned the ignition on, and pulled out of the parking lot. "One thing you should know," he said.

"What's that?" Linda Zacher asked sullenly.

"It's pretty obvious I'm tired. When a person's tired like me, he hasn't got a whole lot of patience. Pull something like that again, and I'll kill you."

"I thought you said you didn't want to hurt me."

He nodded. "I don't. But some things are more important than what I want or don't want."

When she recognized the hunting cabin, Annie started to cry. Mary-Ann hugged her and tried not to cry, herself. "It's okay, Sweetheart. Mommy made a mistake at that fork in the road, but at least now we know which way to go. Come on, I'll carry you." She lifted Annie to her back and started down the road again, gripping Annie's legs on both sides of her hips.

Somehow, carrying Annie like this made her realize how desperately she wanted to stop Billy and that, in turn, transformed her fear to a kind of determined courage.

She plodded along as fast as she could despite the aches building in her back and legs. When they finally arrived back at the fork, Mary-Ann glanced at her watch. It was already past five. She allowed herself only a few minutes to rest and eat a candy bar before setting out again. She didn't want them to be caught in the dark. The road was already sunk in shadow as the sun had gone below the high tree line to the west. A growing anger fueled her determination and masked the increasing desperation she felt. Where was the village? She guessed they'd already covered five or six miles and she couldn't imagine it being much longer.

But an hour later, they still had not found the village.

Dusk was descending to complete darkness.

The moon was out, but periodically it slipped behind a cloud, obscuring Mary-Ann's view of the road. Three or four times, she stumbled, falling hard to the ground with Annie on her back. Her blue jeans were torn and her knees were bleeding badly, but she continued, almost manic in her resolve. *Billy ain't gonna do it. Billy ain't gonna do it. I ain't gonna let him. I ain't.*

Annie slept on and off, whimpering when she was awake. Mary-Ann kept hearing sounds in the woods on both sides of them. She swore to herself that she would die before she'd let a bear get at Annie. She plodded on, her legs like deadened logs, her back screaming in agony.

Finally, through the thick screen of leaves, she saw faint lights. She stumbled ahead as fast as she could, tripping twice. Her knees were a latticework of scrapes and cuts, bleeding onto her torn jeans. Each time, she picked herself up again. She continued forward, saying, "We're there, Annie. We're there. We'll be home soon." She emerged onto a paved road and saw the gas station a hundred yards to her right. With a tiny cry of relief, she staggered toward it. As she neared the pumps, she collapsed to her knees. Pain shot through her like a current of electricity. Annie rolled off her back and sprawled on the ground. Mary-Ann reached over and stroked her daughter's forehead. "It's okay, Annie. It's okay. We made it; we can get help now."

She heard rushing, shuffling footsteps. "Goldang, Lady, what happened to you?" She looked up to see an old man gazing solicitously at her. He extended a macula-spotted hand which she gratefully accepted.

"I ... we ... got lost in the woods," she said, rising painfully to her feet then turning to help Annie up. Her hair was matted against her forehead with sweat.

"What the hell were you doing in the woods?"

"I need to use your telephone. Please."

"Should I call an ambulance for you?"

"No, no. I'll be all right."

"How about I call Homer Dobson? He's old and retired, but he's still a mighty good doctor."

"Please, no," she replied. "I only need to use your phone."

"Sure, sure, Lady. No problem." He led them into the store. Mary-Ann's legs were shot through with pain as she followed the man. "Phone's over theah," he said, pointing to the phone behind the counter. "You gonna call your husband?"

"Can you give my daughter something to eat while I call?"

"Was just about to offer it myself," the old man said. "Got some sandwiches my wife made just this afternoon. Come over heah, little girl, tell me which one you want."

While Annie eagerly followed the man to the cabinet that also housed milk, eggs, and cheese, Mary-Ann pulled out a slip of paper and dialed Matt Cannon's number.

He answered on the third ring. "This is Mary-Ann Scroggs," she said. "You have to stop him. He's on his way to Washington right now."

There was a brief pause, then Matt asked, "Does he have any men with him?"

"No, just Mr. Zacher's daughter."

"Zacher's daughter? Why?"

"He's using her to force Mr. Zacher to help him."

"Where are you now?"

"I ... I don't really know. I'm at a gas station."

"Is there somebody there? Ask where you are."

Mary-Ann asked the old man, then told Matt.

"Wait a minute while I look at a map."

While she waited, she watched Annie eagerly biting into a sandwich. When the old man opened one of his milk cartons and poured Annie a glass, tears of gratitude came to Mary-Ann's eyes.

Matt came back on the phone. "Mrs. Scroggs, there's an airport in Greenville about twenty miles from you. Do you think you can get there?"

"I ... I don't know."

"Listen, I know this has been tough on you and Annie, but you need to find a way to get to Washington by tomorrow morning. I have a feeling we're gonna need you. Is there anyone you can get to help you?"

"Yes, the owner, I think. He's a wonderful, kind man," she said with a catch in her throat.

"Ask him if he can get you to Greenville."

Mary-Ann cradled the phone to her chest and looked at the old man. "It's very, very important that we get to the Greenville airport. Can you help us?" Then she mouthed so Annie couldn't hear, "My husband's in trouble."

"Eyuh, course I'll help. I'll take you there myself. Was about to close up, anyway."

She let out a cry of gratitude. "You're so kind." She put the phone back to her ear. "Yes, this wonderful man will drive us."

"Good. We're going to send a private plane to take you to Washington. He'll need daylight to land, so it'll be sometime around five in the morning. Okay?"

"Okay."

"Have the pilot call me when you're on route with a time of arrival; someone will meet you."

"Okay."

"Great. We'll see you soon."

"Bye." She was about to hang up when something came to her. "Wait, wait. There's something else. Are you still there?"

"I'm here."

"My husband had a piece of paper with an address on it. It fell out of his pocket and I picked it up."

"What was the address?"

"Twenty-ninth Street, Georgetown," she replied. "I remember because Annie was born on April twenty-ninth. I can't remember the number."

"That's okay, we already know about that address. We'll take it from here. See you in Washington."

The old man—his name was Rufus Beecham—closed up his gas station and drove them to his house where his wife made a dinner of spaghetti and Italian sausages that Rufus had brought back from the market. After dinner, Rufus suggested that Mary-Ann and Annie clean up then get some sleep. "If you don't need to be there until five in the morning, we don't need to leave for a while."

Alone in the White House library, Angus Baxter surveyed the bookshelves for a place to start his search for the novel that included a scene in which one of the characters peers out of his cell to see the scaffolding being prepared for his execution. Fortunately, when he took up residence in the White House he'd asked that some of his own books be stored in the library which ordinarily contained only works representing a broad array of American letters. Consequently, there was a good chance the book he wanted, even if by a British or a French writer, was there.

Unable to sleep, he had lain in his bed searching his memory for that long-ago novel he read as a boy. Sometime in the early morning it came to him that it could have been *A Tale of Two Cities*; it came to him because when he glanced at his watch and saw that it was one o'clock, he remembered that Charles Darnay paced the floor of his cell at that time while waiting for his execution which was scheduled for 2:00.

But did Darnay actually look out his cell window and see the scaffolding? Baxter had to know.

He placed the Bloody Mary he had mixed himself on the round, Federal Period table and began to rummage through the bookshelves. After ten futile minutes, he paused, took his Bloody Mary from the table, and walked to the window in the north wall, Beatrice at his heels. He parted the pink drapes and looked out at the sky. It was a clear night and both the big and the little dippers were visible. He knew that at Baxter Island they would, at that moment, be hovering high over the serrated skyline. Often, he and Grace had sat on the porch and challenged each other to name the constellations—a game she always won because he could seldom identify anything beyond the dippers and, perhaps, Orion.

Why was he so eager to find the novel? Why did he so fervently want it to be *A Tale of Two Cities*? Was it that in the end Sydney Carton appeared to rescue Darnay from his execution? Was that what he, Baxter, hoped Matt Cannon would do for him? Or was it that Sydney Carton, in going to his own death under the guillotine, displayed an act of uncompromising and noble courage? Perhaps that was what he was expecting of himself. Perhaps it was time, at long last, to do something far, far better than anything he had done before.

No. He wanted to find the novel to know that his mind was still alive, that his memory was functioning. He wanted to recover that piece of memory and to lodge it in his living, pulsating brain because only a brain that expects to live cares about memory.

He wanted to find the novel because, he realized, he desperately wanted not to die. And when this realization, or this reaffirmation, hit him like a breaking wave, he sank into the chair by the window, Bloody Mary in hand, and wept.

It was nearing midnight as they drove down Constitution Avenue past the Ellipse. Matt looked to his right and saw the White House. He wondered what the president was doing at that moment. He knew it was hopeless, but he couldn't help searching his mind for some way to persuade Baxter to call off the King ceremony or, at least, not attend himself. But he was out of ideas. Everything depended on their ability to find Scroggs and stop him. Before turning right onto 23rd Street toward Georgetown, he saw workers near the reflecting pool making preparations for the ceremony that would begin in less than thirteen hours. Floodlights lit the area. A shiver of fear ran through him.

Zacher's place was a typical Georgetown brick row house with a wide, white door framed by wooden Doric columns. Above the door was an elaborate fanlight. Matt and Alexandra walked up to the door and rang the bell several times until at last a thin, tentative voice came from the other side. "Who is it?"

"Scroggs," Matt said.

The door opened. "Listen, I—" Zacher started to say before stopping with a shocked look on his face. "What the hell?" He was wearing a bathrobe.

"So you were expecting him," Matt said.

"Expecting whom?" Zacher asked. "What do you want?"

"You know damn well whom. When do you expect him?"

"He didn't give me his schedule," Zacher said with a forced defiance.

"Okay, we'll just wait for him to come to us," Alexandra said. "How about inviting us in?"

With a look of defeat, Zacher stepped aside and they entered a small hallway. "In here," Zacher said, gesturing toward an elegantly furnished room. "Listen, we want the same thing. He forced me to sign a false confession that—"

"—We know. We read it," Matt said.

Zacher gave them a surprised look. "You read it? How?"

"You left the file open in your Boothbay Harbor place."

"You broke into my house?"

"So sue us," Alexandra said.

Zacher paused. "Listen, that confession is false."

Matt laughed. "You operate inside the Beltway, Zacher. You know all about plausible deniability and that's something you have precious little of at the moment. I don't know what he's done with the document, but he's a pretty sharp guy. You have no choice but to help us get him to call it off without exposing the president and Senator Haskins, or your sorry ass for that matter. If he talks, everybody loses."

"Erase him."

"Just like that? You don't think he tucked that confession somewhere where it will show up if something happens to him?"

Zacher frowned. "As a matter of fact, that's exactly what he said."

"Of course," Alexandra said. "He's smart. But you know what? You haven't thought it all the way through."

"What do you mean?"

"If we erase him, we have to erase you, too."

Zacher's eyes grew round. "What? Why?"

"He gets killed, the document shows up. The document shows up, you, being the lovely person you are, defend yourself any way you can. That means you charge the president with a set up. The whole thing blows sky high. So you see, if we kill him, we kill you."

Zacher said, "We can fix this, I know we can. How do we fix this?"

"The only way is to convince Scroggs to call it off and let him keep the money," Matt said. "That way he doesn't talk, we don't talk, and you don't talk. The whole thing goes away."

"He has my daughter with him."

"Well, you better hope they show up soon or this is going to be a long night."

At four in the morning, Mary-Ann and Annie started out for Greenville with Rufus Beecham. Rufus chatted amicably all the way to the airport, talking about his five great-grandchildren. "The two youngest are about your little Annie's age." When they arrived at the airport to find no plane—they were a half-hour early—he turned the radio on. "It's been an awful long time since I sat in a car with a pretty lady listening to music," he said. "Eyuh, awful long time."

At exactly five o'clock, a two-engine plane appeared, made a low pass at the abandoned airport, circled around, and came in for a landing. Mary-Ann hugged Rufus and thanked him for his kindness. He blushed. And as Mary-Ann and Annie walked toward the plane, he called out, "Good luck. Hope everything turns out all right."

Matt sat at the kitchen table nursing his third cup of coffee when his cell phone chirped. Glancing at his watch, he hurriedly answered it, listened for a moment, said, "Great. Thanks," and flipped the phone closed. Turning to Alexandra, he said, "Mary-Ann Scroggs and Annie will be landing at Reagan in two hours. One of us should meet her."

"I'll go," Alexandra replied. "Should I bring her back here or go directly to the ceremony?"

"I think here. There's still a chance Scroggs will show up and it would be a hell of a lot easier dealing with him here than out in the middle of a huge crowd. There's no telling what he'd do, and people could get hurt."

"What about my daughter?" Zacher asked.

"Yuh, she could get hurt, too," Matt replied.

"Can't you get him for kidnapping?"

Matt laughed. "And what exactly was it you did with Mary-Ann Scroggs and Annie? Kidnapping is a federal crime. You better hope this all works out."

Zacher wiped his lips with a napkin and stared sullenly into space.

Chapter 24—The Lincoln Memorial

Scroggs slowed the car and scanned the area near the reflecting pool where men were setting up for the ceremony under flood lights. After studying the layout for a few moments, he thought to himself, This will be easier than Iraq.

"What's going on here?" Linda Zacher asked.

"A lot's gonna be happenin'," he replied. "Stay tuned." He accelerated the car and, instead of turning right on 23rd Street, continued onto the Theodore Roosevelt Bridge.

Linda Zacher said, "Wait, I thought we were going to my father's place."

"What? Do you think I'm crazy?" Scroggs asked. "If he's ratted on me, that's exactly where they'll be." At least, that's what I'm hoping, he thought. That way, they're not out here looking for me.

"Who?"

"You don't need to know." They crossed into Arlington and Scroggs headed for the storage place where he, Huey Figg, and Vernon Ludlow had placed the weapons and the protest signs. After retrieving them, he returned to the car and showed Linda Zacher a BAN HANDGUNS sign and asked, "Want one? I have extras."

She frowned, but said nothing.

Laughing, Scroggs placed the signs in the trunk, pulled out of the parking lot, and headed for Arlington Cemetery. As they approached the entrance, Linda Zacher asked, "Why are we going here?"

"We're gonna take a stroll to kill time. In another hour or so, I won't need you anymore."

She gave him a frightened look. "What are you planning to do?"

He pulled into a parking spot, turned the engine off, and walked around to the passenger side. He opened the door and said, "Let's go."

"Where are we going? What are you going to do to me?" Her voice had an edge of panic to it.

"Don't ask," he replied.

Mary-Ann Scroggs followed Alexandra into Zacher's house. Alexandra carried Annie on her hip, the girl's head resting on her shoulder. She was asleep. Alexandra smiled, "She's had a couple of long nights." She looked at Zacher. "Is there a bed we can put her in for a little while?"

"Yes, the guest room. Follow me."

Mary-Ann followed them.

When they returned, Matt noted Mary-Ann's disheveled appearance, her torn jeans, and her badly scarred knees, and asked, "What happened to you?"

She told him about the hunting cabin and about getting lost and about having to find her way in the dark, carrying Annie, until they finally found the gas station.

"Jesus, you're a brave woman," Matt said.

"The old man—his name is Rufus Beecham—was so kind. Billy's not here?"

"I'm afraid not," Matt replied.

Alexandra glanced at her watch. "There's a drug store around the corner. I'm going to get some ointment for those scratches," she said to Mary-Ann.

"Thank you; you're so kind."

"Whatever we can do. You've been through a lot."

Matt followed Alexandra to the door. In a low voice, he said, "We can give Scroggs another hour or so to show up, otherwise we're going to have to find him at the ceremony."

"I hope we don't have to do that," Alexandra replied. "He'll have a gun and there'll be a whole lot of people around.

For more than a half-hour, Scroggs had guided Linda Zacher through Arlington National Cemetery with its cherry trees and ordered rows of tombstones. When he found a section containing soldiers killed in Iraq, he had thought: This is for you guys. This time, we're gonna get the biggest lieutenant of them all. He and Linda Zacher walked along the rows of white headstones until he found the name he had been looking for: Wilford James Thistlewood.

"He was a buddy of mine, who was killed because of a stupid Lieutenant," Scroggs said. He turned to Linda Zacher, "You know anybody who fought in Iraq?"

"No."

"Figures. How old is your father?"

"Sixty-six."

"Then how come he didn't fight in Viet Nam?"

She shrugged.

He gave her a disgusted look. "Yuh, right." Finally, he glanced at his watch and said, "Time to go."

"Where are we going?" Linda Zacher asked, eyeing him warily.

"Back where we came from."

When they returned to the car, Linda Zacher said, "Now where?"

"You're not going anywhere," he replied. "I'm leaving you here. You're young and healthy; it won't take you long to go back and get your father's car keys."

"What do you mean?"

"I left them with Wil Thistlewood. You'll find them behind the tombstone. It's section twenty-eight."

"You're letting me go?"

"I have no quarrel with you," he replied. "By the time you get back I'll be long gone."

He walked back to the car, opened the trunk, withdrew one of the protest signs with the carbon fiber rifle embedded inside, and walked out of the cemetery, eventually joining a group of tourists walking over the Memorial Bridge toward the Lincoln Memorial. Already, he could see crowds gathering near the reflecting pool. Strains of recorded gospel music drifted across the river.

Matt stopped his pacing across the living room floor, glanced at his watch, and said, "Okay, that's it. We have to go."

Alexandra nodded. She turned to Mary-Ann Scroggs. "We need you to come with us. At this point, I think you're the only one who can stop him."

"I'm taking Annie," she said.

Matt and Alexandra exchanged glances. Matt said, "Yuh, I think that makes sense. If we find him and he doesn't listen to you, I don't see how he could go through with it if Annie was there."

Mary-Ann followed Alexandra to the guest room where she gently woke Annie up. Alexandra asked, "How about I give you another ride?"

"Okay," said Annie with a smile as she reached for her.

As the four of them left, Zacher said, "Please don't let any harm come to my daughter."

Over her shoulder, Alexandra said, "Yuh."

When Matt pulled the car up to the curb, Alexandra placed Annie in the back seat and Mary-Ann slid in beside her. Alexandra climbed into the passenger seat. Matt made a U-turn and headed toward the Lincoln Memorial.

Alexandra said, "Listen, Matt, I think it's worth one more call to the president."

"It can't hurt," said Matt as he flipped his cell phone open.

President Baxter was alone in the Oval Office, his mind swamped with a confusion of thoughts, when Doris buzzed him on the intercom. "Time to go, Mister President," she said. "The limousine is waiting for you."

"I'll be along in a moment," he replied. He walked to the sideboard and poured himself a double scotch. He was so practiced at this, he thought, that it wouldn't affect his speech.

If he got to deliver the speech, that is.

He took a large swallow and walked over to his desk where he lovingly fingered his father's Congressional Medal of Honor. He lifted it from the wooden box and held it before his eyes. It swayed gently at the end of its ribbon, picking up flashes of light from the lamp sitting on the corner of the desk. Its oscillation harmonized with the rotation of the anniversary clock's gilded globes, a rhythm like a thudding heart. Like the quickening pulse of his own heart.

He placed the medal back into its case, took one more swallow of scotch, and lifted the picture of Grace from the desk. He studied the familiar features of her face, wishing he believed in an afterlife. How pleasant it would be to see her once again, to hear her voice, see her smile. As the days had ticked down to this day, he'd found himself wanting her with him more and more, wanting her to share with him as she had for all the years of their lives together. He remembered her not the way she was that last time he saw her, but the way she was in the fullness of life. A sense of relentless, rushing time swept over him. He took a last swallow.

The intercom came alive. "It's getting late, Mister President."

"I'm on my way," he replied. He went into his private bathroom, rinsed the glass, and rinsed his mouth out with Listerine. Then he made for the Oval Office door and went through into the outer office.

A touch of superstition, perhaps a vestige of his baseball days in the distant past, caused him not to look back into the Oval Office. He didn't want to give his leaving the air of a final leave taking, an air of special importance. He said "See you later" to Doris as casually as possible, as if he were going to any ordinary event to deliver any ordinary speech, one in hundreds over the last several years. Outside, he returned the marine guards' salutes and climbed into the back of the limousine.

As the motorcade started down the driveway, the back seat phone rang. Baxter lifted the receiver, noticing that his hand was trembling. He answered, breathlessly, "Yes?"

"Mister President, it's Matt."

"I knew you'd call." His voice was flat, empty of emotion.

"We haven't got him," Matt said. "He's probably at the site already. Please, I beg you, don't go."

Baxter said nothing for a long while.

"Mister President? Angus?"

"We've had this discussion," Baxter said. "I have an obligation." Then he hung up the phone.

As he walked over the Arlington Memorial Bridge, shouldering his "BAN ALL GUNS" sign like a cross, Scroggs felt his heart begin to quicken. In the distance, to the right of the Lincoln Memorial, he saw the shining black surfaces of the Vietnam Memorial. Beads of sweat appeared on his brow and blistered on his upper lip in the oppressive August heat. He fixed a determined gaze on the many Doric columns of the memorial, glistening white in the sun. "This is for Annie," he muttered to himself. "Everything is for Annie."

At the end of the bridge, he fell in with a group of sign-carrying protesters making their way toward a security checkpoint near the Korean War Veterans Memorial. In the slow-moving line, people laughed and chatted, speaking of their separate causes. Many were carrying signs similar to the one Scroggs had. There were anti-abortion signs, Mothers-Against-Drunk-Driving signs, other signs calling for the banning of guns. He edged through the crowd to place himself in the center of this later group. He noticed, as he had anticipated, that most of the signs were mounted on lengths of wood far thinner than his. He hoped this didn't cause suspicion in some overzealous guard at the security checkpoint. As he shuffled forward with the crowd, he surveyed the area set up for the ceremony. Already, the crowd in front of the stage was thickening, but he calculated he would have no difficulty finding a spot somewhat to the side so he could set up a temple shot.

"For Annie," he muttered to himself again.

As he neared the security checkpoint, he studied the actions of the guards. They seemed to be taking less time with the protestors than with people not carrying signs. He congratulated himself on his foresight. Edging his way deeper into a cluster of people carrying signs, he waited his turn. When it came, he smiled pleasantly at the young woman who used a metal detector wand along his body and then along the shaft of the sign. A knot of panic started to rise in him as she made several swipes, but then she placed a hand on his elbow and said, "Go on through." He expected to be able to go immediately to his selected spot, but the people ahead of him weren't moving. He raised himself on his toes to see what was going on. Somebody in front of him said to a woman, "Hell, there's another checkpoint! It's like this everywhere since nine-eleven."

Scroggs told himself to stay calm. If he made it through one check, he'd make it through another. His knees trembled. He cursed himself. He'd never felt like that before—not in Iraq, not with Johnny Waters, not with Huey Figg, not with Vernon Ludlow. The difference, he figured, was this was the final act, the culmination of his plans; it was the bottom of the ninth in game seven of the World Series and everyone was more nervous then.

At last, he reached the second checkpoint. The guard here was an older man whose armpits were already wet with sweat. A trickle of sweat ran from his ear to his chin. "Spread your arms, please," he asked Scroggs. Scroggs leaned the sign against his midriff, placard out and facing the guard, as the guard passed the wand up and down first one side, then the other. "Hope you guys make your point," the man said, glancing at the sign. "Our job would be a lot easier if people didn't carry guns around. Okay, go on through. Enjoy the show."

"Thanks," Scroggs said, walking past and heading for the far side of the reflecting pool where he judged he would have a clear shot from the side.

An image of the tin can leaping from its perch when they first tested the carbon fiber rifles came to his mind.

Within minutes, he placed himself in the second row of people on the far right of the stage. Assorted dignitaries and invited guests were already taking their seats on the stage.

He was ready.

All he had to do was wait.

Angus Baxter sat exhausted in the back seat of the limousine. He had eventually found *A Tale of Two Cities* and had stayed up all night thumbing through it, trying to find the scene in which a prisoner views, through his cell window, the scaffolding (or was it a gallows?) intended for his execution. A chill had gone through his bones when he finally found the scene. It was Chapter 13 of the third book and it began: "In the black prison of the Conciergie, the doomed of the day awaited their fate." Baxter read how Charles Darnay had heard his condemnation and had understood, like Baxter himself, that he was sentenced by the millions. And his eyes had moistened when he read: "Nevertheless, it was not easy, with the face of his wife fresh before him, to compose his mind to what it must bear. His hold on life was strong ...."

Died in vain.

And then he had come to the passage: "He had never seen the instrument that was to terminate his life. How high it was from the ground, how many steps it had, where he would be stood, how he would be touched, whether the touching hands would be dyed red, which way his face would be turned ...." Of course the scene in which a prisoner views the gallows from his cell window wasn't in *A Tale of Two Cities* because Darnay was to be guillotined and the guillotine wasn't in the prison yard; it was in the square.

The condemned had to ride to their executions in a cart. A cart such as his presidential limousine that now pulled up to a fenced-off area at the side of the Lincoln Memorial on the 23rd Street side.

Secret Service men surrounded the car and one opened the door for the president. Taking a deep breath—this would be the beginning of his exposure—he stepped from the car and started toward a side entrance to the memorial.

He was surrounded by Secret Service agents and the thought that had haunted him time and again returned: how dare he deliberately expose these men and women to harm, these people whose only concern was his safety? Mike Padilla had already died trying to protect him. Would there be others? His pulse quickened. He felt his heart fluttering against the sides of his throat and the walls of his chest. A sickening feeling rushed at him like a tidal bore, a wall of water breaking over him—it was the certainty that whatever happened from this moment on, he had brought it on himself.

As he emerged from the memorial and descended the wide steps to the stage, he could scarcely breathe. It felt as though his heart was pounding in his ears. Would it happen now? When he was seated? When he was speaking? Would he feel anything? Which way would his face be turned?

He was barely aware of the wave of applause that greeted him as he stepped onto the stage. When several senators came up to him to shake hands, he flinched. His face hot with fear, his hands and knees trembling, he quickly shook hands, gave a weak smile to the others on the stage, and took his seat. He spread the binder containing his prepared remarks on his lap and raised his hands to either side of his head as if in thought. His fingers twitched against his temples. He was on the verge of tears of self pity.

Matt was forced to park on 23rd Street near Washington Circle because the rest of the way was blocked by police barricades. He and the others hurried out of the car, dashed around the barricades, and started to run in the middle of the street the seven or eight blocks to the Lincoln Memorial. Matt carried Annie for several of the blocks before transferring her into Alexandra's arms.

When they got to the intersection with Constitution Avenue, Matt turned left. If they had continued, they would have emerged close to the stage and Scroggs, who must be watching the stage, would see them. Matt was afraid their appearance would trigger him into action. He stopped and, breathing hard, said to the others, "Let's go past the Vietnam Memorial and come in from the back. That way if we see him we have a chance of getting to him before he sees us."

After they passed the southern end of the low, black V-shaped memorial, they turned in toward the reflecting pool. Mary-Ann nearly stumbled down the slope, but recovered her balance. Matt scanned the crowds for protest signs. Mary-Ann had said Scroggs would be carrying a placard saying "Ban All Guns." But there were many signs and they were scattered throughout the crowd. Also, because the signs were facing the stage, he couldn't read the slogans. "I can't tell a thing from here," he said.

"We're just gonna have to rely on recognizing him from the back," Alexandra said. He turned to Mary-Ann and asked, "Do you think you can do that?"

"I don't know," she replied. "I just don't know."

An introductory fanfare came over the speakers mounted on both sides of the stage. At its conclusion, the Marine Band, which was assembled to the right of the stage, began the National Anthem. Along with everybody else, President Baxter stood. He swayed. His legs felt as if he were standing in a tidal bore that was trying to sweep him away, pull him under. The hairs of his sideburns prickled with the anticipation of a bullet. He looked at the musicians and envied them their freedom, their happiness; he imagined each of them would return after the ceremony to their wives and husbands and children to resume their quiet, untroubled lives.

And he thought of Baxter Island and grandchildren and pancakes in the mornings.

At the conclusion of the national anthem, there was a pause, then the giant speakers gave forth with a series of somber chords containing an eerie sense of fatality. It was the beginning of Aaron Copland's Lincoln Portrait. The screen angled to the left of the stage lit up and the National Symphony Orchestra appeared playing the introductory section of the piece. Baxter remembered recording the spoken words of the piece with the orchestra but it still came as a shock to hear his own voice and to see his own image on the huge screen. His face appeared soon after the first section ended on the dying notes of a pleading oboe and his image, looking down on him just as Lincoln's statue looked down on him from behind, said, "Fellow citizens, we cannot escape history. That is what he said. That is what Abraham Lincoln said." And his words were followed by a low, rumbling, ominous sound from the string section. "We—even we here—hold the power and bear the responsibility."

Copland's music, with its swelling chords, spoke of the greatness of the presidency and the greatness of the particular president now looking down on Baxter from his stone perch as if to wonder about this imposter now occupying the office, and Baxter wished fervently, his eyes filling, that he could live and serve out his term and reach some measure of worthiness to it. "We must disenthrall ourselves and then we shall save the country."

How Baxter wished that he could have his years over, to do right a second time that which he had done badly the first time, and it pained him deeply to think of his squandered opportunity for the greatness he and Grace had so wanted. And now it was to end.

"… that these dead shall not have died in vain."

When the music ended, the screen flickered and the face of Martin Luther King appeared, his voice filling the space and echoing from the walls of the memorial. Another man, Baxter thought, of whom he was not worthy.

"Five score years ago, a great American, in whose symbolic shadow we stand, signed the Emancipation Proclamation ...."

Baxter knew the words well, the sonorous voice, the measured cadences. He loved to hear the speech, but this time he couldn't concentrate. He was in a daze as time passed. He scanned the audience. Would he recognize Billy Scroggs?

"I am not unmindful that some of you have come here out of great trials and tribulations ...."

Suddenly, it occurred to Baxter to look for Wayne Haskins. In his dazed state he had forgotten all about the man. He remembered Haskins calling him, urging him not to attend. Was it today that he called? Yesterday? He found Haskins sitting to the far right of the stage. They exchanged glances. A crease of concern was etched in Haskins' forehead. Baxter turned around to face the audience again. He tried to read the text of his remarks spread open in his lap, but he found himself unable to focus. He read the same opening paragraph over and over again. Then he was startled to hear the words:

"I have a dream that one day every valley shall be exalted, every hill and mountain shall be made low, the rough places will be made plain...."

King's speech was almost over. Baxter had had no sense of the time passing so quickly. In moments, he would be introduced and he would have to rise to deliver his remarks.

Is that when it would happen?

The mellifluous voice of Martin Luther King, coming over the speakers, penetrated Matt's consciousness. He was familiar with the speech and knew it was rapidly coming to a conclusion. His heart raced faster.

"This will be the day when all of God's children will be able to sing with a new meaning, 'My country 'tis of thee ....'" The applause on the recording was echoed by the live audience.

Since the Copland piece had started, Matt and the others had been moving through the crowd desperately trying to find Scroggs. Now, Matt was aware of time running out. He guessed that at the conclusion of the recorded King speech, Baxter would deliver his remarks, giving Scroggs the best possible opportunity. He turned to Mary-Ann. "Scan the crowd carefully. Don't panic, do it methodically. Sweep the crowd left to right from the first row back. And concentrate." He was relying on the notion that people can recognize those they love, even at a distance and from behind, by the slope of the shoulders, the tilt of the head, the way of standing. "Do you think you can do it?" he asked.

"I don't know. There are so many people."

"Try. You must try."

"Let freedom ring from the curvaceous peaks of California ...."

Looking toward the stage, Matt saw the president sitting rigidly, staring straight ahead. Soon he would rise from his chair and approach the podium.

"From every mountainside, let freedom ring ...."

Mary-Ann said, "Way down in the front ... on the right ... that could be him."

"Are you sure it's him?"

"No, I can't be sure."

"We may only have one chance at this; you have to be sure!"

They started to move slowly in the man's direction while Mary-Ann focused all her attention on his back.

"Free at last! Free at last!...."

"I can't—" Mary-Ann started to say before stopping and gasping. "Yes, that's him!"

"How can you be sure?"

"He just lowered the sign. See how he's holding it at hip level? That's the way I saw him practicing."

"Practicing?"

"His shot."

Matt looked at the man, then he looked to the stage where a speaker was introducing the president. "It's now or never," he shouted as he and the others barreled through the crowd.

Scroggs' heart started to beat wildly when he saw the president stand and move to the front of the stage. He had stood patiently throughout the video program, listening first to the recording of the president and then to Martin Luther King.

As he awaited his opportunity, he'd become increasingly tense, his heartbeat gradually rising. There was an advantage, he thought, to the way Donnie had done it—a sudden move, little planning, little time for nerves to take over. He was worried his aim wouldn't be steady, certainly not as steady as it was when he first tested the weapon on tin cans.

He wanted to lower the sign, test himself, but he resisted the temptation because he didn't want to telegraph his final move. He was certain Secret Service men were scanning the crowd, certain he had already been spotted several times then passed over. He could feel their eyes on him.

But now, as the president rose, Scroggs took a deep breath and as casually as he could, lowered the sign to the firing position he had practiced so many times in the woods behind his house in Bass Run. "For Annie," he muttered as he waited for the president to present a clear target.

Baxter rose. On wobbly legs, he walked across the stage toward the podium. The sea of people before him was a blur. Out there, he knew, one of those vague points of color, was his assassin.

Watching him.

Waiting.

Was the man directly in front of him? To his left? To his right? His temples buzzed with anticipation. He could almost feel the bullet slamming into his throbbing brain.

Suddenly, there was a commotion. Shouts.

He was abruptly surrounded by Secret Service men, two of whom pushed him roughly to the floor of the stage. He came down hard on his knees. Feet scampered around him as everybody on the stage scurried to the right and the left away from the podium.

Cries of alarm rose up from the audience.

Baxter raised his head and looked out. He saw Matt, Alexandra, and another woman moving toward a spot somewhere to his left. Alexandra, incongruously, was carrying a child. Baxter looked to where they were heading … and he saw his assassin.

Sprawled on the hard wood of the stage, peering through the legs of the men whose job it was to protect him, President Baxter saw him. He saw his self-appointed assassin. There could be no mistaking the brother of Donnie Scroggs. Also, the man was the only person looking directly at him; everybody else was focused on the people moving through the crowd or on the two Secret Service men who were rushing toward them.

He locked eyes with the man and what he saw was unalloyed hatred and a look of betrayal.

Running as if possessed, Mary-Ann passed Matt, and circled round to position herself between the president and her husband. She faced Scroggs and in her expression was a complex mixture of love and fear, pleading and insistence, sadness and despair. Annie came up beside her and placed her small hand in Mary-Ann's. "Daddy?" she said in a weak voice.

"Yes, Sweetheart," Mary-Ann said. "It's Daddy. Go to him. Tell him to come home."

Annie started slowly to walk toward Scroggs. People parted to let her through. Two Secret Service agents appeared but Matt, whom they recognized, held up a hand, begging them not to interfere. Reluctantly, they stopped, bemused and worried expressions on their faces. Perhaps it was because what they saw before them was merely a wife imploring her husband, a young child approaching her father. Besides, they knew the president was already on the ground and shielded by a phalanx of their colleagues. One of the men turned to Matt. "Mr. Cannon, what in hell is this all about? What's going on?"

"It's okay, Tom. I know these people. It's kind of a family thing. Please, I beg you, leave them be."

The agent gave a quizzical look to the other man whom Matt recognized as Scott Fuller, the chief. Fuller nodded. "If Mr. Cannon says it's okay …."

"It's okay," said Matt. "Trust me."

"You better get them away from here, though," Fuller said. "My guys are pretty nervous right now. And I'm coming with you. I have a few questions for this man."

"Of course, Scott. Just give us a few moments to get out of the crowd."

Scroggs had seen Annie coming toward him and his shoulders had sagged. He looked from Annie to Mary-Ann. "Why?" he mouthed. "Why?" He dropped the sign to the ground.

Annie ran the last few steps into her father's arms. He gathered her up and held her close to him. "Mommy and me want you to come home now, Daddy," Annie said. "Will you come?"

His squeezed her tightly.

Mary-Ann appeared before him. "I love you, Billy. I need you. Annie needs you."

He gave her a confused expression. There was a look of betrayal in his eyes.

Mary-Ann stood before him. "Look at me, Billy," she said, gesturing to her battered knees. "Look at me. I carried Annie out of those woods on my back. On my back. That's how important you are to us." She lowered her voice to pleading. "Doesn't that mean anything to you?"

Scroggs stared at her for a long time, his eyes welling.

"Will you come home, Daddy," Annie asked again.

He tightened his hold on her and squeezed his eyes shut. Sunlight glinted from the tear tracking down his cheek. "Yes, Sweetheart, I'll come home now," he said.

Matt approached. "Come on folks, we need to get you out of here." Gently, he pried Annie from Scroggs' arms. Mary-Ann extended a hand to Scroggs and he took it. "Let's go," Matt said, urging them toward Constitution Avenue.

As they started to walk slowly away, Alexandra bent down, picked up Scroggs' sign, nodded to Matt, and followed them away from the reflecting pool.

Matt said to Scroggs. "Well, I guess everything's up to you, now. The Secret Service guys are gonna interview you. What we told Mary-Ann is true. You can keep the money so long as no one is implicated. I hope you're good at coming up with stories."

Epilogue

...yet time serves wherein you may redeem
Your banish'd honors and restore yourselves
Into the good thoughts of the world again.
—William Shakespeare, Henry IV, I, iii

Chapter 25—A Stunning Joint Announcement

One week later, Matt showed his and Alexandra's IDs to a guard and drove through the security gate onto the grounds of Camp David. A canopy of trees created a chiaroscuro light on them and her face went from dark to bright to dark again. "You're certain you want to go through with this?" she asked.

"It was you who told me to get my flesh into the game," he replied.

"True, I did. But you'll be taking a great risk. What if they don't respond the way you hope? What if they force your hand?"

"Who knows what happens then?" he answered. "I could end up being the most hated man in America."

"Or a hero."

They pulled up to Aspen Lodge. Angus Baxter opened the door to let them in. Wayne Haskins was the only other person in the room. Baxter motioned them to seats. "I imagine you both know why Senator Haskins and I wanted to talk with you?"

"You want to make sure the cover-up is leak proof" Matt said.

"That's harsh," replied Baxter.

"Sorry, Mister President, but Zacher and Scroggs are certainly not gonna talk given what they would lose. Sure as hell, you two won't. And, except for Marcie, everybody else who knew about this is dead, and Marcie won't talk. So that leaves me and Alex."

"So how to we buy your silence?" asked Haskins.

"You can't buy it; you can only earn it."

"All right," said Haskins, visibly annoyed. "How do we earn it?"

"Resign," answered Matt.

"Be serious," said Baxter.

"I'm dead serious."

Haskins said, "You're saying if we don't resign you'll blow the lid on this whole thing?"

"That's what I'm saying," replied Matt.

"Go frig yourself."

Baxter said, "You're at least as vulnerable as we are. Have you thought of that?"

"Long and hard. I'm willing to risk it."

"Why?" asked Baxter.

"Because something decent should come of this."

"Something decent …." Echoed Haskins.

"You have something specific in mind," said Baxter. "Tell us."

"There was one area during the campaign you both agreed on: the need for Middle East peace. Each of you was somewhere near the middle. You, Mister President, were slightly on the side of the Palestinians and you, Senator Haskins, slightly on the side of the Israelis."

"Go on," said Baxter.

"Announce that you are both resigning to work full time on the Middle East problem as a team. Otherwise I give CNN an exclusive and we get to see how the game plays out and whether I get immunity for my testimony."

The room fell silent for several long moments. Finally, Baxter turned to Alexandra. "Do you have anything to add, Ms. Lake?"

"Yes. Invite me and Matt to Oslo for the Nobel ceremony."

"Clever," said Baxter ruefully. "But now I'm going to ask you two to leave us."

Two weeks later, Matt and Alexandra were curled up on the sofa watching TV. Alexandra said, "I talked to a doctor this—"

"—Wait, here it is!" said Matt.

The television announcer said "In a stunning joint announcement moments ago at the White House, both President Baxter and Senator Haskins said they would not seek reelection in order to devote themselves exclusively to finding the elusive peace that—"

Matt and Alexandra watched with rapt attention as the announcer explained that the two men would campaign hard for their respective parties but that after the general election, they would begin their Mideast work in ernest.

"Done!" said Matt. He turned the TV off, kissed Alexandra on the cheek, and Asked, "Now what were you saying about a doctor?"

"He's a urologist friend. He told me that often in cases of trauma to the testicles, they're able to salvage some semen and freeze it."

"They would have told me," said Matt.

"Maybe, maybe not. Did you ever see the urologist after the surgery?"

"Come to think of it, no. Another doctor did the follow-up. I don't even know if he was a urologist."

"So you'll call in the morning?"

Matt smiled. "I'll call in the morning."

v

Please visit
www.normanggautreau.com
to see video trailers
an descriptions of the
author's other books.